UNFIT FOR MODEST EARS

By the same author

THE GOLDEN DOOR
WOMEN IN STUART ENGLAND AND AMERICA
SAMUEL PEPYS' PENNY MERRIMENTS (*Editor*)
CONTRAST AND CONNECTION: Bicentennial Essays in Anglo-American History (*Editor with H. C. Allen*)

UNFIT FOR MODEST EARS

A Study of Pornographic, Obscene and Bawdy Works Written or Published in England in the Second Half of the Seventeenth Century

ROGER THOMPSON
University of East Anglia

First published 1979 by
THE MACMILLAN PRESS LTD
London and Basingstoke
Associated companies in Delhi
Dublin Hong Kong Johannesburg Lagos
Melbourne New York Singapore Tokyo

Printed and bound in Great Britain at
William Clowes & Sons Limited
Beccles and London

British Library Cataloguing in Publication Data

Thompson, Roger
Unfit for modest ears
1. English literature — 17th century—
History and criticism 2. Sex in literature
I. Title
820'.9'353 PR439.S

ISBN 0-333-25876-2

FOR
ALLAN SPENCER HOEY

My *Lady* she
Complain'd our Love was course, our *Poetry*
Unfit for modest *Ears*, small *Whores*, and *Play'rs*
Were of our Hair-brain'd *Youth*, the only cares;
Who were too wild for any virtuous *League*,
Too rotten to consummate the Intrigue.

Satyr, *Poems on Several Occasions By the Right Honourable The E. of R—*
('Antwerp', 1680), p. 100.

Contents

Preface

This is a book about dirty books. It deals with some fifty works published during the period of the Interregnum and the Restoration. Between about 1650 and 1690 there were added to the traditional strain of English bawdy two further types of immodest writing: the often outrageous verse connected with the court circle, and pornography, usually of foreign origin, but for the first time published in English.

Although I have attempted to analyse the causes of these developments, I have devoted most of this book to the task of describing the works themselves, partly because most of them are virtually unknown, and partly because they are now often extremely rare. Indeed ten of the most important items survive in unique copies in libraries and private collections in Britain and America. In my analyses of these 'ugly ducklings' of English literature, I have tried to convey a sense of tone and style through frequent quotation, without being unnecessarily offensive.

A word about definitions; the pitfalls here are legion. Henry Miller, who should know, has said: 'To discuss the nature and meaning of obscenity is almost as difficult as to talk about God'. I have rejected judgments based on readers' or my own reactions, on the simple Lawrentian grounds that 'what is pornography to one man is the laughter of genius to another'. Neither the Eysenck scale[1] nor the Kronhausens' list of pornographic characteristics[2] proved practicable yardsticks. Instead, my labels are based on *the intention of the author*. I have normally used four terms to define that intention: (i) *Pornographic*, writing or representation intended to arouse lust, create sexual fantasies or feed auto-erotic desires. The pornographer aims for erection (at least) in the pornophile. (ii) *Obscene*, intended to shock or disgust, or to render the subject of the writing shocking or disgusting. This seems to be the purpose in our period of the use of taboo words or casual descriptions of sexual perversions, and is often a companion of satire. (iii) *Bawdy*, intended to provoke amusement about sex; most dirty jokes, for instance, belong to this category. (iv) *Erotic*, intended to place sex within the context of love, mutuality and affection; orgasm is not the end but the beginning. I occasionally vary these epithets to avoid tedious repetition; thus *ribald* is a synonym for bawdy, and *lewd* for obscene. I use the word *erotica* in its general sense to encompass these four types of writing.

These four terms are not entirely foolproof. There are grey areas between the groups, and isolated passages within a book which are anomalous. It is sometimes difficult to determine what the intention of an anonymous or little-known author was, or to gauge what types of readership he was aiming at. Nonetheless, my four relatively exclusive classifications do have the merit of clarity and simplicity, and I am confident that in the great majority of cases they do reflect the purpose of the texts discussed.

The chapter titles, if occasionally archaic, are, I trust, self-explanatory. Certain well-researched or marginal areas have not been covered here, notably Restoration comedy, ballads, jest-books, drolleries,[3] scatological humour, political and public satire.

My interest in this topic was originally aroused by the discovery that New England Puritans were customers for whore stories and pornography.[4] Part III attempts to extend exploration of the connection between Puritanism and prurience, and to provide a stepping-stone to a wider study of seventeenth-century attitudes towards sexuality.

NOTES

1. H. Eysenck, *Psychology is about People* (London, 1972), pp. 240–50.
2. E. and P. Kronhausen, *Pornography and the Law* (London, 1967), pp. 155–99.
3. C. C. Smith, 'Seventeenth-Century Drolleries', unpublished Ph.D. thesis, Harvard University, 1943.
4. 'Prurience and the Puritans: Aspects of the Restoration Book Trade', H. C. Allen and R. Thompson, eds., *Contrast and Connection* (London, 1976) Ch. II.

Acknowledgments

My debt of gratitude to other scholars and to the 'boffins' of historical research is enormous. It is heartening to experience the sense that the international fraternity of scholarship is as vital, generous and cooperatively dedicated as it has ever been.

I have received liberal assistance from the staffs of the following libraries: Advocates' Library, Edinburgh; Baker Library, Dartmouth, New Hampshire; Beinecke Rare Book Library, Yale University; Bodleian Library, Oxford; Boston Public Library, Massachusetts; British Library, London; Cambridge University Library; Congregational Library, London; Glasgow University Library; Guildhall Library, London; Harvard University Library, particularly Houghton Reading Room; Inner Temple Library; Jesus College Library, Oxford; King's College Library, Cambridge; Lambeth Palace Library, London; Massachusetts Historical Society, Boston; Medical Society of London; Middle Temple Library; Norwich Central Library; Nottingham University Library; Pepys Library, Magdalene College, Cambridge; Princeton University Library; Royal College of Medicine Library, London; Royal College of Physicians Library, London; St Bartholomew's Hospital Library, London; Tavistock Centre Library, London; University College Library, Oxford; University of East Anglia Library, especially Mrs Anne Wood, Inter-Library Loan librarian; University of Illinois Rare Book Library; Victoria and Albert Museum Library.

I am grateful for the help and courtesy of the staffs of the following Record Offices: Borthwick Institute, York; Bristol City; Cambridgeshire; Clwyd; East Devon, Exeter; Ely Diocesan, Cambridge; Hertfordshire; Kent, including Dover Divisional; Lancashire; Middlesex; Norfolk and Norwich; Public Record Office, London.

The American Council of Learned Societies awarded me a generous grant to pursue aspects of my research in the United States. The University of East Anglia granted me two invaluable terms of study leave for research and writing, and has assisted me with research funds. My former pupil, Bill Sadleir, undertook an arduous and urgent piece of research at short notice with painstaking care.

Several scholars eminent in this and allied fields have shared with me their ideas and the fruit of their research: Hugh Amory, Margaret Boddy, John Broadbent, John Carey, David Foxon, David Frantz, Robert Hodge, Robert Latham, Alan Macfarlane, Neil McMaster, Victor Morgan, the late A. N. L. Munby, Stephen Parkes, Lawrence Stone, Keith Thomas, R. G. Walters, T. D. Whittet.

Spouses are the unsung heroes and heroines of any book. Mine has borne with my frequent absences, and even more frequent absence of mind. This book is dedicated to her father, a fine classical scholar, who has been a constant source of encouragement and help.

June 1978

RFT

Part I

Forerunners

1 Classical and Continental

The philosopher John Locke owned only one play by Shakespeare, nothing by his schoolfellow Dryden, but four different editions of Petronius's *Satyricon.*[1] To many bookmen of the later seventeenth century, 'literature' still meant classical literature and 'history' ancient history. As Charles II is an archetypal sexual gymnast to our generation, Heliogabulus, Tiberius or Caligula were to his. Messalina, Lais or Lamia were their 'Nell Gwyns'. It was normal for any educated man to own one or more editions of the great classical masters of the erotic, the obscene, pornography and bawdy: the elegists Ovid, Catullus, Tibullus and Propertius, the epigrammatist Martial, the novelists Petronius and Apuleius and the dramatists Terence and Plautus. Numerous references in other works make it clear that the reputations of these writers were familar to a less sophisticated readership.

For students of the erotic in Stuart England, 'the Professor of extra-marital seduction' was Ovid.[2] *The Elegies, The Art of Love* and *The Remedies of Love* were available in fine editions and unblushing translations.[3] His influence can be seen not only in such coterie poets as Dryden, Rochester, Cowley, Durfey or Sedley, but also in references employed by such hacks as Head, Neville or Brown.[4] The reasons are not far to seek. 'The boy who stayed the course from school to graduation must have known his Ovid from cover to cover', even if, like Milton, he attended that most puritanical of schools, St Paul's.[5] The ambiance of intellectual society in Augustan Rome had so many reflections in Restoration London, and the master's cynical, urbane epicureanism struck a tone admirably suited to the amoral hedonism of the court circle. The seductive ladies' man in Ovid would no doubt have found the crudities and violence of his machismic imitators distasteful, yet he, like the other 'smooth Elegiack Poets', would have recognised much that was familiar in the atmosphere and attitudes at Whitehall. He would hardly have been surprised either at the shocked censoriousness of Puritan moralists – latter-day Catos – at his practical courses in seduction for both sexes.

The seventeenth century was one of the great ages of satire, and two very different Roman satirists had marked influences on their successors. Martial's epigrams had perfected the art of the sexual smear. His stress on the sexual deviances of his victims was tiresomely copied by his graceless pupils, epigrammatists, libellers and lampooners.[6] Similarly the *saeva indignatio* of Juvenal can be traced in the satires on Charles II, his ministers and mistresses, most notably those of Rochester and Oldham.[7]

The vogue for the *Satyricon* of Petronius in the last three decades of the seventeenth century was undoubtedly stimulated by the mid-century discovery of fragments containing the *Cena Trimalchionis* at Drau in Dalmatia.[8] Petronius' footloose anti-heroes had much in common with the roguish extravagant rakes of Restoration stage and court. Such types as the faithless lover, the apparently respectable matron who was in fact a bitch in perpetual heat, the self-made bourgeois with the emphasis on the boor, and the pitiable pedant hack, so popular in Restoration erotica, owed much of their satiric impact to the *Arbiter Elegantiae* of Neronic Rome.

The influence of the other Roman novelist, Apuleius, was rather more indirect. The great exponent of the picaresque was absorbed into English literature through the medium of Spanish rogue tales and the *novelle* of Italian writers like Boccaccio.[9]

Terence was the most popular of the Roman dramatists,[10] read for his style in schools, even though his theme was illicit love. His plots, notably *Eunuchus*, were adapted by Restoration dramatists.[11] Plautus was too bawdy for the classroom and ill-served by publishers, perhaps for this reason.[12] Yet his sharply observed comic characters – itching gallants, windy braggarts, amorous old goats, bitching wives, impudent servants, bourgeois misers and the rest – were models for many a stage or jest-book butt. Plautine anti-Puritanism and scorn for conventional virtues and values chimed perfectly with Restoration licence.[13]

Now that the Moderns have all but driven the Ancients from the field, it is hard to imagine the sway that Roman eroticists exerted over a classics-sodden age. The pervasiveness of their authority is perhaps best demonstrated by the use of tags from Martial, Ovid or Plautus in chapbooks intended for the barely literate,[14] the depth of their impact by the fact that even the greatest writers so often used their models.

The flyblown laurels of leadership in European pornography changed heads in the middle of the seventeenth century. Until the

1650s the dominant influence on English sexual literature and humour had been Italian; since then it has been French. Examination of the causes of this Gallic takeover are beyond the scope of this book; suffice to mention the growth of monarchical despotism, with its attendant political castration of the nobility, and the fierce religious disputes of the period as two of the more obvious stimulants to an obsession with the sexual.

The new accolade was not immediately obvious, however. To most Englishmen of the Restoration, from Charles II to the meanest denizen of Grub Street, the prince of pornographers was still Pietro Aretino, the peak of pornography *Aretine's Postures.*[15] Although Aretino had merely added sixteen *sonetti lussuriosi* to the graphic depiction of sexual gymnastics by Giulio Romano, engraved by Marcantonio Raimondi, his title was nonetheless legitimate. Ironically, his *Ragionamenti* were immensely influential in the development of European pornography. They popularised not only the dialogue form and the sexual satire of the religious, but also the delirious depiction of lust in every imaginable form. Although they were published in London in Italian in 1584 and 1597 – probably for export – no part of the dialogues was Englished until 1658.[16] *La Puttana Errante*, another set of sixteenth-century dialogues, was falsely credited to Aretino and the title and characters were stolen for the ephemeral series *The Wandring Whore* in 1660. The last product of the Italian supremacy was Ferrante Pallavicino's *La Retorica delle Puttane* first published in 1642 and frequently reissued. The author's prurient anti-clericalism and subversive libertinism appealed to his English readership, but the naturalisation into English in 1683 lost much of the subtlety of his sarcasm.[17]

The second great contribution of the Italians to the European erotic tradition lay in their perfection, at the hands of such writers as Boccaccio and Poggio Bracciolini, of the bawdy story in *novella* or *facetia* form. Although these farceurs shared the contempt of the pornographers for the decadence of Roman Catholicism and its clerics, it was their boyish delight in finely engineered plots of cuckoldry which was most influential. Boccaccio was only available in English in heavily bowdlerised form in the seventeenth century,[18] but many of the most ingenious Italian plots were familiar to popular audiences through their appearance in jest-books, drolleries and ballads; similar tales had been filtered through the equally exuberant French collections of *fabliaux*, *Les Cent Nouvelles Nouvelles* (c. 1460) and *Heptameron* (1559).

The brilliant translations of Shelton and Mabbe help to account for the great vogue for Spanish Literature in seventeenth-century England. *Don Quixote, Lazarillo de Tormes* and *Guzman d'Alfariche, The Spanish Rogue*[19] were among the commonest books in English libraries, and the many English imitators of the picaresque novel – often coarsened by gratuitous obscenities – point to the general popularity of the rogue, male or female, as anti-hero. It is also possible that the frequency with which bawds figure in English court verse and ribaldry owes something to De Rojas' brilliant characterisation of Celestina in *The Spanish Bawd*.[20] She eclipsed the meagre creations of Aretino and Pallavicino and was certainly familiar to English readership. Perhaps the unprecedented notoriety of Creswell, Page and Bennet in Restoration London depended as much on literature as on life.

Although France took up the pornographic bays in England after about 1655, the great French master of bawdry, Rabelais, had surprisingly little influence on Restoration England,[21] despite the fact that Urquhart's rumbustious translation of Books I and II had been published in 1653. Indeed Book III was not issued until 1694, when Motteux's continuation appeared. Even if the libertinism of the Abbey of Thélème and the pervasive anti-clericalism of *Gargantua* and *Pantagruel* chimed with Restoration attitudes, the tone and exuberance did not. Rabelaisian humour may have been 'as healthy as the smell of a barnyard on a bright spring morning',[22] but the erotic atmosphere of the later Stuarts was laden with the foetid stench of the city sewer.

The one distinguishing feature of the wide selection of English pornography, obscenity and bawdy to be surveyed here was its lack of originality. With the exception of a few of the court poets, English eroticists and publishers plagiarised and naturalised with increasing despatch as the reign of Charles II progressed. It may have taken over a century for any part of Aretino to be rendered into English, but by the 1680s a few weeks sufficed for the latest French smut to be Englished and put on sale. This brief survey of classical and continental erotica will at least alert the reader to the models which English pedlars so slavishly copied.

NOTES

1. P. Laslett and J. Harrison, eds., *The Library of John Locke* (Oxford, 1965).

2. P. Green, *Essays in Antiquity* (London, 1960), pp. 109–35.
3. J. Carey, 'The Ovidian Love Elegy in England', unpublished D. Phil. thesis, Oxford University, 1961, reviews all editions and translations in the seventeenth century. H. R. Palmer, *List of English Editions of Greek and Latin Classics* (London, 1911).
4. Carey, pp. 398–404.
5. R. Ogilvie, *Latin and Greek* (London, 1964), p. 12; M. L. Clarke, *Classical Education in Britain 1500—1900* (Cambridge, 1959), p. 35.
6. Thomas Farnaby's great edition of Martial was published in London in 1615 and often reprinted. It contained all the epigrams on sodomy, pederasty, fellatio, irrumation, cunnilingus and tribadism. In similar vein, the *Priapeia*, was available in the 1655 Cologne edition, 1664 Leyden, and 1669 Amsterdam. Fifty books of epigrams were produced between 1598 and 1620. *Witts Recreations* went through ten editions between 1640 and 1683.
7. E.g. 'A Ramble in St. James's Park' or 'Sardanapulus'.
8. Editions including the new find appeared first in Paris and Padua in 1664, and subsequently in Uppsala, Leipzig, Amsterdam and London (1963). The English translation by William Burnaby and a collaborator appeared in 1694. On the vogue, see J. Hayward, ed., *The Letters of St-Evremond* (London, 1930), p. 184; A. W. Ward and A. R. Waller, eds., *Cambridge History of English Literature*, Vol. IX (Cambridge, 1912), p. 264.
9. P. D. Walsh, *Roman Novel* (Cambridge, 1970), Ch. 8.
10. Fifty editions are listed in *The Short-Title Catalogue* and Wing.
11. E.g. Sedley's *Bellamira* and Wycherley's *The Country Wife*.
12. A selection, *Colloquia Plautini viginti*, was published in London in 1646; Laurence Eachard's anonymous translation of *Amphitryo, Epidecus* and *Rudens* was published in 1694. Two Elizabethan translations were never reprinted.
13. E. Segal, *Roman Laughter* (Cambridge, Mass., 1968), passim.
14. E.g. R. Head, *The Canting Academy* (London, 1673) or *Select City Quaeries* (London, 1660).
15. D. Foxon, *Libertine Literature in England 1660—1745* (New Hyde Park, 1965), pp. 11–12, hereafter cited as Foxon. The famous Oxford incident of 1675 when undergraduates tried to run off copies on the Clarendon Press is recorded in E. M. Thompson, ed., 'The Letters of Humphrey Prideaux', *Camden Society Publications*, New Series, XV (1875), 30–31.
16. *The Crafty Whore*. Four editions in Italian were published on the continent in the seventeenth century, the most popular with Restoration owners being Cosmopoli (Amsterdam, 1660). *Pornoidascalus*, a Latin translation of the third dialogue, was published abroad in 1623 and 1660.
17. Foxon, pp. 27–9, 10.
18. G. H. McWilliam, *The Decameron* (Harmondsworth, 1972), pp. 25–43.
19. *Lazarillo* was translated by Rowland in 1576. Shelton's *Quixote* appeared in 1612, Mabbe's *Guzman* in 1622.
20. Mabbe's rendering appeared in 1631.
21. H. Brown, *Rabelais in English Literature* (New York, 1967), pp. 133–9.
22. S. Putnam, *The Essential Rabelais* (London, 1946), p. 35.

2 English

A search of earlier published English literature confirms the intuitions of contemporaries and the judgments of recent scholars that 'pornography seems to have been born and grown to maturity in a brief period in the middle of the seventeenth century . . . at this period sex became to some extent intellectualized'.[1] Indeed the only prior candidate for pornographic honours of which I am aware is *Choyce of Valentines* by the avowed admirer of Aretino, Thomas Nashe, which circulated only in manuscript around 1660. 'Good men's hate did it in pieces tear', wrote Davies of Hereford, and Nashe's own shamefaced epilogue suggests that the contemporary tolerance for literary sexual arousal was low.[2] Other evidence, in the form of protests, enforced or voluntary censorship and inhibitions about sexuality all tend to confirm this.

The kinds of works which were condemned for 'lasciviousness', 'paraphrastic obscenity' and 'incitements to lechery' by the pre-Civil War generation turn out to be very thin gruel indeed by Restoration standards. Bishop Hall, for instance, objected to Marlowe's translation of Ovid's *Elegies* and his *Hero and Leander*, to the epigrams of Harrington and Davies, the ephemera of Greene and Nashe and Marston's *Pigmalion's Image*.[3] Some of these lapsed occasionally into bad taste and vulgarity; others described erotic passion with moving eloquence – as did *Venus and Adonis*, Catullus, or Virgil's account of Dido and Aeneas,[4] other targets – but none was written primarily to arouse or shock sexually. Elizabethan apprehension about the decadence of Italy carried over into Jacobean times and encompassed in its condemnation the works we have briefly surveyed. Many of the more exceptionable plays of the early seventeenth century were significantly set in Italy.

Much of the most vocal criticism came of course from Puritans whose standards were scrupulously exacting. Typical of their resentment against licentious publishing was the eighth item of the Root and Branch Petition presented to the Long Parliament on the eve of the Civil War;[5] it condemns

> The swarming of lascivious, idle and unprofitable books and pamphlets, play-books and ballads; and namely Ovid's 'Fits of

> Love', 'The Parliament of Women', which came out at the dissolving of the last Parliament; Barns's 'Poems', Parker's 'Ballads', in disgrace of religion, to the increase of all vice, and withdrawing of people from reading, studying, and hearing the word of God, and other good books.

Ovid's *Ars Amatoria* in Heywood's translation[6] was erotic and immoral, but not pornographic, and the other works were at most bawdy popular songs and satire aiming for a hearty laugh.

The inclusion of play-books in this London pressure-group's protest reminds us that the full force of Puritan loathing was reserved for the stage.[7] Even Ben Jonson admitted of contemporary comedy in 1607 that 'now, especially in drama, or, as they term it, stage poetry, nothing but ribaldry, profanation, blasphemy, all license of offence to God and man is practised . . . foul and unwashed bawdry is now made the food of the scene.'[8] Much pre-Civil War comedy deserved this definition – Beaumont and Fletcher, for instance, Dekker or Shirley – yet it rarely lapsed from bawdry, however foul and unwashed it might be. The penchant of Jacobean tragedians like Webster and Ford for violence, horror and sadism is notorious. The incest theme in *'Tis Pity She's a Whore* or the gratuitous cruelty in *The Duchess of Malfi*, for instance, could qualify as a form of obscenity, but the disgust and horror aimed at is in neither case primarily sexual.

Official reaction, in the forms of legislation and censorship, confirm the impression that exception was taken to works which in the second half of the century would have been regarded as relatively innocent. Neither Lambarde's proposed 'Acte to restrain licentious printing',[9] against works that 'set up an arte of making lascivious ungodly love', nor the Bill of 1604 against importing, printing, buying or selling, popish, vain and lascivious books, was enacted, but Marlowe's translation of Ovid's *Elegies* bound up with the *Epigrams* of Sir John Davies – significantly falsely imprinted 'Middleburgh' – were burnt by order of the Archbishop of Canterbury and the Bishop of London.[10] A ban on publishing epigrams followed. In 1629 the Laudian Imprimatur was introduced, though it seems to have been only fitfully complied with by publishers for the next twelve years.[11] The most detailed evidence of official control occurs in the Office Book of Sir Henry Herbert, Master of the Revels, for the period 1622–42.[12] Herbert saw himself as a tautener of the slack methods of his Jacobean predecessors; he reimposed a tight rein over works for the stage: 'in former time the poetts tooke greater libertie than is allowed them by me'. He took exception often to 'ribaldrie' and 'obsceanes', though his special wrath was reserved for sedition, libels, profanity and commonplace oaths. Similarly, the Licenser of the Press refused to pass some of Donne's Ovidian Elegies in 1633, and censored 'To Julia' and 'A Tale of a Citizen and his Wife' – a mildly bawdy parody of Chaucer – in 1639.[13]

Evidence of internal censorship tends to confirm the impression that the pre-Civil War generation was inhibited about the open discussion of sexuality. Several translations of classical and continental works showed marked prudery. For instance, two versions of Ovid's *Remedia Amoris*, one printed, one in manuscript, stop abruptly at line 365 where Ovid starts to deal explicitly with love-making.[14] One even manages to evade an earlier mention of adultery. The Elizabethan rendering of *The Golden Ass*,[15] reprinted several times in the early years of the century, mixes spoonfuls of bromide into the original, as did Anthony Hodges' translation of Achilles Tatius' romance *Erotikon* in 1638.[16] The anonymous translator of the *Decameron* (1620) omitted or silently altered all the racier tales in his 'version of more decorum than fidelity'.[17] Busby's selection for his *Martialis Epigrammata in usum Scholae Westmonasteriensis* quite naturally left out most of the objectionable pieces for a 'chaste edition', but in two cases he wilfully and silently altered key words totally altering the sense of the original.[18] Two topics plainly embarrass these bowdlerisers: over-explicit descriptions of physical passion, and homosexuality. The first is diluted into mere sentimentality. The second is either omitted, or the situation is altered into a heterosexual one, sometimes with bizarre results.

The taboo against homosexuality is reflected in a dream recorded in Latin in the diary of William Laud on 3 July 1625:[19] 'In my sleep it seemed to me that the Duke of Buckingham got into my bed where he acted towards me most lovingly and it seemed to me that many people entered the room and saw it.' Even more revealing is the plan of William Prynne, scourge of sexual license on the Caroline stage, to use this evidence as a sexual smear at the Archbishop's trial.

When the manuscript verses of Inns of Court wits like Donne, Fletcher, Greville and Campion first came to be printed, significant cuts to the erotic contents were made, probably as concessions to popular taste.[20] Even the privately circulated libels of the court in the 1620s and 1630s showed a restraint quite alien to Restoration lampoons.[21]

The operation of internal censorship is nowhere better displayed than in the diary of Simon Forman, an astrologer in late Elizabethan and Jacobean London. Like that most self-conscious of lechers, Samuel Pepys, Forman recorded his sexual exploits in a private code: 'I did halek cum muher', for instance, or 'halekekeros hariscum tauro', or, more expansively, 'I did halek cum uxore mea et eo tempore fuit illa valde cupida de halek at matrix fuit'. His sexual dreams, violent hostility to whores and delayed onset of sexual activity all suggest a severely repressed personality (though he was later to make up handsomely for lost time). The widespread use of supernatural aids in problems of love and lust recorded in his diary argues a deeply superstitious and trammelled attitude to sexuality among his contemporaries.[22]

Studies of different branches of English literature confirm a marked coarsening of erotic sensibilities in the second half of the century. An examination of prostitutes and women criminals in literature finds the firm moral framework of the early years unhinged by Restoration obsessions with the indecent and the scabrous, with brutality and obscenity.[23] The ballad literature of the century similarly degenerated.[24] So, too, did the poetry influenced by Ovid and other Roman elegists. The witty, brittle, subtle poems of Donne and his contemporaries sank to the dirty-minded, degraded verse of rape, voyeurism and perversion, or, even worse, to the contemptuous iconoclasm of the burlesque.[25]

It remains to ask what was responsible for the onset of this 'filthy run of books', why a bookseller in 1657 should feel that poems 'of late are too much corrupted in the praise of Cupid and Venus'.[26]

The commonest explanation, of course, is that the Restoration was a natural liberating reaction against the sexual repressions of the Interregnum, like Edwardian frivolity after staid and unamused Victorianism. Plainly the general moral tone of Charles II's court was fundamentally different to that of the Cromwellian regime, and the Royal Proclamation against drinking, swearing and debauchery must rank as the supremely ironic gesture of the era.

Yet the mere change of political regime is too simplistic and stark an answer on its own. It does not, for instance, take into account the fact that the 'filthy run' had begun even before

Oliver's death. It exaggerates the suddenness in the change of mores,[27] and neglects the continuity of personnel in positions of power and authority. It underplays the liberating aspects of Cromwell's rule, and forgets that Charles, an avid if indolent admirer of French despotism, established the most repressive system of press censorship since the reign of Elizabeth. Its equation of sexual liberation with the growth of pornography is highly questionable. We must therefore look for additional factors for this trend towards 'the intellectualisation of sex'.

We move closer to the heart of the matter with the contention that

> Restoration society's fault was not so much that it had reacted against Puritanism as that it had retained too much of it. . . . Restoration society had not so much revolted from, as unthinkingly accepted, in company with those very Puritans whom it would otherwise have been right in despising, a great deal of the biblically inspired morality which has always militated against a civilised social order.[26]

In such incompatible melanges of moralities, guilt and shame and perversion may fester. Restoration pornographers 'cannot retain a "pagan" quality. In their treatment of sexual affairs, religious guilt or religious prejudice seem always likely to creep in'.[29]

Apart from the superhuman task of trying to liberate their fellow-men from the slavery of sin, or, at least, vice, the Puritan rulers of England also presided over a partial liberation of women. Sects like the Quakers were no respecters of sexes, and the woman preacher was not uncommon in the 1650s.[30] Within marriage, Puritanism encouraged a greater sense of mutuality between spouses, a respect for 'holy matrimony'. While domesticating sexuality, the counter-culture had marked success in controlling extra-marital licence, which would tend to work for the benefit of women.[31]

The Restoration restored the theory of male mastery, and with it the double standard.[32] A common characteristic of virtually every book and every type that we shall be examining is its underlying contempt for women. Women are created for the satisfaction of men, and satisfaction usually means physical domination. Women are paradoxically depicted as either temptresses or victims, Messalinas or Lucreces, ravenous or ravished. It would be surprising if the more enlightened, and therefore threatening, example of the preceding regime did not give an impetus and edge to the creation of sexual fantasies. Gershon Legman's comments on sexual folklore are apt here:[33]

> Sexual folklore almost always has the air of being humorous. Yet actually it concerns some of the most pressing fears and most destructive life problems of the people who tell the jokes and sing the songs. . . . They are projecting the endemic sexual fears, and problems and defeats of their culture – in which there are very few victories for anyone – on certain standard comedy figures and situations, such as cuckoldry, seduction, impotence, homosexuality, castration and disease, which are obviously not humorous at all. And they are almost always expressing their resistance to authority figures, such as parents, priests and policemen, in stereotyped forms of sexual satisfaction and scatological pranks and vocabulary. It is for these reasons that sexual folklore is generally retailed in a mood of exaggerated horseplay and fun.

For the Restoration one of the leading authority figures to ridicule was the Puritan, his authority deriving not from force but from moral superiority.

The Civil War had not merely been fought on the battlefields, but also in the press. This is reflected in the numbers of pamphlets collected by Thomason: 22 in 1640, over 1000 in 1641 and 1966 in 1642, with a total of 22000 from 1640 to 1660.[34] The routing of royalism not only drove the cavalier pamphleteers underground, it also deprived them of a positive campaigning role. They became an irresponsible opposition. The form their sniping all too often took was sexual satire. In such ephemera as *The Man in the Moon* or *Mercurius Fumigosus* journalists like John Crouch vented their spleen on the alleged lechery of Puritan leaders in lampoons, 'comparable to the most indecent verse of Rochester himself'.[35] The precedent for the tone of Restoration satire had been set years before the King finished his travels.

The years on either side of 1660 and the early 1680s saw two distinct peaks in disreputable publishing, and their common characteristics may help in identifying its causes. Both were times of ominous political stress. Despite repeated triumphs in the field, the problem of legitimising the Cromwellian usurpation was no nearer solution. The attempt to impose the alternative society through the Major-Generals had been a political and social disaster. The King was still over the water, but conspiracies were less of a threat than the obstinate indifference of the masses. Oliver could not go on for ever, nor could army rule. What feuds, what unchecked fanaticism, what fiascos would follow his death? Apprehension, mistrust and disaffection ruled. So with the 1680s. Charles II might have weathered the Exclusion Crisis and the Popish Plot, yet the problem of an inept Catholic successor remained, as illegitimate in the minds of Protestant Englishmen as the rule of the swordsmen. Dutch William was over the water, and so were uncomfortable numbers of English exiles. Conspirators against Charles II might be as incompetent as the Sealed Knot, dissent might appear as muzzled as the Interregnum Royalists, yet the Frenchified court and the Frenchified policies of the government were no more popular than the Major-Generals. The Tory backlash demonstrated that England was no nearer consensus and stability than it had been in the 1650s. Repressed oppositions deprived of legitimate outlets by apprehensive dictatorships in both cases turned to prurience as the dirtiest mud to sling. In the 1650s typical butts were the lasciviousness of women preachers, orgies among the sects and the ravening lusts of preachers and statesmen. The target changed to Roman Catholicism in the 1680s, but the ammunition was much the same: the depravity of cloisters, the seductions of cozening Jesuits and the debauchery of the church leadership.

Other more technical factors probably also encouraged this type of publication. In the increasing anarchy after Oliver's death and the mass of problems facing the newly-restored monarchy, one casualty was the system of censorship. Only when L'Estrange took over control as Surveyor of the Press in August 1663 was the gag reapplied. The Licensing Act expired in 1679 and was not re-enacted until James II's first Parliament. Although authors, printers and publishers were still liable to prosecution under the Common Law, the busy law officers and secretaries of state were chiefly out to catch seditious works, and the merely scandalous had more chance of slipping by.[36]

The economics of the book trade were another important factor. The printing and publishing industries had both expanded during the first half of the century. In 1640 there about twenty-five printing houses in London; by 1649 the number approached sixty. In 1663 the printers themselves and L'Estrange drew attention to the dangerous excess, tempting dangerous excesses,[37] in the trade.

The same problem faced the bookselling side. A year later, Richard Atkyns described the system thus:

> There are at least 600 Booksellers that keep shops in and about London and Two or Three thousand free of the Company of Stationers: the Licensed Books of the Kingdome cannot imploy one third part of them: what shall the rest do? I have heard some of them openly at the Committee of the House of Commons say, They will rather hang than starve; and that a man is not hanged for stealing, but being taken; *necessitas cogit ad turpia*.[38]

Necessitas faced those entering business. It was often they who succumbed to the temptation *ad turpia*.

The devastations of plague and fire, in which Clarendon estimated the London booksellers lost £200 000,[39] eliminated a proportion of the weaker brethren. The number of master-printers fell from seventy in 1665 to thirty-five in 1668.[40] In 1683 Roger North described the situation in Little Britain, one of the bookselling centres of the capital.

> The trade is contracted into the hands of two or three Persons. . . . The rest of the Trade are content to take their Refuse, with which, and the fresh scum of the Press, they furnish one Side of a Shop. . . . They crack their brains to find out selling subjects, and keep Hirelings in garrets, on hard meat, to write and correct by the grate.[41]

L'Estrange recognised a common solution to this brainteaser among stationers: 'the worst books among them bring most profit'. This judgment was supported by the admissions of some of the franker publishers.[42]

Although the dirty story certainly antedated printing, the spread of literacy tended to make popular taste more sophisticated – 'Printing frighted away Robin-goodfellow and the Fayries'[43] – and made the smut-pedlars' prospects of profit more promising. The emergence of a literate public also spawned the Grub Street hack, 'the hireling in a garret'. His 'hard meat' depended on the saleability of his goods; he could hardly compete with the upper end of the market; perforce, he earned his pittance from smut.

The noxious weeds which flourished in the 1680s were far more rank than their predecessors. The French connection had much to do with this, but another degrading influence was surely the court and its hangers-on. Not only was Whitehall a cess-pit of scandals, but its pervasive philosophy of libertinism served to undercut restraint and inhibition. Debauchery had become the badge of loyalty. The superego had a hard time under Charles II.[44]

NOTES

1. Foxon, p. ix.
2. J. B. Steane, ed., *The Unfortunate Traveller and Other Works* (Harmondsworth, 1972), pp. 376, 468. D. O. Frantz, ' "Leud Priapians" and Renaissance Pornography', *Studies in English Literature* XII (1972), 157–172.
3. S. W. Singer, ed., *Satires*, (Chiswick, 1824), p. 6.
4. L. B. Wright, *Middle-Class Culture in Elizabethan England* (London, 1936), pp. 106, 233, and passim; V. F. Calverton, *Sex Expression in Literature* (New York, 1926), Chs. I and II.
5. S. R. Gardiner, ed., *The Constitutional Documents of the Puritan Revolution 1625—1660* (Oxford, 1906), p. 139.
6. Two editions, the second entitled *Loves School*, appeared before the first dated one of 1662.
7. Wright, *Middle-Class Culture*, Ch. VI, has an excellent survey.
8. Introduction to *Volpone.*
9. D. Thomas, *A Long Time Burning* (London, 1969), pp. 15–16.
10. C. A. Duniway, *The Development of the Free Press in Massachusetts* (New York, 1906), p. 10.
11. F. B. Williams, 'The Laudian Imprimatur', *The Library*, 5th Series, XV (1960), 96–104.
12. J. Q. Adams, ed., *The Dramatic Records of Sir Henry Herbert* (New Haven, 1917), pp. 18–56.
13. Carey, 'Ovidian Elegy', pp. 182, 187.
14. Ibid., 265–6.
15. By William Adlington, first published in 1566.
16. Palmer, *List of Classics*, p. 2.
17. McWilliam, *Decameron*, pp. 27, 31, 34, 36; D. Bush, *English Literature in the Earlier Seventeenth Century* (Oxford, 1945), p. 57.
18. London, 1661.
19. Quoted in W. Lamont and S. Oldfield, eds., *Politics, Religion and Literature in the Seventeenth Century* (London, 1975), pp. 44–5. Cf. C. Bingham, 'Seventeenth-century Attitudes to Deviant Sexuality', *Journal of Interdisciplinary History*, I (1970), 447–69.
20. Carey, 'Ovidian Elegy', pp. 137, 148, 167, 182.
21. L. Stone, *Sex, Marriage and the Family 1500—1800* (New York, 1977), p. 538.

22. A. L. Rowse, *Simon Forman: Sex and Society in Shakespeare's Age* (London, 1974), pp. 34, 81, 92, 124.
23. M. Katanka, 'Women of the Underworld', unpublished M.A. Thesis, University of Birmingham, 1973.
24. H. Rollins, *Pepysian Garland* (Cambridge, 1922), p. ix.
25. Carey, 'Ovidian Elegy', Ch. XV, esp. pp. 382, 398–9, 400.
26. D. Thomas, ed., *State Trials*, Vol. I (London, 1972), p. 136; W. London, *Catalogue of Most Vendible Books in England*, p. iii.
27. The early years of Clarendon's supremacy saw some efforts to contain the licentiousness of the court.
28. N. Suckling, 'Molière and English Restoration Comedy', J. R. Brown and B. Harris, eds., *Restoration Theatre* (London, 1965), p. 96.
29. Katanka, 'Women of the Underworld', p. 121.
30. C. Hill, *The World Turned Upside Down* (Harmondsworth, 1975); K. V. Thomas, 'Women and the Civil War Sects', T. Aston, ed., *Crisis in Europe 1560—1660* (London, 1965); R. Thompson, *Women in Stuart England and America* (London, 1974), Ch. III.
31. P. Laslett, *Family Life and Illicit Love* (Cambridge, 1977), Ch. III.
32. K. V. Thomas, 'The Double Standard', *Journal of the History of Ideas*, XX (1959), 206–13.
33. *The Horn Book* (New Hyde Park, 1964) pp. 245–6.
34. F. S. Siebert, *Freedom of the Press in England 1476–1776* (Urbana, 1952), p. 191.
35. J. B. Williams, 'The Beginnings of English Journalism', *CHEL*, VII, p. 358.
36. Cf. the similar situation in 1641 when Star Chamber was abolished. G. Kitchin, *Sir Roger L'Estrange* (London, 1913), p. 138.
37. *Considerations and Proposals in order to the Regulation of the Press.*
38. *The Origins and Growth of Printing* (London, 1664), p. 16; Gervase Disney's father at this time described bookselling as a 'declining trade'; O. C. Watkins, *The Puritan Experience* (London, 1972), p. 63.
39. Kitchin, *L'Estrange*, p. 167.
40. Ibid., p. 178.
41. A. Jessopp, ed., *The Lives of the Norths*, Vol. II (London, 1890), pp. 281–2.
42. See Kirkman's Preface, *The English Rogue* (London, 1671) and Marsh's Preface, *The Wits* (London, 1662).
43. O. L. Dick, ed., *Aubrey's Brief Lives* (Harmondsworth, 1962), p. 17.
44. See, for instance, Pepys' reactions to public debauchery in diary entries for 1 July 1663, 13 July 1667, 30 July 1667, 1 June 1669, 27 June 1669.

Part II

The Works

3 Instructional

The quasi-instructional manual of sexual technique proved a popular medium for pornographic or bawdy writers at least from Aretino's time. Under cover of disseminating necessary information to a novice and of receiving reports of 'practicals', a sense of realism and exciting immediacy could be conjured up, as well as highly explicit details of thrills and spills. The initial dialogue may easily expand into mutual action. It is no surprise therefore to find this technique used in many of the works we shall be examining. The three books in this section are *The School of Venus*, first published in 1655, allegedly at Leyden, but really in Paris, *A Dialogue between a Married Lady and a Maid, Tullia and Octavia*, originally *Aloisiae Sigeae Toletanae Satyra Sotadica de arcanis Amoris et Veneris*, printed in either Lyons of Grenoble in 1659 or 1660, and *The Whores Rhetorick Calculated to the Meridian of London* (1683), a loose English adaptation of Ferrante Pallavicino's *La Retorica delle Puttane* of 1642.[1]

The inclusion of the *Satyra Sotadica* in this group gives it a strong claim to be not only first but foremost. Foxon has rightly called it 'most advanced pornographically' for the seventeenth century. It is significant that these sophisticated pieces of pornography are all of foreign origin. All three were available in foreign language editions in London in the early years of Charles II's reign, and later all were adapted or translated into English: *The School of Venus* in 1680; *Tullia and Octavia* by or in 1684; and *The Whores Rhetorick* in 1683.

All three were prosecuted by the authorities soon after their appearance in English, and the tone of two extant indictments makes it clear that they were thought of as highly pornographic at the time.[2]

In a foray in 1688 Henry Hills, the Messenger of the Press, found six copies of *The School of Venus* ranging in price from 2s 6d to 6s and two of *Tullia and Octavia*. L'Estrange closed the shop of the bookseller Wells in 1677 when he found him with imported Dutch copies of the two books. Benjamin Crayle and Joseph Streater were fined 20s and 40s respectively for printing and selling the two books. In 1683 John Wickens was fined 40s for printing and publishing *The Whores Rhetorick*.[3]

The reactions of private individuals similarly show shock, prurient titillation or outright sexual arousal. Pepys shows all three.

> 13 January 1668. Stopped at Martins my bookseller, where I saw the French book which I did think to have had for my wife to translate, called *Escholle de Filles*; but when I came to look into it, it is the most bawdy, lewd book that ever I saw, rather worse than *putane errante* – so that I was ashamed of reading in it.
> 8 February 1668. Thence away to the Strand to my bookseller's, and there stayed an hour and bought that idle, roguish book *L'escholle des Filles*; which I have bought in plain binding (avoiding the buying of it better bound) because I resolve, as soon as I have read it, to burn it, so that it may not stand in the list of books nor among them, to disgrace them if it should be found.
> 9 February 1668. *Lords day*. We sang till almost night, and drank my good store of wine; and then they parted and I to my chamber, where I did read through *L'escholle des Filles*; a lewd book, but what doth me no wrong to read for information sake (but it did hazer my prick para stand all the while, and una vez to decharger); and after I had done it, I burned it, that it might not be among my books to my shame. [4]

Foxon quotes four literary references to *The School of Venus* and *Tullia and Octavia* all of which clearly class them as pornographic. John Dunton writes of the former twice as a primer 'for teaching and practising diversity of lewdness.'[5] Among the disreputable Tom Brown's library, according to an imaginary witness at a burlesque trial, were 'An Amorous Dialogue between *Tullia* and *Octavia*' and 'An *Italian* Book in octavo in praise of Whoring' which may have been *The Whores Rhetorick*. The other books in the list, like 'Aretino's *Postures*, My Lord *Rochester's* Poems and The Secret History of *Dildos*', indicate their reputation.[6] In a letter to Dr Charles Goodall from Epworth dated 29 October 1698 Samuel Wesley describes schoolboy reading in the early eighties: 'Some of ye Lads had Meursii Elegantiae Aloysia Sigeae Tullia and Octavia, and the most lewd abominable Bookes that ever blasted christian Ey.'[7] A manuscript poem called 'The Deponents', an attack on those who witnessed that James III was not 'a spurious brat', written in 1688, alludes to 'Wrong Fam'd Sigea, or L'Eschole des Filles' implying that their respective authors are both in hell.[8] *The London Bawd* equates a whore-house with 'a School of Venus'.[9] Even the pornographic *Venus in the Cloister* condemned *The School of Venus* and *The Seven Dialogues of Aloisia* (*Tullia and Octavia*) as evil, infamous, a danger, poison, provocatives and incentives. This was expert criticism.[10] Whatever the twentieth century may think of these works, there can be little doubt that the seventeenth equated them with the most pernicious production of the press.

Usually the publication of disreputable books like *The School of Venus* is understandably shrouded in mystery. The birth of this *Venus*, however, triggered the spotlight of investigation by the Parisian authorities and a subsequent trial. Two men, Michel Millot and Jean L'Ange, were deeply implicated in the production of the 300 copies printed in Paris in 1655, but the author is still not known for certain. It was probably someone in the circle of that ostentatious libertine millionaire, Nicolas Fouquet, *Surintendant des Finances* under Mazarin, conceivably that master of 'travesty' Paul Scarron. It was frequently thereafter reprinted in the Netherlands, the European centre of dirty book publishing in the later seventeenth century. It was probably these Dutch editions which made their way on to the English market in the early years of Charles II's reign.[11]

The School of Venus, that is the original English version, has only survived through court records. The indictment of 1680 includes ten exemplary fragments of the first English translation.[12] Much of the 1744 edition is transcribed in the King's Bench Records[13] and this is the earliest extended version in English that is extant. However, there is enough material in the 1680 indictment to suggest that it was a faithful translation from an early French version.

Fortunately there is a modern English edition, translated with an informative introduction by Donald Thomas (London, 1972) based on the excellent modern French edition, edited by Pascal Pia (Paris, 1959).

The work is divided into two dialogues, before and after. The two discutants are Fanchon, a well-developed but totally naive girl of sixteen beloved of Robinet, and Susanne, her older and far more experienced confidante and instructress. Fanchon's ignorance is due to her strict, puritanical mother, whose edicts Susanne quickly sets about undermining. Poor Fanchon has only the dimmest idea of what a male organ looks like – an urinating man once exposed 'something like a white sausage' to her – so after whetting her appetite with a paean to the enormous pleasures she is missing, Susanne begins the lesson with some basic anatomical and linguistic information. Susanne realistically admits that the first insertion may be slightly painful to a virgin. The initial description of orgasm is fairly clinical:

> The boy thrusts to and fro with his rump to insert the yard, while the girl clings to him, feeling the friction and movement of his organ inside her. This, and the other caresses in which they indulge, increases the pleasure. In the end, because of the friction and the movement of their two backsides, both of them grow heated with the excitement which is provoked by the gentle irritation and rubbing along the length of their passages. The boy and girl show each other their feelings about this. It drives them on to harder friction and faster lunging with their bottoms. All the time the excitement and the enjoyment build up, gradually becoming so intense that they gasp with joy and communicate only with movements. Their eyes are half closed and they seem about to breathe their last, clutching each other tighter and tighter. The exquisite sensation overwhelms them to such an extent that you see them almost swoon with ecstasy giving little thrusts towards each other as they discharge the substance which has excited them so much. This substance is a thick, white pulpy liquid with which each infuses the other, provoking the joy that is beyond description.[14]

At Fanchon's insistence, Susanne goes on to describe foreplay, with the girl rather than the boy as the initiator, and the technique of the girl on top. When Fanchon mentions a nightly agitation in her cunny, Susanne shows her how to masturbate. Fanchon then, no doubt remembering her pious upbringing, asks if love-making is not wrong. Susanne laughingly dismisses such doubts. 'There is so much pleasure in it! And no one ever finds out about it, for who is there to tell them?' Omniscient God is also dealt with: 'God, who knows everything, will neither divulge nor reveal anything of this to other people.' And the teachings of the church: 'This is only a tiny peccadillo created by the jealousy of the male sex because they want their women only to belong to them. . . . If women had run the church instead of men, they would have ordered the thing the other way round.' After assuring Fanchon that pleasure is bound to come at the first encounter, Susanne then embarks on a highly explicit description of her own encounters, her lover's foreplay with her, various positions they adopt, the joys of mutual orgasms, ways of ensuring that they climax together, the noise that her vagina makes, and the number of times that they and others have intercourse each night – twice is thought realistic for a steady relationship, though Susanne has heard of twelve times. This highly evocative sequence is interrupted when Robinet is heard arriving. Susanne leaves, promising to tell the ardent young man that Fanchon is at last ready for him.

The second dialogue, subtitled 'The Ladies' Instructor', takes place a few days later, and Fanchon, overjoyed by her experiences, takes up the early running. She gives Susanne a graphic description of their foreplay, Robinet's problems of insertion solved by pomade, their simultaneous orgasms and the postures of their three immediately subsequent bouts. Susanne judges that her pupil has graduated as 'a mistress in the fine art of love'. Fanchon tells of a second session, when Robinet took her on top of a chest, placed different fabrics under her buttocks to teach her how to push and wriggle in different directions and in different rhythms. Susanne then explains flagellation and castration to Fanchon, advises against screaming at orgasm because the neighbours come running with first aid kits, discusses what lovers say to each other during intercourse, and indulges in a schoolmarmish recapitulation. The discussion continues with Fanchon complaining that because her own room is being redecorated she has to sleep in her mother's room. This leads to her describing ways in which she and Robinet have had intercourse in these difficult circumstances: once up against the wall of the entrance hall as she let him in the house, once, unsuccessfully as he leaned against her as she was drying her petticoat over the stove – the petticoat burnt – twice as she sat on his lap at a dance – the burnt hole useful here – and some mutual masturbation while her mother was gazing out of the window. Susanne gets a word in after this excitement to tell Fanchon about the different sizes of penis, but love, she says, is the important thing. Men's desires are always aimed between the thighs, and for girls 'sensual and bodily coupling is the fire that warms us'. Fanchon is worried about pregnancy. 'Go on with you,' says Susanne, 'no need to be afraid of that.' There are, she says vaguely, certain remedies in the highly unlikely event of it happening, or special clothes, or pilgrimages; the father will pay for the child to be nursed and adopted. For the excessively apprehensive or frustrated, there are always dildoes, or even, for royalty, full-scale models of men. If the girl keeps moving during orgasm, conception will not occur, says Susanne, but there are always *coitus interruptus*, linen contraceptives or non-simultaneous orgasms as birth-control techniques. Most of the last thirty pages of the second dialogue are concerned with general ideas, the myth that men and women were originally joined together, the qualities of perfect lovers – Susanne would not give a straw for a man unless his yard was perfect – the relation of reason to passion, the provocative power on men of female modesty, the destruction of Fanchon's mother's creed of virtue and modesty – the lie rules over truth, argument suppresses experience, precedence overcomes what is good – the superiority of older women as mistresses – they have husbands to conceal bastards, as well as experience – and the tongue and mouth as symbols of sexual organs. Susanne does intrude descriptions of masturbating her lover and vigorously riding him; she dismisses with scorn the frigid, passive, sacrificial victim, and delights in 'the sweet cruelty of a man's erect prick ploughing' his beloved. Fanchon by this time has decided to have a lover when she is married, as a change of diet, and Susanne leaves her with the promise that she will take matters in hand. Robinet does not figure as a husband in these plans, though it seems unlikely that his new-found career is at an end.

Donald Thomas argues forcefully that *The School of Venus* is 'not a piece of escapist pornography but a realistic glimpse of sexual happiness.' It is unlike 'the neurotic and sadistic pornography of the last two centuries'; like Milton's nearly contemporaneous depiction of the Garden of Eden, it is a 'vision of a sexual Utopia'. It has 'a strong preoccupation with life as it is really lived, unlike the twilight world of Victorian or modern pornography in which characters are made to act, however improbably, merely to gratify the daydreams of a male readership'.

There are elements of truth in this view. The tone of the dialogue is relatively natural throughout and the two girls are characterised with some care. Descriptions of sexual activity are interrupted by more general topics concerned with love. Deviancy is mentioned occasionally, but not dwelt upon, and mutuality is stressed. The first encounter between the young lovers is not a smooth and mechanical coition, and the joy and delight which love-making offers is enthusiastically praised, without excessiveness or obsessiveness. Susanne is at pains to emphasise that the partners must love one another; the characters are not just copulating robots.

Yet, there is another side. The atmosphere of the two dialogues is almost unrelievedly claustrophobic; hardly ever is the outside world referred to in a concrete way. There is a basic dishonesty in the discussion of pregnancy, evasion when morality is raised and a general idealisation of sex – it is, for instance, less than probable that a girl so sheltered as Fanchon would achieve orgasm with quite the readiness of her account. Susanne's first description of intercourse to the improbably ignorant Fanchon may be straightforward enough, but subsequent renderings attempt greater stimulation in the reader, and Fanchon's techniques for furtive sex in public must have had the intention of titillation, as did the evocative accounts of foreplay and postures. This intention is borne out by the 'Bulle Orthodoxe de Priape' which preceded the first edition. The Bull threatens anathemas against all those who are not emotionally and physically stimulated by the dialogues. There is none of the hypocritical cant in either of the prefaces which English writers habitually employed to disarm criticism; love is a game and a sport to be heartily enjoyed. Yet the message is anarchic and undermining: parental authority, the moral teachings of the church, social mores and the institution of marriage are all attacked. Susanne is the advocate of the pleasure principle, and Fanchon makes an apt pupil. The only sin lies in being found out.

How the twentieth century judges *The School of Venus* is less important for this study than the seventeenth-century reaction, and that, as we have seen, was clear that it was a depraving and corrupting work. My own view is that, despite its redeeming features, it should be classed as pornographic, though relatively speaking a novice in that genre. Imaginatively it does seem to break new ground; there are a few borrowings from Apuleius and incidental similarities with Aretino's *Ragionamenti*, but in general it can claim originality, and this, as we shall see, is a rare redeeming feature among erotica.[15]

To unravel the complex Latin title of *Tullia and Octavia – Aloisiae Sigeae Toletanae Satyra Sotadica de arcanis Amoris et Veneris. Aloisia hispanice scripsit, latinate donavit Ioannis Meursius* – illustrates the lengths to which early pornographers went to camouflage their authorship. Literally translated this reads: The Sotadic Satire on secret Loves and Lusts of Luisa Sigée of Toledo. Luisa wrote in Spanish, Jan de Meurs rendered it into Latin. Almost all of which is false. The book is certainly sotadic, that is to say a coarse satire in the scurrilous manner of the Greek poet Sotades. There is no denying its obsessive fascination for love and lust, mainly the latter. It is emphatically not by Luisa Sigée, the daughter of an expatriate Frenchman, who lived in Toledo from about 1530 to 1560 and was known as 'The Minerva of her Time'. Nor did de Meurs (1579–1639), a respectable professor of Greek and History at Leyden and Soröe, translate it.

Who did write it was unknown in the seventeenth century. The first correct ascription occurred in 1739, when in a burlesque court of Apollo, Nicolas Chorier, well-known as the historian of Dauphiné, was confronted by Luisa Sigée. In 1757 Barbou's edition named Chorier as the author. His memoirs corroborate this; recording his life before 1639, Chorier wrote: 'I then wrote Epistles, Speeches, A Political Dissertation on the French Alliance with the Ottoman Empire, and two Satires, one Menippean, and the other Sotadical.'[16]

Chorier was born in Vienne in 1612, educated at a Jesuit academy and became a Doctor of Law in Vienne. Between 1640 and 1658 he published various historical and philosophical works, including his History of Dauphiné, and grew wealthy from the law. In 1658, however, the Court of Aids was suppressed and Chorier at the age of forty-six was made redundant. He moved at this time to Grenoble, and in 1659 or 1660 his manuscript, written two decades or more before, was secretly printed, either at Grenoble or Lyons. There was some suspicion of his authorship, but in 1666 Du Gué de Bagnols, the Intendant of Lyons, took Chorier under his protection. An edition of 1678 was dedicated to Du Gué. Chorier died at the ripe old age of eighty in 1692 leaving other manuscripts.[17] There were fifteen Latin editions in the next ninety years, and by 1680 the less cumbersome alternative title of *Elegantiae Latini Sermones*, still attributed to poor de Meurs, was commonly used. The first edition in French *L'Academie des Dames*, seems to be the 1680 'Ville-Franche' one in the British Museum; the work was then, as we have seen, quickly Englished by 1684 and Foxon records several subsequent renditions.[18] The French translation is rightly described by Lisieux as 'traduction insipide' but it is impossible to tell from the one exemplary sentence in Cademan's indictment of 1684 whether his English version was from the French or the Latin.

Tullia and Octavia of the common English title refers to the two girls, Tullia, nineteen, married and highly experienced sexually, and her cousin Octavia, who is only fifteen but about to be married to Pamphilius. The seven dialogues are divided into two parts, the long seventh comprising the second part. They each have thematic names, and are of unequal length, the first four being quite short, the fifth and sixth longer.

The first discussion between the girls is called 'The Skirmish'. Tullia wants to know about Octavia's premarital encounters with her fiancé, which evokes a specific and titillating account of petting, and Pamphilius' attempt to enter her, which is prevented by her embarrassment and tightness and the proximity of her mother Sempronia, who, in fact appears, just after the frustrated Pamphilius has spent on her. The second Dialogue, 'Tribadicon', graduates from mere description to action. Octavia opens the conversation by saying 'You have often wished to hold me in your arms when your husband Callias was away'. Tullia, who claims that all women feel some lesbian passions, takes advantage of the opportunity, and excites Octavia by stroking her. As Tullia gets carried away she scratches and pinches her cousin and with 'Ah! Ah! Ah! I'm dying of pleasure' has an orgasm while lying on top of Octavia. In the ensuing calm, she tells Octavia about dildoes. The short third dialogue, 'Anatomy', is concerned with the enormous size of Pamphilius' penis. Tullia explains about male erections and insertion, in a passage that is reminiscent of *The School of Venus* and reassures Octavia, who demands an inspection of Tullia on all fours, and is amazed at her size: a whole man could enter, she says, even one mounted on a horse. 'The Duel', the fourth episode, follows, and this describes Tullia's wedding night with her husband Callias, much as Susanne told Fanchon about her love-making. Callias too is enormous, and so ardent that he explodes as his beam of flesh tries to force its way into the strait gate. Eventually he pierces her up to the seventh rib, and Tullia tastes sexual ecstasy. She goes on to describe how she and Callias experiment with different postures, with her on top, the two on their sides, and how he mounts her in front of her best friend Pomponia, who is suitably orgasmic as she watches. Tullia explains to the still relatively innocent Octavia the difference between the civil law and the law of nature in their teachings on unfaithfulness; cuckolding one's husband is a perfectly natural thing to do.

Between the fourth and fifth meetings there is a gap of two weeks in which Octavia and Pamphilius have got married. 'Lovemaking' finds the two girls in bed together naked. Tullia passionately embraces Octavia, and feeling her amorously discovers that her vagina is enormously enlarged. While she stimulates Octavia with her finger she says her whole hand could now go in, and Octavia describes her husband's impressive armoury, 'the gift of Venus'. She lost her virginity, she explains, in a sitting position. As Tullia grows more and more abandoned she calls Octavia by the name of her lover, Lampridio, and has her lie on her and excite her to mutual but non-simultaneous orgasms. Lying together in the delicious aftermath, Octavia tells more about her wedding, how, as with Robinet in *The School of Venus*, pomade was a vital lubricant, how Pamphilius took enormous pleasure from fellatio, and how they had intercourse three times, which Tullia rates as highly abstemious. Tullia describes her sexual training, her childish experiments with other girls, including cunnilingus, and how Octavia's mother, a libertine and ambisexual, had corrupted her and her friends by having them watch her being ridden by her lover Giocondo. Octavia gives a graphic account of how her mother took her, before her wedding, to a holy man, Father Theodore, who gave her a penance of whipping. He told them that it was perfectly decent for women to strip before him as an act of piety and repentance. Then he flogs Sempronia first heavily, then lightening the blows, then fiercely again, for an hour, which the torn and welted Sempronia calls 'sport, not suffering'. Then he turns his attentions to the neophyte and beats her till the lash drips with blood while she flagellates her own clitoris. Her mother explains that this will increase the voluptuousness of her wedding night. Sempronia comes seven times with Giocondo after this holy disciplining.

Tullia tells Octavia about her mother's and her own lovers. Giocondo is himself married, but Sempronia spent 6000 crowns on a chastity belt for his wife, complete with a portcullis, to which she keeps the key. Giocondo has been allowed intercourse only once with her. Tullia's lover Lampridio used to be an Anchorite, and came three times in a row when he first slept with her, and twice later that day, while Sempronia was in the room keeping guard against the cuckolded Callias. When Lampridio moves in, Callias has a girdle of chastity made for Tullia, who is insatiable for both of them, but Lampridio has a duplicate key cut, and 'made my horse go to the twelfth round in almost a single breath'. A description of a second lashing by the hermit, this time on Tullia, in which the slavering Theodore tore out flesh from her buttocks with his nails and tufts of her pubic hair, and produced in her 'three showers in one coition' leads to the girls' talking about sterility and impotence. The Duchess Leonora could only be brought to venereal delights with her husband by being whipped. Tullia describes seeing the Marquis Alfonso being stimulated by rods, gaining an erection, rushing to his wife, shaking frantically up and down and flooding her with the celestial gifts of Venus. This long episode closes with Tullia confiding that she would like her lover Lampridio to lie with Octavia.

In the last episode of the first part, 'Frolics and Sports', we are into group sex. Both Lampridio and a fourth contestant Rangoni take part with the two girls. Tullia acts as mistress of ceremonies and has Lampridio mount Octavia while herself providing manual stimulation to both of them. Then Rangoni, described as the seediest, meaning most virile, of men, with a huge penis, takes his place on the unwilling Octavia, while Lampridio and Tullia stimulate both of them. It is Tullia's ambition that Lampridio and Rangoni will between them satisfy the girls twenty times that night, and to encourage them in their experimental and increasingly acrobatic posture she tells them how she once in Rome had intercourse twenty-five times with four men in every kind of explicitly drawn posture. As the contortionists discuss the most satisfying positions, Tullia sums up their frolics by saying: 'We delight in the unaccustomed and rush upon the forbidden'.

The cast is greatly expanded for the seventh 'Academic Entertainment', a country party with lascivious diversions. Octavia's lover Alphonse is there; there are young teenagers, too, who are to be initiated, Leonor a frustrated widow, Aloisia who would exhaust Mars and Isabelle who is used to nine times per night. The episode is a melange of stories, increasingly decadent sexual activities and discussions of such topics as artificial stimulants, sodomy, irrumation, incest, frequency, sizes, defloration, postures, homosexuality and lesbianism. Father Theodore and a Tartuffean Father Chrisogon are described first as voyeurs and then as sexual Herculeses. There are stories about the appetites of nuns being satisfied by young men disguised as gardeners, and long-abstemious abbesses achieving fulfilment. The argument that too much sex is unhealthy is laughed to scorn by these record-breakers, and the bigotry of priests who seek to convert husbands to celibacy is assaulted. The motto of the party is Tullia's 'We all live to love and to be loved; that's the intention of Nature.' To this complete anarchy have our two principals come from the opening description of what in retrospect seem innocent adolescent fumblings.

'Aloisia Sigea', Chorier, was plainly a classical scholar of some sophistication, because the text is scattered with references and quotations from Greek and Latin eroticists: Sappho, Aristophanes, Elephantis, Philenis, Hermogenes, the Milesian Tales, Ovid, Petronius, Catullus and *The Priapeia*. There are frequent citations of Greek myths; in the seventh Dialogue, for instance, Tullia answers Octavia's question about women's pleasure in fellatio by the story of Prometheus making man *sans vit*, and fashioning a penis out of mud; he then makes a woman, who drinks from the water in which Prometheus had rinsed his muddy hands. There are also many *doubles entendres* in the Latin text, like the punning of the word *testes*.

'The Divine Aretino' is mentioned more than once by Tullia, and his legacy is particularly marked in the strong anti-clericalism, especially of the seventh Dialogue, which may be a reason why Lisieux speculated that Chorier was a Protestant. Fathers Theodore, Chrisogon and Hippolite are all depicted as rationalising or hypocritical lechers, probably based on actual scandals,[19] and monastic life, as with Aretino, is merely a cover for mass debauchery in secret. One of the many changes towards insipidity in the 1680 French translation occurs on page 89: the original reads 'Even the most pious women are inquisitive about this sort of thing', namely sexual matters. 1680 changes 'pious' to 'chaste', thus losing the slur on apparent saintliness.

The ever-increasing depravity of the sexuality, and particularly the encouragement and lessons which Tullia gives her younger cousin, are justified, as we have seen, on broadly libertine grounds. Honour in love, she says, 'is but a shadow in the light'. Shame, modesty and chastity are inventions of a repressive society; in Nature all things are free. Of course it is common prudence to observe the conventions, but 'whatever thou canst conveniently do, without any scandal to thy husband and family, be fully persuaded that it is permitted to thee'. Assume an appearance of piety, and respect for public rites and common customs, but follow the adage that 'a woman is born for her husband's pleasure, and all other men for hers'. Chorier makes the interesting point through Tullia, that literate woman are rarely virtuous, a view that the authorities in France and England shared in condemning his work and that of others who incited the reading public to lechery. He also justifies the orgiastic and deviant activities of women like Tullia, by having her argue that women of her class can hardly disport themselves in the stews. Although Messalina is more than once mentioned, her example is not to be followed.

Tullia and Octavia, combining instruction with increasingly libidinous relations between teacher, pupil and male auxiliaries, is the most advanced piece of pornography written in the seventeenth century. By some oversight, it omits bestiality, and there is relatively little male homosexuality. However, there is a prevalent emphasis on male brutality. Despite the fact that the girls are almost always willing, usually eager, they are always thrown on to beds, and the men always leap upon them. The enormous size of many of the male organs featured, and the descriptions of defloration and flagellation underline this sense of violence. The only person in the seven dialogues whose character is at all developed is Tullia; from an interested and helpful cousin, she rapidly emerges first as a rampant lesbian, then an unfaithful wife, then as a nymphomaniac orgiast and finally as an insatiable practitioner of every kind of perversion. The *Satyra*, like most pornography, is a fundamentally anti-feminist work.

It is also far more overtly subversive than *The School of Venus*. The usual targets, parents, marriage, social mores, the church, and the ideals of chastity, sanctity, honour and fidelity are degraded with shocking directness; at the end of the book there is nothing left to believe or trust in, except the primal urges of the loins.

Despite superficial similarities with *The School of Venus* – Tullia's initial anatomy lesson, for instance, or the wedding night of

Octavia – the tone is so utterly different that it seems impossible it could have been influenced by *Tullia and Octavia*. Even that boyish enthusiast Aretino would, one suspects, have been shaken by the unrelenting lewdness of his admirer.

Ferrante Pallavicino was an angry young man, who in his short life lambasted the hypocrisies of society, the Roman Catholic church, particularly the Jesuits, tradition and the idea of religious belief in general. He paid for his critical stance by being beheaded for atheism at the age of twenty six at Avignon in 1644. *La Retorica delle Puttane*, satirising the art of rhetoric as another of man's hypocrisies, was first published in 1642 and often republished in his *Opere Scelte*.[21]

Naturalisation and modernisation was a craze in the latter half of the seventeenth century. Along with Homer and Virgil, Pallavicino suffered the fate of being anglicised and dragged into the 1680s. The satire disappears completely in the process, a loss for which the many topical allusions are little recompense.

The title page of *The Whores Rhetorick, Calculated to the Meridian of London And conformed to the Rules of Art. In Two Dialogues* (1683) gives an early clue that the adaptor considered the work dangerously risqué. He writes under a pseudonym, 'Philo-Puttanus', though the imprint, 'Printed for George Shell in Stone-Cutter-Street in Shoe-Lane', may be genuine.[22] His Preface, dedicated 'To the most famous University of London-Courtezans', indulges in numerous antique puns about pens, thorns in the flesh, penetrating precious mines, admission to the pit and allusions to venereal disease. The 'Epistle to the Reader' has the required nod to respectability: 'Read this Book to expose all the tricks and all the finesses you can find therein; carry it in your pockets as some do the pictures of poor Animals rotten with the Venereal distemper, to make you detest these Monsters.' The author, fulfilling this social obligation, 'detests to be bawdy and profane', but 'the nauseous ribaldry is comprised within the terms of a decent civility'. Needless to say, there is no mention of the original.

The Introduction discovers Dorothea,[23] daughter of a cavalier, whom Charles II had smiled upon but 'fair Danae [probably the Duchess of Portsmouth] gets the golden shower'. She is in abject poverty in a room in the red-light district of Covent Garden. This beautiful teenage waif is disturbed by a call from an old woman, whose nose appears to grow moss on it 'like a dog's T——d'. She is a midwife, but for thirty years had served the public from her lovely house in Moor-Fields, providing comfort for the amorous Republic, and having among her worthy and eminent debtors 'King's lieutenants, Lord Mayors and Sheriffs of the City of London'. Dorothea recognises her as 'Lady' Creswell, convicted on 29 November 1681 by a 'Malignant Jury' at Westminister of thirty years of bawdry.[24] She predictably advises Dorothea to go on the game; Dorothea, like Fanchon in *The School of Venus*, protests her total ignorance, but no disinclination, and Creswell accommodatingly offers tuition. The scene is thus set.

The theme throughout the two dialogues that follow is, like Pallavicino's and many of the whore stories of the period, that of avarice. Time and again Creswell returns to this message: 'your avarice must be insatiable', 'ride them more unmercifully than they do their horses, make them greater slaves than Algerines', 'Please others, enrich yourself', 'stolen pleasures will make your dainties yet more highly prized', 'let there be no entry to your Straits until they have disbursed the usual tax', 'Suffer impotents if they show a Lordly generosity', 'the most profitable traffick is with wealthy cits . . . golden lovers' or 'get an impotent old keeper with a bag of money'.[25] Dorothea is advised to beg during orgasm, to have many lovers as well as a keeper and to steal or wheedle everything she can get her hands on. She should never stick at anything 'how licentious soever' provided it is well-rewarded. She must be more mercenary than Danae so hated by the elegists.

The first lesson is mainly concerned with general rules. Dorothea should seem insatiable in pleasing her lover. She should keep the King's peace by night and by day. She is instructed in the stratagems of having two customers in her house at the same time; telling one that she has a 'precise [i.e. Puritan] female friend in the Chamber' or 'a swordy blade' (i.e. a tearaway gallant) is usually enough to frighten a bourgeois customer. She is advised against parading her dainties in public; that is the way to get a flogging in Bridewell – of which Creswell has some recent experience – or being dragged through the city at the tail of a cart. In passing, we are told that old bawds prefer rampant youth, which can 'for once cure their itch by rubbing their superannuated tails'. The author, wishing perhaps to flaunt his literary tastes, quotes or mentions Hobbes, *Heraclitus Ridens, Almanzor and Almahide* and *Oroondates*.

The second dialogue deals specifically with the whore's arts of love-making. Dorothea must 'Frenchifie her Commodities, or, (to avoid ribbaldrie) her Merchandize, not with that Country Pox, but with hard names, and Je ne Sca quois.'[25] She should be tight in her clothes and expose her breasts enough to be titillating, but not so much that her customers will not have an itch to see more. One of the few original Pallavicino jabs is retained when Creswell compares customers to the Jesuits who 'want in their novices a good face'. Given this appearance, 'man's amorous parts soon start to pullulate'. There are detailed instructions about keeping the gate of love literally in good shape, or 'contracting her latitude and longitude into its original and proper bounds'. In an Ovidian echo, the bawd says men think 'the best sailing is in a strait and narrow sea between two pleasant shores'. Old traders tend 'to swallow up a man of war at one morsel and shipwrack the saylors expectation'. A 'Lady of good practice may have each day many clients knocking at her closet door [a common pun, this] with Fee in hand to discharge themselves of their superfluities'. The stairs will be wet and the passage slippery. There follows a long passage on dealing with impotent customers, 'disabled old souldiers with no power to handle their Arms'. She must expect to find them 'hiding under her Petticoats, to raise their decayed appetites by the warm sauce to be found under those Robes . . . sucking pappies' is another means they use 'in matter of erection'. If these prove ineffectual, they will 'blame too much love'. 'As one hand lozenges' and 'tother fumbles with the amorous parts of thy flesh' Dorothea is taught to 'chase him like a mortified piece of flesh, scratch every wrinkle, tickle his flank', even recite to him 'a wanton sonnet'. At long last, he may 'squeeze out a loving tear'. Creswell then deals with Puritan customers, who in their hypocrisy resemble the whore herself, and compares herself to Richard Baxter's lists of lessons from his text 'I come to the nineteenthly'. Floggers are to be treated with reserve, 'the most jealous animal of the whole of creation', and the obdurate lover should be excited with 'lascivious pictures, obscene images and representations . . . the best draughts of Men and Women naked, in sweet caresses and dying postures'. Creswell draws the line at Aretino's Postures; they are 'not necessary to be seen in any Northern clime' but for 'a hot region this side of Sodom'.[27] She does, however, describe some ingenious prints which when hung one way could grace a cathedral, but upside down would drive 'a Hermit into obscene thoughts'. She has advice about Dorothea's reading, too. Romances are out, but modern comedies inculcate the right brand of cynicism. 'For obscenity', she continues, 'I recommend those pieces to you, where you may be supplied with a better stock than I can in conscience expose in this my Rhetorick'. Towards the end of the book there is vague and imprecise mention of various positions, and the need for the whore to move voluptuously and wriggle, though 'Venereal desires are very littel in those parts rubbed twelve time a day'. Dorothea is told about French kissing and reassured that loss of maidenhead is no worse than pricking a pimple. Before the old bawd departs she gives final instructions about practising in front of a mirror. Another 'doe' is ready for the slaughter.[28]

I know of no references in seventeenth-century literature or private writing to this squalid little book. Its printer was, as we have seen, convicted and fined, though it continued to be advertised after this in the *Term Catalogue*, and apparently at least one more edition was published in the 1690s.[29] The second entry in the *Term Catalogue* prints the title as *W—— Rhetorick*.[30]

Apart from cashing in on the topical interest in Creswell's trial and conviction, the author's stance is anti-Puritan; there are attacks on conventicles and the self-righteous lechery of brothers and sisters; many of the bawd's best customers, apart from the recently purged Whig-Presbyterian corporation of the City of London, are said to be in exile in Amsterdam, in their 'cloaks of a Geneva cut'. They are punningly described as 'militant mortal enemies to passive obedience' in a whore, and their devotion is 'enlivened by the prospect of a naked Saint'.

It is hard to think of the author's intention as pornographic, namely sexual arousal on the part of the reader. The general style is one of bawdy, with numerous dirty puns and metaphors. One or two passages lapse into the disgusting and obscene, but on what was thought of as stimulating, precise descriptions of postures, for instance, or evocative descriptions of foreplay, Creswell is vague and general. There is none of the freshness and enjoyment that distinguished *The School of Venus*. Cynicism dominates.

NOTES

1. The involved bibliographies of the three are unravelled in Foxon, pp. 9–10, 30–7, 38–43.
2. See my 'Two Early Editions of Restoration Erotica', *The Library*, 5th Series, XXXII (1977).
3. Foxon, pp. 7–18 gives details of these and other prosecutions.

4. R. Latham and W. Matthews, eds., *The Diary of Samuel Pepys*, Vol. IX (London, 1976), pp. 21, 57–9.
5. *Athenianisme* (London, 1710), pp. 229–30; W. H. Whitemore, ed., *John Dunton's Letters from New England* (Boston, 1867), p. 112.
6. *The Session of the Poets, Holden at the Foot of Parnassus-Hill*, (London, 1969), pp. 6–7. I owe this reference to the kindness of Mr Hugh Amory.
7. H. A. Beecham, 'Samuel Wesley Senior: New Biographical Evidence', *Renaissance and Modern Studies*, VII (1963), 109.
8. Nottingham University, Portland Mss., PwV 42, f. 423.
9. P. 113.
10. *Venus in the Cloister* (London, 1683), pp. 125–7.
11. Foxon, pp. 30–7.
12. Middlesex County Record Office, MJ/SR 1582, published in my 'Two Early Editions'. The earliest reference to an English edition that I have come across occurs in *Erotopolis* (1684), p. 59. This probably refers to the 1680 edition.
13. KB 28/176/19, 20.
14. Thomas translation, pp. 87–8.
15. From Apuleius, pre-coital wine drinking as with Lucius and Photis, p. 102; from Aretino, passing food between mouths, p. 102; preference for coitus on chests, p. 125; female exclamations during intercourse, p. 51; sexual euphemisms, p. 122. The equivalent pages in R. Rosenthal, ed., *Ragionamenti* (London, 1972) are pp. 21, 146, 351, 43–4.
16. I. Lisieux, ed., *Chorier's Memoirs* (Paris, 1880).
17. Foxon, p. 38; I. Lisieux, ed., *Dialogues of Luisa Sigea* (Paris, 1890), pp. v-xii.
18. Foxon, pp. 40–3; Foxon notes the reference in Ravenscroft's *The London Cuckolds* (1682) to 'the beastly bawdy translated booke called *The Schoole of Women*'; this may be a reference to Cademan's edition or an even earlier one.
19. For instance, the Adriaensen affair described in chapter 8 of this book, or the masochism of St Mary Magdalene of Pazzi, who died in 1607. E. J. Dingwall, *Very Peculiar People* (London, 1950), Ch. III.
20. Petronius also attacks rhetoricians at the beginning of the *Satyricon*.
21. *CHEL*, IX, pp. 225–60.
22. The author is unknown; both 'Rolf S. Reade' and Foxon agree that Maidment's attribution to L'Estrange in the Edinburgh edition of 1839 is highly improbable. *Registrum*, II, p. 36; Foxon, p. 10. In the Epistle to the Reader, the author claims to be a university graduate; that is the only clue. There was a young bookseller called George Shell trading in London at this time. He had been freed from apprenticeship in December 1682; he also published a broadside in 1684, but that is all. D. F. McKenzie, *Stationers' Company Apprentices 1641—1700* (Oxford, 1974).
23. A common name for fictional prostitutes at least since *Don Quixote*; used in *The English Rogue* (1668–71).
24. We shall meet this famous bawd again. See Note in Schless, *POAS*, III, p. 384.
25. Pp. 37, 40, 50, 77, 124, 131, 137, 162.
26. P. 114.

27. See under Visual.
28. When Creswell was convicted, *The Impartial Protestant Mercury,* No 64, noted that 'some of her does unkindly testified against her'.
29. Foxon, p. 10.
30. Hilary Term, 1683/4; Vol. II, p. 64 in Arber.

4 Anti-Puritanical

The Restoration was the age of *Hudibras*, *Tartuffe* and the Clarendon Code. Butler's work was not only always in Charles II's pocket; it was required reading for anyone who wished to be thought a loyalist. Molière's canting hypocrite was endlessly copied and adapted on the English stage. Politically, nonconformity, so recently dominant, was harried by a draconian set of vengeful and hobbling statutes. What Richard Head, in a licentious work, called 'those late licentious times' were plainly over, or, at least, a new form of licence ruled.[1]

Richard Baxter, it was alleged later, had foreseen it all. When Monck was considering inviting the King to return in late 1659, he had led a delegation of divines to try to dissuade him. 'Prophaneness is so inseparable from the Royal Party', he had argued, 'that if ever you bring the King back, the power of Godliness will most certainly depart from the Land.'[2] Dissent became the prime target for satire, ridicule, lampoon and libel, more so than that traditional whipping boy, Roman Catholicism. Even, according to Burnet 'Every pulpit turned to raillery of the dissenters to the total neglect of the papists'.[3] As the Vicar of Stratford-on-Avon feelingly noted in his diary, 'Most men are too ready to espie motes in a black cote'.[4] But if that black coat happened to be a Geneva gown, beams were in order. To be a professed Puritan in the Restoration was to be an outcast. As Macaulay wrote of the stage: 'The hero intrigues just as he wears a wig, because if he did not he would be a queer fellow, a city prig, perhaps a puritan . . . .' Weber, Tawney and company notwithstanding, the citizen need not be a Puritan, and there was enough about his values and life-style to raise mirth in an audience of aristocratic or courtly tastes. It was not essential to be a Puritan to sympathise politically with the Good Old Cause, or in Charles II's reign to be counted a Whig. Yet about citizens and Whigs there clung, at least to their enemies, a noxious whiff of sectarianism.

Of course, there was nothing new in the Restoration ridicule of 'saints'. The catonic censor was a Plautine butt, and Apuleius had a field-day with religious enthusiasts in *The Golden Ass*. Chaucer satirised types of humbug and hypocrisy, and the Elizabethans, Jacobeans and Carolines followed suit. Malvolio was Shakespeare's finest contribution to the type; in *Bartholomew Fair* especially, Jonson launched a sustained attack against puritan pretensions. These are only the most famous of a host of scathing stage portraits. [5] Character-writers, epigrammatists, elegists, balladeers, jesters and writers of rogue literature all joined in the attack, even before the Puritan revolution. The effect of Puritan domination, as we have already noted, was to drive their bitterest opponents underground and abroad. Ridicule, previously from a position of dominance and security, was now the resort of the ousted, the hunted and the hopeless. Perhaps this accounts for the sharply accelerated coarseness and obscenity of Interregnum satire. Writers like John Crouch, and the many anonymous libellers become more and more obsessed with the sexual attack. Hardly surprisingly, the good-humoured amusement that had infused a Shakespeare or an Overbury, had been warped into a passion for smearing the regenerate with every kind of lewd and perverted carnality. This approach set the tone for the Restoration; it was its literary revenge, the Royalist author's Clarendon Code.

The archetypal 'fanatick' was a positive flypaper for libels. He spoke through his nose with a snivelling twang; if he preached he rolled his eyes dramatically and looked down his long nose. He was incapable of merriment, and his mirthlessness was reflected in his drab, unfashionable dress, his straggling wigless hair. He was to his marrow disapproving and censorious. His speech was a special sanctified jargon, larded with quotations from his narrow reading, the Bible, sermons and Foxe's *Book of Martyrs*. If he was a Quaker, he would Yea and Nay you, Thee and Thou you and be insolent to his betters, who were almost everybody. The Puritan was clannish and exclusive, consorting only with his brother and sister saints and packing the conventicles to take down interminable sermons in short-hand.

Beneath this appearance of self-righteous earnestness lurked an even more repulsive creature. The caricatured saint was a furtive lecher, a very Jesuit in his ability to procure sisters for his lust and to justify the seduction. This Caiaphas also crept to brothels, where his special predilection was for flagellation or even sodomy. His wife was often as bad as he; though a managing shrew to him, she had an experienced eye for a gallant. The cuckolded husband might even be an accessory to his wife's whoredom if it profited trade. This sanctimonious, impotent, lust-driven pharisee was the image that was conjured up by the satirists in the minds of unregenerate Englishmen in the reign of Charles II.

As always, there were enough backsliders or plain deserters to give a gloss of justification for such a caricature. Even the founders of Protestantism had not been unspotted. Luther's sexual urges had been attacked by Catholic adversaries. Calvin had had compromising relationships with some of his zealous female followers; Beza had 'given a little spice of Wantonness' to his youthful verses.[6] Nor was Knox's name free from scandal, and Marprelate had brought down on English Puritans the charge of vulgarity and ribaldry.

Sexual rumours about the Puritan leadership circulated in surreptitious Royalist publications during the Interregnum. Only a couple of months after the King's return, there appeared a play called *Cromwells Conspiracy* by 'A Person of Honour'. One scene depicted the Protector in his nightshirt after the seduction of Mrs Lambert. Oliver's description of his night of lust with the reluctant beauty is reminiscent of the romantic-cum-lecherous verses of a Sedley, a Buckhurst or a Mulgrave. It must be one of the most improbable speeches in Restoration drama.[7]

The saints had some uncomfortable allies or erstwhile supporters too. John Selden, lawyer, opponent of the Stuarts and member of the Westminster Assembly of Divines, had, according to Aubrey and popular gossip, 'got more by his Prick then he had done by his practice', thanks to his adulterous relationship with the Countess of Kent, not to mention his *affaires* with her waiting-woman and her 'shee-Blackamore'.[8] That 'strenuous puritan', Hugh Peters, pastor in Amsterdam and New England, chaplain to the roundheads and to Cromwell, was dogged by sexual scandal-mongers. In May 1655 a correspondent wrote to Secretary of State Thurlow from Amsterdam: 'I am glad to heare Mr. Peters shows his head againe. It was reported heere that he was found with a whore a bed, and that he grew madd, and said nothing but O blood, blood, that troubles me.' True or not—and it is almost certainly not – this was typical of the inventiveness of anti-puritan libellers.[9]

Several of the regicides were hardly lily-white. Monson had a reputation even before the war as a dissolute rake. Henry Marten was another embarrassment; a rabid republican, spend-thrift, audaciously facetious, he had the doubtful distinction of being called a whoremaster by both Charles I and Cromwell. His reputation as a womaniser led to the allegation that he had written a book on menstruation.[10] After his imprisonment for debt, *Select City Quaeries* wondered 'Whether Henry Marten loves Kings Bench Rules better than *Aretinos* Postures?'[11] Publication of what purported to be his letters to one of his mistresses merely added fuel to the lampooners' flames.[12] Another republican grandee, Thomas Scot, was monotonously smeared with the charge of sexual promiscuity. In 1660, it was rumoured that he was 'impudent acquaintance' with Jane Powell.[13]

Milton's fastidiously tutored nephew and godson, John Phillips, turned renegade during the Interregnum, rather than, more fashionably, after it, and lent his hand to one of the first of the drolleries, *Sportive Wit*. Its obscene pillorying of the elect no doubt owed something to his inside knowledge.[14] His *Satyr against Hypocrites* (1655) was a scathing attack against his former co-religionists and a forerunner of Butler's masterpiece.

The sensation caused by the revelations of the flagellation of his maid by the sadistic Presbyterian divine Zachary Crofton was exploited by Francis Kirkman in *The Presbyterian Lash, or Noctroff's Maid Whipt*. First published in 1661, and reprinted throughout the Restoration, it caught the imagination of John Ward in provincial Stratford-on-Avon, and no doubt helped to fix in the public mind the connotation of Puritanism with sexual deviation.[15] Milton's friend, that discreet bachelor Andrew Marvell, 'the first presbyterian scribbler who sanctified libels and scurrility to the use of the Good Old Cause', in Dryden's phrase,[16] was himself attacked by that renegade Presbyterian, Samuel Parker, as impotent, homosexual and Frenchified.[17]

Shaftesbury, another presbyterian, and according to the famous gibe of Charles II, another 'whoremaster', was persistently and probably groundlessly accused of 'addiction to the brothel'. It was popularly rumoured that his henchman Sir Paul Neal acted as his pimp in Hyde Park; many in the audience may well have identified him with Sir Timothy Treat-All in Behn's *The City Heiress* and with the Podesta in Crowne's *The City Politiques*. The most scabrous similarity was Antonio in Otway's *Venice Preserv'd*; this aged debauchee was shown urging his whore Aquilina to flog him for his sexual satisfaction.

To lewdness every night the Letcher ran,
Shew me, all London, such another man,
Match him at Mother Creswold's if you can.

Haley has argued that all these portraits refer not to Shaftesbury, but his ally, the Chamberlain of the city, Sir Thomas Player, a Presbyterian, who was deeply implicated in the exposure in 1681 of Mrs Creswell's activities. His debt at her brothel in Moorfields was £300. He was, like Rabsheka, 'A Saint that can both flesh and spirit use Alike haunt conventicles and the stews.' Even if Otway intended Renault for his portrait of the Whig leader, he still got in a sexual slur. Renault 'loves fumbling with a wench with all his heart'.[18] Titus Oates, as part of his dressing up for the pillory after the collapse of the Plot and Exclusion Campaign, was accused of sodomy, a crime also urged against Buckingham, quondam ally of dissent.[19] Another embarrassing ally for dissent was the 'debauch'd atheistical bravo', Sir Thomas Armstrong, a crony of Monmouth's. After his execution for complicity in the Rye House Plot in 1684, a mock elegy described how 'The sisters too appear, with snivelling cries. To celebrate their stallion's obsequies.'[20] Finally, among Calvinists of some prominence, there was the scandalous death of Peter Motteux, the translator of Rabelais and prolific author, who died after being flagellated at his own request in a brothel near the Strand in 1719.

There were smaller fry who served the purpose of confirming popular prejudice against 'holy cheats'. Robert Foulkes, a Puritan divine, was found guilty of seducing a young lady, living in sin with her and murdering her bastard by him. Great publicity was given to the case by the intervention of Gilbert Burnet and the resultant publication of Foulkes's *Alarme to Sinners* in 1679, along with a lurid account of the trial. Calamy regretted the hearty sexual appetite of William Farrington, a silk-weaver and preacher, and 'the scandal he brought upon religion by his immoralities'.[21] Henry Hills printed in 1678 George Hickes' *An Account of the Tryal of that most wicked Pharisee, Major Thomas Weir, who was executed for Adultery, Incest and Bestiality*. Weir 'had acquired a particular gracefulness in whining and sighing, above any of the sacred clan' in Edinburgh. In 1670, aged seventy, he confessed to his varied activities and predictably his sect tried to hush the whole affair up. But sin will out, to the delight of cavaliers whom Weir had victimised in the wars, and to the profit no doubt of

Henry Hills. Hickes' introduction gave the impression that Weir's promiscuity was not atypical.

> As for adulteries and fornications, those common failings of these Pharisees, there are more of them committed, and more bastards born within their country, the Western Holy-Land, than in all our nation besides. This is evident from comparing the parish registers and the registries of the presbyteries or rural deaneries of those shires with the rest of the parish and presbytery registers in every diocese of the Church.[22]

John Ward noted the case of "a Scotch Batchelour that had twentie-two children. Hee was not, it seems, very chast.' Nor, it seems, were the Scots troops under Monck who reached London in the winter 1659–60. It was alleged that they scoured 'many English barrels' with their 'Gunsticks' after their arrival.[23]

John Dunton, with his puritan and low-church contacts, and his prurient interest, is himself a splendid example of Pharisaism. In some of the 'characters' which he plagiarised in the New England section of his *Life and Errors* (London, 1705) he gave the impression that some of the inhabitants of 'The City upon a Hill' would have been more at home in Sodom and Gomorrah.[24] He also exposed with typical mealy-mouthed sanctimoniousness the accounts of four dissenting ministers 'lately silenc'd by their Congregations for Whoredom'. With the justification that 'there is scarce a man or woman in the Queen's Dominions who does not know of the lewd Practices' of these lechers, he proceeds to embellish his accounts with every kind of titillating detail, one minister caught *in flagrante delicto* on the kitchen table 'where his church had kept many a day of prayer and fasting', another practising *coitus interruptus* and abortion, another being watched through a chink as 'he was naught' with a whore, and the fourth providing physic for a voracious servant-girl, 'a shoeing horn to draw her on to his lewd embraces', which take place in a closet, after which he potters off to preach a no doubt uplifting sermon.[25] This kind of exposé was popular at the turn of the century, and plainly did nothing to improve the general view of nonconformity.[26]

What Head had found particularly licentious about the Interregnum had been the fact that 'every sordid tradesman took a freedom to prate what he would instead of Preaching' taking place.[27] It was not just trades*men*; it was women too who took up the liberating opportunities which the Civil War and the collapse of church discipline provided. How the world turned upside down has been too well told recently to require a long analysis here. The antinomianism preached by the ranters led to a spirit-inspired overturning of conventional monogamy and morality. *A New Proclamation, or Warning Peece,* (1653) by 'I.F.' attacked 'all Blasphemous Ranters, Quakers and Shakers, Men and Women, who goe up and down teaching that imbraceing ungodlinesse, and wordly lusts, they should live unsoberly, unrighteously, ungodly.' Becoming like little children again, there were men like Abiezer Coppe who preached naked, was 'commonly in bed with two women at a time' and kissed his neighbour's wife 'without sin'. Lawrence Clarkson preached that there was no sin in adultery if it was done in the faith. Believing that 'all is pure to the pure' he proceeded to seduce girls all over the country. Women, too, derived sexual freedom from this libertine counter-culture. Mrs Attaway unilaterally divorced her unbelieving husband and ran off with a member of her congregation.[28] The wife of Chief Justice St John belonged to a sect who met three times a week, blasphemed and cursed for a while, were then silent for half-an-hour and then joined in extempore hymn-singing.[29] The case of James Naylor and his naked female followers, 'my loves, my doves', came towards the end of the Interregnum and was such a sensation that it occupied long hours of parliamentary debate.[30] A print of Thomas Venner, the Fifth-Monarchy Man, showed a 'Conventicula Curiosa Anabaptistarum et Quackerorum' in which the women members of the congregation were stark naked.[31]

Ever since the outbreak of religious and sexual anarchy at Munster in 1534 among the Anabaptists, the more extreme sects had been a source of profound or potential embarrassment to more conventional Puritans. To their opponents, however, they were a gift-horse, which made the peccadilloes of individual celebrities look like spavined mules. English seventeenth-century satirists were no exception. Not only their promiscuity but also their lack of learning added powerful weapons to an already well-stocked armoury.

The bulk of anti-Puritan satire, even that part which deals mainly with their sexual shortcomings, is so enormous, that here we can only examine a few typical examples of various lines of attack. C. M. Webster has gone some way in listing seventeenth-century satires in drama, verse and prose, but his 150 titles are only the tip of the iceberg.[32] There are, for instance, an enormous number in the Thomason Collection in the British Museum which he has not listed. Restoration comedy alone has dozens of take-offs, and the Royalist Drolleries dozens more. The popular theatre also thrived from its lampoons of sectaries, and James Noakes made a speciality of the comic depiction of the Puritan merchant.[33] In the 1660s, as Legman writes, the plethora of 'Rump and Royalist ballads condemn the puritans for every sexual crime'.

Very early in the Long Parliament pamphleteers began attacking women preachers. In *A Discoverie of Six Women Preachers* (London, 1641) the ringleader is depicted in a ludicrous burlesque of a sermon, lasting two hours 'wherefore her longitude might cause a brevitude of her sucking the Aquavitae bottle'. Another, at St Giles's-in-the-Fields, is interrupted in the middle of her extempore prayers by a gentleman calling. 'I think it be the gentleman I was withall at *Salisbury Court*' – a popular theatre off Fleet Street, and also a place of assignation, and on both counts anathema to Puritans – she says, 'whom I promised this day to meet with all' – and we know what for. A third in Kent preached that if husbands crossed their wives' wills they might lawfully be forsaken. From this kind of doctrine it was a small step to all sorts of sexual promiscuity. The female ranter searching for sin too easily finds it in a gentleman's codpiece, to their mutual satisfaction.[34] *The Phanatick Intelligencer* for 24 March 1660 contains a mock petition from Mrs Ives (who had run off with the Earl of Pembroke) to the parliamentary convention:

> In the name of the sisters enlightened by the Light sent from above desiring that the Convention would no longer permit their House to be called the House of Confusion, but that to satisfie their tender consciences it might rather be called a Bawdy-house, for that they had found so much delight and comfort in such houses.

With a cut at Puritan hypocrisy, the convention was alleged to have resolved that it was 'not publickly to be called a Bawdy-house, but that for the satisfaction of the Sisters they might privately use it so when and how they pleased'. In a succeeding list of questions and answers, adultery, fornication, promiscuity, even bestiality, committed by named sectaries are declared doctrinally sound by the most outrageous warping of biblical texts.

Women saints were often portrayed as seeming chaste to the profane, but pantingly ready to receive any brother. Or despite their own predilections they were described as being jealously reserved by the brethren for their own sexual satisfaction, a satisfaction that was not always mutual.

Popular literature has numerous examples of the former types. Typical is the holy sister in a ballad in the Percy Collection who meets a 'puritanicall ladd' carrying his Bible. Their holy greetings quickly lead to more serious business, and after she has gone through the regulation 'Nay pish! Nay fi!' routine that all country girls were expected to utter as a form of token resistance, he 'layd his bible under her breeche and merylye hee kist her'. Their love-making is hampered by positional problems; she complains 'My Buttockes they lye to lowe: I wisht apocrypha were in it.'[35]

The frequently obscene verses which circulated in manuscript around the court and the coffee-houses often featured the sexual antics of Puritan women. Thus 'The Dreame' by Sir C. B., ' 'Twas by no purling streame nor shady grove', describes the encounter of a gallant and 'a bucksome girle'; he accosts her, and when she appears unwilling, he charges her with woman's 'usual Jilting tricks'.

> Young man (quoth shee) thou dost thyselfe abuse
> Thy Carnall weapon I refuse
> But 'tis not trick of Babalonish whore
> For verrily it grieves me sore
> Faine would I copulate but am not free
> The Bretheren have not gifts like thee.
> For thou alas art wanton young and Vaine
> I may not mix with the prophane.

The young man, pitying her lament that 'wee Saints starve for want of Fleshly part', shows in the dream brilliant presence of mind and poses as a convert:

> Sister said I (being resolv'd to win her)
> Yea verrily I am a Sinner

If guifted Men before now sweare and Rant
(Then surely I for Fuck may Cant)
But thou shalt worke my reformation.
I'le be no more a man in Fashion
Short Cloak, plain band, dwarfe Cuffs henceforth I'le ware
And quite cast off all dead mens hair.
The Chase of Vizard masks I will give o're
To Parke and Playhouse goe noe more
Weak bretheren will I help, weak Sisters teach
Then lett mee in thy Pulpitt Preach.
Thou art predestinated to be mine
And I ordained to be thine
Yea thou art Chosen out to swive with me
And I Elected to Fuck thee
But least that shee some Scruple still might have
An other Argument I gave
An Argument noe Sister can withstand
I put my Prick into her hand.[36]

The heroine of one of the obscenest verses ever written in English, Sir Francis Fane's 'Iter Occidentale, or The Wonders of Warm Waters' is 'A Nymph of the inspir'd Train, Some said a Quaker, but most did agree She came to set up C—ts to Fifth Monarchy.' With a seductive sigh, and a 'Friend ar't not free t'increase, is the old man Blunt', she lures a 'well Hung Proselyte' into the water and so begins an aquatic orgy.[37]

The ultimate in this general line of attack against the immorality of female saints was the Puritan whore or bawd, and, equally telling, the prostitute who turned pious. In *Free Parliament Quaeries*, published in April 1660, the question is asked 'Whether that comedie *The Costlie Whore* was not intended for the life of the Lady Sands, and was written by Henry Marten?'[38] In Payne's *The Morning Ramble* (1672) one of the four women rescued by the rakes is the daughter of a Presbyterian minister. She had come up to London to become an actress, and like so many of that profession had ended up a 'Miss', or the kept woman of a courtier or gallant.[39] A year later the *Term Catalogue* for Easter 1673 advertised *The Naked Truth . . . Intrigues of Amorous Fops in Dialogue between a precious Saint-like Sister Terpoli and Minologus a Scoffing Buffoon.* In *The Ape-Gentle-Woman: or Character of an Exchange Wench* (London,

1675) the author gives as two causes for pious-seeming prostitutes, 'a lean vicarage' or 'a broken Phanatick' at home. In this girl's case, her 'Father was busied in the late Civil-Warre; her mother made bold with the brethren' with the result that she had 'more religions in her belly than would furnish a Library'. In the lists of jilts and catalogues of ladies to be sold at auction which were a publishing craze in the 1690s, there are several Puritan women noticed. For instance:

> 12. Mrs. Susan C—n, the errantest shee-Hypocrite, well-versed in bawdry but also the Natural Philosophy, appears a Saint . . .—07–06d.[40]

Mrs Creswell's superficial show of piety was remembered for a generation after her downfall. Tom Brown had her advising Moll Quarles on the need for a church-like atmosphere in her brothel in one of his *Letters from the Dead to the Living* (London, 1702). She claimed to be a benefactress to the church in more ways than one. Not only did she satisfy the daily needs of churchwardens, but it will be remembered, she had pictures in her parlour fit for a cathedral, which when reversed showed erotic postures.[41]

As far as Puritan men were concerned, if they were not naughty fumbling cuckolds, like the 'zealot loath to tumult [against his adulterous wife] least he should be discovered a sinful brother',[42] it was the furtive lecher which particularly caught the satirist's fancy. It was, for example, entirely predictable that the cunning miss, Helena, in *The Practical Part of Love*, should have enticed as her keeper an elder of a Puritan church, 'an old dotard' as she describes him. He rationalised their relationship by calling her his 'handmaid' but made 'unnatural obscene attempts towards her' and paid up guiltily when she threatened to reveal them.[43]

Many of Webster's titles for the Interregnum reveal this libellers' fascination. There is, for instance, *A Description of the Sect called the Family of Love*, which describes their 'revels' graphically and the way in which their leader seduces country maids.[44] Cowley published *The Puritan and the Papist* in 1643, with various vulgar characters of men and women. *The Wiltshire Rant* is an exposé of the amorous career of Thomas Webbe, published in 1652. Another ranter was carved up in *The Life and Death of Stephen Marshall* (1653) and Henry More had much to say about sexuality in his *Enthusiasmus Triumphatus* published three years later. The recall of the Rump led to a bevy of attacks on its members' immorality. These were lovingly listed in *The qualifications of Persons, declared capable by the Rump Parliament*, which came out early in 1660. The rising tide of royalism was seen in *A Perfect Diurnall: or the Daily Proceedings in the Conventicle of the Phanatiques* which Thomason dates March 19, 1660. 'Resolved, That Henry Martin Esq., by Custos Rotten Whorum for the Suburbs of London, and that he enjoy all the delights of that place to all intents and purposes whatsoever occupied them before.'[45] Butler of course set the tone for the Restoration. Throughout England's answer to *Don Quixote* there are sexual innuendoes against the elect. Speaking of Love, Butler writes

> He mounted *synod-men* and rod 'em
> To *Durty Lane*, and *Little-Sodom*
> *Made 'em Corvet, like Spanish* Jenets
> And take the Ring at Madam——.[46]

The seducing minister was a common type; *The English Rogue* has a portrait of a counterfeit libertine minister, who got seven Anabaptist sisters with child in one year, cuckolding three or four of the brethren thereby.[47] The same sort of thing occurs countless times in Restoration bawdy.[48]

The perverted flagellant or masochist was also popularised by Butler.

> I felt the *Blows*, still ply'd as fast,
> As if th' had been by *Lovers* Plac'd,
> In *Raptures of Platonique Lashing*
> And *chast contemplative Bardashing*.[49]

Butler pursued this theme in his character of a Quaker: 'Some old extravagant fornicators find a Lechery in being Whipt.'[50] *The Fifteen Real Comforts*, no doubt plagiarising from Kirkman, retold with glee the story of 'the Presbyterian parson' who had 'taken so much pleasure in whipping his maid'.[51] Later satirists like Ward, Brown and Dunton all employed their rather limited inventiveness in devising scenes in which holy cheats whipped or were whipped. Poor Motteux's death, so near Ward's pub, had a kind of poetic justice about it.

The Quakers were a lampoonist's paradise in the later Interregnum and throughout Charles II's reign. Typical of the sexual slander which the Friends had to sustain was a chapbook called *The Secret Sinners.*[52] The playlet is written 'in their own sanctified language'. With the mistress of the house holding forth at 'the Hill of Sion, that the wicked do prophanely call the Bull-and-Mouth',[53] the Quaker master proceeds to seduce his 'handmaid'. He justifies himself by proclaiming 'the Light within doth say unto me, that Mary is a sister and that God's Lambs may play so that they can keep it secret from the wicked'. The urgency of his rising 'spirit' sweeps aside the confused girl's doubts and she soon 'swims in delight', proclaiming the happiness 'of us Saints above the rest of the Wicked'.[54]

The last type of satire against the Puritans which enjoyed enormous popularity throughout the Interregnum and the Restoration period was the mock sermon. It presented marvellous opportunities to deride the homiletic tone as well as scoring easy sexual points. It was a favourite diversion of Charles II, but the genre had been used at least since 1649, when *Hosanna: or a Song of Thanksgiving, sung by the Children of Zion, and set forth in three notable speeches at Grocers-Hall* was published. The archetype was, needless to say, the luckless Hugh Peters.

The tone is captured in the following extract, on the text 'A lewd woman is a sinful temptation, her eyes are the snares of Satan, and her flesh is the mousetrap of iniquity.'

> I come now to the third and last part, wherein I shall endeavour to handle the mousetrap of iniquity, which I fear (beloved) you have all been handling before me. . . . This trap of Satan lies hid like a coney burrow[55] in the warren of wickedness between the supporters of human frailty, covered over with the fuzzes of iniquity which grow in the very cleft of abomination. A lewd woman (beloved) I say is this warren of wickedness; therefore let not her eyes entice you to be fingering the fuzzes which grow in the cleft of abomination, lest Satan thrust you headlong into the mousetrap of iniquity. Let not Satan with his cloven foot tread upon your tender consciences, but erect your actions upon the pedestal of piety, that Providence may put you in a posture of defence against the devil and all his accomplices.
>
> Thus shall I conclude all with my hearty wishes for the congregation here present: May Providence hedge you and

> ditch you with His mercy and send His dung-carts to fetch away the filthiness from among you. May your actions shine bright in the sunshine of piety, or else remain covered with the shadow of perfection that whatsoever you do may be much to your own praise and the glory of us double-refined Christians. Thus shall you live secure from the vile touch of the envious serpent, moated round about with the flowing tide of perpetual happiness. That you may bathe your sinful flesh in the streams of repentance! That you may enter undefiled into the congregation of the righteous![56]

The peak of venom in Royalist spite against the Puritans was in the 1650s and the 1660s. Seeing turncoat Presbyterians still enjoying positions of influence and wealth after the Restoration while loyal cavaliers continued to suffer no doubt added to their natural bile. As the reign progressed the immediacy of hatred declined; true, Dissenters suffered for their faith as much as Royalists had before, perhaps more so. Contemptuous ridicule took the place of hatred, and the emphasis on sexual perversion among the 'Pharisees' increased. Webster comments on the interesting fact that although Puritanism and manners changed greatly through the century, yet 'certain fundamental concepts of the Dissenters were apparently consistently held by their enemies'. One of these was that they were grossly immoral and hypocritically excused their lust, while loudly and self-righteously accusing 'the prophane'. Thus forty years after the pathetic Naylor flashed across the national scene, Tom Brown saw a laugh in including him in his *Letters from the Dead to the Living*; the greatest Puritan scapegoat of an earlier generation is likewise there, in a letter from Hugh Peters to D–l B–s, of Covent Garden, the red-light district.[57]

Some of the reasons for this sustained sexual attack on Puritanism are obvious. If ever a group asked for it, it was they. In the beginning of our period, the Interregnum, demoralised Royalists would seize any weapon of abuse in their despair. They set a theme which an occasional Puritan scandal would revive. Yet why sex? Why should a man like Peters, who for all his other irritating traits, appears to have been totally blameless sexually, be charged with voracious lechery? Perhaps part of the reason is contained in a point which has already been made: the very emphasis which the Puritans placed on marital fidelity and premarital chastity; this was most strikingly demonstrated through their so-called Adultery Act of 1650, which stipulated death for the crime, and their increased penalties for fornication, but more positively through their teaching on self-denial in youth, and a loving mutuality and trust within marriage. A male-dominated, non-Puritan culture would probably have broadly agreed with Charles II's remark to the rather Puritan Burnet that 'he could not think that God would make a man miserable for taking a little pleasure out of the way'.[58] Yet there were doubts about the Almighty's reactions, especially after more than a century of Protestant proselytising. Even in the works of that outrageous libertine Tom Brown 'a sense of sin is always with us'.[59] Rochester's dying repentance was better known to most Englishmen than his obscene verse. If those wasps of the English conscience could somehow be destroyed by the fumes of the very sexual scandal they attacked, then the nagging doubt might be laid.

NOTES

1. *Nugae Venales*, p. 217.
2. Roger L'Estrange, *Observator*, 4 February 1682.
3. Kitchin, *L'Estrange*, p. 267.
4. Ward, Diary, II, p. 308.
5. For a full list see Calverton, *Sex Expression*, pp. 55–7.
6. Steane, ed., *Nashe*, p. 311.
7. Cf. Aphra Behn, *The Good Old Cause* (1681).
8. *Brief Lives*, pp. 330–2.
9. T. Birch, ed., *Thurlow State Papers* (London, 1742) Vol. IV, p. 734.
10. *Practical Part of Love* (1660), p. 69.
11. Part I (1660), p. 1.
12. *Henry Marten's Familiar Letters to his Lady of Delight* (London, 1662, reprinted 1685).
13. *Select City Quaeries*, Part III (1660), p. 1. Marten, Scot and Peters are all lampooned in the fifth part of *The Wandring Whore* (1661), p. 6.
14. *D.N.B.*
15. S. Gibson, *Bibliography of Francis Kirkman* (Oxford, 1947), pp. 58, 116; Ward, Diary, I, p. 146; II, p. 519. It was alluded to in *Fifteen Real Comforts of Matrimony* (1683), p. 53.
16. *Religio Laici* (1683), p. 20.
17. Samuel Parker, *A Reproof to the Rehearsal Transprosed* (1673), p. 157.
18. K. H. D. Haley, *The First Earl of Shaftesbury* (Oxford, 1967), pp. 211–14; *POAS*, III, p. 294.
19. Narcissus Luttrell, *A Brief Historical Relation of State Affairs* (Oxford, 1857) Vol. I, pp. 271, 44–5; G. de F. Lord, ed., *POAS*, I, p. 178; *POAS*, III,

pp. 283, 368, 578, The charge against Oates quickly became coffee-house jest material. In Alexander Oldys, *The Fair Extravagant* (1682), p. 11, a Whig says 'Pity our poor President isn't here. Let him take a boat with his Boys.' Tom Brown returned to the obscene attack when Oates married the widow Mary Wells in 1693, with *The Salamanca Wedding* (1693).

20. *POAS*, III, p. 569.
21. *Calamy Revised*, p. 191, cited in *POAS*, III, p. 467.
22. Printed with *Ravillac Redivivus*, p. 53.
23. Ward, Diary, IV, p. 912; *The Man in the Moon* (13–20 August 1660).
24. Cf. Edward Ward, *A Trip to New England* (London, 1698). Ward is far more blatant, though, unlike Dunton, he had never actually visited New England.
25. *Athenianisme* (1710), pp. 219–38.
26. E.g. *The Secret Mercury*, September 1702, 'The Character of the Rev. Mr. F———d.'
27. *Nugae Venales*, p. 217.
28. C. Hill, *The World Turned Upside Down* (Harmondsworth, 1975); K. V. Thomas, 'Women and the Civil War Sects,' T. Aston, ed., *Crisis in Europe 1560–1660* (London, 1965) has other examples.
29. *Clarendon State Papers*, Vol. III, pp. 505–6.
30. J. T. Rutt, ed., *Diary of Thomas Burton* (London, 1828) Vol. I, *passim*.
31. J. G. Muddiman, *The King's Journalist* (London, 1923) has a reproduction of the original in the British Museum, opp. p. 136.
32. 'Swift's *Tale of a Tub* compared with earlier Satires of Puritans', *Proceedings of Modern Language Association*, XLVII (1932), 158–81; 'The Satiric Background of the Attack on the Puritans in Swift's *A Tale of a Tub*', *PMLA*, L (1935), 210–23.
33. Hotson, *Stage*, p. 214.
34. Hill, *World Turned*, p. 318.
35. Atkins, *Sex in Literature*, p. 333. For other examples, see Chapter 6.
36. Harvard Mss. Eng., 636 F*, ff. 280–2.
37. V. and A. Dyce 43, ff. 248–54; the poem is further discussed in Chapter 7.
38. She was the third daughter of Lord Salisbury. She is described in *The Practical Part of Love*, p. 72, as 'alamode Sandys', who 'strains sack through the fore part of her smock and drinks a health to the best in Christendome'. Her reputation as an 'infamous woman' had reached Ward in Stratford. Diary, II, p. 360.
39. This may have reflected the brief career of Jane Roberts as mistress of Charles II in 1668; she was the daughter of a Presbyterian clergyman.
40. *A Catalogue of Jilts* (1691), p. 2.
41. *The Whores Rhetorick*, p. 172.
42. *Strange and True Newes from Bartholomew Fair* (1661), p. 5.
43. P. 77.
44. *Harleian Miscellany*, Vol. III.
45. Occupation was a common metaphor for copulation. Thus 'Old Tredeskin the Puritan whoremonger' was 'reputed a decayed occupier' in *Strange and True Conference Between Two Bawds* (1660); see below, Chapter 5.
46. J. Wilders, ed., *Hudibras* (Oxford, 1967) Part II, Canto i, lines 367–70. Durty Lane and Little Sodom were both famous as red-light areas. The missing name is that of Madam Bennet, a notorious bawd. Riding the ring was common slang for intercourse.

47. Part IV (1671), p. 180.
48. E.g. the Saint who gets his maid with child in *Fifteen Real Comforts of Matrimony* (1683), p. 61.
49. Wilders, *Hudibras*, Part III, canto i, lines 275–8. Bardashing is sodomy.
50. A. R. Waller, ed., *Characters and Passages from the Notebooks of Samuel Butler* (Cambridge, 1908), p. 149.
51. P. 53.
52. London, n.d., *c.* 1675; reprinted in part in my edition of *Samuel Pepys' Penny Merriments* (London, 1976), pp. 147–52.
53. In Bloomsbury.
54. Cf. *Practical Part of Love* (1660) sig. A5, where a Quaker is similarly charged with having 'rejoyc'd in spirit with a new adopted sister' with utmost freedom; *Session of the Poets* (1696) p. 5, has a passage on a Quaker castrated because of 'his having too excellent a Faculty in propagating too many Yeas and Nays.'
55. The pun on cunny was a chestnut of ancient usage.
56. Reprinted from Harleian Mss. 7312, ff. 113–17, by J. H. Wilson, *A Rake and his Times* (London, 1954), pp. 104–6. Buckingham was charged by Clarendon with 'repeating and acting what the preachers said in their sermons and turning it into ridicule'. A less bawdy example is in *Proteus Redivivus* (1675). Mock sermons continued to enjoy popularity into the eighteenth century. A piece entitled *Asarias*, a parody of Quaker testifying and prayer, was published in 1710.
57. B. Boyce, *Tom Brown of Facetious Memory* (Cambridge, Mass., 1939), pp. 163–7; Webster, 'Satiric Background', 221.
58. Cited in G. Davies, *Essays in the Later Stuarts* (San Marino, 1958), p. 30.
59. Boyce, *Brown*, p. 102.

5 Prostitutional

It is a curiosity of history that more is usually known about whores in literature, a Nanna, a Julietta, a Moll Flanders or a Fanny Hill, than about the real-life girls and women who plied their trade in London or the provinces. There are, for instance no accurate contemporary statistics or estimates before the middle of the eighteenth century about the number of whores working in London. *The Wandring Whore*, an ephemeral periodical published in 1660 and 1661, had lists of whores working in London appended at the end of each part. Part Five, published early in 1661, lists 138 bawds, 269 common whores, and sundry male foylers, kidnappers, decoys, pimps, hectors and trapanners. In the third part however Julietta had claimed that those listed were 'but a handful in comparison of those are yet to enter themselves amongst us'. *The Ladies Champion*, a rival publication to *The Wandring Whore*, estimated the number of this type of 'caterpillars and poysonous vermine' as 1500 in 1660. *The Practical Part of Love* published in the same year stated that a full list would cover thirty pages, which at a rough computation based on the lists in *The Wandring Whore* would add up to a total of 3600. None of these sources can be regarded as anything more than educated guesses, but they are the nearest we come to fact in an age when statistics were only just coming to be used and valued.

I have elsewhere discussed the continuing problem of arriving at some estimate of the numbers of prostitutes in London at the end of the century, even with the additional evidence furnished by the Societies for the Reformation of Manners in the last decade of the century. At the turn of the century the London societies were claiming to prosecute about 700 bawds and prostitutes annually, but there are sound reasons for thinking that this was only the tip of the iceberg.[1]

There is not even agreement about the level of prostitution in the capital during the Interregnum, when one might have expected a closer record of their activities to have been kept. Before the outbreak of the Civil War prostitution seems to have been common enough. *The First and Large Petition of the City of London* to the Long Parliament in 1641 deplored the 'great increase and frequency of whoredoms and adulteries'.[2] When the King moved his headquarters to Oxford there was a considerable migration of camp-followers from London. John Ward recounts in his Diary, on the authority of his barber, that 'for every returne allmost of ye waggon there came whole loads from London'. Indeed 'much about this time there was a report that ye parliament had a designe to send poccy whores to spoyle ye [Royalist] souldiers, uppon which account an order was made to turne all ye whores out of ye towne' of Oxford.[3] An intriguing example of early 'biological' warfare.

This migration was a matter of economic necessity, if a pamphlet called *St. Hillaries Teares* (1642) is to be believed.

> If you step aside into Coven Garden, long Acre, and Drury Lane, where those Doves of Venus, those birds of youth and beauty, (the wanton Ladies) doe build their nests, you shall finde them in such a dump of amazement, to see the hopes of their Trading frustrate.

Whereas, before 1642, 'ten or twentie pound Suppers were but trifles to them', they are now forced to make do on a diet of cheese and onions, hardly very appealing to the stray customer. This 'ruination of whoring' was why the London Bawd 'hated '41 like an old cavalier.'[4]

After the King's defeat and the capture of Oxford the whores probably drifted back to London, but the impression given by Royalist pamphleteers is that customers were scarce. *A Dialogue Between Mistris Macquerella, a Suburb Bawd, Mistris Scolopendra, a Noted Curtezan, and Mr. Pimpinello, an Usher . . . Bemoaning the Act against Adultery and Fornication*, published by Edward Crouch in 1650, bewails their lack of trade. Whores are forced to pawn their stuffs, and pimps to search for an honest living. Because of the fierce penalties of 'hanging, burning, carting, whipping or so', 'she that keeps a shop of publike Brothelrie' is forced to keep sentries at her door to warn against raids. There is 'No fee for ——— now to be had'. The nostalgia for the good old days comes out in a final song

> When the Priests came simpring in
> Resolv'd to turn the pin.

When Lords and Knights of fame
To dance Levaltoes came.
When citizens each day
Were glad to pray and pay:
Most eager for to sease
Upon the French disease. . . .

Whether this bleak rule of public morality was maintained for the next decade is debated. Damaris Page is alleged to have said in 1660 that 'our sister-hood hath been routed by the Rumpers all weathers'. On the other hand, Cavalier propaganda made much, as we have seen, of the secret lechery of the rule of the saints, in which whores as well as 'sisters' played their parts. J. B. Williams argues that 'one effect of a standing army of 30 000 men in London had been the crowding of the outskirts of the city with brothels' and paradoxically argues that after the Restoration, 'London was at least a cleaner and sweeter city for ordinary folk to dwell in when Cromwell's army was disbanded by Charles II'.[5] Certainly the attempts in the Interregnum to crush the popular theatre, which was a haunt of prostitutes looking for customers, had the effect of driving the players out to the safer villages like Knightsbridge, where they continued to give performances. In February, 1654, *Mercurius Fumigosus* reported that 'The Bawdes in the Suburbs are Petitioning against the putting down of the poor *Actors*'.[6] This was, of course, Royalist propaganda, too. Williams, who does not cite the source for his claim, may have generalised from the sexual needs of normal armies to those of Cromwell's—a dangerous assumption.[7]

If it is difficult to get an impression of the levels of prostitution in London at different periods of the seventeenth century, it is well-nigh impossible for the provinces. When Humphrey Prideaux arrived in Norwich in 1681 he reported to Ellis: 'This town swarms with alehouses, and every one of them they tell is alsoe a bawdy house.'[8] A search for prostitutes in Leith in 1692 netted eighty.[9] Another major port town, Deal, was claimed to have twenty-six whores in 1703.[10] Wrightson's researches in the court records of Essex and Southwest Lancashire suggest, however, that prostitution was relatively rare in country districts. 'Examples of whoring at festivals' like church-ales, harvest-homes or May-days, he writes, 'stand out in court records by their lurid rarity'. Some 'vulnerable and underprivileged' amateurs' in certain villages might provide sexual gratification for young men between puberty and marriage, but the pretty shepherdess waiting for a bundle in the hay with the passing gallant seems to be a myth created by erotic pastoral poets.[11] When Charles II stayed at Lord Cornwallis' place at Culford in Suffolk in May 1668, his lordship was commanded to procure a whore for his royal guest, and the only pretty enough girl that he could find was the vicar's daughter who, leaping to escape, was killed. There were no professionals apparently in the neighbourhood of Newmarket, even at race meeting times.[12] One development of the century which may have increased the opportunities for prostitution in the provinces was the apparent decline of rural festivals— they were prohibited, of course, during the Interregnum— to be replaced by the alehouse as a social meeting-point, but a far more fragmented and uncontrollable and potentially even furtive one.[13] Certainly alehouses were associated in the popular mind with prostitution, especially in large market towns, busy seaports and important communications junctions.[14]

Another development in the early years of the Restoration period had the effect of making contemporary estimation even more unreliable. This was colourfully described by Gusman, the pimping hector, in the sixth part of *The Wandring Whore* (1663):

> Now the privat Whores have got the knack on't to knock in corners, so that all our Cattel in Dog and Bitch Yard, Drury-Lane, Luterners-Lane, Parkhurst-Lane, Bloomsbury, Hatten-Wall, &c. cannot with all their painting, perfuming, clean linnen or sweetest Oratory or loudest calling, persuade a Gallant to enter their Forts, notwithstanding there hangs out white Colours to draw on to a treaty all weathers, Ergo, Publick trading is destroy'd by privat correspondencies and actings, which was not formerly when our lists of whores were printed.

These forerunners of call-girls, maintaining outward respectability if they followed the advice of their literary tutors, would have been far more difficult to identify and count than the employees of brothels or the street-walkers whose very livelihood depended on their calling attention to themselves.

The Restoration period is remarkable for the frequency with which actual madams and prostitutes are mentioned in literature. We have already encountered Mrs Creswell, the canting bawd of Moorfields in *Venice Preserv'd* and *The Whores Rhetorick*. Her bequest of £10 in 1684 for a funeral sermon in which 'nothing but what was well should be said of her' led the ingenious preacher to pronounce what appeared to be the outrageously generous valediction 'She was born well, lived well and died well'. This he justified by the unimpeachable argument that 'she was born with the name of Creswell, she lived in Clerkenwell and died in Bridewell'.[15] In company with 'the great bawd of the seamen', Damaris Page, who was once visited by the Duke of York, she signed two fictional 'Poor Whores' Petitions', one addressed to Lady Castlemaine, the King's whore. Mrs Page had earlier gained some notoriety in letters from *A Strange and True Conference Between Two Notorious Bawds, Damarose Page and Pris Fotheringham* published in 1660.[16] Fotheringham, in turn, was the heroine of a series of pamphlets like *Strange and true Nevves From Jack-a-Newberries Six Windmills* (1660). Mother Temple, Sue Lemming and Betty Lawrence also became household words through the ephemera that poured from the presses at the end of the Interregnum, and Betty Lucas was awarded the international accolade of *La Puttana Errante* in the third part of *Select City Quaeries* (1660). Two famous whores of the 1670s, Betty Bewly and Jenny Cromwell (what symbolism in a name) were named in the Epilogue to Nathaniel Lee's *Gloriana* (1676). Both seem to have specialised in flagellation. *The Plain Dealer* was ironically dedicated to another famous brothel-keeper, 'Lady' Bennet, already immortalised in *Hudibras*. A sexual gymnast who has come down to us only as 'Posture Moll' was also renowned in the latter part of Charles II's reign.[17] The craze for auctions, with their catalogues, brought forth a batch of broadsides which were, to all intents and purposes, 'Ladies Directories', like the lists at the end of the first five parts of *The Wandring Whore*. In 1691, for instance, there appeared *A Catalogue of Jilts, Cracks, Prostitutes, Night walkers, Whores, She-friends, King Women and others of the Linnen-lifting Tribe, who are to be seen every Night in the Cloysters in Smithfield from eight to eleven during the time of the Fair*. The twenty-two names which follow, including 'Posture Moll', who, 'as N. Culpeper says of some Herbs and Plants needs no description', are of actual prostitutes with their going rates. In the same year came out *An Auction of Whores*, again listing real-life practitioners.[18]

These references to actual prostitutes could be multiplied if manuscript verse and prose were also included,[19] and this perhaps is a clue to the reason for their frequency. As James Sutherland has pointed out 'the literary world of the Restoration period was more closely organised than it had ever been before'. It was 'a compact society', a collection of 'literary coteries', which 'naturally produced the lampoon, the epigram, the private joke and . . . outbursts of satirical wit'.[20] Among the choice topics of gossip in the clubs and coffee-houses frequented by these overgrown schoolboys who thought of themselves as wits were 'the girls of the game'. Seamier publishers 'cracking their brains to find out selling subjects' could always turn a dishonest penny by catering to this audience.

We have so far spoken of prostitutes generically, but there were in that hierarchical society ranks and degrees among ladies of pleasure, as Ames's *Catalogue* suggests, and the price list confirms. At the pinnacle were the King's mistresses, Castlemaine, Gwyn, Portsmouth and the rest; these were often women of noble or gentle birth, themselves and their offspring ennobled, handsomely rewarded for their favours out of the secret service and other funds, and sometimes politically influential. Next followed the 'Misses' of the courtiers, often lodged near Whitehall in Pall Mall or King Street, like Mrs Lane, whom the Duke of Norfolk took with him up to Norwich in 1696, or Sue Willis, who so captivated Lord Culpeper that he took her with him on a spending spree in Paris. Any woman who was the kept mistress of one man was designated a miss; thus in Ames's *Catalogue*, item 21 is 'Mrs. W——by, formerly Miss to Col. S—field in Ireland'. Moll Flanders was more of a miss than a whore, despite Defoe's subtitle. Misses were much more of a mixed bag than the royal mistresses. They might occasionally have been maids of honour and girls of breeding seduced by a Rochester or a Mulgrave, but more often they were Nell Gwyn types, pretty, pert and poor, ex-actresses or procured by the likes of Bennet, Page and Creswell for their customers. Next came the real professionals, the whores or jilts, as current slang went, who either had their own establishments and regular customers, with possibly a pimp or hector and a maid who acted as 'maitresse d'hotel', or worked for a madam. At the bottom of the heap were the street-walkers, bulkers and drabs, who solicited in the red-light areas or taverns, depended on the customer to find a bed, or performed her services on some dark bulk. A miss or whore with some foresight and business sense would save up and transfer into the bawdy-house business; she might perhaps employ a girl or two 'newly come upon the town' or even take a waif or two off the hands of the parish overseers of the poor for future employment. Usually, though, it was downhill all the way in the profession; Mrs W——by, once a miss, now a night-walker, soon beating hemp in Bridewell, not long after dead from untreated V.D. and malnutrition, was the normal pattern.

The customer in search of a whore would be heading in the right direction down the Strand towards Fleet Street and the City. On his left he would soon come to the maze of narrow streets and alleyways of the Covent Garden district, with its bagnios and brothels and walkers, or just beyond Drury Lane, the notorious Whetstones Park, which despite its name was an alley to the north of Lincolns Inn Fields, which themselves pullulated on warm summer nights. If nothing took his fancy there, there was always Saffron Hill and Turnmill Street, a half mile on, or Moorfields a mile further on down Holborn and off to the left, or the Tower Hill area down towards the river to the right. In the spring and summer St James's Park, or Vauxhall or Spring Gardens, would be a happy hunting-ground, or even across London Bridge in Southwark, or Alsatia as it was known, famous for its stews and 'Winchester Geese' since the Middle Ages. This was where the famous Dutch bawd, popularised by Goodman's *Holland's Leaguer* (1632) and numerous imitations, had had her establishment in the early years of the century.

Literally, pornography is writing about prostitutes, and bawdy about bawds; there was plenty of both in the Interregnum and Restoration. I have divided the literature on whores into three parts: Dialogues, Whore Stories as a branch of rogue literature and 'characters' and descriptions.

The first two sets of dialogues were part of a rash of ephemera which welled from the presses in the spring of 1660, and flowed for the rest of that year, a period when, according to the sober Puritan Henry Newcome, 'the people make a business of playing the fool with sabbath-breaking, health-drinking, morris-dancing and the raising of maypoles'.[21] Another way of demonstrating discontent at the rule of the saints and delight at the imminent return of the King was to celebrate the high-jinks of ladies of pleasure who had been under a cloud of official disapproval for so long in London.

The particular bit of obscene fool-playing which gave rise to the first of our dialogues took place in the Six Windmills, a pub-cum-brothel earlier known as the Jack-a-Newberry, in the notorious neighbourhood of Upper Moorfields. This establishment was presided over by Pris Fotheringham, whose party trick was 'to stand upon (her) head with a naked Breech, bare Belly, spread Legs, with the orifice of her *Rima Magna* open whilst several Cully-Rumpers chuck in sixteen half-crowns into it [*sic*] for their pleasure and my profit'. This original variation on tiddly-winks or chuck-farthing earned her *Rima Magna* the title of 'the chuck office' and Mrs Fotheringham a spell in Newgate, where Mrs Damrose Page was already incarcerated. Their shared inactivity inspired *A Strange and True Conference Between two Notorious Bawds, Damarose Page and Pris Fotheringham, During their Imprisonment and lying together in Newgate; With the Newest Orders and Customs of the Half-Crown Chuck-Office, And the Officers thereunto belonging. With the practice of the Prick Office.* By Megg. Spenser, Over-seer of the Whores and Hectors on the Bank-Side, 1660.[22]

Mrs Fotheringham blames her pockified and cornuted husband for charging her, her crime being 'drawing a sword-cutler's blade out of his belly and putting it in my own'.[23] There is some extremely bawdy gossip between the two about the sexual antics of the town, of Mrs Cater and her daughter who specialise in three-in-a-bed and Hammond in the Prick Office at the Last and Lyon in East Smithfield, 'whose females do every one of them buss the end of his Trap-stick as he lies naked upon the bed and his face and standing T—— upwards'.[24] There follow the twenty rules and orders for the chuck office. Apart from Pris's patent to her new trick and punishments for rule-breaking—castration for hectors, and for whores, 'their water-gaps sowed up tighter than any Italian padlock—this is also an opportunity for more in-jokes. The escapade of Ben Ross the draper's apprentice is mentioned; he had stolen two gowns from his master and conveyed them to two famous whores Sue Lemming and Betty Orange in his codpiece; so is Shepard, the impotent butcher of Saffron Hill, with puns on flesh, John Heyden, the lecherous Rosicrucian and astrologer, whose exploits in 1657 and 1658 were a blot on Puritan morality[25] and Betty Lawrence '(who loves whipping so well)' and 'caused Butterfield the woodmonger in Thames St. to drink and drabb away two loads of faggots at a sitting with some of the sisters'. S. H. is given a monopoly to provide 'books of venery and midwifery'[26] and George Simpleton 'to make baudy drollery for the Sportive Wits amongst us.'[27] The conference ends with Page asking Fotheringham to read her the chapter from the Proverbs of Solomon against whoredom!

This conference provoked a further small pamphlet with an

even more grandiose title, *Strange and true Nevves From Jack-a-Newberries Six Windmills* . . . allegedly written by none other than 'Peter Aretine, Cardinall of Rome' and 'Printed for Rodericus e Castro' in 1660. Much of it is a plagiarism of the original *Conference*; some of the rules are changed, with such additions as 'No one of this society refuse to do the deed of nature either backwards or any other of Peter Aretine's postures so long as she's pay'd for't.' At the end there is a threat to name any customer who causes trouble. The interesting difference between the two pamphlets lies not in their content but in their tone. In the latter there is mock shock at the activities of the 'Chuck Office', and it claims to be 'Publish'd by way of admonition to all persons to beware of that house of Darkness'. The title contains epithets like 'impudent' and 'unparallelled' and the pamphlet ends with a series of hypocritical sentiments. This was a common ruse of pornographers and smut-merchants in the Restoration, but it is curious that the second piece, which is, by the way, no less bawdy than the first, should employ this face-saving technique. Possibly it appeared just after the actual Restoration when the policy of the new government headed by Clarendon towards the press was unknown, and playing safe was thought a wise precaution.[28]

The second set of dialogues are Numbers 1–6 of *The Wandring Whore: A Dialogue Between Magdalena a Crafty Bawd, Julietta an Exquisite Whore, Francion a Lascivious Gallant, and Gusman a Pimping Hector*. 1660–1663. These squalid sixteen-page pamphlets are extremely rare and in many ways elusive.[29]

The appearance of the first five numbers provoked the authorities into a search for those responsible. The State Papers Domestic for 5 October 1661 has 'A List of Numerous prisoners now in Newgate, with the charges against them and the dates of their commital', which includes the name of John Garfield, charged with writing *The Wandring Whore.*[30] His arrest is corroborated in *The Ladies Champion* (1660)[31] and the sixth part of *The Wandring Whore*. The former hints that John Heyden was the real culprit,[32] but this charge against 'Eugenius Theodidactus' seems groundless.[33] The sixth number bears the imprint 'London Printed for John Johnson 1663'. Johnson may have been related to Thomas and Marmaduke Johnson, who were closely connected with the Brooke-Marsh-Kirkman group responsible for many of the dirty books published in London around the period of the Restoration.[34]

The first number of *The Wandring Whore* appeared on 28 November 1660, and the next three followed at weekly intervals. The fifth was delayed for some three months, perhaps by the activities of the authorities. The title and cast are taken from *La Puttana Errante* ascribed to Aretino, but in fact written by an imitator.[35] The Italian work had been published by the Elzevir Press in 1660 to accompany an edition of the *Ragionamenti*. Several of the pamphlets already mentioned published in 1660 bear the name of 'Peter Aretine' as alleged author. The prince of pornographers was enjoying a new lease of life under whatever false colours he appeared.

The narrative line of *The Wandring Whore* is, to say the least, weak. Julietta, the exquisite whore, has just arrived from the capital of whoredom, Venice, in its aspiring competitor, London. She is prized by Magdalena, the crafty bawd, and Gusman the pimping hector. Between them they gull Francion, the gallant cully, of increasingly exorbitant sums of money. Francion is not Hercules, however, nor are the lists of whores and their henchmen at the end of each number sufficient to fill sixteen pages. So the gaps are filled with discussions of sex, or as Magdalena puts it at the beginning of the first number, 'talk [of] a little bawdery and drollery'. These discussions are either about the most advanced sexual techniques and aids, or the latest scandals of the town. In the first number, the former include the strummulo or merkin, forms of false pubic hair for whores worn bald by overwork, various cures of venereal disease, the Italian padlock, or chastity belt, described in loving detail of Julietta, different postures, dealing with 'bastards and by-blows' so as not to bring down the wrath of the parish authorities, aphrodisiacs, and Scotch-spurs (a metaphor for the penis). The latter give the author opportunity to expatiate on the Chuck Office, which proves the truth of 'the poulterers cry and rules for keepers and whores No Mony No Cony, a cunny being the deerest piece of flesh in the whole world'.[36] We also hear about the Dutch wench who had Rhenish wine poured down more than one orifice, the drunken whore 'layed belly naked on a table with a candle stuck in her commodity' which caused a small forest fire, only extinguished by a 'codpiece engine', and the girl with crablice 'arising from inbred lechery' cured by a gentleman using a pipe of tobacco in a highly original way 'at her Cinque ports'. Julietta's 'combate upon back and belly' with Francion occurs offstage, with Gusman 'pimping and peeping at their door'. Francion, boastful of the size of his organ, feared about 'beating the bottom of Julietta's belly out, wrapped an ell of Holland neer the root of his P——'. But Julietta 'snatcht it off and cool'd his courage quickly'. After a post-coital tale of cuckoldry in which Julietta tells of a wife who managed intercourse with her lover while playing whist or picquet with her husband, the bill is presented:

		£	s	d
Imprimis	broaching belly unwemmed and unboared	1	–	–
Item	Magdalena's fee		10	–
Item	Gusman's fee		2	6
Item	Julietta's smock		10	–
Item	For dressing, painting & perfuming her		5	–
Item	Pictures as B: S: does		5	–
Item	Occupying most convenient and close box in room		5	–
Item	Oysters, anchovies, olives and capers		10	–
Item	Wine	1	–	–
Item	Sweet meats		10	–
Item	Musick	1	–	–
	Summa Totalis	5	12	6

To which exploitation, Francion responds with Ovidian nonchalence: 'Hang mony, my father took pleasure in getting and griping it, and I'le spend it freely.'

Number Two fails to sustain the inventiveness of the first. Leading whores and their specialities are punningly discussed; Francion bewails the absence, even for £5, of 'pure untoucht Maidenhead' and Gusman suggests possible locations in an armchair tour of the vice-spots of London. Typical is the description of whore's excitation of customers:

> They kiss with their mouths open, and put their tongues in his mouth and suck it. Their left hand is in his Cod-piece, their right in his pocket; they commend his Trap stick, and pluck

> their coats above their thighs, their smocks above their knees, bidding him thrust his hand into the best C— in christendom, tickling the knobs thereof till they burst out with laughing, as W—— the Butchers son in Stocks did Honor Brooks, the rammish Scotch whore at D—— between her legs, not forgetting that Ursula had 2/6d for shewing her twit-twat there and 2/6d for stroaking the marrow out of mans gristle.

The number ends with Julietta describing the luxurious bordellos of Venice and their visual aids.

The third number begins with action, which the second had sadly lacked. Julietta uses her arts to arouse Francion:

> Come (sweet heart) wilt thou do-a-little, the fitts come on me now. I'll show you a pure pair of naked breasts, smooth Buttocks, Lovely and ivory thighes, the best red-lipt C— in Christendom. . . . *Francion*: You would tempt a *Saint* especially such a one as I am . . . make my P—— rise with your perfum'd Cabinet. I'll enter its Port with a full spring tyde between thy bums riding safe at Anchor within thy harbour.

After this Ovidian conceit, Francion ejaculates precipitately, and is reminded of baudy Martial's verses. The two of them swap yarns about whores picking pockets, especially Mall Savory who stole a man's watch and hid it in her commodity, only to be embarrasingly discovered when the alarm went off. Several of these pranks had already been told in *A Strange and True Conference*. The feeble Francion ends the business with 'I find no Motions to a Second Rancounter with you, Julietta.' A somewhat churlish youth.

Topical gossip is even more prevalent in the fourth number. Fellow-traders like Sue Lemming, Betty Orange, Mary Marten, Honor Brooks, Mal Savory (Thom Player's mob) are anatomised disdainfully; they are 'common jades or jakes, that like as well a Broom man, a Tucker or a Dung-hill raker as a gentleman, but a T—— is as good for such sowes as a Pancake . . . idle Whores who F— for necessity, not pleasure'. It is implied that when they cannot get custom at 'their usual rendezvouses' they join conventicles and dance naked and pick up their customers that way. And trade, according to Magdalena, *is* bad, because so many amateurs, citizen's wives—all named, of course—are horning in on the game. Gusman tells a horrific story of a drunken gentleman picked up by a whore:

> He fell to feeling her with freedom in a dark passage; after which she felt him likewise, and, because he was drunk, had much ado to cause an erection, yet did it . . . holding his P—— close by the root she cut it clear and sheer off, leaving his member and the knife together. He took up his P—— and put it in his Fob and went to a Chirurgeon to stitch it on, but he just put a quill up the pissing place to keep it open. The gentleman died two days later. The whore when apprehended said that he had given a wench the running of the reins and she returned him for her pains.

The episode ends with the grand gulling of Francion by persuading him that Julietta is pregnant by him. This time the bill, including payments to a substitute father, to the parish, the midwife, for clothes, nurse and lying in, totals £135 and Francion gaily signs away yet more of his father's ill-gotten gains.

The next number is described on the title-page as 'The Fifth and last Part'. Magdalena, unsatisfied with £135 extracted from Francion, proposes that they should gull him into marrying Julietta, whose 'very teeth water at the contrivance'. They draw up an outrageous settlement, including £300 per annum for life for the bride, a coach and four horses, a lusty black servant, and freedom to entertain any man and choose her own chambermaids. Gusman points out that even if the settlement does not take with Francion, Julietta once married to him will be able to extract alimony or keep a gentleman-usher to serve her lascivious whims.

While they wait for their quarry to arrive, they 'drive away the tedious night' with 'some pleasant tales'. Gusman recounts a case heard at Salisbury Assizes in which a rebuffed lover spread the rumour that 'a bouncing Girl . . . had no C—— and scarce a pissing place'. The spokeswoman of a jury of women who had examined the girl reported to the judge that 'she had a good thing', or 'a very good commodity', but he was dissatisfied with these euphemisms and demanded a clear statement. Which provoked 'She hath a C—— large enough for the beggest (*sic*) mans P—— in the Parish' which in turn provoked general laughter and damages to the plaintiff of £60. Julietta tells of a young man who wore a sample from a lady's pubic hair as 'a Bravido in his hat', and Magdalena of a lady who finally rebuffed an unwelcome courter by showing him 'her breast naked, ranckled, rotted and corrupted'. This leads to a discussion of the role of clothes, cosmetics and coquetry as 'provocations to lust and Lechery'.

When Francion arrives, the three rogues set about convincing him that Julietta is weary of her whoring life and wishes to turn virtuous, if only Francion will marry her. The gull, however, is not that gullible: 'marry I may not'. In a hurried compromise, Magdalena accepts his offer of £50 per annum, *durante vita*, and Julietta declares herself 'Content till our next days meeting'.

That next meeting took two years to take place. *The Sixth Part of the Wandring Whore Revived* was set on a different press; Julietta has become Julia, Francion is identified as French, Eubulus is added to the cast, and the eight pages, lacking the lists of bawds, whores and pimps, is credited to 'Peter Aretine'. Even in comparison with the previous parts this is a very poor thing. There is reference to the lists, which Francion and Gusman agree have done wonders for trade and made London whores 'famous for infamy'. Most of the rest is composed of Magdalena's and Julia's discussion of a famous Roman whore, her appearance, her beguiling charms and subtle salesmanship. This is heavily reliant on similar passages in the *Ragionamenti*, and the plagiarism is the more evident because the setting shifts to Rome. There is no action; Francion is merely another discutant. The last sentence promises a seventh part, but I know of no evidence that Johnson ever published one.

These ephemera are such a mish-mash of material that they are hard to classify. Much of their contents is bawdy, ammunition for dirty-jokesters— 'Have you heard the latest one about Sue Lemming?' But in the detailed discussion of sexual techniques and the 'rancounters' of Francion and Julietta, there is a plain attempt to arouse the reader sexually; by Aretine standards, it is not very good, but it is there.

The tone is thoroughly sordid; it is Grub Street stuff at its most obsessive. There is none of the bumptious exuberance of the Italians here. What makes it more distasteful are the protestations of the author that rather than 'the propagating of whoreing and tempting customers to go amongst them', he is intent on 'destroying them . . . of routing them and giving the Magistrates notice of their villainous Practices.'

In the small world of Grub Street *The Wandring Whore* provoked responses like *The Ladies Champion* (1660) and imitations like *The Wandring Whores Complaint for Want of Trading*, which is a dialogue full of underworld slang and rogueries, like the hector rushing in disguised as the whore's husband and demanding blackmail of the customer caught *in flagrante delicto.* The relatively new institution of the coffee-house, and the growth in the number of private whores are blamed by the street-walkers for their lack of customers. The thieves' cant points to Richard Head as a possible author of this bawdry, though 'Mercurius Democritus' claims it as his.

The other offshoot just worth a mention is *Strange News from Bartholomew Fair, or The Wandring Whore Discovered* by 'Peter Aretine', 1661. The gossips are three whores, Bonny Bessie of Whore and Bacon Lane, Merry Moll of Duck Street and Pritty Peg of Py-Corner and their conversation is again in thieves' cant and refers to the ways of picking pockets and maximising profits. The chuck office is alluded to, though it seems to be in decline.

All of this is essentially ephemeral, stimulated by Restoration madness, the revival of Aretino and the sexual scandals of the town. The hunt for the author of *The Wandring Whore* was the usual heaven-sent free publicity for Grub Street and they kept the bubble going for two years. In the history of Restoration bawdry it suggests the speed with which continental publications were taken up or exploited by English smut-pedlars; the response of the authorities was also a warning to them that the policy of the new regime was not going to be markedly different from that of the Protectorate.

The other dialogue is of considerably greater importance. Its full title reveals the kind of hypocrisy with which English publishers habitually glossed their seamier offerings:

> The Crafty Whore: or, The Mistery and Iniquity of Bawdy Houses Laid open, In a dialogue between two SUBTLE BAWDS, wherein, as in a mirrour, our City-Curtesans may see their soul-destroying Art, and Crafty devices, whereby they Insnare and Beguile Youth, portraied to the life, By the Pensell of one of their late, (but now penitent) Captives, for the benefit of all, but especially the younger sort. Whereunto is added Dehortations from Lust Drawn from the Sad and Lamentable consequences it produceth.
>
> London. Printed for Henry Marsh —— 1658.

A manuscript note on the title-page of the British Museum copy gives May as the month of publication. There is no evidence of action being taken against Marsh.

Which is a pity, because before his unlamented death in the 1665 Plague, he was responsible for a string of indecent publications and knavish practices. He was the son of a clockmaker, Michael Marsh, and had only been a freeman since October 1657.[37] At the end of *The Wits: or, Sport upon Sport*, a collections of Drolls, some highly indecent and obscene, which he published in 1662, is appended a list of some 135 of Marsh's publications. It is a mixed bag, with theology and poetry represented, but the bulk of the catalogue is made up of plays, romances, questionable medical works and several unquestionably disreputable titles like *Venus Undrest, Overbury Reviv'd* and *Natures Chief Rarities*. He was described as a man of 'so much cunning and knavery', and one side of this was his pirating of plays copyrighted by Humphrey Robinson and Anne Moseley. He was a frequent partner with Nathaniel Brooke who also realised the profitability of books on sex, and with Francis Kirkman, part author of *The English Rogue*. Despite his eagerness for 'ready money', however, Marsh did not prosper. Kirkman seems to have taken over his business in the early 1660s, and when he died he was heavily in debt.[38]

The Crafty Whore is a naturalisation of the famous dialogue between Nanna and Antonia, 'The Life of the Whores', on the third day of the first part of the *Ragionamenti* of Aretino. This part was often published separately from the rest under the Latin title of *Pornodidasculus*, first published in a Latin translation from a Spanish translation of the Italian original at Frankfurt in 1623 and soon to be reprinted in 1660. In 1655 there had appeared a German rendering, which may have been the immediate stimulus for an English version, though the Latin edition was quite common in England.[39]

The scene for *The Crafty Whore* is Rome, and the whore is renamed Thais, though the bawd retains the name of Antonia. The Aretine model is followed fairly closely. The kinds of tricks which an accomplished whore plays on her customers maddened by lust, like holding out until they have promised more and more presents, feigning pregnancy, having several customers on the same night (once with a rival asleep in the same bed) or pretending to withdraw to a convent in order to raise prices or get a husband, are all reproduced. So are some of the arcaner tricks of the trade, like the shrinking of vaginas to counterfeit virginity, the circumvention of chastity belts, the employment of hectors to steal customers' belongings, and the national characteristics of customers. Her account of her later career is also copied: bawd, doctoress to cracked maidenheads, astrologer and receiver of stolen goods. Some of these items from the original probably influenced the choice of conversation in *The Wandring Whore* and *The Strange and True Conference.*

The English intrusions are mainly tiresome topical slang and chapbook jokes, which utterly destroy the Roman ambiance and completely vulgarise Aretino's realism. *The Crafty Whore* is unconscious burlesque. One piece of jingoism is the addition of comments about English customers, which does not appear in the original. The typical Englishman, says Thais, after criticising the urgency of the French and insufficiency of the Spaniards, 'spends freely on and in me'. This generosity unfortunately extends to 'giving me the clap'. She also praises Englishwomen's beauty and relative liberty, repeating the old adage that if there were a bridge over the Channel all the women of Europe would flock across it.

The fact that the Latin tags in the text are usually translated suggests that Marsh intended *The Crafty Whore* for a general, non-intellectual readership. His offering verges on the pornographic in the account of Thais's titillation and frustration of her ardent lover on their first night together. Aretino set the original more in the context of roguery and cony-catching stratagems than erotic arousal. The hackneyed English metaphors are just bad bawdry.

The vogue of treating whores as female rogues dates back at least to late-Elizabethan times, and was popular throughout the first half of the seventeenth century. In this phase it is the roguishness, the wit of trickery, that is emphasised; the sexual side of the profession is played down. There is not a great deal of difference in the treatment of Moll Cutpurse, the pickpocket, or Long Meg of Westminster, the amazon barmaid, and Dona Britanica Hollandia, the anti-heroine of Goodman's *Hollands Leaguer*, who presided over a moated bordello on the south bank. Indeed Longa Margarita is referred to in Goodman as the keeper 'for many years of a famous infamous house of open Hospitality' in the same neighbourhood. Yet in the chapbook accounts of her there is no mention of her sexual activities at all.[40]

This balance is dramatically upset in the Restoration period. Frank Chandler, the easily-scandalised historian of rogue literature, stresses this in reference to the influential *English Rogue*. One of Richard Head's main departures from the great Spanish tradition is his 'exaggeration of the erotic element' in the first part. When Kirkman produced a pirated second part, 'the erotic element was for him supreme, and in this and later additions obscenity rules'.

The first of the whore stories I have selected was published anonymously by Henry Marsh in 1660, in August according to Thomason, and was entitled *The Practical Part of Love. Extracted out of the Extravagant and Lascivious Life of a Fair but Subtle Female.* Marsh's list of 1662, re-titles the book *Venus Undrest*, with the original as a sub-title.

The plot of the book is about the lives of not one but two subtle females, Lucia and her daughter Helena. Lucia is the daughter of a poor publican. Her beauty is such, that although 'she stiffly held her Maiden-Castle', yet 'scaling ladders were erected, guns planted ready to make a breach' by the various gallants who patronised her father's pub. The most feverish for her is Lovit, who implores Lucia to act as his doctor and 'quickly apply something (a cupping-glasse if you will have it) that would extract out of him that humour which was the cause of his hot distemper'. His promise to marry her, and a little pishing and fying on her part, act as a prelude to the storming. Lovit however loves it rather than her, and when she becomes pregnant he deserts her and marries a wealthy but ugly woman. Lucia gets her revenge by sending the bailies round on his wedding morning and demanding a large sum of money or threatening an action for breach of promise. With this capital and that typical female disease of 'furor uterinus' or voraciousness for sex, she embarks on the game. After a hectic career she dies, leaving Helena to the knowing guardian Mother Cunny—the nickname of an actual London bawd. Her elementary lessons are on such topics as to 'seem chast and modest, with alluring smiles, commanding looks and Celestial Glances', the graces of affability, singing, dancing and playing the lute. Having graduated after more advanced studies, Helena resolves to escape from the old bawd. She steals off to Croydon, where she meets another old woman who proceeds to tell her the story of Gillian of Croydon, subject of country dance, who had been the proud but secret mistress of a local gentleman, but had been deserted by him and become 'the arrantest whore in all our country'. Helena also contracts the green sickness there, a common complaint of adolescent girls burdened with an unwanted maidenhead. She goes to London where she is quickly cured, and cured again and again. 'To omit all the lewd practices of our Helena', she lures an 'old dotard . . . an Elder . . . an old sinke-kater' into marriage. When she gives birth after only five months 'he taxed her for it'. She having 'quite cured my Gentleman of his old Itch and Lechery, and made him scratch where it needed not' makes off with £500 obtained on his credit to Tunbridge Wells, whence she institutes a claim for alimony in which 'she exagitated and urged some obscene unnatural attempts of his towards her; a practice that had pretty well succeeded in the court before'. He escaped this final humiliation by dying, 'and left Helena a most triumphant, rich now regnant whore'.[41]

Despite the diversion of Gillian of Croydon's story, typical of rogue literature—Meriton Latroon, the English Rogue, disappears for whole books—this account makes the narrative of Helena and her mother appear reasonably straightforward and unified. It is not. The distractions are endless. For instance, when Mother Cunny is giving Helena her elementary education, fifteen pages are given over to a sexual parody of Lilly's Latin Grammar and the description of 'Love's University'. This gives the author an opportunity for the most outrageous *doubles entendres*, for instance

> A *Noun Adjectival* cannot stand long by itself, (because its property is to fall) and earnestly desires other things to be joined with it; as *Foemina*, a woman. A *Noun Substantive* standeth by it self, till it requireth another *thing to be joyn'd* with it to shew its power and effect, and doth decline as *Vir*, a Man, *Priapus* a thing called by that name.

He has a field-day with the genitive and with conjunctions. The comparatives and superlatives he chooses are long, longer, longest, thick, thicker thickest. The noun chosen to demonstrate the meaning of preposition is thighs, and the example for the accusative is *eum coenaverim*. Apart from these schoolboy jokes there are also topical puns in the grammar; the genitive plural is declined as a-rumP. This precursor of the atrocities committed on Kennedy's *Latin Primer* then moves on to higher education without elevating the wit. Arithmetic is 'all multiplication'; 'the young Proficient with the Geometric Staff can take the Longitude, Latitude and Profundity of any Cavity'. In music lessons we meet those old chestnuts pricksong and the virginholes, the cliffe (cleft) men practise on and the quavers with which women respond, whether their mates are breef or semi-breef. The contents of the library are an interesting catalogue of what the age considered indecent.[62] Pride of place is given to a folio volume of Aretino's postures, a chained *Emblemmata amoris* and a mysterious much used volume, which turns out to be a metaphor for the female pudendum.

The red herrings in *The Practical Part of Love* do not end with this excursus into education. There are many topical allusions. The ideal bawdy house is compared to 'our late Commonwealth where all share alike and sweat with their Rumps for their dayly provision'. The King's Declaration of Indulgence proclaims that the courtiers 'never yet made conscience to dispense and indulge with their codpiece'. In treating Helena's green sickness the contemporary medical world is guyed. Lady Sandys is alleged to strain sack through the fore part of her smock, Harry Martin to have written a 'very learned Treatise *de Menstruis*' and a certain old lord to be 'a notorious smel-smock'.

There are jokes. Lovit's marriage to the ugly heiress turns into a well-known *fabliau* farce, where the experienced Lovit thinking that at least he has got a virgin discovers that his new wife has been 'daily exercising what a lusty lad showed me six years ago'. When Helena falls 'in company of some Maids that used to meet in the Evening and there talk of their Sweethearts and tell bawdy stories' she is treated to a variant of an old jest. A village idiot 'with a very large Bawble' has perfected a trick: 'he layed a bean on top of his ——— and yerked it a great way'. A maid sees this performance, and 'had a longing mind to employ it to better exercise'. She therefore takes the fool into a barn 'to ly with her, and they did it two or three times'. The fool, however, 'set up a great howl because this made his tool limber and out of order'. When the maid asked him what he was making such a fuss about, he replied that 'Jone had quite spoyled his Bean-Slapper'.

On most pages the reader finds himself led into scampering after one hare or another: the seduction of young apprentices by stale old servant-maids, who need to rub their itching gums with a child's coral, or a set of 'Bawdy Lectures' with questions and answers provided by Lucia, a long disquisition, partly in Latin 'for modesty sake' on 'Furor uterinus', classical allusions to Messalina and her like, and highly involved metaphors about girls ripe for harvesting or their dry combustible materials mounting to a flame.

The author of this extraordinary potpourri is not known. Indeed it seems quite probable that there was more than one author. The style of the parodied grammar is quite different from that of the recounting of the story of Gillian of Croydon. One of the writers was plainly a man of some education, probably a university graduate, who knew something of contemporary medical practice. His appeal was not to the chapbook-ballad-ephemera readership, but to a more intellectual appreciation. There is more originality in this than in many of the rogue stories, but the author(s) cannot resist the temptation to flog a good idea to death. Amidst a plethora of dirty jokes and unsubtle suggestiveness it is strange to come across a piece left in Latin 'for modesty sake' or for the same reason, the phrase 'to omit all the lewd practices of our Helena'. The preface, on the other hand, is refreshingly free from the usual cant about the moral intention of the work. Yet *The Practical Part of Love* does not seem to me to have been written with a pornographic intention; there is no loving dwelling on the details of sexual intimacy, for instance, or on perversions or experimentation. It is dirty-minded in a hearty kind of way—redolent of the merriment of coffee-house or tavern, rather than the solitary tumescent Pepys locked in his cabinet.

The London Jilt: or, The politick Whore. Shewing, All the Artifices and Stratagems which the Ladies of Pleasure make use of for the Intreaguing and Decoying of Men; Interwoven with Several Pleasant Stories of the Misses Ingenious Performances was published by Henry Rhodes at the height of the 1680s festival of filth in 1683. A second part followed in 1684, suggesting its popularity, which is borne out by its frequent appearance in auction catalogues and its being ordered from New England. It was, however, never reprinted, and the only known copy is at Harvard.

I have written at some length on this typical example of a Restoration whore story elsewhere, disproving, among other points, the attribution to the poet and romancier Alexander Oldys.[43] My comments here can therefore be brief. As rogue tales go, *The London Jilt* has the great and rare advantage of a strong unified narrative thread and a sustained attempt to develop the jilt's character through the first person. It is, too, relatively realistic; the knowing whore much prefers the wealthy middle-aged customer to the eager but penurious young blade; she counterfeits ecstasy to bring her customer the quicker to orgasm so as to get rid of him and make room for the next in line; she is constantly worried about pregnancy and violence from cheated customers—she keeps a mastiff, which finally gets ripped up in a sadistic scene. There are several interesting comments on birth control techniques, including a description of some kind of dutch cap.[44]

Some of the situations in which she finds herself smack of the *novelle* of Poggio, like discovering herself in bed in the dark in a brothel with her husband, who is meant to be out of town, and substituting her maid in order to wreak revenge on him. Lovers are forced to flee, like Jack Churchill from Castlemaine's rooms, clad only in their shirt tails. Skinflint cits are informed upon to the officers of the spiritual courts and duly caught in flagrant adultery with the informant, who pockets a reward. Maidenheads are sold and repaired and resold. The pregnancy trick buys a £60 annuity. There are moments of tension when her keeper, who thinks she is his alone, stays longer than expected and threatens to discover one of her fifteen other regulars arriving. The stock character of the voracious widow is much in evidence; the Jilt's mother—herself a superannuated whore—is one such, who finally in desperation marries a young bully and comes quickly to regret it. One encounter, in fact the Jilt's first, is somewhat less common. This is her bedding with a young gallant of wealthy family who proves to be not only impotent, but 'gelt'. His disability is described in specific detail by the frustrated maid who hoped to be relieved of her maidenhead.

We leave the anti-heroine the affluent owner of a lace shop, with a 'miss' in her employ, and some hypocritical sentiments to her readers, similar to those of the author in the preface. Again, the intention of the anonymous author seems to be to tell a racy tale of low life, rather than to stimulate. Occasionally he intentionally disgusts; invariably he delights in the latest and the not so novel sexual puns; but I can find no passages in the 243 pages of narrative in which he deliberately sets out to arouse sexual fantasies. As usual, this roguery is bawdy rather than pornography.

The fourth edition of *The London Bawd* was printed for John Gwillim in 1711. I have been unable to discover the dates of the earlier editions, but the text bears all the marks of its having been written in the 1680s or 1690s. Gwillim had been publishing since 1684 when he put his first advertisement in the *Term Catalogues*. Dunton describes him as a rich man by the beginning of the eighteenth century.[45]

The anonymous author begins with a character of a bawd, a loathsome superannuated whore, riddled with the pox, her teeth fallen out, her breath like a bear-garden, her nose and chin meeting, her wares well-worn. As an alternative to beating hemp in Bridewell, she acquires a bed, a plaister box, a looking-glass, three bottles of strong waters, two ounces of tobacco and a couple of country wenches and proceeds to procure new flesh for old customers, preserve maidenheads and wish the mathematics (increase and multiply) well. This medlar, never ripe till rotten, is 'the Chief Instrument of Evil'.

The author then copies *The Wandring Whore* format and has an inconclusive discussion between a whore, an old bawd, a pimp, a pander and a prodigal spendthrift about which of this unsavoury crew is most vital to trade and should therefore have pre-eminence. The pander tells of a colleague who prostituted his own wife when he found himself with two customers and only one whore.

Chapter III moves on to the real business of the book which is a series of 'Droll Tales'. The first is an anglicised version of a *Decameron* story[46] about an impotent old man who catches his young wife preparing for the arrival of her lover. She is tied to a post in a pond, but a bawd takes her place. The husband is amazed and humiliated when the punishments he thinks he has been inflicting on his wife leave no mark on her. The next tale had close similiarities with one of Nanna's on the third day of the *Ragionamenti*; it describes the methods a whore uses to beggar her keeper. Other farces have Irish footmen broguing their way into trouble in a whorehouse, a steward evicted from a brothel down a shute in his shirt, leaving £50 behind, a tale reminiscent of *The London Jilt* of a husband and wife who meet in a bagnio and a rehash of the Poggio story of the man who borrows £50 from a goldsmith with his ring as a pledge, pays the goldsmith's wife £50 for her favours, and then gets his ring back by telling the goldsmith in front of his wife that he has returned the money to her. The point of view changes when the Bawd starts to tell her own life-story, but the tricks and stratagems continue to be plagiarised. There are the topical touches of a visit by a spy from the Society for the Reformation of Manners, a canting do-gooder who uses vile Billingsgate to slander the whores, and the cataloguing of 'the jolly crew of active dames who will perform such Leacherous Agilities as will stir you up to take the other touch'. We learn that the girls go to church on Sundays to show themselves off to the gallants, and read play-books so as to make witty discourses to their guests. By an act of poetic justice the dreary recital of regurgitated farces ends suddenly, in mid-sentence, in the one original story in the whole 168 pages, that of a draper's wife who entertains her Thames sculler to lunch at the Three Cranes and then pays him a guinea for 'doing a Lady's Business' in an adjoining room.

Some whore stories appeared under the aegis of male rogue tales; it was almost inconceivable that the Restoration rogue would not sooner or later, usually sooner, fall in with a whore, and such was the rambling nature of the genre that once met, the whore must be allowed to tell her story, and probably the stories of other whores she had known, before the confused reader was reminded scores of pages later that the hero, a heroic listener, was alive and, all things considered, well, and about to continue his story, until, of course, the next lengthy diversion.

Such, as has been mentioned, was the fate of Meriton Latroon, *The English Rogue*, invented by Richard Head in 1665, stolen by Francis Kirkman in 1668, and shared as a profitable subject by the two of them in the third and fourth parts which appeared in 1671. Meriton dominates the stage in the first, and, it is generally agreed, best part; his story is a mixture of jests and the cheats indulged in by various trades, a favourite topic of Head's. When Kirkman stole the story, however, the whores steal the limelight. Mistress Mary's story in the later chapters of Part II is fairly slight and unimportant, but Kirkman craftily leaves Mistress Dorothy on stage at the end so that her story must be taken up at the beginning of the third part; in fact it takes up two-thirds of the joint enterprise.

Mistress Dorothy's whore story starts in a conventional enough way. Poor but beautiful with the predictable teenager's itch to part with her maidenhead, she accumulates gallants as customers and becomes pregnant. Enter the oldest cheat in the book: 'She made all that had to do with her contribute to her Expences'. Off in the country for her lying in, Dorothy meets an old woman, alias a procurer. She just has an opportunity to smother the bastard, before the old bawd takes up the story-telling. Her description of her seduction by a sailor is fairly typical of her style of narration, indeed that of all the participants:

> He being somewhat tipsie, I sat in his lap, and as cunningly as I could slipt my hand into his Pocket . . . as slyly he conveyed one of his hands into another place. Having not yet been at the sport, I squeeked out, which made him rise and me withdraw my hand, and both of us leave our Prizes.

After this fumbling start, there is no looking back. She has a bastard by a blackamoor, which is duly smothered. With her vagina expertly repaired, 'she goes as a maid' and marries an innkeeper. When this unfortunate is discovered with the servant-maid, his inn is fired and his lover drowned in the well. A passing gallant offers a chance of further revenge on her husband, but when he proves false to the bawd, she arranges for him to creep into her bed at night where her forewarned husband is lying in wait. She, meantime, is pleasuring herself with a new gallant. When both these beaux become tiresome, the bawd arranges a situation in which they fight, and conveniently kill each other. Dorothy is allowed back into the narrative when the bawd's services are requested by a barren woman of the neighbourhood. Several chapters are spent in the experiments of these two sexual scientists with various stallions.

Dorothy's interrupted account of her cheats and villainies is told in the third part in the East Indies and on the voyage to Surat. The fourth, and as it turned out, last, part finds the wandering rogues in Italy on the road from Messina to Naples. This gives the opportunity to dust over some tatty cuckolding tales—one of which is also a 'novel' in *Nugae Venales*, where it is described with blatant cheek as 'new' – and the old favourite of the wealthy widow determined to marry only a wealthy second husband, who is tricked into a match with a penniless poet.

Both Head and Kirkman were devotees of romances and rogueries. Indeed Kirkman's first venture in the world of bookselling—he had been apprenticed to a scrivener, though his pious mother wanted him to be a clergyman and his father had told him that the only two books he ever needed to read were the Bible and *The Practice of Piety*—was a circulating library of English and French Histories, i.e. novels and rogue stories, romances and poetry.[47] No doubt his involvement in the seedy activities of Marsh, Brooke and the printer Thomas Johnson gave him an insight into the profitability of sexual adventures. These two influences account for the increasing emphasis on the erotic in the four parts of *The English Rogue*. Chandler's analysis of the stories so bewilderingly recounted by the series of narrators leaves no doubt of the wholesale piracy that the two authors had committed on Spanish, French and Italian originals. Perhaps Starkey's successful adaptation of Castillo Salorzano's famous Spanish whore story *La Picara* in 1665 had some influences on Kirkman's second part, which introduces Mary and Dorothy as major figures, whereas before they had merely been passing victims of Meriton Latroon's sexual cheats. However, both Kirkman and Head were so saturated in this kind of literature that they could just as easily have decided on this course independently. They do steal situations from Salorzano, but their policy of wholesale borrowing is far more catholic than this one source.

No English whore story would be complete without the author's casuistical claims that the contents were intended not as encouragement to vices but as a warning against them. Thus Kirkman in his preface to Part II:

> I hope all persons who make use of this book to practice debaucheries will be induced to forebear and decline their wickedness, lest a just judgment overtake them, as they will find it hath done these extravagants.

Since the fifth and last part advertised at the end of the fourth never materialised, we shall never know the fate of the crew of rogues still happily tricking and cheating their way through southern Italy.[48]

One of the ingredients of *The English Rogue* which introduces a disturbing note to the English whore story is that of violence and cold-blooded sadism. It had not theretofore been usual for the 'by-blows' of the prostitutes' profession to be conveniently removed from the scene by infanticide, though perhaps in real life this solution was resorted to.

This element is present in the last of our rogue tales, *The London Bully, Or The Prodigal Son, Displaying the Principal Cheats of Our Modern Debauchees; With The Secret Practices and Cabals of the Lewd Apprentices of the Town: Discovered In The Life and Actions of an Eminent Citizens Son.* London, Printed by Henry Clarke for Thomas Malthus . . . 1683.[49] The prostitute in *The London Bully* is a spirited girl called Isabel. Her relationship with the bully is full of cheats and counter-cheats, and that staple of rogue literature, revenge. When Isabel throws a burning faggot at the bully which sparks his shirt and singes his penis[50] he responds by giving her *aqua fortis* for removing her freckles which instead turns her face yellow.[51] She in return lures him to her chamber. 'She lay there with her bosom all naked, and . . . excited so much desire that I could constrain myself no longer.' When he is fully engaged Isabel's hector appears and administers a well-deserved bullying to the Bully. His counter is to arrange that all Isabel's clothes are stolen and that she is left only with rags to cover her nakedness.

Intruded among these pranks, however, are some distinctly unsavoury episodes. The bully for instance is persuaded by the promise of a miss to have intercourse with an aged (i.e. 36 or 37 years old) bawd, who 'was well-nigh an hour busied with erecting the standard, which otherwise was always vigorous upon such game'. There is also an encounter with a deformed woman, with among other handicaps 'breasts like cow's udders; and the shattering denouement to the evocative seduction of an Italian perriwig-maker's wife, when removal of her smock—which, according to the bully, was an unusual precursor to intercourse—suddenly reveals that she 'was locked up after the mode of Italy'. By far the nastiest incident in the whole book occurs on Hampstead Heath. A gang of drunken bullies catch sight of a finely dressed woman taking the air with a bumpkin in her train. They surround her, and taunt her with her company, and the terrified woman in order to escape says that the servant is her husband. At this, the bullies force them 'to do their business in our presence'. The bumpkin is ordered to 'make himself ready for the attack'. The bully 'made the Lady alight and had put her into a posture to receive the Cavalier at one jump into his Seat . . . the fellow mounted . . . the Lady whispered 'Ah Peter for the love of God put it aside . . . but he took much pleasure in it or was afraid' and the beastly business was done. Subsequently the bully does show some remorse, and excuses himself on the grounds of drink. Nevertheless this vicarious rape is an obscene example of sexual violence and this intention on the part of the anonymous author is always in the background of the book.

Dialogue and narrative are two vital ingredients of the fictional form; the third is character. The writing of 'characters', generally with a satiric bias, was one of the most popular forms of fictional exercise in the seventeenth century. Sir Thomas Overbury's Characters were among the best-sellers of the century and were reprinted over and over again. The two great Restoration antiquaries Aubrey and Wood both used a 'characters' approach in their most memorable works and Dryden adapted it to devastating effect in *Absalom and Achitophel*. Countless others followed the Overbury example, notably John Earle, John Taylor, the 'Water-poet', Thomas Fuller, Francis Osborn, Richard Flecknoe, Samuel Butler, and that arch-plagiariser John Dunton.[52]

In low literature, which was nothing if not imitative of its betters, the character was applied to the whore, the bawd, the pimp, the hector and their customers. Apart from the bawdy baskets so racily described by Greene and his fellows in the late Elizabethan cony-catching romps, two pre-Restoration characterisers deserve mention. The first is John Taylor, the Thames waterman, who had considerable first-hand knowledge from his trade of the various classes of ladies of pleasure. His verse portraits include *A Common Whore, with all her Graces graced*, published by Gosson in 1622, and *A Bawd*, which was probably written and published about the same time, but whose first extant copy is dated 1635. The character of a bawd in *The London Bawd*, which we have already noticed, bears a suspicious resemblance to Taylor's original. Ballads and chapbooks contained many descriptions of prostitutes and their lackeys throughout the century.[53] The other characteriser is the rather more sinister Humphrey Mill, whose *A Night Search. Discovering the Nature of All Sorts of Nightwalkers*, first appeared in 1640. It is a goulash of characters, rogueries and realism, with some obscenely specific details, about, for instance, the disposal of unwanted bastards. A second part appeared in 1646, and this fits more obviously in the whore story category. Mill's book was alleged to be required reading in bawdy-houses two decades later, and more significantly may have given Dunton the idea for his *Night-Walker* which began to appear as a sixpenny monthly serial in September 1696, and under a gloss of transparent cant of which he was a past master, gave the reader a titillating account of a tour of the London hot-spots, in the rather uncomfortable company of a couple of disguised clergymen. A decade later Dunton was to try his hand at another similar venture, *The Whoring Pacquet*, exploiting the well-worked convention of secret news and letters being broken open and revealed to the curious reader, and with his inveterate zeal for projects advertised for the future, *The Concubines Pacquet*, which thankfully never materialised.[54] *The Secret Mercury*, which began its serial appearances in September 1702, followed the example of the *Night-Walker* in a less contortedly Grundyish way, and its early contents included such gems as 'The Character of Madame L—— of Hackney', 'A Conference with a Night-Walker', 'A Discovery in More-Fields' and 'The Cheats of the Cloysters'.[55] At this time, two other hacks with expert knowledge of the seamy characters of London's underworld were unashamedly putting that expertise to profitable use. Ned Ward's *London Spy* (1704–6), a series of steps and rambles round the town, is littered with whores; his *The*

Insinuating Whore and the Repenting Harlot (1700) is described by Katanka as 'the most explicit and discursive examination of a whore in the whole century'.[56] Tom Brown's prime weakness was for claret, but he too often portrayed prostitutes. We have already mentioned their appearance in his *Letters from the Dead to the Living*; his *Amusements Serious and Comical, Calculated for the Meridian of London* extract plenty of low comedy from the doings and personalities of members of the profession.

From the many characters and sketches of misses and their professional elders and inferiors, I have taken three different but in their separate ways typical examples. The first treats the whore as a member of the criminal classes generally; it is Richard Head's anonymously written *Canting Academy, or, The Devil's Cabinet Opened*, published by Matthew Drew in 1673. Rather more specialised than his book of wheedling characters, *Proteus Redivivus*, it sets out to decipher the slang or cant which 'the more debauched and looser sort of people' employ among themselves. There is a 'Compleat Canting Dictionary', poems in cant with English translations, and to set the tone there is a frontispiece that shows a whore and customer kissing on the ground, with her saying 'I'll smoke your lackam' and he 'I'le wap your bite'. Either slang did not change much over the century, or, far more probably, Head plagiarised wholeheartedly from Greene, but many Elizabethan words appear. Thus a dell is still a young girl, ripe for whoredom but not yet inducted into its arts, and doxies are, as before, 'destructive Queans, and oftentimes secretly Murderers of the Infants which are illegitimately begotten of their bodies'. Surprisingly a gilt, popular slang for a prostitute or miss during the Restoration, is still given as a lock-pick, especially in inns. There are many slang terms connected with the 'falling sickness' or V.D., with the tricks whores use for picking customers' pockets or substituting copper for gold coins. Head cannot sustain this etymological approach for the whole length of book, however, and it declines into a miscellany with songs, 'The Vicious and remarkable Lives of Mother Craftsby and Mr. Wheedler', a canter's 'Academy of Complements' burlesquing the popular books of etiquette and address of the day, and rambling disquisitions on lechery, gluttony and covetousness.

The Character of a Town-Miss, which came out as a penny broadsheet in 1675, with a companion about a town-gallant, and provoked a reply in defence, *The Town Miss's Declaration* (1675), is an altogether more literary production.[57] It is attractively written from a satirical point of view, but though quietly telling, the author's amusement at her rise and fall, her pretences and airs, never descends to bilious bludgeoning. The opening gives the flavour:

> A miss is a new name, which the civility of this age bestows on one that our unmannerly ancestors called whore and strumpet. A certain help mate for a gentleman, instead of a wife; serving either for prevention of the sin of marrying, or else as a little side pillow, to render the yoke of matrimony more easy. She is an excellent convenience for those that have more money than wit, to spend their estates upon; [The hack could never have resisted the temptation for a pun on spend, however dog-eared.] and the most that can be said in her commendation, is that she will infallibly bring a man to repentance. Yet you may call her an honest courtesan, or at least a common inclosed; for though she is an outlier, yet she seems to be confined within the pale, and differs from your ordinary prostitute, as a wholesale men from retailers; one perhaps has a hundred customers, and the other but two or three, and yet this gets most by her trade. Indeed, she may well thrive, seeing she carries her stock above her, and every man is desirous to deal in her commodity: for she is a gallant's business, a citizen's recreation, a lawyer's estate in fee-tail; a young doctor's necessary experiment, and a parson's comfortable importance.[58]

Although she 'talks high of her family . . . ruined by the late wars' she is a country wench, debauched by a ploughman and a booby squire at thirteen, pregnant at fourteen, and packed off by the latter to London 'the goodliest forest in England, to shelter a great belly'. Her 'bantling' is left in a handbasket, for the parish to discover and maintain, and the midwife-procuress helps her to her first keeper, a third-rate gentleman. By pocket-picking she accumulates some capital, and begins to blossom as a miss. She hires a 'maid (forgive me, for I lie, I mean a she-servant)', rents 'noble rooms' and decks herself in expensive finery. This display decoys a rich young gallant whom she proceeds to bleed of his inheritance, at the same time entertaining two or three other private customers. She excites his jealousy, she sulks and pouts, she pretends debt, she must have presents, she appears indifferent, she scolds and nags. There are plenty more cullies once he is beggared. With the next she will have nothing to do until a £300 annuity is signed, sealed and delivered, and in a month he is abandoned. By now she has a coach, a box at the theatre, her boys in livery, her blackamoor and her dog, a she-secretary, an old trot, and a dildo-merchant or a pair of able stallions to satisfy the needs her present cully cannot. She has more pride 'than would have served six of Queen Elizabeth's countess'. Her speech is a flow of affected gallantry and she addresses ladies of the best quality as though she were their equal. Each year she sails down to Tunbridge or Epsom, 'to wash and tallow, and refit her leaky bottom'.

But the ravages of time catch up with her,

> and engraves wrinkles, where she once painted roses. Then her former adorers despise her, the world hates her, and she becomes a loathsome thing, too unclean to enter into heaven; too diseased to continue long upon earth; and too foul to be touched with anything but a pen, or a pair of tongs; and therefore it is time to leave her:—for, foh, how she stinks.

The third piece is in verse: *The Female Fire-Ships. A Satyr Against Whoring In a Letter to a Friend just come to Town.* It was published by E. Richardson in 1691; it is nineteen pages long, and was almost certainly the work of Richard Ames. Ames was a minor poet of some aspirations but little talent. He was a graduate of Oxford and his works are listed at the end of the second edition of *The Folly of Love* (1693). He seems to have had to make do on hack-work, and to have made a speciality of the catalogues of whores and jilts, unmarried ladies and enfeebled bachelors that Dunton and his rival Randal Taylor published in the 1690s. He is very briefly noticed as a denizen of Grub Street in Dunton's *Life and Errors* (1704) and appears to have died about 1693.[59]

Whatever Ames' real motives for *The Female Fire-Ships*, he warns the suspicious reader

> Think not that any sad mishap
> Of swelling groin, or weeping Clap,
> Or Bubo, or venereous shanker
> Occasioned this Poetic Anger.

No, rather, it was the fate of a fellow Oxonian, 'A Friend of mine, young, airy, witty/Rich, Gallant, Well-belov'd and Pretty', who all innocent of the snares of London, this 'pious town' more vicious than any in Europe, was enmeshed by whores, 'poxt and clapt' and within two years dead.

With this provocation Ames launches into a sustained tirade against these cannibals devouring a dozen men an hour who are egged on by a frightful fiend within who whets their lewd desires. He runs through a venomous catalogue of the hierarchy: the 'Pentionary Miss,' who samples 'the dainties of the East' to 'heighten her salacious Itch'; 'Whores of the Second Rate', 'Play-house punks' who seek out some 'rustick cully' and after a token show of resistance, unrig themselves for one poor shilling; then come the 'Nocturnal Privateers', the street-walkers, who 'Board you and clap you underneath their Hatches'. Then there are the brothel whores 'Of fam'd Report, The religious Nuns of Salisbury Court, Who daily standing at their Convent door, And plying, seem to cry Next Whore, Next Whore.' Or the religious whores who show themselves off at church, but at prayer have 'One eye up to wink an Assignation'. These seem chaste Lucretias by day and 'Blush when they hear a word they judge obscene, While a thousand lewd ideas lurk within.' But after dark they reveal their true colours, 'Like Jezebels whose Arts some holy pages fill, They wipe their Mouths and say they've done no ill.' With a passing word on coffee-houses which are mere fronts for brothels, for the swearing bullies who take the whore's one obsession, her profit, and the assertion than none of the bawds who own 'vaulting houses', 'Bewly, Swatford, Temple, Whipple, Creswell nor Cozens who so loved the nipple' has an ounce of compassion for the 'clapt sparks in Fluxes, who penitently stew' in the Lock in Southwark, he completes his anatomy of abuses.

James Sutherland argues that to 'read the work of such a satirist as Richard Ames is to scrape the very bottom of a muddy barrel'. He does, however, grant that 'his vigorous and often obscene doggerel satisfied the crude taste of a masculine public'. *The Female Fire-Ships* does have the merit of maintaining a sense of outrage and moral indignation with greater success and sincerity than the usual hackney work, which nodded in a preface in the direction of morality, only to wallow in a slough of dirty jokes and *doubles entendres* in the text. Ames, despite his pathetic limitations, does make some effort to sustain an artistic tone.

There are relatively few accounts of brothels in the libertine literature of the Restoration.[60] Head has Meriton Latroon visit Madam Creswell's establishment in Moorfields in the first part of

The English Rogue. Tom Brown's letter from Creswell to Moll Quarles gives some details of management. Neither, however, is particularly life-like. A frequently transcribed manuscript poem, 'The last Night's Ramble', dated 1687, gives a vivid impression of a rather high-class establishment.

> Warm'd with the pleasures, which Debauches yeild
> Brain, stufft with fumes, Excesse of Wine had fill'd,
> I took last Night a Ramble being drunk
> To visit old Accquaintance Bawd and Punk.
> 'Twas madam *Southcot* near old Dunkirk square,
> That House of ease for many a Rampant peer
> For only the lewd Quality f—k there. —
> The first divertisement I found was this,
> I heard the Treble note of yeilding Misse.
> Whisp'ring, Lord, Sr what pleasant Tales you Tell!
> You'l find th'Enjoyment worth your mony well.
> Then in Base viol voice I heard him swear
> Dam me a Guiney Madam's very fair.
> The utmost Fee I ever gave to swive,
> She answer'd, How d'ye think that we can live?
> I'le Swear Sr *William R—ch* sr gave me five.
> While thus I listned I observ'd at last,
> Tho' she ask't more, she held the Guinea fast.
> When Grand procuresse to each standing *P—k*
> Came in half fluster'd from her Stallion *Dick*
> With Varnish'd Face of paint three Inches Thick,
> Daub'd on by Art and wise Industry laid
> To hide the wrinkles Envious tyme had made.
> This necessary friend I wou'd have staid;
> When came an Implement she call'd her Maid,
> Bred in the Art and skillfull in the Trade,
> And whisper'd her away. I guess'd the matter,
> And at a little distance Saunter'd a'ter:
> Anon I heard one knocking at the door
> Who entring, cry'd give me a ready Whore;
> Let her be clean and sound, and bring her strait,
> You know me (Bawd) I am not us'd to wait.
> At *Grayden's* such a dam'd defeat I've had
> With *Lady Mary Ratcl*— I am mad,
> And must the fflame that's kindled by her Eyes,

Quench 'twixt some co͞mon vulgar Beauties Thighs.
And to advance my Gust of Lechery
Just in the Act, dear *Ratcl*— I will cry
ffancying at least I swive with Quality.
By that same Cock't up nose (thought I) and Mein
That haughty spark shou'd be Lord Chamberl—
To be convinc'd I follow but mistook,
The Room, and did into another look.
Where who the divel doe you think I found?
But one (Oh Frailty) of the Reverend Gown.
Stinking mouth'd *Chest*— to my best discerning
Who gravely was a fine young Whore Confirming.
Nay If't be soe cry'd I, we need not doubt,
Since our good Clergymen are soe devout
But we shall keep all fears of Pop'ry out.

Then down I went and thro' a Wainscot flaw
Wallowing upon a Tir'd out Whore I saw,
Fumbling in vain, old Griping *Renel—h*,
With whores and pox, These forty years worn out
He sweats and stinks for one poor single 'Bout.
'Till Wench half stifl'd cry'd, my Lord, I'le Fr–g
You[r] P–k's too short, your Belly is too big.[61]

There is little doubt that the problem of prostitution became progressively more severe during the reign of Charles II. Those writers who turned a dishonest penny by describing the tricks, cheats and sexual prowess of whores all admit as much in their disingenuous addresses to the reader, especially in the 1680s and 1690s. To non-Londoners, the capital was looked upon as a horrendous assault course for virtue, male or female. Its corrupting influence vied in the popular mind with that of Sodom and Gomorrah.

It is difficult to gauge popular reaction to prostitution and its growth in London. There were many overt signs of opposition. The most obvious were the attacks on the bawdy-houses by the London apprentices. Traditionally these took place on Shrove Tuesday, but a more serious riot occurred in Easter week 1668. On 24 March, Pepys reported

Back to Whitehall, where great talk of the tumult at the other end of the town about Moorefields among the prentices, taking

> the liberty of these holidays to pull down bawdy-houses. . . . And some young men we saw brought by soldiers to the guard at White-hall, and overheard others that stood by say that it was only for pulling down bawdy-houses. And none of the bystanders finding fault with them, but rather of the soldiers for hindering them. And we heard a Justice of Peace this morning say to the King that he had been endeavouring to suppress this tumult, but could not; and that imprisoning some in the new prison at Clerkenwell, the rest did come and break open the prison and release them. And that they do give out that they are for pulling down of bawdy-houses, which is one of the great grievances of the nation. To which the King made a very, poor, cold, insipid answer: 'Why, why, do they go to them then?', and that was all, and had no mind to go on with the discourse. . . .
> *25 March* . . . The Duke of York and all with him this morning were full of the talk of the prentices, who are not yet down, though the guards and militia of the town have been in arms all this night and the night before; and the prentices have made fools of them, sometimes by running from them and flinging stones at them. Some blood has been spilt, but a great many houses pulled down; and among others, the Duke of York was mighty merry at that of Damaris Page's, the great bawd of the seamen. . . . But here it was said how these idle fellows have had the confidence to say that they did ill in contenting themselves in pulling down the little bawdy-houses and did not go and pull down the great bawdy-house in Whitehall. And some of them have had a word among them, and it was 'Reformation and Reducement!' This doth make the courtiers ill at ease to see this spirit among the people, though they think this matter will not come to much; but it speaks people's minds. And then they say that there are men of understanding among them, that have been of Cromwell's army; but how true that is I know not.

This annual saturnalia had plainly got out of hand, and its motives were more complicated that the usual springtime release of youthful high spirits. Nonetheless the comments of the J.P. and the bystanders are indicative. The attacks on brothels continued throughout the reign. Luttrell reports an attack on Moorfields and Whetstone Park in April 1679, and another by two or three hundred prentices on the latter on 2 September 1682; these were over and above the normal Shrove Tuesday assaults.

These displays of popular distaste for the most tangible symbols of Restoration immorality led some enterprising publisher to produce mock petitions from the whores. In the aftermath of the 1668 riot, there appeared two broadsheets: *The Whores' Petition to the London Prentices*, which was a moderately witty attempt to justify the oldest profession and to argue that lust was less serious a sin than thieving, which apprentices were renowned for. The second was *The Poor Whores' Petition to the Countess of Castlemayne*, which appeared in April. This was signed by Damaris Page and Mrs Creswell and sought protection from, by implication, the leading strumpet in the land.[62] L'Estrange, the Surveyor of the Press, took exception to it, but did not prosecute, because as he wrote to Secretary of State Arlington 'I can fasten nothing on The Poor Whores' Petition that a jury will take notice of. He went on to complain of the change in seditious styles between 1663 and 1668. Then it was 'heavy pious stuff. Now it is chiefly satirical and not a little indecent, and as such much more difficult to get a conviction on.'[63] Presumably the potential jurymen of London or Middlesex were not unsympathetic to the implications of the petition.

When members of the court circle ventured out of the privileged confines of the West End, they were liable to feel the popular disapproval for the example which they gave. Thus in Norwich:

> The Duke of Norfolk brought down one Mrs. Lane, his mis, with him, who made a great show here. But all that have any regard to their reputations here think it scandalous to accept his invitations. . . . She carries herself here as such cattell use to doe, without shame or modesty.[64]

Mrs Gwyn might divert the barrage of the Oxford mob in 1681, yelling to them that she was the *Protestant* whore, but she was liable to insults when she ventured abroad even in London. On 26 January 1681 Luttrell records

> Mrs. Ellen Gwyn being at the dukes playhouse, was affronted by a person who came into the pitt and called her whore; whom Mr. Herbert, the Earl of Pembroke's brother, vindicating, there were many swords drawn and a great hubbub in the house.[65]

The support which the campaign for a reformation of manners gained in the 1690s in its attack on brothels suggests that there was a deep-seated disgust among ordinary people in London and the provinces at the depths to which public morality had sunk. A formal puritanism had bitten deep into English attitudes. It might, like the prefaces of the purveyors of bawdry, be hypocritical—Pepys, after recording the King's insipid, but nonetheless pertinent question, proceeded the next day to one of his naughty fondling sessions in his coach with young Mrs Daniel—yet it does seem clear that there was a sense of affront and outrage over 'the wickedness of this age', and that a merry, Mediterranean tolerance of harlotry was alien to the seventeenth-century English temperament.

NOTES

1. Thompson, *Women*, pp. 241–3.
2. Hill, *World Turned*, p. 301; Gardiner, *Documents*, p. 142.
3. Vol. V, p. 1172.
4. *London Bawd*, p. 5.
5. *History of Journalism*, p. 145.
6. Hutson, *Stage*, pp. 17–44.
7. *History of Journalism*, p. 146.
8. Thompson, ed., 'Prideaux Letters', p. 120. The same claim is made about London taverns in *The London Jilt*, Part II (1684), p. 48.
9. W. H. Blumenthal, *Brides from Bridewell* (Rutland, Vt., 1962), p. 25.
10. B. Bahlmann, *The Moral Revolution of 1688* (New Haven, 1957), p. 104.
11. K. Wrightson, 'The Puritan Reformation of Manners', unpublished Ph.D. thesis, Cambridge University, cf. P. Laslett. *Family Life and Illicit Love* (Cambridge, 1977), pp. 107, 147–51.
12. Wilson, *Rake*, p. 103.
13. Wrightson, 'The Puritan Reformation of Manners', pp. 31, 38, 49, 174.
14. Mrs Dorothy in *The English Rogue*, was a hostess, *sc.* procuress, in a country inn.
15. A. L. Hayward, ed., *Tom Brown's Amusements Serious and Comical* (London, 1927), p. 442.
16. Page is also alluded to in one of Pepys' *Penny Merriments, The Womans Brawl* (N.d.), Vol. II, No. 1.
17. *London Bawd*, p. 149; *Catalogue of Jilts*, p. 2.
18. I owe these two references to Mr Hugh Amory, who ascribes the first to Richard Ames and the second to John Dunton.
19. One Lampoon, 'Though Ladys of Quallities C—ts often Itch' names thirteen whores alone. Harvard, Mss. Eng. 636 F*, ff. 274–5.
20. *Eng. Lit. Late Seventeenth Century*, pp. 27–8.
21. Quoted in Wrightson, 'Puritan Reformation', pp. 286, 288.
22. Chuck Office is a pun, possibly on the Poultry Office; chuck was slang for chicken.
23. This profession had two years earlier gained a mention in *The Crafty Whore*, p. 46.
24. Tarse was a common slang term for penis in the seventeenth century.
25. Hill, *World Turned*, p. 298.

26. The titles are: *Lusty Drollery, Venus Cabinet Unlockt, The Crafty Whore, A Night Search, The Venereal Spy, The Practical Part of Love*, and *The Wandring Whore*. The identity of 'S.H.' is discussed below.
27. 'Pimp Singleton' is described as 'the extemporary poet' in a list at the end of *The Wandring Whore*, Part V.
28. The location of these two very rare pamphlets is the Guildhall Library , London; a note dated 1974 adds that there are also copies in the Bodleian; they are not in the Thomason Collection.
29. Parts I–III are in the Guildhall Library, London, A1.1 No 56; Parts II–IV are in the Thomason Collection, British Museum, E. 1053.3, E. 1053.6, E. 1053.8; Part V is in the Bodleian, Wood 654A; Part VI is also in the Bodleian, Douce A253(1).
30. Williams, *History of Journalism*, p. 146.
31. McKenzie, *Apprentices*. Garfield became a freeman in 1655. He was the son of Rev. Thomas Garfield, of Tickhill, Yorks.
32. K. V. Thomas, *Religion and the Decline of Magic* (Harmondsworth, 1973), p. 445.
33. Theodidactus is described as 'Powder-Monkey, Roqui Crucian, Pump-master-general, Universal Mountebank, Mathematician, Lawyer, Fortune-Teller, Secretary to the Naturals, and Scribber of that infamous piece of Non-sense, Advice to a Daughter against Advice to a Son'. *Select City Quaeries*, Part I, Q. 6 also notices him.
34. Thompson, *Contrast and Connection*, p. 40.
35. Niccolo Franco, Aretino's secretary, is a possible candidate; Foxon, pp. 28–30.
36. Part of the sub-title is 'Discovering their diabolical Practises at the Half-Crown Chuck Office'.
37. McKenzie, *Apprentices*.
38. Gibson, *Kirkman*, pp. 52, 144. *The Wits* list is reprinted in Elson's edition, p. 257.
39. Foxon, p. 26; an edition of the complete *Ragionamenti*, n.p., had last been published in 1649 or 1651.
40. *The Life of Long Meg of Westminster*, published by G. Conyers, is in Pepys' *Penny Merriments*. Vol. II, No. 26.
41. The stratagem of extracting alimony from a tricked husband had recently been employed in real life; see the fascinating *Alimony Arraign'd: Or The Remonstrance and Humble Appeal of Thomas Ivie, Esq*. (1654).
42. The complete catalogue is: *Venus Undrest, Life of Mother Cunny, Anatomy of Cuckoldry, Luteners Lane Decipher'd, Francion's Bawdy History, Jovial Drollery, Venus and Adonis, Lusty Drollery, Venus her Cabinet Unlockt, Ovids Art of loving, Natures Chief Rarities, The crafty whore reprinted, The English Bawd, The errant Rogue, Catalogue of all the Whores of the Citty covering thirty sheets of paper*, all sorts of books of midwifery. Pp. 39–40.
43. *Harvard Library Quarterly*, XXIII (1975), 289–94.
44. Pp. 80, 93.
45. H. R. Plomer, *Dictionary of Printers and Booksellers* 1668–1725 (London, 1968). There are references to the societies for the reformation of manners, pp. 158–9, 161, which may have been added to later editions to give a sense of topicality. All the allusions to prostitutes belong to the latter part of

Charles II's reign. Gwillim's list is respectable apart from this title; it could have been a youthful venture to raise capital.

46. VII, viii.
47. Gibson, *Kirkman*, p. 52.
48. With similar monitory sentiments, Head tried his hand at a straight whore story in 1675, *The Miss Display'd* reprinted as *Madam Wheedle, or The Fashionable Miss Display'd* in 1678, published anonymously. This piece is set mainly in Head's birthplace, Ireland, which he later briefly visited, and much of the action is lifted bodily from Goodman's *Hollands Leaguer* and *The Practical Part of Love*.
49. Malthus was also responsible for *Fifteen Real Comforts of Matrimony*, see under Matrimonial. He published only between 1682 and 1685, when according to Dunton he emigrated to Holland in 'perplext circumstances'.
50. This may be an elaborate figure for her giving him V.D.
51. This was the chief disadvantage of its common use for treating whores for V.D. Cf. *London Jilt*, Part II, pp. 97–9; *London Bawd*, p. 139.
52. G. Murphy, *Bibliography of English Character-Books* (London, 1925); C. N. Greenough and J. M. French, *Bibliography of Theophrastian Character in English* (Cambridge, Mass., 1947).
53. These are well surveyed in Katanka, 'Women of the Underworld'.
54. P. Pinkus, *Grub Street Stripp'd Bare* (London, 1968), p. 107; I am grateful to Dr Stephen Parks, the bibliographer of Dunton, for assistance with this important but often unreliable character.
55. Walter Graham, *Beginnings of English Literary Periodicals* (New York, 1926), p. 41.
56. 'Women of the Underworld', p. 82.
57. Both Miss pieces are in the Bodleian, Wood 654A. *The Character* is reproduced in Pinkus, *Grub Street*, pp. 280-4.
58. Pinkus has modernised the spelling.
59. I owe this information to Mr Hugh Amory, who has an article forthcoming on Ames.
60. Beljame, *Men of Letters*, p. 52, gives four examples of brothel scenes in Restoration comedy.
61. Bodleian Firth Mss. c. 15, ff. 268–74; Nottingham, PwV 42, ff. 324–32; V. and A. Dyce 43, ff. 784–8.
62. There were other *Whores Petitions* in the reign; one, for instance, to the apprentices of London 1672, was a plea for custom since so many regular clients had gone off to the war. Another, in manuscript, addressed to the King, thanked him for the profitable trade they enjoyed thanks to his example. V. and A. Dyce 43, f. 552.
63. *Calendar of State Papers Domestic, Charles II*, Vol. III, 1667–1668, p. 357.
64. Thompson, ed., 'Prideaux Letters', 184.
65. *Historical Relation*, Vol. I, p. 34.

6 Matrimonial

The maids' catechism asked 'What is the chief end of a maid?' and generations of maids learnt the answer: 'To be married'.[1] Most adults entered this 'inevitable state' – many, given the hazards of life, more than once. Yet, to writers of bawdry, people did not marry and live happily ever after. Wedding nights, which then as now were the source of much prurient exaggeration, were a brief interlude of sensual release.[2] The usual approach was that of the author of *Ten Pleasures of Marriage* (1683): 'Now you may outdo Aretin and all her (sic) light companions in all their several postures.' *The Presbyterian Wedding*, a ballad of the later years of the century, had the minister in the bridal chamber, 'And while they strove in mutual love, The parson sang a psalm'. At Dunton's wedding, a wag attached a bell to the bed, and there followed much ribald comment about the jangling and juddering.[3] This 'cavalcade of love' was merely the overture; the opera was about cuckoldry.[4]

The horned husband had been a figure of fun since classical times. Thus Plautus subverted Catonic puritanism, and Ovid Augustan *virtus*. Thus Boccaccio and Poggio ridiculed the hypocrisies of clerical celibacy and Christian monogamy. Thus French farceurs undermined the courtly love ideal. The emphasis of these Latins, however, is not on the adultery. They stress the guile and quick-wittedness of the lovers; the husband is usually merely an obstacle to be cunningly circumvented. He may even emerge blindly grateful for his worsting: 'cocu, battu et content'.

The English, by contrast, feel impelled to justify. Adultery may still be a joke in Stuart times, but there is a cloud of guilt about it. Infidelity is no longer an ingenious jape; it is a joke at someone's expense. So that someone, the husband, has to be shown to be deserving of his fate. In the numberless English cuckolding situations, then, we have numberless and exhausting explanations. Impotence, whether or not due to senility, is by far the commonest, frequently connected with the arranged marriage. The husband might be unspeakable in other ways: jealous, mean, drunken, womanising, boring, bourgeois or, rarely, brutal. Whatever his faults, the reader must be made to share the sentiments of Sir Henry Savile about a lady: 'Since . . . she has to do with such a hound [her husband] . . . she cannot possibly be in the wrong, considering who she has to deal with, but in not cuckolding him.'[5] Given that prerequisite, guiltless mirth can flow at the prospect of the whey-faced fool, with his huge stag's horns, drying the bastard's clouts on the points, or having them tipped with silver by his profitable spouse.

The other impetus must, of course, come from the wife's sexual needs. These, like the greensick maid's or Aesop's archetypal widow's, are typically ravenous, 'tumbling and tossing in a good Feather-bed, sometimes on one side, and sometimes on the other: sighing and groaning, as if her very twatling-strings would break, making her moan to the curtains, fumbling, and biting, and tearing the sheets and by no means [able to] ease her oppressed body and mind.'[6]

There are intriguing parallels here with traditional white American attitudes to the Negro. 'Sambo' was conventionally seen as inherently inferior: indolent, wasteful, irresponsible, childishly silly and wilful. Yet he was paradoxically credited with superhuman sexual prowess and appetites. The Diary of John Ward, bachelor vicar of Stratford-on-Avon, reflects the same kind of typical Restoration ambivalence towards women. On the one hand he gleefully instances their inherent infantile wilfulness. There is the wife of the gentleman, forbidden to ride upon the dog; this is the first thing she does when opportunity offers, and, predictably, she gets bitten. He recounts how Sir John Hotham had four of his wife's teeth forcibly extracted to teach her proper subordination. He copies Erasmus, Euripides and the Strasbourg scholar Stahl in derogation of the weaker sex, and approvingly notes the adage 'A Wife, a Knife and a Walnut Tree, The more they're Beaten, the Better they be'. On the other hand, he records a description of the irregular longings of women and maids, the signs of potency of women in Albertus Magnus, a recipe for cold water as an antidote to woman's lust and the story of a woman who coupled with a dog; her offspring always circled before lying down. Women may be wilful, silly, irresponsible and generally contemptible, but at the same time they are sexually dangerous, mysterious and suspect.

How often these sex-crazed simpletons betrayed their lords and masters in real life it is impossible to measure. The evidence from the court of Charles II discussed below suggests that there sexual immorality for women was much commoner after marriage than before. Literary references portray the same pattern among the middle classes. The *bon bourgeois* could lock up his daughters, but his wife defied incarceration. Neither source is particularly reliable.

It is far easier to suggest why this might have been the case. A bastard was a serious threat to any community. It had to be supported for years out of the poor rate; it was a moral blot. Every conceivable social, moral and economic pressure was therefore exerted to prevent such a direful accident from happening. On the other hand, an ignorant or complaisant husband who would 'Christen the froward buntling once a year/And carefully thy spurious issue rear', dealt most conveniently with all these problems and pressures. Ironically, fornication was faced with far greater sanctions, including the ultimate deterrent of discovery, than discreet adultery by a wife. It is intriguing that this justification is the least mentioned in literary treatments of cuckoldry. The great majority of Pepys' extramarital couplings were with married women, typically the wives of subordinates. After the scare that Betty Lane might be pregnant, the diarist insisted that she must get married before their sexual relationship could be resumed. With unmarried girls he normally contented himself with gropings and fondlings.[7]

Of course, in real life cuckoldry is not funny at all, any more than impotence or nymphomania, defloration or prostitution, widowhood or venereal disease. In thinking about cuckoldry it is wise to recall Legman's remarks on folk humour.

> Sexual folklore almost always concerns some of the most pressing fears and the most destructive life problems of the people. . . . they are projecting the endemic sexual fears, and problems, and defeats of their culture . . . on certain standard comedy figures and situations like cuckoldry. . . .

Why this obsession with adultery and its attendant guilt? What were the fears, and problems and defeats of Restoration culture which made the cuckold such a popular object of projection?.

Holy matrimony legitimised sexuality. 'The most modest and chaste Virgin.

> who would not have showed (a man) her Foot before, without her shoe and stocking on . . . now without the least breach of

> Modesty freely strips off her clothes in the Room with him, and goes into what we call the naked bed with him, lies in his arms, and in his Bosom and sleeps safely and with security to her Virtue with him All the Night.[9]

This idyllic transformation hardly conveyed the complexity of either sexuality or marriage, however. Sexuality had several functions: practically it served to produce offspring; emotionally it could be an expression of love; physically it satisfied lust. The main purpose of marital sex, according to traditional theologians, was the reproductive. Marriage was more than the subjugation of a maidenhead, the end of a prolonged period of sexual restraint for the happy couple. It marked the formation of a new household, an economic unit, a means of raising, supporting and disciplining legitimate children, a new unit of government, a little church and a little common wealth. In canon and common law, it represented a new tutelage for the bride, 'given away' by her patriarchal father to a new patriarch whom she promised to obey. For people of any substance it was an important property negotiation, a source of capital, a means of perpetuating ownership within a family line; with such issues at stake, 'prudential matches' must be made. Many parents thought these too crucial to be left to the whims of love-lorn youth.

These prevailing views on marriage and marital sexuality were, as we have noted, under challenge in the seventeenth century. Some Puritan and Anglican idealists, for instance, preached that marriage should be 'a friendship', 'a union of souls rather than sexes', a matter of 'I choose' rather than 'I take', a partnership of loving mutuality rather than a legal and proprietorial relationship of superior husband and inferior wife.[10] Milton went so far as to advocate divorce on the grounds of incompatibility, though the judge of that would be the husband. Puritans in England in the 1650s and in New England extended Anglican separation into full divorce, and in 1670 Lord Roos was given the right to remarry by his peers. Charles II attended the debates not just because they were 'better than a play'; Buckingham and others had seriously advanced divorce and remarriage as a solution to the succession problem.

Another more radical alternative to traditional marriage was polygamy. For fundamentalists this was justified by Old Testament precedent. Luther had been driven by political pressures to endorse the bigamy of Philip of Hesse; Clement VII and Cardinal

Cajetan had both suggested the same solution for Henry VIII's 'great matter'. The English publication of Bernardo Ochino's *Protestant Dialogue of Polygamy*[11] in 1657 further stimulated serious argument about the topic, which the imbalance of the sexes in the middle years of the century had made an important issue.[12] Probably provoked by this, Henry Neville, a writer of previously sullied reputation, brought out his utopian novellette *The Isle of Pines* (1668), describing the polygamous peopling of an island in the Indian Ocean by a shipwrecked book-keeper George Pine and four women castaways, one a negress. Apart from one mildly erotic scene, it is a straightforward account of the production of 565 offspring in a period of forty years. The third generation has become debauched by decadence, whoredoms, incests, adulteries and wantonness—perhaps a veiled attack against Restoration morals.[13] Against this background it is hardly surprising to find bigamy offered as another way out of the succession problem of the 1670s.

Something approaching this solution was in fact indulged in by both the King and Buckingham, whose wife also proved barren: the mock marriage to a mistress. In 1670 the Duke went through such a ceremony with the Countess of Shrewsbury. It was alleged that Sprat, the Duke's chaplain and later Bishop of Rochester, officiated at the ceremony; afterwards the poor Duchess was popularly known as the 'dowager duchess'. The King followed suit at Euston on 4 October 1671 with a mock marriage to Louise de Kerouaille.[14] Behind these bizarre ceremonies lay the suggestion that a marriage should be a love-match.

It was the ranters and other extreme sects who were most wildly experimental. A few groups dispensed with marriage and even polygamy altogether and indulged in 'standaway divorces' and free love; in fiction these became hall-marks of conventiclers. The preachments of a Coppe or Clarkson threatened to overturn the whole social structure, a terrifying prospect, but also a powerfully titillating one. In this, they joined hands with extremists at the other end of the spectrum, the libertines, who, despising convention, preached the cult of obedience to natural appetites and celebrated an Ovidian, prelapsarian sexual promiscuity. In their inverted world, not only is marrying a sin,[15] but

> Marriage is but a licensed way to sin,
> A nooze to catch religious woodcocks in,
> Or the nick name of some malicious Fiend,

Begot in Hell to prosecute mankind.
'Tis the destroyer of our peace and health
Misspender of our precious time and wealth,
The enemy to wit, valour, mirth, all
That we can virtuous good or pleasant call.[16]

The emergence of these conflicting ideas reflected larger economic, intellectual and cultural developments, like the rise of the urban middle class and of individualism, to be discussed in the Conclusion. Both the concept of marriage as union of soul-mates, feasibly terminable, and the extremer alternatives placed traditional ideas in jeopardy, and in some cases would have had the effect of usurping patriarchal authority. To cavalier machismo, the doctrine of inviting the slaves up from the quarters to share the big house was a ludicrous betrayal. Only impotent, Puritan, bourgeois husbands would thus lose their grip on the naturally uppity womenfolk; only they would be weak-minded enough to imagine that marriage could be a permanent friendship, or that the emancipated wife could remain faithful. Thus the groupings into which satire and bawdy about marriage during the Interregnum and Restoration naturally fall: marriage as conflict, cuckoldry as propaganda, the myths of male inadequacy and female wantonness and male sexuality.

Happy marriages rarely make the literary headlines. It is trouble and strife which is newsworthy, and popular representations of this were flytings, or spousal scolding matches. There are three examples of this in Pepys' collection of chapbooks, *Penny Merriments*, and many more in ballads and broadsides. In *Worm-wood Lectures* by the famous balladeer Martin Parker, and *Vinegar and Mustard*, the wives open the battling in prose, and the husbands respond in verse. Tavern haunting, dalliance with wenches, idleness, or blindness to the new light of the sects are typical of the hysterical indictments these shrews fling at their husbands, who, when their turns come, are calmly reasonable, but firmly dominant. The wife who enters the pub like a wasp, leaves it reeling on her spouse's unsteady arm; the Quakeress abandons the Friends; the merry miller's wife is put in her subordinate place by being reminded that she once happily sacrificed her own maidenhead to him, 'and for the same I made amends'. Altogether more verbally violent is *The Womans Brawl* in which Jack and Doll harangue each other for fourteen unremittingly scabrous pages.[17]

The conflict in *Ten Pleasures of Marriage* and its sequel *Confessions of a New-Married Couple* by 'A. Marsh, Typogr.' published in 1682 and 1683 respectively, probably in the Netherlands, is less frenetic but equally inexorable. In twenty painful chapters we are led along the primrose path from courting bliss to costive separation. With a direful predictability the apparently simpering and innocent fiancée gradually manoeuvres until she 'hath got the breeches', and that is the beginning of the end. She employs every opportunity in her campaign. First she thinks she is barren, and her neuroses extract concessions from her husband (who may, after all, prove impotent). Then she becomes pregnant, and yearns for 'exoticks' which her thankful cully cannot deny her. Her allies the midwife and nurse make further demands, and the agony of labour extracts still more from her pitying spouse. The husband's business requires him to travel, and he leaves his wife in charge of the cash. Her servant-maids prove 'base-conditioned' and defraud the family funds. Their business slumps. Their son proves a wastrel. The husband in his distress grows negligent and takes to drink. Soon the purse is empty, and the disillusioned husband seeks divorce from his breeches-clad wife. If only he had known what his attraction to her 'snow white breasts' would lead him to.

Sometimes a husband tried to impose special provisions on his prospective wife, as in Restoration comedy proviso scenes. Thus Tom the Taylor:

> First, you shall kiss my hand and swear that you will acknowledge me to be your Lord and Master.
>
> Secondly, when I come home drunk a nights, you shall be diligent to make me unready and get me to bed, and if I chance to befoul myself, you are to make me clean without chiding me.
>
> Thirdly, if any Gentle Woman comes to have me take measure of her, you must forthwith go out of the Room, and leave us together and not be jealous.
>
> Fourthly you must not let any man kiss you but your husband, but if any should offer any such thing to you, you must be sure to let me know what they say and do to you.
>
> Fifthly and lastly, you must promise not to spend nor waste your Husbands Money nor Goods, and observe alwaies in Cow-cumber-time, to put less meat in the Pot than at other time, because you know that then we have always a Bad Trade:

> And one thing I had almost forgot, which is, that you shall be sure every day once or twice in the day to muster the Flees and the Lice that have taken possession in our Bedding and wearing Apparel: I say once again (and be sure to remember this last Article of our agreement) you must destroy, kill, and slay them all, if possible.

Joan humbly agrees to these conditions, in return asking only that she may choose her own maid and receive visits from a young male 'Cozen', to which Tom accedes. When, however, he gets drunk on his wedding night and is incapable of giving his new wife her due benevolence, she and her knowing maid force the shame-faced tailor to let her 'make void all those promises I made you before marriage, and next that you shall not lye with me, nor desire to lye with me at any time but when I please'. So much for insurance policies.[18]

It is surely no coincidence that the cuckoldry theme was employed as a major propaganda weapon by anti-Puritans during the Civil War and Interregnum without the usual English sense of guilt. One of Anthony a Wood's collections of pamphlets in the Bodleian contains several examples of this genre.[19] There are firstly the mock petitions. *The City-Dames Petition in behalf of the long-afflicted but well-affected Cavaliers* was allegedly presented to the House of Commons in 1647. The case of such citizens' wives as Mary Lecher, Sarah Lovesicke, Rachel Wantall, Dorothy Swivewell or Priscilla Tooly was desperate. Since '42 when the cavaliers departed, their trading has been mightily impeded. Their poor husbands, hard at work all day, are now forced to labour at night as well. In the good old days 'Cavaliers alwaies stood stiffe to the City', but now the dames' only custom is from a 'mouse-hair'd fellow, with a long thing God blesse us by his side as rusty as himself'. Sexual potency is the last refuge of the defeated.

Henry Neville, gentleman, republican, rumoured atheist and recruiter to Parliament in 1645, fastened on an Aristophanean idea to broadcast libels. His parody of the business of the House of Commons, *The Parliament of Ladies* (1647), involved an assembly of cavalier ladies of rather questionable reputation, like Lady Newport, Lady Stanhope and Lady Carlisle. Various mock orders are passed, for instance 'No round-head should come into any of their quarters'; complaints are heard, like that of the famous bawd

'Lady' Foster about the current decay of trade, and the disposition of certain favoured men, cavalier and roundhead, is debated and agreed upon. Great play is made on 'standing forces', 'disposal of baggages', 'purging malignancy'—i.e. venereal disease— and the 'occupation' of various towns which also happen to be the titular names of various ladies. It is all good undergraduate bawdry, execrably and anonymously printed, as it was anonymously written. The satire became more cutting in a second part as the ladies agree to revenge themselves on their husbands' hunting of forbidden game by themselves hunting 'in their own——berries'. Various parliamentary generals and senior officers are assessed and assigned, including Cromwell and Fairfax, certain ministers are offered the freedom of the ladies' pulpits and some questions are forwarded to the synod about sexual irregularities in the Old Testament, which contemporaries would certainly have thought of as blasphemous. With his third pamphlet, *Newes from the New Exchange, or The Common-wealth of Ladies* (1650) Neville is scraping a very slimy barrel. The alleged sexual proclivities and equipment of cavalier, Presbyterian and roundhead ladies are vulgarly set out, and the illicit liaisons of many leading politicians of the commonwealth rumoured. Peters, Scot and Marten are there, along with Cromwell, Ireton, Rainsborough, Jephson, Bradshaw and Lenthall. The excuse for this parade of filth is the new freedom of women; the opening paragraph reads

> There was a time in *England*, when men *wore the Breeches*, and debar'd women of their *Liberty*; which brought many grievances and oppressions upon the *weaker vessels*. . . . In consideration whereof, and divers other inconveniences, by the tyranny of men the *Ladies Rampant* of the times, in their last *Parliament*, knowing themselves to be a part of the *free people* of this Nation, unanimously resolved to assert their own *freedoms* and casting off the intolerable yoak of their *Lords* and *Husbands*, have voted themselves the *Supreme Authority* both at home and abroad, and settled themselves in the posture of a *Free-State*, as may appear by their *Practises*.

Select City Quaeries: Discovering several Cheats, Abuses and Subtilties of the City Bawds, Whores and Trepanners, by Mercurius Philalethes, was published in three parts, March 9, 19 and April 11, 1660. Despite its subtitle, it is a catalogue in question form of the sexual irregularities of London citizens and their wives, mainly centring on cuckoldry:

> XII Whether Mr. Simpson, the Apothecary in Cornhill was as careful to give his wife due benevolence, as he was to give his Sister Butler a Glyster; whether Mr. Butler was abused when another takes on his Occupation?
> XXVII Whether the Lowsie Barber's Wife in the Postern by Moorgate did ever handle the Ironmonger's man's ware in one hand, and his Master's in t'other; whether the Deceiver and Receiver are not alike?[20]

This format had a brief but rapidly tiring vogue in the first half of 1660 before grinding itself into the dirt. It might have raised a few smiles and blushes in the coffee-houses and taverns at the time, when men were beginning to adjust to a rather different morality. Such libels were essentially fugitive pieces, and their only interest for us is the weapons they use.

Masculine impotence or at least inadequacy was a seventeenth-century obsession. Occasionally it is explored for its own sake, usually lubricious, as in *The London Jilt*, where the sufferer is a young country gentleman, a Squire Limberham. In pornographic books, it is the rationale for the exploration of perversions like flagellation or sadism.[21] Yet in the majority of cases it is the disability of two groups: the aged and the bourgeoisie, often Puritan. Like cuckoldry, it is a form of insult, less important in itself than for what it symbolises. The insult to age is a symbol both of anti-authoritarianism and the changes in social mores that the second half of the century witnessed. In real life, men of years tended to be controllers of wealth and power, arrangers of marriages, financers of apprenticeships and dowries, armed with the powerful weapon of disinheritance. Conventionally, age meant experience and experience meant wisdom. It is no coincidence that the Restoration wits and satirists were young men, or, as they aged, continued to act like young men. In a stable society they would have deferred to and imitated their elders and betters. In the zig-zags of seventeenth-century politics, however, the traditional relationships between the generations suffered. A young man's father in the 1660s would either be tainted with at least condonation of the Good Old Cause, or else, like Clarendon or Ormonde, be an old cavalier, ridiculously out of place relics from an era that the Puritan revolution had destroyed, or, more likely, embittered by what seemed neglect for their loyalty. So age, while still demanding deference customarily, and still wielding power, in the family, for instance, and in many areas of local and central government, was either suspect or pathetic or ridiculous.[22] While this disjunction between the generations is reflected in serious literature in the number of 'Advices' to the young and the endless moans of sermons about the rising generation, in satire and bawdry the potency and poverty of youth are set against the wealth, but impotence, of age. The more or less easy seduction of May is the obvious way of ridiculing January.

We have already mentioned several times the reasons for the vilification of the urban middle classes. It was the pose of men of breeding, or of those who hoped for their patronage or approval. It reflected not only a social and intellectual dichotomy, but also the inexorable and frightening course of economic development. While the gallants were about their wives, the bourgeoisie, like Quomodo in *Michaelmas Term*, were about their—the gentlemen's—estates. The careers of those arch wits of the Restoration, Buckingham and Rochester, are nicely symbolic. The Duke, with £20,000 per year at the Restoration, dies penniless, and in popular report at least, in squalor in a mean inn in Kirby Moorside.[23] The Earl is burnt out by wild excess at thirty. Compare their lives and deaths with Pepys, the essential bourgeois, accumulating, accounting, collecting, investing, auditing, burgeoning—and probably sexually inadequate.[24]

The incidence of impotence in seventeenth-century bawdry is so frequent, that, were it true, the population must have declined sharply. Not even Charles II escaped the taunt. Very few of the dirty books we discuss in this book do not make some reference to it. Here we can only deal with one or two pieces in which it plays the major part.

Fumblers-Hall, kept and holden in Feeble-Court, at the sign of the Labour-in-vain, in Doe-little-lane is one of the chapbooks in Pepys' *Penny Merriments*. It employs the popular trial format, like Sessions of the Poets, in this case before the Master and Corporation of Fumblers Hall, a building made entirely of horn of one kind or another, and similarly decorated. A series of 'females of Cornucopia' present their cases against their husbands, whose sexual assets are dismissed as 'a straw in the Nostrils of a Cow, a very slug, a meer fible' or 'a meer Gut, a Chitterling, a Fiddle-string that will make no musick to a Womans Instrument'. The women allege the taunts of their neighbours, envy of their friends' beautiful children, as well as sexual frustration, as grounds for their pleas. Though one husband offers to counter his wife's assertions with an exhibit, the men's responses are generally feeble and evasive—one, for instance, arguing 'that every Night she Farts in her sleep'. The court usually finds for the plaintiffs, granting them 'licence of freedom' to find extramural satisfaction.

The Parliament of Women, not to be confused with Neville's libels, was first published in 1640, and reprinted during the Restoration. It is based on a Roman jest—and indeed, nominally set in Roman times—derived from the *Ecclesiazudsai* of Aristophanes, about the rumour that the Senate had decreed that men in Rome could have two wives. The women gather together to discuss this outrage, and quickly come to the conclusion that it is they who should have 'two strings to their bow . . . keeping one for delight and the other for drudgery'. But this needs some justification, and so a queue of tradesmen's wives forms up to catalogue the sexual shortcomings of their husbands: a tailor's wife[25], a feltmaker's, a horse-courser's, a goldsmith's, a silkman's, a comfit-maker's, a braisier's, an apothecary's, a mason's, a wire-drawer's. The sexual puns are outrageous and bawdy; oh that any was original. After exhausting the possibilities of *double entendre*, the women enact a series of laws, which as well as allowing them two or even for the 'greatest Vessels' three husbands, give them all kinds of other freedoms and dominance and lay down exhausting duties for whichever male is on the night shift.

The plots of many jests and stories involving adultery likewise turn on the husband's impotence. Margery Wiseakers and Cisly Doelittle in *The Female Ramblers* (1683) are married to 'Jealous-pated Fumbling Coxcombs . . . who long after fluttering like Cock-Sparrows, tire themselves and us with doing e'ne nothing'. They persuade their bourgeois husbands to take them to the fair, rather than the cheaper and less dangerous expedition to get may-blossom which the husbands prefer. Sure enough, once at the fair, two seductive gallants, Horner and Doewell, inebriate the boorish husbands, and live up to their names with the ladies. Similarly the four 'Intriegues' in *The Art of Cuckoldom*, published anonymously in 1697, all involve beautiful and sprightly young women being married against their wills to elderly, wealthy citizens. Since Phillis, in the first story, has already gladly parted with her maidenhead to her lover Strephon, 'Bridal Night drudgery is not like to be too hard a tug for his fifty-eight years'. The prentice knowingly opines that 'an old husband could not be overextraordinary satisfactory to such young veins'. So with the city mercer in the next farce: 'his reverend and superannuated manhood was overmatched' by his twenty-year-old wife, whose 'fair soil was but weakly tilled at home'. All poor Urania, married to a fifty-year-old merchant, gets after her arranged marriage are 'wedding-night embraces, though not the transports of Wedlock'.

In Ames's catalogues some attempt is made to prevent such disasters. In *A Catalogue of Ladies to be set up by Auction* (1691) it is stipulated that only those 'Gentlemen will be accepted [as Bidders] who have clear limbs and Members entire upon due Examination'. A subsequent list of the 'Batchelors Attenders in the Womens Auction' does not however suggest the ladies went to stallions; the men have names like Mr. Feeble Fainwood or Mr. Jasper Flutter. Perhaps this was why so few of the ladies were bought.

The myth of female wantonness, a pornographer's stock-in-trade, has usually been a necessary component of male fantasising. Not only did the concept of the hungry woman ease guilt about men's promiscuous urges, and provide a rationale for the sexual battle of the classes, but, more seriously, it rationalised and excused man's frequent fall from grace. Ward records a story in his diary about a young woman in the agony of labour asking Lady Pickering why it was that women had to endure this pain. Her ladyship replied that it came from 'our Grandmother Eve eating of the apple', to which the sufferer replied that she wished that it had choked her. Woman as temptress and agent of the devil was a particularly useful symbol when an influential group in society was stressing with embarrassing urgency the divinely ordained duty of matrimonial love and fidelity.

The pattern set by Joseph Swetnam bit deep. His *The Arraignment of Lewd, Idle, Froward and Unconstant Women* first came out in 1615 and was frequently reissued in various forms throughout the century. Swetnam's Juvenalian *saeva indignatio* against women led him to drag up every example in classical literature and biblical story of the ways their 'continuall desire' and 'amorous glances of lust' had led otherwise virtuous, noble or wise men astray. His hatred of women seems to be almost pathological; they were all like Semiramis who 'waxed so insatiable in carnal lust that two men at one time could not satisfie her desire'. With the passion of an early Christian father he warned against innocent appearances. 'If she carry it never so cleane, Yet in the end she will be accounted but a cunny-catching Queane.' If love for woman was a 'sore', curable perhaps by a close study of Ovid's *Remedia Amoris*, 'Woe be unto the unfortunate Man that matcheth himself with a Widdow'. Swetnam's torrent stimulated a pamphlet war in which the fair sex found their defenders, yet it was his message that most men probably wanted to hear.

The departure of men from London to fight for the parliamentary cause on the battlefield evoked plenty of snide allusions to women's sexual starvation. Typical was *The Virgins Complaint for the losse of their Sweet-Hearts by these present Wars, and their owne long solitude and keeping their Virginities against their Wills* (1642). The 200 000 mature maids or supposed virgins are distracted by green sickness, eating 'clay-wall, morter and small coales' in their frustration. The wars, pressing men who should be pressing their necessities, are even more ravenous and greedy of man's flesh than the signers. The poor maids are driven by desperation to the archetypal inadequates, 'frosty bearded usurers', 'bungling fumblers that cannot stand without the helpe of crutches', 'idle and useless old members' and effeminate tailors and musicians. Most galling is the thought of the suttlers' wives in camp, or the 'Daughters and Damsels of the townes where they are billetted in garrison' who have more than even they can cope with. A year later, the midwives followed suit in a mock petition for peace, again filled with hoary military-sexual puns both about their own lack of 'comfort and benevolence' and the decline of their trade.[26]

Once the war was over, the focus turned to the sexual inability of the bourgeoisie to satisfy the lusts of emancipated citoyennes. *Now or Never: Or a New Parliament of Women* which George Horton published in 1656' showed a singular lack of originality. The session, which met in the seamy area of Moorfields, adopted certain rules which they called to the attention of 'All London Prentices, Young-men, Batchelours and others'. These gave their lusts *carte blanche*. No man was to call his wife whore 'unlesse she hath been taken naught in an open market place'. Aphrodisiacs and 'sperm-makers' were to be fed to 'men of abilitie'. 'No maids or married women be denied the thing they love . . . either at bed or board.'

Apart from lusting after lusty gallants, bourgeois women were commonly depicted as the seducers of apprentices. This was how the innocent young Jack of Newbury, the great clothier, began his climb to fame and wealth, according to Delony's ballad which in various forms was a Stuart best-seller. The apprentice in *John and His Mistris . . . the Wanton Wife and her Handsom Prentice*, an undated chapbook, is so comically ignorant of the facts of life that the mistress has to adopt all kinds of ruses to get him upstairs to the garret. He is a fast learner, however.

Then up stairs they did go,
Where she taught him to wooe,
The bashful Young-man she outfac'd
Come Iohnny she said,
Prethee be not afraid
By me thou shalt ne'r be disgrac'd.

She taught him to bill
And to kiss her his fill,
Till his Courage began for to move,
Oh then she did cry
Sweet Iohnny I dye,
These these are the pleasures of Love.

Sweet Mistris, said John,
I'le never lye alone,
'Tis so sweet and so pleasant a pain,
Thus panting to lye,
Dear Mistris let's try
For I long till I dye once again.

Her Johnny and she,
Very well did agree,
But now he begun to be cloy'd
The maid cal'd him down,
And he left her alone,
But he thank'd her for what he enjoy'd,[27]

Professional stallions were also available for those women who found even those discreet Drury Lane brothels for married women smacking too much of Messalina.[28] *The Towne-Miss* at the height of her success had two, it will be remembered. In a popular droll, or scene acted in the non-coterie theatre, called *The Stallion*,[29] Ruttilio gets the job, apparently enviable, of satisfying a famous bawd. In this extremely lewd piece, however, the strapping, well-hung stud is rapidly drained dry by his mistress's demands, and is only saved from complete collapse by a timely rescue. It was not only whores—in respect of appetite merely super-women—but wives as well who allegedly had these potent servants. *The Floating Island*, published anonymously in 1673, and written under the pseudonym of Frank Careless by Richard Head, is a description of a 'voyage of discovery' from Lambeth to east of 'Terra del Templo' along the Thames. In one passage he describes the feminine need for 'men of great naturall parts . . . that can afford to spend five hundreds pounds perannum'. As insurance for their mistresses in the household, 'and that their strength may be thoroughly discovered . . . before they are admitted as Menials for venerial Service, some chamber-maid must take them to task who must make report what meer nature hath performed, without help of Jellies, or any such-like provocations.'[30]

For every mistress who seduced an apprentice in real life there must have been scores of masters who led servant-girls astray.[31] Ward notes the paradox of a favourite chambermaid's exclamation 'As I am honest', meaning chaste. The definition of 'A dishonest maid' was one who had been 'crusht betwixt her Master and a feather bed'. This kind of pressed-meat sandwich, though starting Moll Flanders' career, is pretty rare in low literature; there are only two cases in the 115 chapbooks that make up the *Penny Merriments*, and in each case the master is severely worsted by the maid. In whore stories it is much commoner for girls to be born to the trade and copy their mothers' examples than for the Harlot's Progress to begin with a cart trip up to London from the countryside, there to be met by an insinuating bawd or pimp, or to take to prostitution after induction by the master of the household.

The argument of this chapter can best be summarised by two Restoration contributions to the *querelle des femmes: XV Comforts of Rash and Inconsiderate Marriage, or Select Animadversions Upon the Miscarriages of a Wedded State*. Done out of French. It was first published in 1681, with new editions in the following two years, published by Heyrick, Crooke and Gillyflower. The response, allegedly by 'A Person of Quality of the Female Sex', was advertised as *The Womans Advocate* in the *Term Catalogue* but published, by Alsop and Malthus, with the title *Fifteen Real Comforts of Matrimony, Being in requital of the late Fifteen Sham-Comforts. With Satyrical Reflections on Whoring, And the Debauchery of this Age* (1683).

The origins of this Restoration rugby match go back to the first half of the fifteenth century. The cult of chivalry was rapidly being eroded by a steady stream of mysogynistic or cicisbeistic books, usually bawdy and scatological, of which the most famous was *Cent Nouvelles Nouvelles* of the circle of Margaret of Navarre. One of these anti-matrimonial works was *Les Quinze Joies de Mariage*, sometimes ascribed to Antoine la Salle, tutor of the future Louis XI, though the evidence for his authorship is extremely shakey. The title was a profane parody of the pious *Fifteen Joys of the Virgin*, and the whole tone is satirical and combative.[32]

The fifteen so-called comforts are not all sexually promiscuous wives, quite. Two are scolds, and another is a super-scold who produces four scolding daughters. The rest are all sexual exploiters. One uses the withdrawal of her favours to get fine clothes, which bankrupts her husband. An apparently happy marriage is shipwrecked when the middle-aged wife develops a curiosity about other men's weapons, finds many 'sufficiently tool'd for her Salaciousness', and having sworn her fidelity, finally gives her husband V.D. Two use the obsessions of pregnancy and the pain of childbirth to subdue their husbands to the role of unpaid servants, and then gad abroad after gallants. A young girl made pregnant by a rake, deceives a young widgeon with the help of her mother—'in the Oven before'—simulates virginity on her wedding night, and presents him with a miraculously premature bouncing baby after only three months. A pretty young wife persuades her husband to take her to a party, where all the men are her secret lovers, giving her 'a gentle tread on the toe, an amorous squeeze of the hand and a languishing eye'. The husband's discovery sends him into a melancholy, which she uses to justify further amours. There are plenty of impotents. A cuckoldy old goat without *humidum radicale* who must be up and at his young brisk and wanton wife is the butt of an old, old *novella* plot. His wife give her favours to a gallant for £50, but in the end it is the old goat who pays. Another husband, with a 'Lean and Meager parcel of Carpenters Tools' dismisses his roving wife, who 'requires more milk' and goes to 'lap elsewhere'. He repents, allows her back home and catches 'a swinging clap' for his pains.

As good a husband 'as ever laid Leg over a woman' is relegated to an errand-boy while his wife enjoys herself with a gallant, and a young widower who seeks solace with an older widow finds he has both a nag and 'a lascivious draining old wife' on his enfeebled hands. In the 1682 edition three extra 'comforts' were added. In one story a childless couple cannot decide whether the husband is impotent or the wife barren. He begins experiments with a 'She-Gallant', and she with a gallant; in their ensuing penury, he becomes a 'pad' and she a 'buttock and file', a pocket-picking whore in thieves' cant. The message is hardly obscure: marriage is a net, a snare, a trap.

The riposte begins as though it were a counter-attack against men, who are described in the 'Preface to the Injur'd Ladies' as 'by-hole-hunters'. If woman ruled, there would be no taverns, gunsmiths or bawdy-houses, we are told; and 'women seldom think ill, till their husbands dream it first'. Certainly male sexuality is ridiculed throughout the fifteen episodes. His lust is so consuming that a whore has been known to make a customer re-dress during foreplay and go out to get the 2s 6d he lacks for £20 worth of all-night dalliance, which may cost him another £200 to avoid the blackmail of a bantling being laid at his door. Man's fatal 'scapeloytring . . . frequently brings the lascivious Prodigal more than Circumcis'd from the Surgeon, and sends him Noseless to the Grave'.[33] A surgeon claims to have 'Nuts of Priapus anow (the spoils of Venerial Combats) to button a Leaguer coat'. The perversions of the impotent— 'an old Dottrel with no more pith to his back than an elder-gun'— are lovingly dwelt on; these 'sapless . . . half-pint lechers, who fornicate with their eyes, when their other Tackle fails', sometimes demand special discipline: 'a sturdy Quean belabours their buttocks, till their impotent wimbles peep out of their bellies to beg a reprieve for their Tayles'. Thanks to this kind of treatment, 'the naked hanches of a strapping black-browed Quean . . . are all bedript with the fat of his Infant-offerings'. Another 'father in sin' is pictured like a dog under a table while two naked whores eat above; he snaps at their legs and they throw him bones.[34] There are plenty of cuckolds too. One, returning embarrassingly unannounced, is sent out by his wife to the apothecary's in her rich lover's breeches while the paramour makes his escape. She then has the gall to accuse her husband of picking up the trousers at a whore-house in mistake for his own. When another Actaeon finds his wife in bed with her lover, she brazenly tells him that she gives him all he wants; why should she waste the surplus?

Yet, if this is *The Womans Advocate*, Lord protect her from her friends. For rather than emerging from this melange of obscenity and borrowed bawdy[35] as an innocent sufferer from male promiscuity, woman is set in a male-made mould. Typically, she is in 'a continual famine, yawning and stretching for more . . . hardly the spout of a whale's neck will serve to send forth streams sufficient to quench her inward fire.' She uses her attractions mercilessly, in and out of wedlock; she enslaves men by her temptations; her chief virtue is a quick wit to escape the consequences of her voracious appetites. All women are whores at heart.

Although many married for the money or the maidenhead, 'more belonged to housekeeping than foure bare legges in bed'[36] and most of that was acutely unpleasant. Much of the satire on marriage was of well-worn antiquity, but an important innovation of the Interregnum, perpetuated in the Restoration, was the literary reversal of traditional sex roles. Males tended to be depicted either as sexually unsatisfying or as gigolos, obediently servicing their mistresses. Females are the huntresses, the sexual activists; it is their wanton urges which generate the plots. This is in striking contrast to the many tales of cuckoldry in the *Decameron* or Poggio's *Facetiae*, where a lovelorn gallant typically provides the motive force. Although this reversal was surely a wild distortion of reality, it does reflect both the well-documented emancipation of urban middle-class women and the new ideas about marriage as more than an arranged property deal and perpetuator of the species. To those who had been soundly whipped in battle after battle by the proponents of these ideas—and what more telling test of male potency than war?—the last resort was to ridicule and libel their conquerors as hag-ridden cuckolds and eunuchs.

NOTES

1. Quoted in D. Defoe, *Conjugal Lewdness or Matrimonial Whoredom* (London, 1727), p. 32.
2. Average age of marriage, except for the aristocracy, was the middle or late twenties. Louis de Gaya, *Ceremonies Nuptiales* (1679), a scholarly but sometimes titillating account, was translated into English by I.S.S. in 1685, and again by Tom Brown in 1697, reaching a third edition by 1704.

3. *Life and Errors* (London, 1705), p. 99.
4. The origins of this word were discussed, often bawdily, in G. Rogers, *The Horn Exalted* (London, 1659). Cf. L. Norell, 'The Cuckold in Restoration Comedy', unpublished Ph.D. dissertation, University of Florida, 1962.
5. W. D. Cooper, ed., 'Savile Correspondence', *Camden Society*, First Series, LXXI (1858), 116.
6. *The Parliament of Women* (London, 1640); reprinted in Thompson, ed., *Penny Merriments*, p. 256.
7. A. Bryant, *Samuel Pepys: The Man in the Making* (London, 1952), p. 64; J. H. Wilson, *The Private Life of Mr. Pepys* (London, 1959), passim.
8. *The Horn Book*, pp. 245–6.
9. Defoe, *Conjugal Lewdness*, p. 58.
10. Ibid., pp. 27, 43, 114.
11. Published by Garfield. G. Bullough, 'Polygamy Among the Reformers', G. R. Hibbard, ed., *Renaissance and Modern Essays presented to V. de S. Pinto* (London, 1966), pp. 5–23. *The Isle of Pines* is reproduced in part in *Shorter Novels of the Seventeenth Century* (London, 1930).
12. R. Thompson, 'Seventeenth-Century Sex Ratios', *Population Studies*, XXVIII (1974).
13. R. Thompson, 'Prurience and the Puritans', H. C. Allen and R. Thompson, eds., *Contrast and Connection* (London, 1976), p. 40.
14. Wilson, *Rake and his Times*, pp. 142, 160.
15. *Character of a Towne-Miss*, p. 2.
16. *A Satyr against Marriage* (1682).
17. Thompson, ed., *Penny Merriments*, pp. 249–51.
18. Ibid., pp. 267–72; for marital conflict in Restoration comedy, see G. S. Alleman, *Matrimonial Law and the Materials of Restoration Comedy* (Wallingford, 1942) and E. J. Gagan, *The New Woman* (New York, 1954).
19. Wood 654A; Thomason has many more.
20. Part I.
21. Crayle, the porn-pedlar, published a translation of Cornelius Gallus, *Impotent Love* (1689).
22. See Norell, 'Cuckold in Restoration Comedy', Ch. III.
23. Wilson, *Rake and his Times*, denies the squalor, but not the poverty.
24. Sir D'Arcy Power, *The Medical History of Mr. and Mrs. Pepys*, Abernethian Society, 1895.
25. A traditionally ill-equipped profession, vide Feeble in Falstaff's recruiting scene.
26. *The Midwives Just Petition* (1643) in Thomason and Wood 654A.
27. Thompson, ed., *Penny Merriments*, pp. 277–9; cf. *Tom Stitch*, ibid., pp. 280–2.
28. *The London Jilt*, part I, pp. 20–4; *The London Bawd*, pp. 70–1; Hayward, ed. *Tom Brown*, p. 443.
29. Excerpted from Beaumont and Fletcher, *The Custom of the Country*, in *The Wits* (1662). Beljame, *Men of Letters*, p. 47, has references to stallions in Restoration comedy.
30. Pp. 11–12. Women are often portrayed as administering aphrodisiac foods or wines to men. Cantharides (spanish fly) and satyrion (orchis) were also quite familiar. Rabelais alludes to them, as does Tom Brown. Boyce, *Brown*, p. 163.
31. Wrightson, 'Puritan Reformation', p. 57.

32. R. Aldington, ed., *The Fifteen Joys of Marriage* (London, n.d.), pp. 3–40; it was first published in England by de Worde (1509) and popularised by *The Batchelar's Banquet* (1603), probably by Robert Tofte.
33. Allusions to the effects of V.D.
34. Cf. *The Wandring Whore*, No. 3, p. 9 and *Erotopolis* (1684), p. 105.
35. Two of the farces are from the *Decameron*, two from Poggio and one from *Michaelmas Term*.
36. Swetnam, *Arraignment*, p. 35.

7 Aristocratical

The absence so far in this study of licentious literature of any discussion of a court renowned for its licentiousness may seem strange. Yet the court, though far more public than nowadays was in many ways isolated from the rest of the country, like a luxury liner moored at Westminster. It had its tourist spots in the West End: the Parks, the theatres, the gaming-houses like Lockets, its bagnios in Drury Lane, its Misses' lodgings in Pall Mall and King Street, its great courtiers' houses along the Thames. Nonetheless Temple Bar, the western edge of the City of London, was not just a physical barrier; it marked a psychological barrier between the court and 'the country'.[1]

The rampant depravity of some of the denizens of this hothouse is notorious. The sexual rapacities and public obscenities of Buckingham, Monmouth, Killigrew, Montagu, Oxford, Rochester, Jermyn, Sedley, Buckhurst, Lady Castlemaine, Lady Arundel and Lady Shrewsbury are well attested.[2] Rumour implicated many more. The King, 'Old Rowley', proclaimed his god-given privilege for 'a little pleasure out of the way', and shamelessly pardoned atrocities committed by his courtiers.[3]

Yet before we equate 'the great bawdy house of Whitehall' with the worst excesses of Caligulan Rome, we should note some mitigating factors. The most vivid account of court life, Hamilton's, paints a picture of high-spirited frivolity and triviality, a boisterous and silly adolescence. For all the ogling that went on—the Duke of York was particularly unsubtle at 'giving the eye'—the number of pre-marital conquests, even by the King, was slight. For maids, as St. Evremond cautioned, 'serious intentions and landed property are required here'.[4] Commenting on a caesarian operation, the King opined that 'most husbands had rather make use of a needle and thread than a knife', but not all courtier husbands were as complaisant as Castlemaine. Nor did all offenders escape royal censure unscathed.[5] Gossip probably exaggerated or invented many lewd incidents;[6] others, blamed on courtiers, were perpetrated by unattached gallants, hectors and bravoes. Some scepticism is therefore in order.

The principal cause of this debauched tone was the King. 'His immoderate delight in empty, effeminate and vulgar conversations' had become set in his exiled twenties.[7] Clarendon, who so fatally misread the political realities for the monarchy in 1660, thought that the intractability of problems facing the ill-prepared cynic drove him into the diverting round of pleasure. That the pleasure would be taken with ravening jades like Castlemaine was inevitable after the disaster of the Portuguese match.[8] Others followed eagerly where the 'facetious fascist' ambled. Many Restoration courtiers, like Buckingham, had thrown in their lot with the Protectorate; debauchery for them might serve the dual purposes of purgation and symbol of loyalty. Others had taken to furtive licentiousness under Oliver as an escape for their powerlessness to change a hopeless situation.[9] Younger men had picked up 'epicurean' and 'lickorish' habits at university or inn of court; this tuition would continue.[10]

Profounder influences were also at work. A plausible case has been made out for the importation of Mediterranean culture and values via France, with its courtesans, its machismo, its carnival, its sexual guiltlessness and experimentation.[11] Certainly the sun-belt philosophy of libertinism, encouraged by Hobbesian Pyrrhonism and materialism, enjoyed a heady vogue among the Whitehall playboys.[12] Its instinctual celebration was encapsulated by Crowne: 'The order of Nature is to follow my appetite; am I to eat at Noon, because it is noon, or because I am hungry? . . . The world is Nature's house of entertainment, where men of wit and pleasure are her free guests, ty'd to no rules, or orders.' Such convenient beliefs turned sex into a matter of 'touch and go', women into sex-objects.[13] 'What is there to be had of a woman more than the possessing her?' demanded Sedley.[14] The often-noted conscious refinement of manners at the Restoration may well have emphasised superficial polish at the cost of deeper attachments; 'the comedy of manners was essentially the comedy of sex', not of love.[15] Other commentators point to more conjectural causes such as a generational revolt against earnest parents of the Civil War era, to the changing balance between 'matrism' and 'patrism',[16] or to a 'dissociation of sensibility' in the generation of Milton and Dryden.[17] The causes of the decadence are complex and debatable; what is certain is that after the tasteful chastity of Charles I's ménage and the staid rusticity of Oliver's, Charles II's court provided a heyday for rakes and wits.

A few of the authors of 'satyrs', lampoons, libels, litanies or songs which circulated around 'Sodom-on-Thames' among these self-styled scourges achieved more than passing fame: Rochester, Oldham, Sedley, Etherege, Dorset. For most, though, an ephemeral ripple, a topical hit, was the best they could manage. Theirs is the wit of the school magazine, the satire of the student newspaper, the smutty parody or obscenity of the lavatory wall, parochial, personal, adolescent. Their main literary aim was to shock and demean. Recklessness, excess, impulsiveness, promiscuity, extravagance they admired; they affected an arrogant contempt for convention, morality, responsibility, authority, prudence or profundity. Their satire is never on the grand scale of a Marvell, a Dryden, an Ayloffe; they prefer cheap abuse, squalid scandal, revolting perversions and the shattering of taboos. They are manic, monotonous hooligans of letters.[18]

The ingrown effluent of these scribblers normally circulated in manuscript, except for an occasional surreptitious printing like *Poems on Several Occasions* in 1680. 'Not one in forty libels comes to press, though by the help of manuscripts they are well-nigh as public,' wrote the frustrated L'Estrange in 1677.[19] The original draft might be copied by a scrivener, or by admirers in coffee-houses, The Groom-Porter's Lodge or the Wits' Drawing Room at Whitehall. The lampoon craze spawned specialist distributors like Julian, 'Secretary to the Muses', Warcup, his rival as 'a Treasury of Spite' or Somerton, and scriptoria which produced whole manuscript anthologies covering several decades.[20] Several of these miscellany volumes have survived.[21]

The task of describing and classifying the large number of court verses that has survived has been lightened by the recent publication of J. H. Wilson's *Court Satires of the Restoration*, with exhaustive notes and bibliographies.[22] His selection, however, omits such disgusting pieces as Fane's 'Iter Occidentale', *Sodom* or verses, like Rochester's 'Ramble in St. James's Park', printed in *Poems on Several Occasions*. It is dominated by personal libels against either court ladies or mistresses or rival halfwits and fops. Here we will comment briefly on three popular topics of the miscellanies: satires against Charles II, attitudes to male and female sexuality and *The Farce of Sodom*.

The main burden of attacks on 'the father of his people' was His

Majesty's enslavement to lust. The King, and thus the country, is ruled by his penis:

> To Reigne, and give that lawlesse member Swing. . . .
> Out Flyes his Pintle for the Royall Cause
> Prick foams and swears he will be absolute.[23]

In such powerful satires as Rochester's 'In the Isle of Great Brittain', Lacy's 'Preserv'd by Wonder in the Oak, O Charles', Freke's 'History of the Insipids', 'The Lady of Pleasure' and others less memorable, the message of Oldham's indignant 'Sardanapulus' is reiterated,

> C—t was the Star that rul'd thy Fate,
> C—t the sole business and Affair of State,
> And C—t the only Field to make thee Great;
> C—t thy whole Life's fair Center whither did bend
> All thy Designs, and all thy Lines of Empire tend:
> And C—t the sure unerring Card
> Which plac'd at Helm, the mighty Vessel and its motion steer'd.[24]

That the revulsion against this 'cunt-struck' libertine (misspending his time, energy and the nation's money as well as his seed)[25] was basically political is borne out by two points: Rochester, Dorset and Sedley consistently voted with the Whig lobby in the late 1670s.[26] Secondly, although Castlemaine is smeared for her undiscriminating promiscuity, and Gwyn for her gutter origins, the real venom is reserved for the King's last great mistress, the French papist Portsmouth. As 'Carwell' is politically most dangerous, so no obscenity, about her sex organs, her 'whites' or the stale royal seed in her vagina, is spared. The fact that she was the most seemly, dignified and emotionally steadying of all the royal whores is of no moment.[27]

It will come as no surprise that the attitudes towards sexuality in the court verses were at best unconventional and at worst depraved. Marriage is scorned. Vaughan's view that 'A Wife's but an orthodox Whore' was too flattering for some.[28] She was an intolerable millstone: 'The clog of all Pleasure, the luggage of Life, Her portion but small, and her C—t very wide.'[29] The prevailing cult is for youth, free to follow natural instincts, untrammelled by the monotony, the jealousies, the duties of matrimony.[30] Marriage to Tom Brown was 'The Greatest cheat that Priesthood E're contriv'd';[31] a husband 'a dull Temperate Fool who's always dead'.[32] 'To be married and live in the country' was, according to Rochester, a curse fit only for a cur. Fothergill's libertine, 'Give me, ye Gods, each day an active Whore', was the rakes' manifesto.[33]

Women, 'the silliest part of God's Creation',[34] are frequently epitomised as their sex organs; indeed this was their only interesting feature. 'By God, there is nothing to be beloved *propter se* but a cunt,' the startled Pepys was informed.[35] One wit, known only as 'Watt', wrote a long encomium 'In Prayse of Twatt, By a faire Ladys Command'.[36] Rochester anathematised his mistress' 'lewd cunt' in a dozen enraged lines.[37] The King's poverty was caused by 'Imbezling Cunt, That wide-mouthed greedy Monster'.[38] Dorset summed up typical female appeal:

> Cunts whose strong charmes the world bewitches
> The Joy of Kings! The Beggars Riches!
> The Courtiers Business! The Statesmans Leisure!
> The tired Tinkers Ease and Pleasure.[30]

Even this beneficence was evanescent, however. Distension turned celebration into execration. Not only were the most nauseous secretions and diseases attributed to these organs, discarded at last even by pages and footmen, but their devouring lust—whining like 'a dog-drawn bitch'—can only be assuaged by dildoes. These artificial phalli exerted extraordinary fascination over the wits' imaginations, in the case of Rochester, Butler and Dorset with rollicking results. Usually, however, dildoes serve only as a means of abuse, symbols of self-abuse.[40]

In this surreal, cartoonists' world populated by animated sex organs, 'Squire Pego', the penis, is similarly anthropomorphised. His commands are insistent, imperative, justifying rape and reckless promiscuity. Thus Etherege addressed his as 'the sneaking Varlet'[41] and Buckhurst puns;

> Dreaming last night of Mistris Harley
> My Prick was up this morning Earley
> And I was fain without my gowne
> To rise i'th' Cold to gett him downe.[42]

Sometimes the squire disgraced himself by over-eagerness. *Ejaculatio praecox* had been Nashe's problem; it was inherited by

Rochester, 'Sir C.B.' and Mulgrave.[43] The inability to control the 'Boistrous Tarse who never knew Command'[44] is akin to impotence, which is likewise frequently charged—even against Charles II—and less frequently admitted.[45] In both cases, anathemas rain on the over-audacious or the inadequate:

> Base metled Hanger by thy Masters Thigh,
> Eternal Shame to all P—cks Heraldry,
> Hide thy despised Head, and do not dare
> To Peep, no, not so much as take the Ayr
> But through a Button Hole, but Pine and dye
> Confin'd within this Codpiece Monastry.
> The little Childish Boy that scarcely knows
> The Channell through which his Urine flows,
> Touch't by my Mistresse her Magnetic Hand
> His little needle presently will Stand;
> Did she not clap her Leggs about thy Back,
> Her Porthole ope; Damn'd P—ck what dis't Lack?
> Henceforth stand stiff, and gain thy Honour lost,
> Or I'le ne're draw thee but against a Post.[46]

The frequent bemoaning of one's impotence—so different from bawdy 'country' humour—may well have had bases in reality. Alcoholism and venereal disease both tend to depress sexual performance.[47] In some cases, Rochester's for instance, deeper psychological repressions may have been at work. The slur of inadequacy against the King or leading statesmen, on the other hand, suggests political dimensions: the impotence of 'Louis XIV's poodle', the failure of domestic policies and the boding problem of the succession. The *plenum potestatis* of God's vicegerent on earth becomes ludicrous when the vice-gerent can only produce 'dry-bobs'.[48]

With men and women being wagged by their own tails—to adapt a contemporary cliché—it follows that that staple of pornography, copulation in risky, improbable places, will be popular. Thus we meet couples pullulating in a lottery booth at Tonbridge, in the playhouse and in coaches.[49] The most outrageous orgy, however, occurs in Sir Francis Fane's 'Iter Occidentale, Or the Wonder of Warm Waters' (1674).[50] The tone is set by the opening landscape:

> Deep in an unctious Vale, 'twixt Swelling Hills,
> Curl'd o're with Shady Tufts, Spending hot Kills,
> Lyes Englands C—t, call'd Bath by modest Brittish.

After a catalogue of the 'sound and sickly C—ts of Christendome' that 'on Pilgrimage to St. Pego come', the action opens when

> Upstarts a Nymph of the inspir'd Train
> Some said a Quaker, but most did agree
> She came to set up C—ts to Fifth Monarchy. . . .
> Sooner shall Hares the Dogs and Horses hunt
> And sooner shall a P—ck tire out a C—t,
> Then I forget the memorable Dame,
> Or Quench in Lethe's Flood that glorious Name,
> That mov'd thee to divest thy covering Carnall
> Sin Shelt'ring Smock, and Shew thy Pit Infernall:
> The Hunt is up; the artfull Dame divides
> With naked Strokes, the more inflamed Tydes:
> All zealous Youths that Drawers had about them,
> As much asham'd as Adam was without them
> Cast off their Conscious Raggs by her Example,
> The Scent attractive, and the view was ample,
> Out plunge the Blust'ring Water Dogs to o'retake
> The steddy Duck that skims the Creamy Lake. . . .

Exhausting these,

> at last She Stops and lyes
> On Back becalm'd but who dare take the Prize:
> From C—t embossed at Bay, Frighted they fly,
> But holy Sister with inlightned Eye
> Leer'd on a Master P—ck, and groan'd a Sigh,
> Friend ar't not free t'increase, is the old man Blunt?
> Why dos't thou fear the Creature call'd C—t.
> It is long-suffering, under Pressures meek,
> Box it on one, 'twill turn the other Cheek.

'The well-hung Proselyte' proceeds to mount her as she swims on her back, but after battering, goring and 'Fighting Whale C—t, at Backsword, and at Rapier . . . the Patriarch is Slain', while 'C—t like well train'd Souldier do's sustain The shock, and Still makes up the Breach again. . .' . The next assailant enters with 'Stewd P—ck no bigger than Anchove' and after vain efforts 'Enrag'd he then with double Fist do's F—gg her'. This insult to manhood provokes a mass male response: 'then twice twelve P—cks attack'd Severall Ways, and twice Twelve tymes C—t Militant bore the Bays'. An elegy with political overtones spoken by an attentive matron ends the poem:

> P—ck, Natures Pump, C—ts Pioneer,
> Love under Sail, Lifes Harbinger . . .
> The Virgins Bait, the Womans Hook:
> To Save the Trouble to Create,
> The worlds great Axis on whose Poles
> Turn Kingdoms, Churches, Bodyes, Souls,
> How Great a Soveraign would'st thou be
> If Poor C—t did not Master Thee.

Whether Fane intends a conscious attack on female liberation among the sects or a second blast of the trumpet against the monstrous regiment of women, it is difficult to say. No allegorical purpose, however, can mask his degrading of sexuality to a combat between waterborne sex organs. 'Iter Occidentale' must rank as one of the obscenest exercises even of that insensitive age.

The other staple of pornography, sexual deviance or perversion, is also well represented. There is some slight evidence of adolescent lesbianism among maids of honour at Whitehall,[51] but to the wits the dildo vogue opened up altogether lewder possibilities. Jaded, discarded raveners are depicted using dildoes *à deux* to assuage their itches.[52] The unfortunate Lady Harvey, endowed by rumour, if not by nature, with a prodigious clitoris, was alleged to use 'her long-cunted muscle' in the satisfaction of her female friends.[53]

The wits' favorite perversion, however, was sodomy, certainly in verse, and probably in practice. This crime was punishable by death and still profoundly taboo, as the political smear campaigns against both Buckingham and Oates suggest.[54] Pepys was shocked both by the fact that Sedley had publicly 'acted all postures of lust and buggery that could be imagined' and the reported pervasiveness of the practice 'among our gallants'.[55] In 1698 it was claimed that 'Nothing is more ordinary in England than this unnatural vice',[56] and a Sodomite Club with forty-three catamites or 'sukeys' flourished about this time in London.[57] The evidence for that trendsetter, Rochester's preference for sodomy with both boys and women, occurs in his poetry and his letters.[58]

Those charged in libels with 'unnatural vice' include the Bishop of London, 'the bishops', John Dryden, James Noakes the comedian, Charles II, Nathaniel Lee the playwright, the Dukes of

Vendôme and York, Lords Falkland, Mordaunt, Talbot and Berkeley, the terror of linkboys and footmen. Among the assortment of named victims were Ladies Felton, Arundel, Stamford, Portsmouth and Shrewsbury, the Misses Gwyn, Temple and Jenny Dee, William Mountfort the actor, the Earl of Arran, a judge of the high court, a turkey and a rotten door. Sometimes these libels included three-in-a-bed routines.[59]

In most cases, of course, the intention is merely to outrage contemporary mores, much as Italian works aimed 'to applaud and canonize unnatural sodomitrie' had appalled Elizabethan and early Stuart generations. The fact that these had been recently republished,[60] and that sodomy was also practised at Louis XIV's court,[61] raises the possibility that English fascination may reflect the 'mediterraneanisation' of Charles II's court. If sodomy was also intended as a thrust against Roman Catholicism—several practitioners were papists[62]—it is never articulated. The fear of venereal disease or the lack of satisfaction from distended vaginas, advanced as justification in some verses, rings false and feeble; anal sex as contraceptive device is not even mentioned. The spur to the Restoration obsession with sodomy is most probably that reckless, restless passion for experimentation, fostered both by the old Italian and the new French pornography, the philosophy of libertinism and the cult of the extravagant rake. Though psychological explanations are easier to present than to prove, it is undeniable that sodomy as a diversion is profoundly misogynistic; the female catamite is reduced to the role of the last alleged victim: a knothole in a rotten door.

From sodomy we descend finally to *Sodom*. This playlet survives only in various manuscript copies.[63] It was thrice printed at the time, but no published copies have survived.[64] One of the major mysteries about *Sodom* is its authorship. It was usually attributed in the 1680s to Rochester, but this merely demonstrates the power of his reputation for obscenity. The recent nomination of Christopher Fishbourne is no more convincing.[65] Responsibility for this repulsive work must remain an open question.

The action of the six scenes can be very quickly described.[66] The king of Sodom, Bolloxinian, more probably Charles II than James I, opens the play with the famous mock-heroic lines

> Thus in the zenith of my Lust I Reigne
> I drink to swive, and Swive to drink again.

The king announces that because he is tired of cunts, a declaration of indulgence is to be proclaimed:

> Let Conscience have its force of Liberty.
> I do proclaim that Buggery may be us'd
> O're all the Land, so Cunt be not abus'd.

After hearing of a plot between Pene, one of the pimps of honour, and Queen Cuntigratia, the king and his favourite Pockanello depart to enjoy the provisions of the new dispensation.

The second scene in a portico beside a garden filled with erotic statuary introduces the women. The distraught queen is comforted by her four maids of honour, both with the suggestion that she take the general, Buggeranthus, as a lover, and more immediately a dildo, but it is paltry ware and fails to satisfy her. The scene ends with an obscene song and group sex by a dozen naked dancers.

Next comes the seduction by Princess Swivia of her young brother Prince Pricket. The queen interrupts a second attempt, and a fight develops between mother and daughter over who should stimulate the prince, in which he again spends, and is led off exhausted.

The fourth scene brings Cuntigratia and Buggeranthus together. They have coupled once, and the queen tries unsuccessfully to rally the spent commander to another bout, but he struggles off to recuperate. The king and his entourage enter and discuss the situation. He has graduated to turkeys; the general announces that the troops are delighted with the new proclamation, and by buggering one another save their fortnight's pay. The women of the realm are making do with dogs; one who tried to coax a reluctant cart-horse is made 'Mistress of the Elephant'. An ambassador from Gomorrah arrives with a present of forty striplings from King Tarsehole; his letter is made up of biblical tags. *Exeunt omnes* with striplings.

The fifth scene finds the maids with Virtuoso, dildo- and merkin-maker to the court. They are highly critical of his products, and demand to see his genuine article, which puts them into such a frenzy that they fight to have the first go; all this excitement causes Virtuoso to ejaculate, and again they leave the stage in frustrated dejection.

Bolloxinian's determination to invade heaven and bugger all the gods, proves to be the hubris preceding swift nemesis. Flux, the physician-in-ordinary to the king, announces an epidemic among the nation's sexual organs, male from overuse, female from neglect. The children complain about being abused; the queen is dead, the prince and princess have the clap. Flux prescribes an immediate return to the course of love and nature, but the king persists. Faustine demons appear, followed by the ghost of Cuntigratia, who announces the day of doom. The unrepentant monarch closes the sixth and final scene with

> Let Heav'ns Descend, Set the world on Fire
> We, to some darker caverns will retyre,
> There, on thy bugger'd Arse I will expire.
> Lears all the while on Pockanello.
>
> Enter Fire and Brimstone a Cloud of Smoak arises
> The curtain's Drawne. Finis.

The written text fits our definition of Sodom as obscene, designed to shock and disgust. A surviving prologue, however, assumes a pornographic intention.[67]

> I do presume there are no women here,
> 'Tis too debauch'd for their fair sex I fear,
> Sure they will not in petticoats appear.
> And yet I am informed here's many a lass
> Come for to ease the itching of her arse,
> Damn'd pocky jades, whose cunts are hot as fire,
> Yet they must see this play to increase desire,
> Before three acts are done of this our farce,
> They'll scrape acquaintance with a standing tarse,
> And impudently move it to their arse. . . .

Certainly if the farce were ever performed, obeying stage directions and mounting the tableaux, then the obscenity of the written word would merely heighten the visual pornography. That this melange of adultery, incest, sodomy, bestiality, pederasty and masturbation plumbed the depths of depravity is proved by that rare and ultimate accolade, translation into French.[68]

Soundings of the general revulsion for the real and rumoured debauchery of the court demonstrate the chasm yawning between Whitehall and the country at large, and help to explain not only the movement to reform manners but also the Revolution itself. William III replaced 'the borrowed south' with 'hyperborean seemliness'.[69]

Puritans and good-old-causers were predictably shaken. Milton's allegorical picture of the court of the Philistines in *Samson Agonistes* is famous. His friend Andrew Marvell, apart from his poetic recriminations, wrote in 1670: 'The Court is at the highest pitch of wanton luxury and the People full of discontent.'[70] We have already seen the mob in the Easter week riots of 1668 referring to Whitehall as 'the great bawdy-house'.[71] Canny Dutch propagandists distributed pamphlets among English seamen describing the licentiousness of King and Court.[72] In a prediction of the pelting of mistresses' coaches at Oxford in 1681, a wit described popular reactions to Nell Gwyn's elevation:

> And every day they do the Monster see,
> They let ten thousand Curses fly at thee:
> Aloud in public streets, they use thee thus,
> And none dare quell 'em they're so numerous.[73]

John Ward was plainly as fascinated as he was repelled by the sexual abandon, the extravagance, the atheism and violence of the court. Mere vicars were not the only Anglican critics.[74] Even the easy-going Archbishop of Canterbury, Gilbert Sheldon, felt moved to expostulate with his friend the King about his flagrant affaire with Castlemaine, and inveigh from the pulpit against the licentiousness of the court. He even refused the King communion.[75]

The dependent and deferential Pepys was impelled to compose his 'Great Letter of Reproof' to Lord Sandwich about his infatuation with a whore. His catalogue of criticisms concludes thus: 'Lastly (my Lord), I find a general coldness in all persons towards your Lordship; such as, from my first dependence on you, I never yet knew. . . .'[76]

The reactions of ordinary people occasionally survive through official records. In 1664, a Londoner's seditious charge that 'The King is a Rogue and a Knave. . . . The King keepeth whores' was followed by 'drinking a Health to the King and all whores'.[77] In 1683 an informer was told that 'I should inform against the King for lying with so many women'.[78] Less than a month later two Somerset magistrates wrote to the Secretary of State about 'a percel of vermin' which sang and spread among the people at Bridgwater Fair scandalous ballads abusing the government and the Duke of York.[79] In 1671 a servant of Rochester's was informed

'Thy Lord is a Hector and a Shabb, and you are a rogue for serving him'. The Middlesex jury apparently agreed.[80]

The most striking example of popular revulsion against the gross immorality of courtiers was given by Parliament's treatment of Buckingham's flagrant adultery with Lady Shrewsbury. The Commons described him as a public scandal, and reminded that neither adulterer nor fornicator shall enter the Kingdom of Heaven. On 5 February 1674 the Lords solemnly cautioned him on a surety of £10 000 not to 'converse nor cohabit with the said Anna-Maria, Countess of Shrewsbury, for the future'. It was a public reprimand from his peers to a leading courtier who had thought with impunity to flout conventional morality.[81]

The obverse of this rebuke is shown in the enormous popular interest in Rochester's penitent death. Burnet's account of his conversion and Parson's funeral oration were both best-sellers, and one senses a national feeling of relief that the General of the Ballers has renounced his ribald following in favour of the church militant, and, hopefully, the church triumphant.[82] For that ageing roué and indolent condoner of vice, Charles II, there was to be no such spectacular change of heart; only the sour comment of Evelyn after seeing him on Sunday publicly fondling his mistresses, 'six days after all was in dust'.[83]

Rochester symbolised then, and since, what was brilliant and what was disgraceful about the court wits. The epitaph of a critic

> But obscene words too grosse to move Desire
> Like heaps of fuel do but choak the fire;
> That Authors name has undeserved Praise
> Who palled the Appetite he meant to raise.[84]

is perhaps too severe for him. It is hardly severe enough for those who so lamely aped him.

NOTES

1. Rochester's impersonation of Dr Bendo or court ladies' of orange wenches in the city were recounted like expeditions into a foreign country.
2. J. H. Wilson, *The Court Wits of the Restoration* (London, 1948), *Nell Gwyn* (London, 1952) and *All the King's Ladies* (London, 1958) present abundant evidence. Cf. V. de S. Pinto, *Sir Charles Sedley* (London, 1927), pp. 61, 307, 309; Pepys' *Diary*, 25 Dec. 1662, 14 Oct. 1660, 9 Nov. 1663, 26 Apr. 1667, 16 Feb. 1668.

3. The nickname was derived either from a stallion in the royal stables or a particularly lecherous goat. The phrase was addressed to Burnet. G. Davies, *Essays on the Later Stuarts* (San Marino, 1958), p. 25.
4. Anthony Hamilton, *Memoirs of the Comte de Gramont* (London, 1963), p. 78.
5. Chesterfield and Robartes removed their wives to the country; Denham was rumoured to have poisoned his after her involvement with the Duke of York. Rochester, Jermyn, Montagu and Killigrew were all banished from court; Lady Shrewsbury was forced to flee twice and even la Castlemaine prudently withdrew on one occasion.
6. J. H. Wilson, *A Rake and his Times* (London, 1954), p. 94; V. de S. Pinto, *Enthusiast in Wit* (London, 1962), p. 101; V. Sackville West, *Knole and the Sackvilles* (London, 1934), pp. 114–16; V. D. Sutch, *Gilbert Sheldon* (The Hague, 1973), p. 167.
7. Davies, *Essays*, p. 25. It is interesting to compare Charles with Louis XIV, also a potential sybarite, who was called to power in his early twenties, before habits of adult pleasure-seeking were set. *Gramont*, p. 68.
8. G. Huehns, ed., *Selections from Clarendon* (London, 1955), p. 401.
9. Ibid., p. 378; *Correspondence of the Second Earl of Chesterfield* (London, 1829), p. 97; *The Yellow Book* (1656), p. 2; *Trial of the Ladies* (1656), p. 5; Pinto, *Sedley*, pp. 44–6.
10. H. A. Beecham, 'Samuel Wesley senior: New Biographical Evidence', *Renaissance and Modern Studies*, VII (1963), 103; Pinto, *Sedley*, p. 47; Thompson, ed., 'Prideaux Letters', p. 5; *Confessions of a New-Married Couple* (1683) Ch. VIII; Pinto, *Enthusiast*, pp. 7–9.
11. H. Love, ed. *Restoration Literature* (London, 1972), p. vii.
12. D. Underwood, *Etherege and the Seventeenth-Century Comedy of Manners* (New Haven, 1957); T. H. Fujimura, *The Restoration Comedy of Wit* (Princeton, 1952), p. 49; Norell, Restoration Cuckold, Ch IV; L. Bredvold, *The Intellectual Milieu of John Dryden* (Ann Arbor, 1934).
13. R. Jordan. 'The Extravagant Rake in Restoration Comedy', Love, ed., *Restoration Literature*, pp. 87–9.
14. Pepys' *Diary*, 4 Oct. 1664.
15. H. Hunt, 'Restoration Acting', J. R. Brown and B. Harris, eds., *Restoration Theatre* (London, 1965), p. 184.
16. G. R. Taylor, *Sex in History* (London, 1959), p. 189.
17. T. S. Eliot, *Selected Essays* (London, 1951), pp. 286–9; S. K. Sen, *The Metaphysical Tradition and T. S. Eliot* (Calcutta, 1965), pp. 40ff; Foxon, p. ix.
18. See the Yale edition of *Poems on Affairs of State*; G. de F. Lord, 'Satire and Sedition: The Life and Works of John Ayloffe', *Huntington Library Quarterly*, XXIX (1966), 255–73; Wilson, *Wits*, passim.
19. Lord, ed., *P.O.A.S.*, I. p. xxxvii.
20. Ibid., p. xxxvii; W. J. Cameron, 'A Late Seventeenth-Century Scriptorium', *Renaissance and Modern Studies*, VII (1963), 29; B. Harris, 'Captain Robert Julian', *English Literary History*, X (1943), 294–309.
21. I have consulted Victoria and Albert Museum, Dyce 43; Nottingham University, Portland PwV 42; Harvard University Mss. Eng. 636 F*; *The Duchess of Portsmouth's Garland* (1837); Yale University Osborn f.b. 66; J. H. Wilson, ed., *Court Satires of the Restoration* (Columbus, 1966); *Poems on Several Occasions by the E. of R.* ('Antwerp', 1680).

22. This and *P.O.A.S.* volumes have excellent discussions of the various texts surviving.
23. 'The Whore of Babylon', Dyce 43, ff. 31–4.
24. Dyce 43, ff. 333–40; cf. ff. 110–3, 274, 76–85, 326, 309, 324, 358; Mss. Eng. 636 F*, 283–4; Osborn f.b. 66, f. 29; *P.O.A.S.*, I, p. 146.
25. The enormous disbursements on the royal mistresses are recorded in J. K. Akerman, ed., 'Secret Service money', *Camden Society,* LII (1851) passim. Stone, *Family, Sex and Marriage*, p. 515, suggests that the emphasis on sexual 'spending' of seed would be particularly psychologically offensive to the 'saving' bourgeoisie.
26. D. M. Vieth, ed., *The Complete Poems of John Wilmot, Earl of Rochester* (New Haven, 1968), p. xxxi; Pinto, *Sedley*, p. 140.
27. *Garland*, passim; Dyce 43, ff. 208, 275, 26, 31, 4, 50, 96, 111, 215, 229, 437, 556. Cf. J. P. Kenyon, *The Stuarts* (London, 1963), pp. 127–8, 135–7, 154–6.
28. Dyce 43, ff. 27–8.
29. Dyce 43, ff. 56–8; cf. ff. 395, 480–2.
30. Dyce 43, f. 371.
31. Dyce 43 ff. 731–2.
32. Dyce 43, f. 246.
33. Ibid. An inside view of the rake's world is given in Etherege's *Man of Mode*, analysed in Pinto, *Sedley*, pp. 71ff.
34. Vieth, ed., *Rochester*, p. 51.
35. *Diary*, 30 July, 1667.
36. Osborn f.b. 66, f. 6.
37. Vieth, ed., *Rochester*, p. 45.
38. Wilson, *Satires*, p. 63.
39. Osborn, f.b. 66, f. 30.
40. Vieth, ed., *Rochester*, pp. 54–9; Dyce 43, ff. 113–19; *P.O.S.O.*, pp. 34–9. Cf. *Garland*, p. ix; Dyce 43, ff. 331–3. J. Atkins, *Sex in Literature* has a rather poor chapter on dildoes, pp. 389–400.
41. Mss. Eng. 636 F*, f. 99.
42. Mss. Eng. 636 F*, f. 105.
43. Steane, ed., *Traveller*, p. 466; *P.O.S.O.*, p. 28; Mss. Eng. 636 F*, ff. 280–1; Dyce 43, ff. 243–4.
44. Mss. Eng. 636 F*, ff. 282–3.
45. Dyce 43, f. 312; *P.O.A.S.*, I, p. 169.
46. Dyce 43, ff. 243–4.
47. Wilson, *Rake*, p. 149; Pinto, *Enthusiast*, p. 98.
48. *P.O.A.S.*, I, p. 169.
49. Dyce 43, ff. 478, 596, 622.
50. Dyce 43, ff. 248–55. The court visited Bath in 1670 or 1671 for an attempted warm water cure for the queen's barrenness. *Gramont*, p. 235.
51. *Gramont*, p. 170.
52. Dyce 43, f. 27.
53. Wilson, *Satire*, p. 125; Dyce 43, ff. 26–7.
54. Dyce 43, ff. 7, 171–6; Wilson, *Rake*, p. 210; Dyce 43, f. 718.
55. *Diary,* 1 July 1663.
56. Taylor, *Sex in History*, p. 189.
57. J. Dunton, *Athenianisme* (4th. Ed., 1710), pp. 93–8.

58. J. H. Wilson, ed., *The Rochester-Savile Letters 1671–1680* (London, 1941), p. 189; Vieth, ed., *Rochester*, p. 51; *P.O.S.O.*, pp. 27, 54, 32.
59. E.g. the King, Miss Temple and the Bishop of London! Cf. *P.O.S.O.*, p. 53.
60. Giovanni della Casa, *Capitolo del Forno* (1538), and *De laudibus sodomia sev Pederastiae* (1550), privately reissued by Hadrian Beverland 1673–5, E. J. Dingwall, *Very peculiar People* (London, 1950), pp. 149–50. Ferrante Pallavicino's version of *Alcibiade Fanciullo a Scola*, a dialogue in praise of sodomy, was published in Oranges in 1652. R. P. Sinistrari, *De Sodomia Tractatus* was also published in the seventeenth century.
61. Ashbee, *Catena*, p. 26.
62. Dukes of York and Vendôme, Lord Talbot, Ladies Shrewsbury, Norfolk, Portsmouth.
63. Dyce 43, ff. 133–62; B. M. Harleian Mss. 7312; Stadtbibliothek, Hamburg; Princeton AM 14401, a commonplace book, has two versions; Hayward's papers record a copy in the Portland Papers at Nottingham University, King's College, Cambridge, Hayward Papers, Rochester Box 1; Ashbee vaguely mentions another copy in private hands, P. Fryer, *Forbidden Books of the Victorians* (London, 1970), pp. 190–5.
64. 1684, 1689, 1707, Foxon, pp. 11, 13.
65. R. M. Baine, 'Rochester or Fishbourne: A Question of Authorship', *Review of English Studies*, XXII (1946), 201–6. Fishbourne's only known obscene verse in Mss. Eng. 636 F* f. 76 is just not in the same class as *Sodom.*
66. Fryer, *Forbidden Books*, pp. 190–5, has Ashbee's epitome.
67. Ibid., p. 190.
68. 1682 and early eighteenth century, ibid., p. 195.
69. Love, ed., *Restoration Literature*, p. vii. The number of obscene lampoons declined rapidly after 1689; Wilson, *Satire*, p. xii.
70. Quoted in Brown and Harris, eds., *Restoration Theatre*, p. 12.
71. Pepys, *Diary*, 25 March 1668.
72. Kitchin, *L'Estrange*, p. 170.
73. Dyce 43, f. 275.
74. Diary, II, pp. 360, 414, 547, 580, 593; IV, 850a, 991.
75. Sutch, *Sheldon*, pp. 102–3; Ward, Diary, IV, p. 1031.
76. 17 Nov. 1663.
77. Jeaffreson, ed., *Middx. Records,* III, p. 339.
78. *C.S.P.D.*, C.II, 1683, p. 77.
79. Ibid., p. 94.
80. Jeaffreson, ed., III, p. 29.
81. Wilson, *Rake*, pp. 196–204.
82. Pinto, *Enthusiast*, pp. 209–23.
83. E. S. de Beer, ed., *Diary of John Evelyn* (Oxford, 1955), Vol. IV, p. 403.
84. *Ars Poetica* (1680–85) cited in Hayward, Rochester Box I.

8 Anti-Papistical

When Nell Gwyn pulled down the window of her coach and yelled to the hostile Oxford mob 'Peace, good people, I am the *Protestant* whore', she was adroitly playing on a century and a half of English history. Much anti-Catholicism was firmly embedded in folk-memory, by rituals like pope-burning processions, the celebration of Queen Elizabeth's accession, by perennially popular works like Foxe's *Book of Martyrs* and nostalgic sentiment for King Henry VIII, illustrated by the numerous chapbook and ballad stories about him.

From the viewpoint of this tradition, going back at least to Wycliffe, the reigns of Charles II and his brother were appalling aberrations. When a sabot was found in the Speaker's chair in the House of Commons in 1673, everyone knew that it was meant as a symbol of 'Popery and wooden shoes', the rallying cry of Protestants. If what Charles II did can be dignified with the name of a policy, it flew in the face of deep-seated English prejudice. He sold Dunkirk; he married a papist; he fought Protestants in alliance with Catholics; he allowed his brother and successor to desert the Church of England, to marry an Italian papist, and his own court to be riddled with secret or open romanists. He concluded a menacing secret treaty with that terrifying fanatic Louis XIV, the callous persecutor of French and foreign Protestants; he was swayed by the insidious blandishments of his French Catholic mistress; he tried to extend toleration to her co-religionists, a dangerous and furtive fifth-column. It was not only the might and ambition of Louis XIV which made Catholicism such a threat. Its spiritual and intellectual appeal won considerable numbers of influential English converts. Contemporary English paranoia about popery is reflected not only in the Test Acts and the Exclusion Bills, but also in the belief held by educated men as well as the vulgar, that agents of Rome were responsible for the Great Fire and that Titus Oates's fabrications were credible. In what other circumstances could such a contemptible crook have thrown the nation into three years of chaos?[1] How else would the outrageous rumour that there were 3000 priests in England in Charles II's reign have been swallowed? The short disaster of James II's reign confirmed all the fears that had been voiced by prophets like Marvell and Ayloffe in their political verse.

This chapter will deal only with predominantly sexual attacks on Roman Catholicism during the Restoration. In this area there was likewise a strong tradition to draw on; much of the most telling sexual satire on Catholicism had the added force of coming, not from imaginative outsiders, but from often knowledgeable insiders. Boccaccio had been a student of canon law and an ambassador to the papal court at Avignon. Poggio Bracciolini was a papal secretary, and Aretino a papal protégé and servant. Rabelais was an ordained priest, and had been both a Franciscan and a Benedictine. Several of the authors of the often bitterly anti-clerical *fabliaux* appear to have had priestly backgrounds, as did some of the members of the intellectual circle of Margaret of Navarre. Henri Estienne, whose *Apologie pour Herodote* (Geneva, 1566) was translated by Richard Carew and published in England in 1607 as *The World of Wonders*, borrowed from orthodox preachers for his satires on the vices of the clergy. In Charles II's reign some of the most violent attacks on the sexual behaviour of the establishment of the French church came from Jansenists.[2] The pornographer Chorier, whom we have already met as an anti-clericalist, had been educated by the Jesuits, and another acquaintance, Ferrante Pallavicino, who was beheaded at the age of twenty-six in 1644 for his attacks on the priests, had been himself a priest and one of the canons of the Lateran. Louis-Henri de Loménie, Comte de Brienne, who published *Recueil de Poésies chrestiennes et diverses* (1670), some of which were highly erotic and others hardly complimentary of the religious orders, was himself a member of the Oratorians.[3]

Two other renegades from Rome provided the Restoration with considerable sexual ammunition. James Salgado, a Spanish convert to Protestantism, had suffered at the hands of the Inquisition. He was in England from *c.* 1678 to 1684, and among his works published in English were *Symbiosis, or an intimate conversation between the Pope and the Devil* (1681) and *The Fryer*, to which we refer later. Gregorio Leti, sprung from a prelatical Milanese family, was won to Calvinism at the age of twenty-nine. His pathological intemperance led to his expulsion in turn from Geneva, London and Paris. He died after twenty years' residence in Amsterdam in 1701. His venomous anti-Catholicism was given free rein in *Il Nipotisma di Roma* (Amsterdam, 1667) and lives of Sixtus V (Lausanne, 1669) and Donna Olympia, discussed below. Particularly influential was his *Il Putanismo Romano*, appearing under the pseudonym of Marforio. Thomas Buel published it in Italian in London in 1669, reprinting in 1670 and 1675. It was rendered into French in 1670 (Cologne) and an English version entitled *The History of the Whores and Whoredoms of the Popes, Cardinals and Clergy of Rome*, translated by I.D., followed in 1678. This collection of sexual improprieties by a man who, according to Bayle, saw himself as a latter-day Aretino, provided a happy hunting-ground for English satirists and controversialists.[4]

One important distinction of aim must be made about this group of expert insiders. Some of them were primarily concerned to attack various aspects of church life, and incidentally, used sexual weapons in their offensive. The Jansenists are obvious examples of this main intention. Others, like Aretino and Chorier, were first and foremost pornographers, who found in monastic life or the priesthood ideal quasi-taboo subjects for the projection of erotic fantasies; the idea of a sex-crazed nun or a sadist confessor was perfect arousal material.

The English had contributed a steady stream of sexual mud-flinging against Roman Catholicism in the sixty years before the Restoration. Its volume is such that only a few examples can be mentioned here. John Taylor, the self-styled water poet, was strongly anti-Catholic, and his *Common Whore* (1622) and *A Bawd* (?1625) both reflect this in the sexual sphere.[5] In 1628 was published anonymously *The Unmasking of all Popish monks, friers and Jesuits*, a fruitful model for Restoration writers.[6] D. S. Barnard has argued persuasively that the plot of Goodman's *Hollands Leaguer* (1632) was an allegory in which Protestantism, in the not altogether complimentary disguise of the madam, Donna Britanica Hollandia, is besieged by Catholicism, led by the fiendishly cunning chaplain Ignatius.[7] Prynne's *Histriomastix* (1633), among its plethora of citations and hates, employs not very subtle innuendo against the sexual failings of the Whore of Babylon. Though normally inhibited by their strict sense of decorum and avoiding the trap of being tarred with same brush as the unregenerate, the Puritans let their natural hair down when it came to attacking Catholicism. The sexual chinks in Rome's armour had been pretty closely explored by the time Charles II tactfully commented on the Bible presented to him at Dover.

The most frequently mooted criticism of Roman Catholic sexual attitudes concerned the teaching that fornication was a venial rather than a mortal sin. Time and again carping Protestants threw this apparent tolerance of sexual incontinence in the face of the papacy. 'The Pope stands our friend', says the crafty Roman whore, citing this decree, 'and the Cardinals too.'[8] A West Country bawd tells the young wife of an old husband that keeping a gallant in such circumstances is 'accounted but a venial sin'. Later the London bawd reassures her pupil Dorothea that the keeping of gigolos and misses is 'scarce a crime; all the devout doctors of the Roman church, including the Pope' agree on this. Old Mother Creswell therefore decides to join the Church of Rome, which allows us 'most pleasure while we live'.[9] When the converted Countess of Castlemaine allegedly delivered her *Gracious Answer to the Poor Whores Petition* (London, 1668) she too dwelt on the veniality of mere copulation, in her case, of course, extending the license from fornication to adultery. This teaching, and the apparent ease with which absolution could be obtained from confessors, led Sir Walter Raleigh to call 'the Romane . . . the religion for licentiousness', and led John Ward to note that pearl in his diary.[10] The shameless adultery of Anna-Maria, Countess of Shrewsbury, daughter of a leading Catholic family in England, and the equally scandalous behaviour of another leading court Catholic, the 'epicurish' Jermyn, served only to confirm this prejudice.[11]

The celibacy of the clergy was a second area of muck-raking. Rabelais, in Urquhart's translation, put the objection with his usual bluntness: 'There are plenty of good stiff broad and short-swords that inhibit cloistral codpieces', and what was true of the cloister was true of the secular priesthood too. Bayle commented in more restrained style in his article on Launoi:

> Either clergymen should be permitted to marry, or forbidden to keep young servant maids; for the prodigious concubinage of priests, which has scandalised the public for so many ages, owes its origin to the permission of having women about them, to manage their houses. The intention of the superiors was that they should confine themselves to the business of servant

> maids; but they are easily suffered to be persuaded to serve some other purposes. . . .[12]

The example set by the Papacy, College of Cardinals and the Curia in this area—and others—was wearisomely rehearsed by critics.

The prodigious concubinage of the priesthood was eagerly advertised by Protestants. Ward noted the well-known fact, derived from Poggio, that there were 450 harlots helping to service the Council of Constance in 1414. He also smugly recorded that the so-called reforming Council of Trent had placed priests' concubines under ecclesiastical jurisdiction. One of the more unfortunate fruits of these liaisions he discovered, was the bastard Bishop Bonner.[13] The pervasive nepotism, especially in Rome, which these 'by-blows' encouraged was, of course, a time-honoured scandal.

To the Duke of Buckingham, who presumably knew about these things from his mistress, the main danger lay not in the fate of serving-maids, but in that of women in the confessional. He confided to his commonplace book, 'It cannot choose but make priests lascivious to feel thus the privy parts of a woman's soul.' Or again: 'I should be afraid she should not deny the secrets of her body to whom she discovers the secrets of her soul.' And, similarly: 'Upon this condition of absolving a woman from a thousand sins, 'tis easy to persuade her to commit one new one.'[14] Explaining 'the growth of atheisme and infidelitie' in Restoration England, Ward argued that it had moved northward from Italy, through France. It thrived in Italy, 'because those who profes most, the churchmen, carrie themselves so badly and so vitiously.'[15] Any reader of the *Facetiae* of Poggio, or its many derivatives, would have no difficulty in finding examples of the behaviour that worried Ward and Buckingham. 'The Pilgrimage' written in the 1680s, told how the priests had made a pilgrimage throughout England to warn friars and nuns—even the Lady Abbess—to cease their indiscretions.[16]

The mere seduction of servants or penitents was the least shocking of the sexual aberrations of priesthood and cloister. Sex-starvation could produce every kind of perversion among this privileged class. According to the Preface of *The Horn Exalted*, 'Beware of a Monk before and behind' had become a common

Italian proverb. The strongly anti-Catholic Ashbee was nevertheless not exaggerating when he wrote, 'That the rod has been used in all Roman Catholic countries by priests as an instrument to serve their own lubricity is not of course to be denied.'[17] Ward recorded the case of a transvestite cardinal in the papacy of Alexander VII, and we shall meet many other examples of unconventional behaviour.[18]

A perennially popular target was the Society of Jesus, seen by Protestants, and some of their co-religionists, as casuists who could justify any sexual aberration. Ward records how they went about persuading certain Swiss cantons to join the Catholic League in the sixteenth century by adjuring wives not to grant their favours to their husbands until they agreed to the reinforcement of the League.[19] The Jesuits' blandishments and moral relativism figure largely in attacks on them made in mid-century France by Pascal and the Jansenists, and was gleefully taken up by writers of fiction as a condoning cause of Catholic sexual deviations and libertinism. Apart from 'squibs' like *Ignatian Fireworks, A History of the Jesuits* published in 1667, the most widely-read attacks on the Society were firstly *Jesuits' Morals*, a translation by Tongue which appeared in 1670 of *Morale Pratique des Jesuites*, published in Cologne in 1669, and the fiercely ridiculing and at times obscene *Satires against the Jesuits*, by John Oldham which came out in 1681.[20]

The last common butt of Catholicism was the excessive gullibility about miracles among the faithful, and the improper uses to which this could be put by the designing cynic. This is a popular theme with both Poggio and Boccaccio, and was used too by Protestant Englishmen. In his *Voyage to the Levant* (1636) Sir Henry Blunt, for instance, made much of an apparent miracle with a turd. This conjunction of the sublime and the scatological helped confirm that deep-seated English belief that Romanism played mercilessly on the superstitions of its devotees.

I have divided the Restoration sexual attacks on the Roman Catholic church into three groups: general attacks, attacks on specific scandals, both of which had some basis of fact; the third group is composed of fictional works which portray licentiousness within the church.

Romes Rarities, or, The popes Cabinet Unlock'd was published by J. Norris in 1684. It is subdivided into various vices: lust, cupidity, cruelty and so on. The anonymous author at one stage admits 'I blush to think that I have offended the chaste ears of the Protestant Reader', but this sense of shame does not inhibit him from producing another 160 pages of often blush-making evidence.[21] Lust is the largest section by far, and sexual matters intrude frequently among the other deadly sins. Thus, among cupidities, we learn that Pope Paul III lived on the income of 45 000 courtesans. The smut-seeking author travels without any consideration for chronology; debauches of the Dark Ages are described cheek by jowl with tales from the *Cent Nouvelles Nouvelles, Scoggins Jests* and Boccaccio. Old favourites like Pope Joan, a great Protestant stand-by, make their appearance, including her giving birth in the street during a procession. The jest of the friar caught in bed with his concubine and declaring all four legs at the bottom of the bed to be his—a veritable miracle—is recounted, as is the *mot* of Henri IV that the barn ought to be near the threshers, when he stopped by a convent with a monastery nearby. The abbess who leaves her minorite stallion to surprise a nun and her lover is embarrassed to find that she has the minorite's breeches on her head instead of her coif. Various priestly lechers are depicted: Thomas of Abingdon who had two children by a sister, and three more by his concubines; the curé of Vienne who was caught *in flagrante delicto* behind the altar on Good Friday, of all days, with a notable strumpet and received a mild sentence which was later further commuted. Franciscans are particularly prone: one group of them keep a butcher's wife in their house and dress her as a friar; another makes love to a woman only three weeks after she has given birth in a complicatedly furtive plot; two others, playing too wantonly on their mendicancy, offer to pay a ferry-woman by lying with her. The dangers of celibacy are urged in the epigram of John Hayward, which was reported to Queen Elizabeth, that if priests were not allowed to marry they would keep lemans. Other father confessors euphemise kissing a pretty penitent as 'imprinting a blessing upon her lips', or warn the males in their care that deflowering of virgins or sleeping with one's neighbour's wife is perfectly acceptable, provided they leave the nuns for the priesthood. The perversions of the papal court are much in evidence, with, for instance, an account of Pietro Aloisio, the son of Pope Paul III, who rightly earned the title of 'The prince of Sodomy'. The Italian soldiers besieging Lyons during the civil wars, we learn, paid four pistolets to the local herdsmen to bugger their goats, and one more, perhaps, for marrying them. There is even a necrophiliac, Sigismund Malatesta, the Lord of Romagnola. This amazingly uncritical mish-mash concludes with a paraphrase of *An Anatomy of the English Nunnery in Lisbon*, writ by a young brother of that Order. There is a place in the wall of the convent garden that is full of the bones of the nuns' bastards; the Jesuit confessor of the house is admitted to a sick lady's chamber, and is shortly afterwards espied by the chambermaid providing therapy in bed with Mistress Anne. The grates in the confessional cells are all loosened so that with a slight wrench the nuns can pass through them and spend the night with their confessors, light penance indeed. The nuns sit at meals either singing bawdy songs and obscene catches to please their confessor, or else play loose and wanton tunes upon their instruments. It all sounds like an Aretinesque establishment.

Similar in format to *Romes Rarities* was A. Gavin's anonymously written *Frauds of the Romish Monks and Priests* which was published in 1691.[22] Rather more imaginatively put together was *The Popish Courant*, a serial which accompanied the venomously anti-papist *Weekly Pacquet of Advice from Rome*, probably the work of Henry Care, put out weekly from 3 December 1679 by the Whig publisher Langley Curtis.[23] It is, as George Kitchin observed, a strange amalgamation; the *Weekly Pacquet* is earnestness in the most wearing Puritan manner, whereas the *Courant* is a series of 'joco-serious reflections on Roman Fopperies'. One imagines that divines like Baxter felt the same kind of embarrassment at the bawdy *Courant* that their predecessors a century before had felt about *The Martin Marprelate Tracts*.

The message is not dissimilar from *Romes Rarities*, though the serial organisation makes its randomness more acceptable. The *Courant* allegedly came each week from a different papist centre, Rome or Douai or Paris, but the local scandal is padded out with dips into the bran-tub of Romish sins. The typical convent, we learn in the second number, is a 'religious coneyborough' with usually an active father at work. Among rare sights, one of the rarest is a chaste nun, and the stews are 'more chast, sober and modest than some monasteries'. The secular priests, says No 6, 'keep Misses, Concubines and Common Strumpets . . . and the Devil has given them Nephews in abominable abundance'. The keeping of concubines by monks is, we learn to our surprise, 'but a venial sin'. The law of Sweden that all priests caught in the act shall be gelded 'strikes sad thought into our Nunneries'. The subtle policy of sending an army of Catholic courtesans to England to achieve its reclamation to Rome is controverted by the argument that the country is already figuratively, and no doubt in many cases literally, bulging with consecrated smocks. The popes are favourite Aunt Sallies. Though the great doctor of the church, St Jerome, compared whores to a privy or the bilges in a ship, popes less austere than himself made profits out of the building of stews in the holy city and the licensing of 3000 harlots. Pope Gregory, instigator of attacks on England's Virgin Queen, had a bastard, as did Cardinal Cremensis, way back in 1125, though he committed the added mistake of being caught begetting it. Sixtus IV granted a licence for sodomy; Innocent VII, ineptly named, had sixteen bastards, and Paul II was 'strangled by the Divel in the very act of Uncleanness'. The same Sixtus had built the stews for multitudes of strumpets who thronged in Rome and had licensed sodomy to favoured cardinals and courtiers during the three hottest months of the summer. The Jesuits, too, come in for regular sniping, as, for instance, in the account of one Mena, who falls for an innocent girl in Valladolid in 1607 and secretly marries her. Some 'ladies and gentlewomen in England', we are titillatingly told, 'have done no less'. The *coup de grace* of the *Courant* was the so-called miracle of Alamis de Rupe in Germany. He had a vision that 'the Virgin Mary entered his cell, and made a ring of her hair, and with it married herself to him, offering herself unto him to be kissed and her breasts to be handled and sucked in as familiar a manner as a Wife to a Husband'. Disgusting, even if you did not, as a good Protestant, have any truck with the cult of the Virgin.[24]

Nothing delighted an anti-Catholic audience better than the revelation of specific scandals within the church. Two ladies who rivalled the faded reputation of Pope Joan were Lolla Paulina and Donna Olympia Maldachini. The former is referred to in some detail by Goodman in *Hollands Leaguer*. She was 'the greatest whore and the most declared bawd that ever Rome acknowledged'. She became the mistress of the Cardinal D'Este, the brother of the Duke of Ferrara and builder of the Villa d'Este at Tivoli in the middle of the sixteenth century. Donna Olympia was the latest in this line of influential courtesans. Her lover was Pope Innocent X, and her hold over him from 1644 to 1655 was allegedly so great that she was painted by Protestants as the *de facto* ruler of the papacy. Her life by Abbot Gualdi, a pseudonym for Gregorio Leti, was published in an English translation in 1666.[25] She was alleged to have left 'two million crowns in gold and land and moveables inestimable'. This was one reason, no doubt, why popery and wooden shoes went together.[26]

What really made the Protestant propagandist's mouth water, however, was the exposure of perversions and sexual scandals, preferably within cloisters. One of the longest-playing hits in this area was the saga of Cornelius Adriaensen. He was born in Dordrecht in 1521, became a Franciscan and by 1548 had established a fine reputation as a preacher in Bruges. He was particularly persuasive in his praise of celibacy and condemnation of marriage. He became something of a cult figure among the women of Bruges and set up a secret order among them. His *dévotaires* would come to him in a private room where they would be persuaded to undress and by their nudity surmount all sense of shame. Adriansen would give them some soft blows; in cold weather, or if a follower had slipped away briefly from home, he would merely lift their skirts to chastise them. This order lasted for several years until two young and beautiful novices, Betteken Maes and Celleken Pieters, could not, despite his coaxing and showing them other *dévotaires* naked, bring themselves to strip for him. They were excommunicated from the order, and eventually betrayed it to the magistrates. Adriaensen escaped from Bruges in 1563 to Ypres and died in 1581. Some accounts say that he used obscene expressions during these sessions, and that he had sexual relations with chosen disciples.[27]

An account of these activities was published in Ghedrucht in 1569 and this quickly passed into English anti-Catholic folklore. He was still making the running in 1688 as the anti-hero of a ballad called *The Lusty Fryar of Flanders*; by this time as well as whipping, he had also become a convent stallion and had got thirty nuns with child in three weeks.[28]

A not dissimilar case which achieved notoriety during the Restoration was that of Father Rock. Although his story was described as 'A Famous Novel' in the English edition of 1683, *The Adamite, or The Loves of Father Rock and His Intrigues with the Nuns*[29] was in fact translated from a French account of an actual episode.

Father Rock was a Jesuit, impotent and about sixty years old when 'some moments of meditation made him bring forth that fine and easie doctrine . . . that the habit acquired by the viewing of nudity, which does not sollicite, is a certain proof of the recovery of that primitive justice' of Adam. He set about enrolling votaries in the convent to which he was confessor. The thirteen nuns who joined his order of the Adamites were pledged to secrecy, and divided into degrees according to powers of insensibility. The highest were Adamites, that were able 'to be felt without any sense of titillation and that likewise acquired the power of contemplating in the same posture the nakedness and groping of Father Rock'. The more susceptible or modest were called pensionaries and novices. Rock invented an elaborate code for parts of the female body: the bosom was called 'the stomacher', the belly 'the apron' and the thighs 'the unities'; those who uncovered their bosoms were called 'favourites', the belly and legs 'easy', the thighs 'free', and those who stripped naked 'predestinated'. Father Rock had two particular favourites (in the conventional sense). One was the sacristine of the convent, a mature woman of strong suppressed sexuality. One of his decoded letters to her illustrates their relationship:

> It will not be requisite that henceforward you take such pains to undress yourself, and it will be sufficient for you that you wear no Drawers by my example. Remember to be more diligent in pulling up your gown and petticoats, for yesterday methought you fumbled a long time at that office; you see how nimbly I opened my Robe in your presence. Do not put so many pins in your breastcloth, endeavour to obtain leave to go to the waters at Bourbon . . . we will enjoy the softest pleasures of Love, without feeling the pains, since we are proof against its stings . . . you must have pretty firm sight since you remarked as you say that Men are larger above and . . . women are below better furnished.

Even more sought-after than the sacristine was Nanon, an innocent and beautiful novice of fifteen 'with a high bosom and firm beyond her age . . . her gait was loose and wanton'. The father's gradual breaking down of her modesty is similarly revealed in decoded letters between the two. At an early encounter he explains his doctrine about achieving the soul's 'Empire over the Body to subdue the flesh and achieve a Primitive and Original Innocence'. Nanon's eagerness for perfection allows the confessor to touch her face, hands, neck and bosom before the bell goes for dinner. He then proceeds to encourage her to expose her stomacher, praising her 'demi-globes, which Nature has placed so prominently, meaning them to be seen'. But she proves a slow disciple. 'Why', he asks her in his next note, 'does she have no ambition to show her Unities? That which is nearest to the centre of the body is the more perfect. If you cannot support the sight of mine, it is a sign of your imperfection'. Nanon promises to try harder, but confesses that the sight of his unities filled her with horror, trembling and astonishment. 'When she only lifts her skirt a little the next day to show the unities she receives some gentle reproaches, and the order 'Too morrow come only in your Night Gown to the Parlour and leave me to do the rest'. Accordingly she is persuaded to undress.

> with an extream trouble and the highest confusion . . . though she was not strong enough to support the sight of such an object with a motion of extream pleasure. The Insensible by this discovery became sensible opening his Robe before her, justified in that pleasant posture that he had recovered the Original Innocence.

Nanon, who does not emerge as very sharp, fails to reap the benefits of insensibility. 'You have rendred me so ticklish, that the sight of Objects which do but weakly solicite others excite Motions in me which I am not always Mistress of.' Even she is growing suspicious of his motives. 'A certain Mother shewed you freely and at the first command her Unities which you laughing interpreted her . . . an Impostor.' The sacristine too turns sour, the authorities become concerned about the impudence and levity of some of the younger nuns, and the whole shocking affair is exposed when Nanon and the sacristine call him 'Impostor, Lustful, Prostituted Suborner of Virgins' in the parlour. In the ensuing inquiry, the Jesuits outwardly try to maintain the innocence of their colleague, but the Archbishop of Rheims drives away 'the Devouring Wolf', who cools his ardour on a diet of bread and water. The convent undergoes painful penances and mortifications, as well they might for the ammunition that they have presented to their religious enemies.[30]

The Nunns Complaint Against the Fryars was another French exposé of licentiousness behind cloister walls. It was a declaration, written for the nuns of St Clare near Provins forty miles east-south-east of Paris by Alexandre Louis Varet. It outlines the crisis at the convent between the years 1663 and 1667, when the nuns were in conflict with the Cordeliers or Franciscans, who provided their confessors. It eventually involved the Archbishop of Sens, the papacy and Louis XIV. *The Complaint* was first published in France in 1667, and twice after reissued, but once the nuns won their case, Louis XIV ordered the book suppressed and set a watch on the booksellers. It first appeared in an English version in 1676, published by Robert Pawlett.

The Epistle from the translator to the reader is full of the wholesome lessons that can be learnt from it. English Catholics will be warned against sending their daughters to French convents even as pensionaries. Non-Catholics will be able to breathe a sigh of relief that England does not have what Milton once unkindly called 'convenient stowage for your withered daughters'. Finally all will be warned about the control by religious orders, Franciscans and Jesuits in particular, of the upbringing of the young, and will no doubt shun any institution with which they have anything to do.

The first part of the book tells of the attempts of various abbesses to reform and remoralise the house, and the machinations of the Cordeliers to frustrate them. This included a great deal of politicking at the elections of abbesses, and beguiling of floating voters by 'a thousand idle expressions of love and fondness', embraces and kisses and caresses. The complex battle between the reforming faction and the Cordeliers and the nuns in their spell is recited, including appeals and counter-appeals to higher and higher authorities.

What is to our purpose is the section of the 'Factum' or Declaration covering 'Spiritual Disorders'. The translator frequently states that he is omitting anything which violates modesty. The basic case of the nuns is that the Cordeliers acted as a corrupting influence, and sought to perpetuate their control by placing their converts in positions of authority. It was usually the young whom the confessors sought to entice, newly professed nuns, novices and pensioners, that is girls from Catholic families staying at the convent, but not intending to proceed to vows. The friars induced a spirit of wantonness and libertinism by numerous devices. They would caress and court the more suggestible girls with 'a hundred idle complements of love': one addressed Sister N as 'his sweeting, his inclination, his faithful confident'; another proposed to one of the novices 'that she should be his own'. A professed nun deposed that her confessor had told her that she was 'too well made both in body and mind to hide herself from the world'. It was alleged that they sought to deprave the minds of their spiritual charges by allowing lascivious books in the convent, romances and plays, *The Maxims of Love*, our old friend *L'Escholle des Filles* or *The Catechism of Love*, and by singing erotic and bawdy songs at the grate. Several examples of the passionate love-letters that some of the confessors sent to the girls are entered as evidence; one asked for the particular disposal of the middle and upward of a particular friend, the handling or sight of bosom, mouth and hands. Mock marriages between friars and nuns were performed, and 'he and she went alone to another grate to consummate the marriage together'. They had devices to lift up the sisters' neckcloths, and sometimes threw off their habits to reveal satin suits underneath. They exchanged habits with the sisters. One of their ways of 'exciting the nuns to imitate the debauches of other convents' was to persuade them to dress as women of the world, in décolletage with patches and paint. They played cards till five in the morning with kisses as wagers, and 'brake the very grates to doe things with more ease'. The letters reproduced are said to be the least 'impudent, impious and beastly'; nonetheless, one ardent Franciscan declares that he is 'never cold in the private parts'. Sometimes the confessor would arrive for his penitents drunk, or when drunk later reveal their confessions. One sister, who had joined in the antics, fully expected the fate of Sodom and Gomorrah to overtake the house. And no wonder when there were

> secret and nocturnal entries into the Garden and Monastery by the help of false keys, ladders of cord, and in baskets . . . dances in the refectory . . . and at nun's funerals, the Cordeliers would run after those they fancy, take them in their arms, kiss them, play the fool with them, go to their private chambers, feast it there, be frolick, stay whole hours there, father and nun alone by themselves with a pensioner as sentinel.

Eyewitnesses reported insolences even when confessing the sick, fathers cooped up with nuns in small closets, others kissing and putting their hands in sisters' bosoms, and horrid contrivances to deal with the outcomes of the 'last act of incontinence'.

The temporal mismanagement of the convent by the nominees—and mistresses—of the Cordeliers pales into insignificance after this orgiastic catalogue. It is hardly surprising that Louis XIV should have sought to suppress this evidence, and even less so that publishers in the Netherlands and England should have frustrated his attempts.

By contrast, [Pierre du Moulin] *The Monk's Hood Pull'd Off: or the Capucin Fryar Described*, published by James Collins in 1671 would have been dull and untitillating fare. Apart from occasional references to group flagellation to mortify the flesh—flagellation or rolling in the snow had been St Francis's way of dealing with erections, we learn—and the over-ascetic friar who gelded himself, there are slim pickings here for the critic in search of salacious details.[31] That this exposé of scandals continued for many years to be material in demand is borne out by an advertisement by Edmund Curll in 1724 for *A Case of Seduction, or The Late Proceedings in Paris against the Rev. Abbé des Rues for committing Rapes Upon One Hundred and Thirty-Three Virgins, Written by Himself.*[32]

After the extraordinary performances of Father Rock or the Cordeliers of Provins fictional representations of the sexual exploitation of the Roman Catholic church might seem both redundant and a good deal less stimulating than the real thing. This, however, would be an unwarranted slur on the inventiveness of their authors.

Seventeenth-century publishers were already pretty sophisticated in the use of sucker-trap titles.[33] It seems likely that many unwary buyers would have been disappointed both by *The Amorous Abbess: or, Love in a Nunnery*, published by R. Bentley in 1684, and the series of love letters which passed between a nun and a cavalier, which Bentley, in partnership with Magnes, published during the Restoration period.[34] Both of these works are pure sentiment, novellettish love stories, in which the convent is seen merely as an insuperable obstacle, rather than an orgiastic love-nest.

Of the four fictional representations of sexual depravity in the Catholic church discussed here, two are rogue stories, and two dialogues. One of the rogue stories we have already alluded to as a whore story: Richard Head's *The Miss Display'd* (London, 1675). The anti-heroine, Cornelia, is the daughter of an English gentlemen in Ulster and his beautiful Irish Roman Catholic wife. Cornelia, wicked, wilful and beautiful, persuades her parents to allow her to go to live in Dublin as serving-woman to a noblewoman. It is here that, in a plot closely following Goodman's *Hollands Leaguer*, she encounters the nobleman's chaplain, significantly names Ignatius. He is the archetypal subtle and insinuating

Jesuit. He is already acting as an *adjutor tori*, or assistant for feeble husbands, to her ladyship, or 'his Lady-Miss' as he calls her, when the relatively innocent Cornelia joins the household. This 'precious, deforming, non-conforming, dissembling holder-forth', 'devil-instructed', with 'lust kindled by the devil's bellows', quickly sets about the seduction of Cornelia, who has not escaped her far from impotent master's eye either. She withstands on prudential rather than moral grounds Ignatian proposals for an affair and then marriage. She is beguiled, however, by his idea that they should celebrate a 'holy day on St. Valentine's Day for Cupid's and Hymen's sake . . . a celebration of Venus vigil'. The plot becomes complicated by the designs of the master and Ignatius' surprising incompetence. He creeps into the wrong bed, the Lady's, and is discovered there by the master en route to Cornelia. The next morning he receives apt punishment; before he is expelled from the household, he has his foreskin removed with a razor.[35]

The second rogue story is invitingly entitled *Eve Revived, or The Fair One Stark-Naked.* It was published by William Downing in 1684, and was translated by 'G.R.' out of French.[36] Its interest for us here is that the anti-heroine is an ex-Ursuline novice, and once more the important man in her life is a Jesuit. She is called Angelica and lives in Lyons with her widowed mother and younger sister. Her mother is rich, but wants to marry a younger man, and is therefore intent on removing the nubile Angelica, already courted by a cavalier, from the scene; thus she can appear with her other daughter to be younger than she really is. To cajole Angelica, whose (sexual) blood is already 'boyling', she employs Father Stanislas, the Jesuit of typically commodious morals. He succeeds, but in the process falls for his convert, who makes an increasingly pitiful sight in the cloister. Her melancholy makes her ill, and the ardent Stanislas comes to her chamber; she pleads with him to help her escape, increasing her persuasiveness by 'exposing certain Nudities capable of kindling Flames in the heart of the most Insensible'. Stanislas is no Father Rock, and 'falls to hugging and embracing' her. He organises a perilous escape, after writing her passionate love-letters, but is not allowed to consummate his passion. A susceptible cavalier who lodges the runaways steals both Angelica and a large sum of money from Stanislas. The cavalier, 'though given some liberty to his hands' and 'granted certain liberties which she thought might have mollified his flames' is denied 'the last Favour' until they can get married in Geneva. Angelica's virtue is frequently assaulted, but she is inhibited by maidenly modesty and her Ursuline training. The frustrated man finally employs an extraordinary strategem for relief of 'the Impurity of his Desires':

> He paid a servant-maid, and flung her upon the bed, and made Angelica lye down by her, whom he obliged to open her Bosom, he lifted up the Petticoats and Smocks of both of 'em, and lying a little a cross upon the Maid, having placed one of his hands upon Angelica's Breasts, and the other upon her Tuzzy-Muzzy, and applyed his Mouth upon hers also, he enjoyed the one and embraced the other, with as much Pleasure and Delight as if all the Misterious Commerce had passed between Angelica and himself. Angelica felt Delights so approaching those that he enjoyed that she breathed out tender sighs.

In her ensuing adventures she is cozened by an Italian ex-monk, 'an insinuating cheat', both of her maidenhead and the money she had taken from Stanislas. She experiments with dildoes, is watched shaving her pubic hair by a voyeur, and becomes the transvestite minion of a young prince, who is inevitably suspected of 'the Italian vice'. Eventually, as the member of a brothel in The Hague, she is visited by a customer who turns out to be Father Stanislas. He pretends to forgive her, and the next day takes her for a walk by the sea at Scheveling.

> The water being warm, he suggested to our Innocent *Fair One* Bathing. . . . He was already Stark-Naked, and had already wantoned in the Water, when that seeing Angelica come in with her smock on, he lifted it up and took it from her, with so sweet a violence, that she would then have been taken for our First Mother. . . . They wash'd, Kiss'd, whipt and a hundred other little Toyings.

Pretending chill, Stanislas gets out of the water, but persuades Angelica to stay in. He dresses unhurriedly. The last she sees of him is his form disappearing at speed over the dune clutching all her clothes, 'leaving thus that *Fair One Stark-Naked* . . . a perfect Model of *Eve Revived*'. This, even for a Jesuit, is a remarkably guileful revenge, especially as Stanislas has discovered where Angelica's savings are hidden.

The first of the dialogues is really a swapping of stories between a monk and two nuns, Angelica and Placidia. It is called *Conversation at the Grate, or The Monk in the Parlor* and forms an appendix to *The Adamite.*[37] The monk tells the story in the first person. He had 'continually wantoned away my time as a youth with an infinite number of young ladies . . . taking a certain little liberty which my Age took an innocent delight in'. His mother persuaded him to enter a monastery, 'where Love and Ambition reigns'. Monks counterfeit piety before profane persons, but, like him, are famished for the sight of beauties. 'The sight of a woman's backside pretty neat . . . furiously seized upon me so that I had much ado so to master my Passion.' Hearing, as 'I fed myself with ideas a thousand times more tickling', that a beautiful old flame had entered the Convent of Montmartre, he inveigles his way into the convent parlour for two hours conversation with Sister Angelica and her friend, neither of whom have yet achieved 'the gift of mortification'. Most of the jokes they swap are on a pretty puerile level. For instance a young pensionary asks what the slang term 'tail' means, and is told that it is 'the immodest part'. When she is later sick, she puts her illness down to her having eaten 'the immodest part of a fish'. A novice who shows too much bosom replies to the abbess's scolding, by arguing that two-year-olds are shown off naked, and her breasts are only two years old. This causes Placidia to wet herself laughing. Other accounts are slightly more titillating: a naked nun flagellating herself, especially as she had 'the finest, smoothest, whitest, plumpest Body that ever was seen'; there is one of the commonly told clyster stories, containing a hint of lesbianism; two nuns fight each other, and bite and tear out pieces of each other's buttocks; a cat gets under a monk's habit as he talks with some ladies by the fire and begins to 'play with his you know what', which gives him an erection 'redoubling that I know not what'. The monk's attempts to remove the cat lead to its sinking its teeth into its plaything, and in the end the rescuing ladies are treated to an eyeful. The monk responds that he prefers to be bitten there with a 'mouth without teeth', which Angelica to do her credit, does not understand. The common run, however, tells of ladies who use bungs to stop them farting, Jesuits given aperients and surprised when 'meditating' in a wood for the fifth time, or ladies of quality revealing their naked buttocks inadvertently to visiting Archbishops. It is distinctly shopworn bawdy, but, of course, even bawdy should have been far from the minds of the dedictated religious.

The last of the anti-Catholic books is by far the most noteworthy: *Venus in the Cloister or the Nun in her Smock*. It was first published in French in 1683 with a Cologne imprint, with a sixth edition by 1692, and rapidly translated and published in London in the same year by a young bookseller called Henry Rhodes, who had already brought out the first part of *The London Jilt* in 1683 and was to make a speciality of plays, romances, rogueries, jest-books and 'mild pornography' during his long and prolific career.[38]

The English editions of *Venus in the Cloister* are extremely rare. The Bodleian bought the unique survivor of Rhodes' edition in the Mostyn Hall sale at Christie's in October 1974.[36] The British Museum has a copy of the unique copy of Curll's 1725 edition, owned by Mr R. Edgar Cox of Bournemouth.

Although the title-page gives the author as the Abbé Duprat, Barbier's ascription to Jean Barrin is usually accepted. Barrin was a cleric, precentor of Nantes Cathedral and vicar-general of the diocese. He translated the Elegies and Epistles of Ovid in his youth, and this was published in Paris in 1676, with subsequent Hague editions in 1692 and 1701.

Venus in the Cloister, which plainly owes a good deal both to Aretino's first dialogue in the *Ragionamenti* and to Chorier's *Satyra Sotadica*, consists of five dialogues between Sister Angelica, a professed nun of nineteen or twenty, and Agnes, an inexperienced novice to the enclosed order. That Agnes will be an apt pupil is suggested by the fact that she is discovered on the first page masturbating. Like Tullia, Angelica quickly emerges as a lesbian; throughout the book Barrin describes passionate 'Florentine kissing', fondling and mutual stimulation between the two nuns. Some semblance of a narrative line in the first two dialogues is maintained by Angelica arranging for Agnes to meet an abbé, a monk and a friar at the grate, and the younger girl, as in the instructional pattern, reporting back her experiences after Angelica emerges from an eight-day retreat. Throughout even the opening dialogues, however, this unity is punctuated by anecdotes, philosophising and passionate love-play between the two. Dialogues III and IV are completely rambling affairs, but some sense of process is recovered in the last dialogue which is completely taken up with a *novella* plot, adapted from Aretino.

The author's interest in sexual deviancy suggested early by Angelica's passionate lesbianism is confirmed throughout the dialogues. He constantly returns to sado-masochism, with a climax at the end of Dialogue IV in a ten-page description of a flagellation scene. A scourge is prominently displayed in the frontispiece, and a favourite form of perverted stimulation among the nuns is using this instrument of mortification to induce orgasm. The story of St Alexis who was immune to his Wife's charms on his wedding night until she flayed herself is told to demonstrate the strange powers of the lash over men. The subtitle implies, and the text frequently explores, a prurient, voyeuristic obsession with nakedness; Angelica often lifts up Agnes's smock to dote on her body, or describes seeing nuns and their lovers in the nude through cracks in cell doors. There is even a blasphemous comment on a painting of the naked child Jesus. Beside these delights, masturbation with or without dildoes – the latter more commonly to hand than the rosary – reading dirty books brought in by confessors, and even coupling with priests, monks, friars or gardeners are so many 'bagatelles . . . peccadilloes'.

Sexual intercourse is subject to severe frustrations. There is the grille separating the visitors' room from the nuns' parlour for instance. One over-ardent visitor wrenched away part of the grille only to become embarrassingly stuck as he tried to wriggle through to his beloved. The cognoscenti are aware that this obstacle can be circumvented by two loose floorboards, known as the Straits of Gibraltar, which lead to the desired Pillars of Hercules. Then there are the interruptions caused by prying, prurient nuns nudging cell doors open or spying through peep-holes and chinks. The watchfulness of the abbess is a constant danger too. Though she is the Patroness of the lascivious Knights of the Grille, she is jealous of her inferiors' similar 'Ecstatic Intromissions and profane Exercises'. Indeed the whole of the last dialogue underlines her qualities. A young man smuggles himself into the convent to be with his beloved. His valuable services are terminated during an intimate inspection by the abbess when an uncontrollable erection snaps the garter that has been maintaining his appearance of feminity. Some of the sisters regard this metamorphosis as a miracle, but the abbess locks the intruder in the room next to hers: 'so sweet a Morsel was worthy the Mouth of an Abbess'.

Venus in the Cloister seems to me plainly intended to stimulate sexual excitement in the reader and arouse his imagination by specificity of detail, fantasy situations within a taboo area and a canine interest in abnormal sexuality. Here I disagree with Mr

Foxon's verdict that it is hardly distinguishable from *histoires galantes.*[40] Barrin is as obviously hostile to many aspects of contemporary church life. Angelica, for instance, gives Agnes an example of a generalised confession which conceals far more than it reveals. Several male orders come in for satirical condemnation. The Jesuits are attacked both for pederasty and for justifying lechery provided it is committed with prudence and circumspection; Capuchins are depicted as sadists, and Carthusians as masturbators—warriors in 'the battle of five fingers against one'; Benedictines are snobbishly exclusive, opposing sexual relations with other orders as 'promiscuity'. Spiritual directors are uniformly protrayed as 'goats in heat'; one of them has a reliquary containing locks of hair of all his conquests, punningly called 'The Relicks of Ste. Barbe'. The first four members admitted to 'The Order of the Grille' are a bishop, two abbés and a prior. With exemplars like these it is hardly surprising that the nuns are so depraved.

Nonetheless, the author goes to some lengths to furnish justification for the nuns' behaviour. In his dedicatory epistle to Madam D.L.R. (?de la Roche), the Lady Abbess of Beaulieu, he jokingly interprets the vows of poverty, chastity and obedience as willingly stripping down to the smock, taking for her rule pure nature, and being as docile (sexually) as any novice. This unconventional type of chastity recurs frequently. As early as page 3, Agnes describes herself as 'an Enemy to all Restraint', a girl who 'would always act with Liberty . . . be guided by that pure and innocent Nature, by following entirely the inclinations which She gives us'. Angelica cites a Jesuit who condones sinning as 'Liberty of Conscience', a phrase which would raise ironic laughter among Englishmen in Charles II's and James II's reigns. Another line is advanced in Dialogue II: chastity is a gift of God, and therefore the ungifted, even if cloistered, cannot be expected to achieve it, especially if they enter orders under parental or priestly pressure in early adolescence. Both principals are apostles of libertinism; they obey the commands of Nature, and spurn man-made conventions. Yet Angelica condemns the sheer debauchery 'of those who never taste perfect pleasure' described in such works as *L'Escholle des Filles* and *Satyra Sotadica*, both of which she has read in the convent. She recognises some restraints in the message of Christ and the need for prudence. Her motto is 'Let us love, let us seek Pleasure where it is lawful'.

My reading of *Venus in the Cloister* is that the pornographic intention of Barrin is primary. He set his account in a convent because sexy nuns were likely to titillate his readers; criticism of his church's shortcomings was incidental to his main purpose. Projection on religious is a time-honoured slant.[41]

Barrin's style is in marked contrast to English bawdy, and even further removed from the lewd obscenity of court satire. He aspires to a more erotic evocation, and his circumlocutions make some claim to elegance. The abbess's handkerchief after a visit by a Jesuit is 'moisten'd in certain places with a liquor somewhat viscuous (sic)'. A spiritual director 'pushed Devotion so far into the souls of two of our sisters that they found themselves very much incommoded for nine months after'. Or, Angelica offers the novice: 'My hand shall now perform that office which thine own did just now so charitably to another part of thy Body.' There is a fastidiousness, a dryness about his nonetheless stimulating indirections that would elude English pornographers until Cleland.

The 'Abbé Duprat's' dedication alludes to the embarrassment that would be caused if his 'curous entertainments' were ever made public. They would 'provide new subjects of criticism and furnish with Arms those who would attack us'. With particular irony for English readers he quotes Quevedo's dictum: 'He that rightly comprehends the Morality of the Discourse shall never repent the Reading of it.' In his report on the trial of Curll for publishing *Venus in the Cloister*, Lord Fortescue opined: 'I thought it rather to be published, on purpose to expose the Romish priests, the father confessors, and the Popish religion.'[42] It is certainly arguable that the apparently apolitical Henry Rhodes did far more damage to the cause of James II than all the frenzied efforts of Whig publishers like Curtis, 'Elephant' Smith or Benjamin Harris. It is surprising that the cynically anti-Jacobite administration in 1725 prosecuted rather than encouraged the unspeakable Curll in that particular venture. Even in the dying days of the *ancien régime*, *Venus in the Cloister*, along with *Monastic News, or the Diverting Adventures of Brother Maurice*, were circulating in the guise of 'Philosophical Books' among the fiercely anti-clerical opposition.[43] The connection between subversion and pornography was here demonstrably strong.

With 'friends' like Barrin, Aretino, Poggio, Boccaccio, Leti, Chorier or Pallavicino, what need had the Roman Catholic church for enemies? Protestant attacks pale beside their exposés. The Stuarts might appear impregnable at the death of Charles II, with his Catholic queen, his Catholic mistress, his Catholic confessor and his Catholic cousin of France at the centre of the web. Yet the fact that his Catholic brother was resuming his travels within four short years demonstrates the deep and abiding distrust of the vast majority of the English nation for his religion and what it stood for. Perhaps it was not so much what that silly man did as what his people had been schooled to expect from him that caused his downfall. The books we have been discussing in this chapter played some part in that schooling process.

NOTES

1. John Ward, for instance, Oxford graduate, vicar, student of medicine, and an informed follower of national and international affairs, was convinced in the validity of both rumours. Diary, Vol. V, pp. 1130–1, 1300–20.
2. N. MacMaster, 'The Extremist Jansenists 1630–1703', unpublished Ph.D. Thesis, Cambridge University, 1972. He cites titles such as *Profession de Foy de M. l'Archevesque de Paris, Le Moine Secularisé* and *Le Clerc Tonsuré*. The leaders of the extreme Jansenist groups, whose particular targets were Harlay, Archbishop of Paris, and the Assembly of the Clergy, were Le Noir and Bordin. It appears that Gilles Dubois, Du Pré, an ecclesiastic from Lyons, and Minutoli, a friend of Bayle, had a hand in their composition.
3. He was expelled from the order in 1670, and proceeded to plunge into a life 'of scandalous dissipation'. R. Birley, 'The Library of . . . Comte de Brienne', *The Library*, 5th Series, XVII (1962), 105–31. He had been a member of Fouquet's circle, from which, as we have seen, *L'Escholle des Filles* emerged.
4. *Biographie Universelle* (Paris, 1825). His *Del Teatro Britannica* was ordered seized by the authorities in London in 1682. *CSPD CII*, 6 February 1682.
5. Katanka, 'Women of the Underworld', p. 3.
6. Bennett, *English Books*, p. 88.
7. D. S. Barnard, ed., *Hollands Leaguer* (Atlantic Highlands, N.J., 1971), pp. xiv–xxii.
8. *The Crafty Whore* (1658), pp. 59–60.
9. *London Bawd*, pp. 10, 118.
10. Vol. V, p. 1231.
11. The epithet is Sir Edward Walker's; he was a fellow royalist in exile with Jermyn, later Earl of St Albans, and a crony of John Ward's. Diary, Vol. IV, p. 991. Gramont commented on the sexual prowess of the wealthy but otherwise unprepossessing lover of the Queen-Mother. *Memoirs,* pp. 75–6, 83–6.
12. *Dictionnaire Historique et Critique* (1697–1702) cited in Atkins, *Sex in Literature*, pp. 56–7.
13. Diary, Vol. II, pp. 314, 603; Vol. IV, p. 1073.

14. Wilson, *Rake*, pp. 44, 45. Oldham, *Works* (1684) described the confessional as 'the lechery office'. Cf. 'Utile Dulce' (1681): 'Be fond in private, but in Publick grave. . . . Be wise as Maids which are in Cloysters Blest, Come veil'd to th' World, but Naked to the Priest.' Nottingham, PwV 42, f. 136.
15. Diary, Vol. III, p. 768.
16. *Poems on Affairs of State*, Vol. III (1704), p. 299.
17. Fryer, *Forbidden Books*, p. 22. For priests, also read monks.
18. Diary, Vol. IV, p. 997.
19. Diary, Vol. IV, pp. 1079–80.
20. Israel Tongue was the nonconformist collaborator of Oates. Wing has thirty-five entries under Jesuits, all but one of which are derogatory.
21. P. 30.
22. Cf. *The True History of the Lives of the Popes of Rome* (London, 1679) which was in demand in New England.
23. This thorn in the flesh of the Stuarts makes frequent appearances in *CSPD* in the late 1670s and early 1680s. In January 1683, for instance, an informer writes to the secretary of state that among Curtis' stock are *The Perplext Prince, Articles of Impeachment against the Duchess of Portsmouth, Julian the Apostate* and *Weekly Pacquets of Advice from Rome*. Curtis suffered in the Tory backlash when he was fined the unprecedented sum of £500 for *The Night-Walker of Bloomsbury*, after the execution of William, Lord Russell in 1684. Kitchin, *L'Estrange*, pp. 234, 322.
24. That this kind of material remained popular into the eighteenth century is suggested by the inclusion of 'Cheats of the Cloyster' in the new serial publication *The Secret Mercury* in September 1702. Graham, *Periodicals*, p. 41.
25. The Bodleian copy, published by Robert Littlebury, is bound with *Romes Rarities*. The original Italian edition had come out in the same year in Geneva, under the false imprint of 'Raguse'.
26. Donna Olympia is also mentioned in Head's *The Miss Display'd* pp. 24–6.
27. This account follows Ashbee, *Index Librorum Prohibitorum* (London, 1877), pp. xl, 415, 422, 463. Dingwall, *Peculiar People*, p. 140, cites J. Gretser, S.J., *De Spontanea Disciplarum* (1608).
28. Bodleian, Douce Ballads, Vol. II, No 143.
29. Published by the well-known popular market stationer, Dorman Newman.
30. The unique surviving copy of *The Adamite* is in the library of the University of Illinois at Urbana-Champaign. It also contains general comments about the way the confessional is abused, especially in convents, and the reputation of the Jesuits for casuistry and persuasion.
31. More general and more specific is James Salgado, *History of the Fryers Idle and Vicious Lives* (London, 1682).
32. Atkins, *Sex in Literature*, p. 59.
33. Foxon, p. 40, has an example of Tonson using the title *Aloisia, or the amours of Octavia Englished* (1681) as a come-on for what turns out to be a mere piece of bawdry.
34. The latter were first published in French in 1669, and were written by Marianna Alcoforado, a Portuguese nun. Who the author of the cavalier's letters was is not certain, but it may have been Guilleraques. The English translator of the nun's letters was L'Estrange (1678, 1680, 1684). Aphra Behn Englished the cavalier's (1683). V. Mylne, 'Changing Attitudes to

Truth in Fiction', *Renaissance and Modern Studies*, VII (1963), 53–77; Kitchin, *L'Estrange*, p. 416.

35. Pp. 17–37.
36. *Eve ressucité, ou la belle sans Chemise* was published in Holland, with the false imprint of 'Cologne, chez Louis le Sincère, 1683'.
37. Its pagination continues that of *The Adamite*. It is, I think, an English production; several of its story plots are taken from *Nugae Venales*.
38. C. Blagden, 'The Memorandum Book of Henry Rhodes 1695–1720', *Book Collector*, III (1954), 28–39, 103–17. There were two apprentices who could have fitted our man. The more probable was freed by redemption in 1680. McKenzie, *Apprentices*, p. 140. He may have been related to a bookseller called John Rhodes, born about 1600, trading as late as 1668 in St-Martin-in-the-Fields, who also worked in the theatre. Hotson, *Stage*, pp. 95, 99, 216. R. B. McKerrow, *Dictionary of Printers and Booksellers 1557–1640* (London, 1968) also notices a Matthew Rhodes, who traded as a freeman of the Stationers' Company 1622–33. Rhodes' unhindered publication of *Venus in the Cloister* was used by Curll as an argument against conviction for publishing a new edition in 1725. Foxon, p. 14.
39. I am grateful to Mr Julian Roberts for bringing this to my attention.
40. Foxon, p. 43.
41. W. Young, *Eros Denied* (London, 1968), p. 256.
42. Thomas, *State Trials*, Vol. I, p. 140.
43. R. Darnton, 'Literary Low Life in Pre-Revolutionary France', *Past and Present*, No LI (1971), 81–115.

9 'Medical'

'Physic' in Restoration England was still at a frighteningly elementary stage. Quite simply 'medical science was helpless before most contemporary hazards to health'.[1] Treatment of serious illnesses was hindered by reliance on the classical theory of the humours, leading to bleeding or purging to bring the humours back into balance, by the inability of doctors to discover the root cause of an illness through lack of instruments and equipment, lack of professionalism, practical training and hospital facilities, or laboratories. Surgeons had no anaesthetics or concept of antisepsis. The standard textbook by Richard Wiseman, *Severall Chirurgicall Treatises* (1676), was known, especially no doubt by patients, as 'Wiseman's Book of Martyrs'. Consulting a qualified physician was an expensive business, even if you could find one, especially in London where the Royal College used its monopoly of licensing in a very restrictive way. In the commonest trauma of family life, childbirth, the midwife was likely to be totally unqualified. Typically the greatest advance in this area, the Chamberlen forceps, remained a closely guarded secret.

Given this lamentable situation it is hardly surprising to find Pepys treating the anniversary of his survival from being cut for the stone as some kind of miraculous event. Or to read Muggleton's opinion that doctors were 'the greatest cheats in the world. If there were never a doctor of physic in the world, people would live longer and live better in health.' This view was supported by no less an authority than Thomas Sydenham, the leading physician of the century. The greatest scourge of the age, bubonic plague, was never understood; it just very conveniently went away. The very general lack of faith in doctors appears in several drolleries. In 'A Close-stool and a Chamber-pot chuse out a Doctour' in *Sportive Wit*, most London practitioners are alleged to be only interested in one piece of female anatomy. Dr. Turner 'first kills the man, then treads the hen'; certainly the charge of killing the man, albeit unwittingly, was hardly baseless. Similarly in 'A Colledge of Doctors' in the same collection, the fellows and licentiates typically use their clyster pipes in the wrong hole, and there is dreadful punning on knives in sheaths, injections and pulse-taking. Ordinary people would be more likely to consult an apothecary, or a quack, or wise man or woman, or rely on familiar folk-wisdom within the family or the community.

The diary of John Ward, vicar of Stratford-on-Avon, gives a revealing impression of this side of medicine. From his undergraduate days at Oxford, Ward had been interested in the apothecary's art. As a young man, he visited herb gardens in London, met the great simplers, Bates and Bowles, and all his life read and recorded case-histories and recipes. He was frequently consulted by his parishioners for cures. Some may have been effective; others were hair-raising. One cure for venereal disease in men, for instance, was to sleep as soon and as often as possible with 'a sound woman'. Another was protracted galloping on horseback. Primitive psychology is recorded:

> Dr. Trig cured a woman that was troubled with hysterical fitts this way: he laid her uppon the ground with her face downwards, then took up her coats and gave her three or four slaps on the arse; he did this before much companie, which I scarcely believe.[2]

His wide reading and expertise are matched throughout the diary by his ignorance, misinformation and credulity. He accounts for imperfections in children, for instance, 'because men use copulation with their wives when ye woman hath her Menstruous flowing'. Or, he has heard that 'the testicles of hysterical virgins are bigger than a man's fist'. He is a proponent of mercurial fluxing 'for ye ffrench pox', which D'Arcy Power, his transcriber, describes as 'a remedy certainly as bad as the disease', though this was, of course, one of the commonest forms of treatment. Other cures he notes include a stag's pizzle, aurum potabile, purging pills, raisins and nutmegs in the white of an egg, guajacum, or vipers drowned in wine.[3] He is keen on oddities and wonders.[4] He twice records seeing the body of a drowned man which had an erection; he gives a long description of an hermaphrodite that he has heard about; he reports on a Spanish cup of clay that is alleged to stop conception; he is interested in some women whose alae or nymphae are so large that they hang out of their privities in a strange manner and others who have not had their periods for years, or never stop. In fact much of his medical interest centres on women's complaints, which is somewhat strange in a man who never married. His four favourites are hysteria, or the suffocation of the mother, the green sickness, the 'whites' or leucorrheia, and menstruation; he notes several conflicting theories about the precise medical definition of virginity. There is, unexpectedly, less on childbirth and miscarriages, but stray references to the female testes and female circumcision. He copies down a rumour that Queen Catherine's barrenness arises from 'a too eager flowing of her courses'. He notes several aphrodisiacs including powdered testicles, Montague's caudle, astringent pills taken with an encouraging electuary, herrings, boars' testicles, but not, surprisingly, a stag's pizzle. He rarely alludes to impotence, and then only when it afflicts some celebrity like the King of Poland or the Duke of Bavaria, who cured his own with pills from Rome, only to bequeath it to his three sons. His views on copulation are coloured by his mild mysogyny and the belief that women get far more pleasure out of it than men. He records several tell-tale signs of those over-given to venery, like a blue circle round the eyes or thin urine; for Ward, there is such a state of having too much of a good thing. If a person of Ward's intelligence, education and reading could give credence to some of these descriptions and prescriptions, it is positively terrifying to think what poisons and exacerbaters an ignorant apothecary or quack might confidently dispense.

One topic to which Ward never refers, despite his gynecological interests, is abortion. His silence is typical. Although the temptation to terminate unwanted pregnancies in a generally pre-contraceptive age should have been strong, it would appear that among ordinary people the religious sanctions against it were stronger. We have already met one or two references to infanticide committed by whores on their unwelcome bastards.[5] I have only come across four references to abortion. The first, already mentioned, occurs in *The School Of Venus* when Francion is reassured about the consequences of taking Robinet as her lover. All that Susanne says is 'I'm fond enough of you to look after you if that should happen. In cases like that I've got certain remedies which leave absolutely nothing to be desired'.[6] The second is *Erotopolis*, where it is reported that the Empiricks of Betty-Land 'teach the shepherdesses how to shun the pains of the harvest and yet enjoy the full content of the Pleasures of Tillage'.[7] 'The Ladyes Mistake or the Physicians Puzzle', in Dyce 43, has the physician claim that he has 'kill'd fifty the belly within'.[8] Doctor Alexander Frazier, the

King's principal physician, was described by Pepys as 'being so great with my Lady Castlemaine and Stewart at court in helping to slip their calves when there is occasion'.[9]

'The less sophisticated [reader of pornography] has in the past turned to manuals of sexual instruction and psychology. Here he is allowed to read (and privately to wallow in) fairly frank accounts of sexual activity and the difficulties encountered by others.'[10] The past certainly includes our period. Frequently ostensible medical books were regarded as objects of suspicion or prurience. In *The Practical Part of Love*, whose very title is a parody of a technical instruction manual, the library of 'Love's University' contains along with blatantly dirty books, such titles as *Culpepper's Midwife, The Compleat Midwife* and *The Birth of Mankind*.[11] In a print called *The Compleat Auctioner*, by Sutton Nicholls dated about 1700, the first of these works and *Aristotles Master-Piece* are side by side with *Aretine's Postures, Satyra Sotadica* and other pornography.[12] Tom Brown similarly relegated medical and pseudo-medical works to the most disreputable category. In his attack on Dryden, *Reasons for Mr. Bays changing his Religion* (1688), he writes of the poet laureate translating 'certain luscious pieces of Lucretius fit only to keep company with *Culpepper's Midwife* and *Aloisia Sigea*'.[13] In the 'Compleat Catalogue of choice, learned and ingenious Books' which Brown himself abandoned when he allegedly eluded a dunning landlord, were the same *Tullia and Octavia, Aretine's Postures* alongside Salmon's *Cure of the Lues Venerea Anglice French Pox* and a little tract explaining 'how to prevent Miscarriages in the Female Sex'.[14]

There was a detectable defensiveness on the part of authors of serious or pseudo-serious medical works on these sensitive topics about the motivation of some of their readers. This often followed the logic of Wye Saltonstall's *Picturae Loquentes* (London, 1631): 'Nor should they read . . . such as Nature's secrets do discover, since still desire doth but from knowledge grow.'[15] The son of John Henry Meibomius, professor of physic at the University of Juliers and 'reckoned among the Principal Ornaments of the Age', was initially unwilling to reprint his father's *Treatise on the Use of Flogging in Venereal Affairs* because he might 'incur the censure of such to whom these papers tinctured with a tickling Salt might seem too ludicrous and libertine'. He salved his conscience with the thoughts that it was written for physicians and 'in Language only familiar to the Learned'.[16] Curll, who brought out an English translation in 1718, and usually weighed up the pornographic possibilities of his ventures, argued that 'The Fault is not in the Subject Matter but in the Inclination of the Reader. . . . The Chastest Ear in the World is not polluted by a Relation of the *Prodigies of Lewdness*.' This did not prevent him from trying, however.

In the second Intrigue in *The Art of Cuckoldom* the cuckolder mentions another medical work, *Aristotles Problems*, and the context and bawdy puns that follow the title imply that it was commonly regarded as a disreputable book. *Aristotles Master-piece*, 'very necessary for all Midwives, Nurses and Young-Married Women', declares its purpose as being for 'The Benefit and Advantage of the Modest of either Sex; not desiring that this book should fall in to the Hands of any Obscene or Wanton Person. . .'. This intention is repeated half-way through the text. 'This book is for the Publick Good, and in no wise intended to convert them to obscenity.'

The longest discussion of the motives of readers of this kind of work occurs at the beginning of the first English selections of Sinibaldi's *Geneanthropeia*, entitled *Rare Verities* (London, 1658). The translator[17] imagines that

> It may be some seemingly modest, will hold me for a Capitall offender for Transcribing those things into English, which should have remained still in the obscurity of an unknown tongue. To which I answer; that I hold it very unjust that scholars should monopolize the trade of Drollery to themselves, and that they should be so uncharitable as not to let their Countreymen partake of those sublime secrets they understand, unlesse they puzzle their braines with Latine and Greek. I think such men, had they their ends, would make such sots of Englishmen, as that they should either forget, or never know the manner of generation; and that when they are married, they must be forced to come to them to be taught the way of copulation.

Furthermore, foreseeing that 'some jerks' will be laid on him by the censorious, he solicits from a friend a testimonial for the work. This friend 'singles out some objections' which he afterwards silences. The first is that the translator has been a modern Clodius going to the presence chamber at the secret sacrifice of Bona Dea in the disguise of a woman. Others may criticise *Rare Verities* on the grounds that it is written

> rather to incite an itching or titillation whereby women may be disposed to conception, then to stir up the conception of learned mens brains. The Chamber-maid is like to receive great satisfaction in making a scrutiny, whether she enjoys the integrity of her Hymen, and so be resolved, *quid poterit salva virginite rapi*. She will roul over your pages to see whether she hath forfeited the notes of her virginity, by petulancy, whilest others (I mean the profoundly learned) make strict inquisition into abstruse Philosophical verities. Here shall both sexes view their several postures, how to fight in Venus her battalia, beyond all dull books of fencing and fighting. And now you are arrived at the amphibious sort of Objectors, that *curios simulant, & vivunt Bacchanalia*: such as carry the *Practice of Piety* in their hands, this in their pocket, and yet make publick exclamations against it for obscene language &c. while their fancies immerg'd in its luxurious imbracements commit adulteries with their own Chimera'.

Such imagined objections came without doubt from experience of similar works being thus received, rather than from the friend's fertile imagination. His policy of fore-arming was justified by the description of Sinibaldi's work as 'sportive' in *Proteus Redivivus.*[18] The best documented account of this kind of misuse of medical material comes from a different continent and a different century, but it concerns books that were current in the seventeenth century. The trouble broke out in 1744 in the Massachusetts township of Northampton, of which Jonathan Edwards, the finest intellect of colonial New England, was pastor. Its cause was 'bad books'. These, on examination, proved to be a doctor's book which contained prints of 'the private parts of woman's body'; this work was known popularly as 'the young folk's bible'. Another savoury read among the young was a book 'about women's having children' 'a nasty book about woman kind'. The boys who got hold of these works, which proved to be *Aristotles Master-Piece* and *The Midwife Rightly Instructed*, were given to making lewd and suggestive remarks to girls of the town 'about Girls things concerning Girls that it is unclean to speak of', saying 'you do not need to be scared we know as much about ye as you and more too'. Such books were, claimed one self-righteous young woman, 'exceeding unclean to the top of Baseness', a remarkable paradox. One witness described how

> John Lancton a fortnight ago last Friday was at the farm where I was and was talking of such things and he boasted That he had read Aristotle he talked about his reading the book more than once talked about the things that was in that book in a most unclean manner a long time Betty Jenks and Moll Waters there he spoke of the book as a Granny Book when I checked him he Laughed and he talked exceeding uncleanly. and Lasciviously so that I never heard any fellow go so far after he was gone we the young women that were there agreed that we never heard any such talk come out of any mans mouth whatsoever. it seem'd to me to be almost as bad as tongue could express.

After numerous witnesses had been heard, one with the marvellously appropriate name of Clap, the ringleaders were sifted out and punished, and the town relapsed into more mundane disputes. The whole affair provides a perfect example of the type of misuse of material with which we began this section.[19]

The results of this perversion of author's intention by readers —pornography in the eye of the beholder—were twofold. On the one hand serious books on sensitive topics went in danger of misuse not only by readers, but also by disreputable publishers. On the other, books which sought to titillate through quasi-medical information were put on the market to exploit this audience. At this distance it is sometimes difficult to know which group a particular work was intended for, especially given the unprofessional state of the medical profession.

A work like *A Rational Account of the Natural Weaknesss of Woman . . . By a Physician* (London, 2nd ed., 1716) plainly belongs among the serious works. It is a pretty rudimentary description of the sort of complaints that Ward showed such interest in, with no attempt at titillation. It is sprinkled with recipes for cures and letters from satisfied customers; the last page contains a list of the physician's own medicines with their prices, ranging from 3s 6d to 5s. Similarly Rodericus de Castro's *de morbis Mulierum* is a genuine medical work. Yet to the author of *Select City Quaeries* de Castro is 'the Bawdy Author'.[20] I place John Henry Meibomius' *De Usu Flagrorum* in this category with greater diffidence. Meibomius (1590–1655) was, as we have seen, a leading physician of his generation. His treatise was first published in 1639 at Leyden, and a second authorised edition, corrected by his son Henry, appeared at Frankfurt in 1670 after an unauthorised reprint a year or two before. This Latin edition was reasonably well known in Restoration England. In 1718 Curll published a translation by George Sewell, 'A Physician', including letters that passed between Thomas Bartholin and Henry Meibomius, and with a pornographic *Treatise of Hermaphrodites* added.

The original Meibomius treatise, which had been privately printed at Leyden by Cassius, 'bears the marks' of a serious investigation of a topic admittedly 'very entertaining and alluring'. The opening section contains examples from classical literature and medical writings and from more recent works and observation of men—and some women—incapable of intercourse without flogging. Picus of Mirandola and Coelius are both quoted in the second section which examines the causes of this; both believe that it arises from whipping among schoolboys 'when a reciprocal frication among his school-fellows used to be provoked by the Titulation of stripes'. Juvenal, Persius and Tibullus, Apuleius and Petronius all provide evidence of songs and dances and the figure of Priapus producing erections in audiences. Meibomius supports the theory that it is warmth in the loins and reins which produces erections. Those who take part in erotic dances described by the ancients would by their movement excite just this heat; similarly nocturnal emissions occur when men lie on their backs in bed, thus overheating their kidneys. Galen prescribed a cold plaister on the loins to cure priapisms, and Virgil's diagnosis of impotence derives from coldness in kidneys and sides. What flogging does, according to Meibomius, is to heat otherwise frigid areas and produce 'aptness for venery'. The author's descriptions are straightforward, but, in the nature of the case, many of his quotations are inevitably erotic.

Curll, however, was plainly intent on dressing the production up into something positively titillating. Apart from the hermaphrodite piece, he added a frontispiece showing a woman beating a man with his breeches down in front of a mirror, while he gazed over his shoulder at a girl clad in a smock with her hand at her breasts and her legs displayed. Beside her bed is a picture of Leda and the swan; two men peer at the scene through a window. Bartholin's letter adds further modern examples of men being flogged sexually. A note from the translator denies that the previous edition's latinity was a 'charm against infirmity'; it merely restricted knowledge to the learned. Curll's window-dressing of this slight essay no doubt explains why he was arrested for publishing *A Treatise of the Use of Flogging in Venereal Affairs* and *Venus in the Cloister* in November 1725. Even so the prosecution probably realised that it was on fairly weak ground with Meibomius and concentrated entirely on *Venus in the Cloister* in making its case.[21]

The three quasi-medical books of unsavoury reputation during the Restoration and after are in one sense part of the folk-lore of medicine. Both the *Master-Piece* and the *Problems* used the name of Aristotle on the slenderest of grounds. A few passages are traceable to his work on the generation of animals, a few more to pupils of his, like Aphrodiseus. Medieval physicians like Averroes and Albertus Magnus are often quoted, and the works of Sylvius and Pareus of the sixteenth and seventeenth centuries are also plagiarised. The mixture was concocted by one or more English hacks in the seventeenth century and plainly aimed at a popular audience, 'the innocent and the prurient'. The predominance of intimate material dealing with women suggests too that it was a male readership that was being courted. It was certainly one of the most successful ventures of the century, and the *Master-Piece* may have reached as many as a hundred editions in England and America by the 1830s.[22]

I have used the 1694 edition of *Aristotles Master-Piece: or, the Secrets of Generation Displayed in all the Parts thereof* published by W. B. Medically it is greatly superior to the *Problems* and some of its advice, for instance to midwives about the process of childbirth, is excellent. It takes a moral line about marriage, opposing fornication almost homiletically, likewise adultery, patronage of whores and excessive lust. It deplores the possibility that the description of the genitals in women 'may be turned by some Lascivious and Lewd Persons into ridicule'. Of speaking about copulation, it advises people 'to cloath it in that modest Dress that the Chastest Ear may hear, without being put to the trouble of a Blush'. Occasionally it falls into the patois of bawdy. When describing the problems of old men married to young women, for instance, we read 'he strives and vainly strains to please her' and finally has 'the Honour to be dubbed a Knight of the Forked Order, and have their Names inrolled in the colony of Cuckoldom'. This could well come from *Fifteen Comforts* or Pepys' chapbooks. The woodcut on the opening page is of a naked women clearly showing her sex organs. The popular notions that girls become broody after menarche, and that women derive far more pleasure from sex than men, are spelled out. Various aphrodisiacs are listed from powdered acorns to sea-food, and hen's eggs, game, nuts, raisins and strong wines, it appears, all help in the generation of seed. The common belief that women's imaginations affect the appearance of their children is confirmed by the story of the women who had a bastard resembling her husband because she was so fearful of him catching her while her lover was in the saddle.[23] This idea is also seen as a cause for monsters—several of which are illustrated in the crude woodcuts–but more common is intercourse during 'time of terms', i.e. periods, which is often resorted to by impatient sailors returned from long voyages. Instructions are given about widening the neck of the womb if it proves too tight for the yard, and about how to know when the hymen is ruptured. The clitoris is rightly described as the seat of feminine pleasure, though its normal dimensions are exaggerated; women are advised to refrain from sex for most of pregnancy, and given infallible tests to determine whether the child they are carrying will be a boy or a girl. Rather quaintly, men are recommended to stay within women after intercourse in order to keep the draughts out of the womb. Midwives are warned against dealing with women with V.D. since they might transfer the disease to another woman who will then infect her husband, which will cause them to 'think hard of each other'. In the main there is little evidence of intentional titillation in the *Master-Piece*; anatomical descriptions are straightforward and free of erotic undertones. It is hardly surprising that it became something of a bible for ordinary people, in the same way that Nicolas Venette's *Le Tableau de la Vie Conjugale* (1696) did for the French peasantry in the eighteenth century.[24] The titillation of the uninitiated or the perverted seems to have been an incidental service.

The Problems of Aristotle; with other Philosophers and Physicians. Wherein are contained divers Questions with their Answers Touching the Estate of Mans Body, was published by J. Wright, the well-known ballad and chapbook stationer, in partnership with Richard Chiswell, whom Dunton was to describe as 'the Metropolitan bookseller to the World' in 1684.[25] As its sub-title states, it is a series of questions, with, unannounced, a remarkable quantity of wrong answers. Its pathology is based on notions of humidity, heat and cold, and it places great faith in the purgative effect of menstruation; this is why women have longer hair than men, no hair on their chests or faces (until after menopause, when, logically, they should all start to grow heavy beards!), why they are smooth and fair and why they do not go bald. Men, on the other hand, become bald through venery, excess of which 'causeth more hurt than immoderate letting of blood'. Fat women rarely conceive because the sperm slips out of their wombs; fat men 'cast forth little seed'. Men with long organs rarely beget children because the seed has so far to travel. We learn why men wink during carnal copulation, why birds do not piss, why children 'take pleasure in the act of venery seeing they do not cast forth any seed' and 'women's wits are unapt in good things, and most prompt in naughty things'. As to why 'Every living creature is sad after carnal copulation', the answer is that 'this act is filthy and unclean, and so every living creature doth abhor it; and when men doe think upon it they are ashamed and sad'.

It is amazing that this innocent trash should have assumed such a seamy reputation. Its readership must have been among the least sophisticated—suggested also by its leading publisher and his successors in later editions, Wotton and Conyers—and the sexually ingenuous. It is certainly an inferior monument to the Greeks than even the so-called *Master-Piece.*[26]

The translator, or rather adaptor, of *Rare Verities. The Cabinet of Venus Unlocked and Her Secrets laid open. Being a Translation of part of Sinibaldus his Geneanthropeia*,[27] was aiming at a far more sophisticated audience. The title page bears tags from Horace and Martial, and the Epistle, signed 'Erotodidascalus', is addressed 'To the Amorous Readers . . . the devout Adorers of *Venus* . . . the tried Champions of Venus'. He refers to Sinibaldus as a 'Pornodidascalian' and delivers himself of several anti-Puritan sentiments. This is going to be a racier read than Dod and Sibbes or some voluminous Rabbin. 'If I write anything obscene,' he titillatingly warns, 'it is because my Authors wrote so, from whom I Collected this miscellany.' In a burst of humility, he admits that his genius does not deserve 'to kisse Pegasus his ——'. In his letter to his friend seeking a testimonial he puns on being 'the pick-lock of Venus her Cabinet, to let you with more ease enter and rifle and despoile her inestimable treasure' and predicts trouble from the precise. 'For my part I expect no less than to be whipt by every squint-eyed fellow, worse then Dr. Gill lash'd his maids Bumbgillion when

He took up her smock
And then whip'd her nock.[28]

His friend's reply is replete with tags and mentions Harvey's discoveries, but he too allows himself some abstruse jokes about chastity belts and *Aristotles Problems* making 'every Lady a Peripatetick, and sworn Philosopher', implying looseness and libertinism. Some idea of the nature of the selection is given by the selection headings in the Index, which include:

> What is copulation?
> What is Venereal Love?
> Concerning those things that increase love.
> Concerning love-potions and philters.
> Whether females may change their sex.
> Which is most lustful a man or a beast?
> Which of the two is more lustful, a man or a woman?
> Which is more lustful a woman or a maid?
> Physiognomic signs of lust.
> Examples of such men and women that have been very lustful and lecherous.
> Concerning a mans Genitals, and their apt conformation.
> From whence proceeds the erection of the yard?
> Whether too long or too short a yard be obnoxious to generation.
> How to shorten the yard being too long.
> Of venereal impotency.
> Concerning some men that have had wonderful great Genitals.
> Concerning castrating men and women.
> A brief description of Womans Genitalls.
> Concerning the Clytoris.
> How to contract the vulva being too large and wide.
> Whether there be any signs of corrupted virginity.
> Concerning night pollutions.
> Whether to copulate backwards after the manner of beasts is best.
> Concerning pendulous venery, as also many other fantastical venereal postures.
> Of the good and the bad that comes by venery.

From this excerpt, and the general tone of the prefatory remarks, there is little doubt that the author of *Rare Verities*—and it is more accurate to think of this English version as a new work, rather than blackening Sinibaldi's reputation—was aiming at titillation, if not arousal, of his readership. Sometimes he is merely vulgar, but more often he chooses topics or illustrations to his points which would appeal to the lubricious. When he defines copulation, he gratuitously points out the obvious that sodomy and bestiality do not qualify. He takes a highly cynical view of love, in keeping with his numerous quotations from Ovid, Martial, Catullus, Juvenal, Apuleius and Lucretius. Like most of his contemporaries he is fascinated by wonders, but his are almost always calculated to be sexually exciting. Thus we hear of women in the East Indies who had such a burning itch to copulate that they surrounded European explorers imploring their favours; or the island of L'Amory where the inhabitants all go naked and free love is practised; or the Spaniard who was wont to make love ten times each day; or the Indian, who by means of an aphrodisiac ejaculated twelve times in one hour and in all seventy times till only blood came; there is the man with the penis six feet long which could bear a weight of thirty pounds, and the inevitable reference to Messalina, whom a hundred couplings in a day might weary but would not satisfy. He has a long section on ancients like Sardanapulus, Tiberius, Nero, Cyrene—a forerunner of Aretino in posturing—or Darius whose lusts were legendary and another on characters who practised bestiality. Lesbianism is a topic on which he dwells. He has three different sections on different kinds of aphrodisiacs; a man who is usually less than satisfying to his wife is fed cock's testicles, and goes on a sexual rampage. Unlike his master, Ovid, however, he has no remedy for the unfortunate state of love. Satyriasis, or an uncontrollable itch in women's privities, obviously fascinates him. For form's sake, he includes a few accounts of chaste women, but his attitude to females is usually disdainful. He comments on one heroic tale of chastity, 'an example rarely to be parallelled in these our times'. His motto is 'A man excels a woman in all things'. This belief seems the main ground for his rejection of certain postures: they are uncomfortable for men. He has imbibed some Puritan values: idleness is the commonest cause of lechery; physical beauty should not be the only or even the main quality attracting a man. He repeats many of the folklore myths, on women receiving ten times greater pleasure from sexual intercourse than men, on telepathic influences of the mother on the foetus, the lechery of the bald, long noses and large mouths as signs of large penises or pudenda, the voraciousness of redheads and barren women. Several of the commonplaces of whore stories are included, like the art of shrinking girls' vulvas to make them appear virgins, the common practice of infanticide among prostitutes and the poor, the frequency of cuckoldry. He accepts the contemporary medical theory that sperm or its catalyst travels down the spinal canal to the scrotum, which explains why hunch-backs are such fast workers.[29] He also repeats the idea that the retention of sperm in men or of sexual discharges in women is physically and mentally debilitating, thus the melancholy of bachelors or the neuroses of maids or the madness of widows.[30]

Under the gloss of a medical treatise, *Rare Verities* set out to cater for an audience who wanted rather more than mere gynecological or physiological instruction. The 'translator' may have hoped to 'deprave and corrupt' the uninitiated reader—though he claims in his epistle that the mere title will scare them away—but he certainly intended titillation for the more sophisticated. For the seventeenth century, it seems to be on the verges of pornography, though not of the class of *Tullia and Octavia* or *Venus in the Cloister*.[31] A derivative work, John Martin's *Gonosologium Novum*, was prosecuted at the Middlesex Quarter Sessions on 20 July 1709 and the case was remanded to the Queen's Bench.[32] The indictment called it 'scandalous'. This is endorsed by references to *Venus Cabinet Unlockt* both in the library of the University of Love in *The Practical Part of Love*, and in *Select City Quaeries*; the inferences are that it was contemporaneously regarded as erotic and salacious.

The extent to which the perversion of medical works had been carried by the early eighteenth century is demonstrated by *Tractatus Hermaphroditus, or a Treatise of Hermaphrodites* which Curll published along with Meibomius in 1718. He was no doubt relying on the proven seventeenth-century interest in these very rare freaks, which went along with the general credulity of the age about natural wonders. Details about female anatomy serve as a preface to highly explicit and voyeuristic scenes of lesbianism using dildoes and other forms of stimulation. This pornographic section dominates the book, though towards the end there is a return to a more scientific gloss, much of which is a paraphrase of 'Aristotle'. The brief section on 'Extraordinary Conceptions' plagiarises the unlikely tale from the *Problems* of the girl who got into a bath in which a man had masturbated, and thereby conceived. Even more outlandish is the account of the girl who became pregnant after climbing into the bed in which her father had polluted himself. Were they charged with incest? Compared with this kind of concentrated perversion masquerading under a physiological banner, the popular works we have been discussing were relatively harmless, however much they might have teased and tickled their unsophisticated readership at the time.

There is not space here to more than mention medical publications on what was, at least to the bawdy-minded, the commonest ailment of the age, venereal disease. In Pepys' *Penny Merriments*, for instance, there are countless ribald references to syphilis and gonorrhoea. The effect of the latter on sufferers' noses caused repeated merriment, as did the thought of patients sweating it out in Cornelius Tubs or undergoing fearful fluxes brought on by mercury treatments at 'Thomas his Spital'. Similarly Ward has numerous references to symptoms and cures, though he only mentions two of his parishioners as actually having contracted the disease. It is arguable that the penchant for defloration in the period and in the eighteenth century was connected with the fear of contracting the disease. Court wits, as we have seen, used V.D. as a justification for sodomy among men and the use of dildoes among women. Of the many works on the *Lues Venerea*,[33] as it was technically called, one of the most popular was Gideon Harvey's *Little Venus Unmask'd. Being a Discourse of the French Pox, with all its Kinds, Causes, Signs and Prognosticles. Also the Running of the Reins, Shanker, Bubo, Gleets, with their Cures*. Harvey lived from about 1640 to about 1700, and appears to have been born in the Netherlands. He matriculated at Exeter College, Oxford in 1655, but his medical training and degree came from Leyden, with Padua the leading medical school in Europe. Harvey was strongly opposed both to the College of Physicians and the Apothecaries' Company and engaged in heated public disputes with both bodies. This did not prevent him from having some form of semi-official practice at the court of Charles II. He first published *Little Venus Unmask'd* in 1670 as a digest of his weightier *Great Venus Unmask'd*. The former had reached a sixth edition by 1700. To purists, Harvey's work was marred by his penchant for slang and puns. This is how he describes the spread of the disease in the late fifteenth century, when the French were besieging the already infected Spaniards in Naples:

> Forced to dismiss their Mistresses already sufficiently rubbed with the Indian lodestone into the Enemy's camp, these hungry Mushrooms, almost starved for want of Womens Flesh . . .

> which was so well seasoned and daubed with Mustard, that in a few weeks it took them all by the Nose. . . .

Despite his bawdy bent, Harvey was a leading authority on the treatment of a disease, which was far less of a scourge during the Restoration than it had been in the Tudor period.[34] He was a proponent of sweet mercury, which was the least damaging form of treatment until guayacum, an imported drug, became common at the end of the century. Harvey claims that 'the pox at this present is more propagated in one day than a Hundred Years ago it was in a month'. The commonest form seems to have been the less dangerous though more painful gonorrhoea. That the seventeenth century made a joke of this disease may be another reflection of those social neuroses which snigger at what in fact frightens, or it may imply that a killer was after a century under some kind of control. At this range it is exceedingly difficult to disentangle the facts from the fiction, a problem which readers of all medical works must have encountered during the Restoration period.

The apprehensions of genuine writers, the exploitation of medical topics by pedlars of filth, the common equation of gynecological and instructional manuals with pornography, and the numerous editions such works achieved all point to a considerable readership which found these books sexually titillating. The young and sexually unsophisticated are often identified as customers, and our analysis of high-brow readership, plus the fact that it was usual in such works to translate classical tags into English, demonstrates that the intelligentsia rarely favoured such works. On the other hand, the relative subtlety of style and allusions in *Rare Verities* or *Aristotles Master-Piece* argues an audience more intellectually mature than chapbook or ballad readers. Why a middle-brow readership should find a misused or abused 'medical' approach attractive we can only conjecture. The Northampton evidence and the depiction of carnal copulation as filthy and shameful in *Aristotles Problems* suggests sexual repression as a major cause. A youthful readership may further argue a breakdown of the transmission of sexual knowledge from one generation to the next and a sense of sexual tension due to prolonged adolescent celibacy. The resort to genuine medical manuals implies as much of an intellectualisation of sexuality as the reading of pornography under a transparent 'scientific' disguise.

NOTES

1. Thomas, *Religion and Decline of Magic*, pp. 9–17; this is the best brief introduction to the subject, which I follow here.
2. Trig was a well-known woman's doctor in London, who is alluded to in *Practical Part of Love*, p. 47.
3. Mrs Creswell's letter to Moll Quarles suggests viper wine as an aphrodisiac for 'a fumbler'. Hayward, ed., *Brown, Amusements*, p. 444.
4. Many popular books catered for this kind of interest; e.g. T.R., *The Amazement of Future Ages* (1684), an early venture of John Dunton's with its titillating accounts of sex-changes and transvestism.
5. E.g. *English Rogue*, Mrs Dorothy's Story, Parts II and III.
6. Thomas, p. 144.
7. P. 122; on pp. 159–63 there is a further discussion of the sexual advances the doctors make when they are examining the shepherdesses.
8. F. 689.
9. Quoted by Wall, 'Restoration Rake', p. 43. Frazier and Dr Fourcade also treated courtiers for V.D. L. Stone, *Family, Sex and Marriage 1500–1800* (New York, 1977), pp. 73, 423, states that midwives were popularly thought of as abortionists, and quotes early eighteenth-century advertisements for abortive pills.
10. Atkins, *Sex in Literature*, p. 68.
11. P. 40.
12. B.M. 1415; for an inexpert discussion, see *Catalogue of Prints and Drawings: Political and Personal Satires* (London, 1873) Vol. II, Part I. The print is reproduced in Pinkus, *Grub Street*, and on the dust-jacket of this book.
13. Foxon, p. 6; *Aloisia Sigea* is an alternative title to *Satyra Sotadica*, our *Tullia and Octavia*.
14. *Session of the Poets*, pp. 6–7.
15. Sig. B1^{v}.
16. The author of *Practical Part of Love* had self-righteously left an account of the 'furor uterinus' in Latin.
17. W. T. Lowndes, *Bibliographer's Manual* (London, 1834) Vol. II, p. 89, attributes the translation to Richard Head. Head referred to it in *Proteus Redivivus*.
18. P.214.
19. This account is based on T. H. Johnson, 'Jonathan Edwards and the "Young Folks' Bible" ', *New England Quarterly*, V (1932), 37–54.
20. Part II, Q.XXVI.
21. Foxon, p. 14.
22. This paragraph is based on O. T. Beale, '*Aristotle's Master-Piece* in America: A Landmark in the Folklore of Medicine', *William and Mary Quarterly*, 3rd Series, XX (1963), 207–22. Palmer, *List of Classics*, has a Latin edition published in London in 1583, an English translation published in Edinburgh in 1595, and further editions from London 1597 and 1607. I have not explored the bibliography of either work. Beale further mentions other pseudo-Aristotelian medical works like the *Last Legacy* brought out in different editions by Borman and Salmon in 1690 and 1700 respectively, and *The*

Compleat and Experienced Midwife, which was one of the books which caused Edwards such consternation in Northampton.

23. This telepathy is also mentioned in *The London Jilt*, Part I, p. 78; Aretino knew of the theory, Rosenthal, ed., *Ragionamenti*, p. 72.
24. Foxon, p. 13 has a note on the bibliography of this best-seller.
25. An earlier edition was advertised by them in the *Term Catalogue* for Trinity 1679.
26. Nathaniel Brooke also took the name of an ancient in vain with his *Oedipus: or, A Resolver of Secrets of Nature and Resolution of Amorous Naturall Problems* by C. M. I have been unable to trace any surviving copies of this work advertised in *Sportive Wit*.
27. Published by P. Briggs, London, 1658. J. B. Sinibaldi was a Neapolitan physician, born at Lionessa, who practised in Rome around the turn of the sixteenth and seventeenth centuries.
28. Gill was High-Master of St Paul's; nock is slang for the cleft between the buttocks, and gillian slang for a wench. This libel is reminiscent of Kirkman's jibes at Zachary Crofton.
29. Cf. *Sportive Wit*, p. 4.
30. This idea was advanced by serious medical writers, e.g. Thomas Cogan, *Haven of Health* (London, 1589), p. 241; Sir Theodore Mayerne, James I's physician also supported it in *Opera Medica* (1703 ed.), p. 83. These sources are cited in L. Stone, *The Crisis of the Aristocracy 1558–1641* (Oxford, 1966), p. 620. In his *An Elizabethan: Sir Horatio Pallavicino* (Oxford, 1956), p. 29, he argues that the widower Sir Horatio was induced to an early remarriage because his aches and pains were exacerbated by a lack of ejaculation. Others were no doubt less 'moral' in satisfying this need. Whether this theory had any part in the apparent growth of masturbation in the seventeenth century is an intriguing question. Less reputable works also referred to the dangers of retaining sperm. *Practical Part of Love*, pp. 13–14.
31. Ashbee claimed that there was a copy of this very rare work in the British Museum, *Index*, p. 264. Wing located only one surviving copy, that in Glasgow University Library.
32. KB 28/31/20; Foxon, p. 13; Hayward Papers, Rochester Box II.
33. Others included John Wynell's *Lues Veneria*, J. Joynel's *Treatise of the French Disease* (1670), Bumoorth's *New Discovery of the French Disease* (1682) and Culpeper's *Treatise*.
34. L. Clarkson, *Death, Disease and Famine* (London, 1975), pp. 40–1.

10 Visual

When he rhetorically asked himself 'Through what part is love [which he had just defined as lust] at first received in', the translator of *Rare Verities* unhesitatingly answered

> The receptacle, and habitation of love is the eye. . . . Love wounding through the eye of a lover, easily laieth open a passage to penetrate the heart. . . . In a word, its the eye which is all in all to the lover; Its his sentinel to perceive all things for his advantage.[1]

The impact of visual imagery, particularly the erotic, is, in comparison with the literary, immediate, even sudden. The relationship between visual receptivity and the ability or willingness to read is a complex one. Presumably societies or groups in which the written word plays an unimportant part place a greater emphasis on the visual, and its impact is relatively greater. Since large portions of Stuart society could not or would not read for pleasure, we might expect therefore that pictures would play an important part in their imaginative lives, and that erotic representations would form a major source for sexual fantasising. Usually this expectation can only be inferred from literary evidence because the pictures themselves have seldom survived; other displays, of course, are known only by report. Nonetheless the seventeenth century appears to have envisaged as wide a gamut of visual erotica as the 1970s, and this inventiveness inevitably conjured up warnings and protests, which in themselves are negative evidence of its pervasiveness and effectiveness.

Admonitions against the effects of looking at erotic images were for Puritans, at least, part of their greater distrust of any works which played upon the imagination: the stage, romances or lyric poetry. This may have been partly because such productions were, taken literally, lies, and more generally because the 'fancy' was a faculty which must be rigidly controlled by right reason and the fear of the Lord rather than being allowed to run riot, especially in the sexual sphere.[2] It is not then surprising to find William Prynne, that arch-Jeremiah of Caroline England, inveighing against 'obscene pictures' among a long list of other evils including lascivious songs, bonfires, grand Christmasses, long hair and laughter. 'Magistrates', he continues 'must take care that no Filthinesse or obscenity be shewed neither in Shewes, nor Pictures. . . .'[3] Goodman's preface to *Hollands Leaguer* cites the most notorious of these obscene pictures: 'Vertue is seldom found to spring from Lacedaemonian Tables, and Chastity much less from *Aretines* pictures.'[4] In May 1649 an ordinance of the Long Parliament was issued against 'scandalous, seditious and libellous pamphlets, papers and pictures'.[5]

It was not only Puritans who attacked scandalous pictures. Robert Carr, an Anglican divine, warned that 'lust works in the eye gazing upon Beauty'. He quoted Clement Alexander's *Admonition to Grace* on the Greeks:

> Nothing was more usual with them than to hang their Rooms with the Pictures of the Gods drawn in the most lascivious postures, engaged in the most filthy and dishonest actions, enough to shame even lust itself.

The lesson to the faithful was plain: 'They must shut their eyes against all uncomely objects, all wanton and lascivious pictures.'[6] The Swiss theologian, J. F. Ostervald, the pastor of Neuchâtel, wrote that 'the infallible sign of an unchast Person' was his 'fixing the sight upon such objects as promote Impurity'. 'A man, though innocent of open sin, who allows himself in all sort of Impurities, has polluted both Body and heart by a hundred shameful Actions, by forbidden looks and dangerous Readings etc.' Rather than closing the eyes, 'Unchast Pictures, obscene and lascivious Draughts and Representations must be utterly banished'.[7] The French, too, seem to have been worried at the beginning of Louis XIV's personal rule about dirty drawings. Chorier twice mentions misanthropes and Catos who have objected to the drawing of postures and forbidden nudity in paintings.[8]

Very few of these condemned pieces have survived. None of the original engravings of 'Aretino's Postures', except an innocuous one in the British Museum, has come down to us.[9] A few sets of cavalier playing cards with titillating engravings still exist.[10]

Among the sale catalogues of libraries sold by auction in the last quarter of the century are one or two appendices or separate catalogues of engravings and prints. The largest collection offered for sale belonged to Richard, Lord Maitland, who also owned a significant amount of literary pornography. Many of the works are impossible to identify because of the vagueness of the entries compiled by Walford, the auctioneer. There are, for instance, 'Antiqitates Romanae, 90 fig. de Sacrific. Baccinal Ludes Priapeia Balneis per Marc Anton, Sylv de Ravenna Bonazon &c.'; or 'Veneres, Gratiae, Cupidines, 54 fig.'; or 'Galenteria by Little Masters 68 fig.'; or 'Priapi Sacra by Lasner after Caratz'. It seems likely from these titles that some of Maitland's large collection depicted at least erotic subjects, if not positively arousing ones.[11] John Dunstan's pictures include such items as 'Sacra Priapi &c well done by Becket', '2 Amorous Drawings by Laroon', '4 large Droll Pieces' and '10 Drawings of several postures', which in this context probably means poses.[12] Typical of the tantalising nature of this evidence is an entry in the catalogue of Dr Rugeley of a painting entitled 'The Woman Taken in Adultery'.[13] It may be a profoundly religious depiction, or it may be profoundly sensual; mere titles are too little to go on.

Occasionally a frontispiece in a book will give some idea of form and style of popular visual eroticism. These would probably be a good deal more innocent and restrained than separately printed cuts, since the eye of the Surveyor of the Imprimerie or licenser would be most likely to fall on the page facing the title-page. *The Practical Part of Love* has a set of four engravings as a frontispiece. In the top left, a man is playing a cello while a woman with protruding bust presents herself to two visiting men; in the top right, a similarly alluringly clad woman, with patches, is sitting on a man's lap beside a bed; they are kissing; in the bottom left, a group sits round a table; wine is flowing and cards being played. One of the men in the mixed group is wearing a pair of horns. In the bottom right, a man is paying a woman in the background, while in the foreground a woman is already in bed and a man is undressing. These are descriptive rather than particularly evocative, except to the most innocent and sheltered of eyes. It is doubtful, too, whether the crude woodcut of a naked women showing her genitalia at the beginning of *Aristotles Master-Piece* would be much more arousing. Some of the cuts which adorned ballads and broadsides might have been faintly titillating. The illustration to *Whipping Tom*, for instance, shows a flagellation scene with naked women being whipped by other women.[14] *The Wanton Virgins Frighted* has a woodcut of a group of naked women and some men, one of whom is clearly making not very subtle sexual advances.[15] Perhaps, in the absence of photographs and sophisticated reproductions of drawings, such crudely executed pictures would turn people on; it is not very easy to imagine. It may be this kind of thing that is meant in 'Lampoon, Though Ladys of Quality's C—ts often itch' in the lines 'Like a Damn'd Debauch Picture upon Alehouse wall/Soe James is ill painted and Expos'd to all.'[16] A case before the Middlesex Justices in 1658 describes a painting by Peter Gnast of a 'deboised [debauched] man and woman' worth15s and belonging to Robert Wright.[17] While in Edinburgh, the London Bully stole a picture of 'A Lady with her breasts half-naked and petticoats up as high as her knees, wielding a net for the trawling of men'.[18]

There is very little information about the trade in dirty pictures. Though the woodcuts we have referred to were of English origin, it is probable that more sophisticated engravings of erotic or pornographic subjects were imported from abroad. *Romes Rarities* (1684) claims that 'pictures are printed in Rome to provoke Lust',[19] and though this is a suspect anti-Catholic source, it gains plausibility from the fact that an Italian called Barnardi seems to have been one of the main dealers in London during the period. He was prosecuted at the Middlesex Quarter Sessions in 1684 for 'exposing, selling, uttering and publishing . . . a packe of cards on which are represented divers obscene postures and figures not fit to be expressed among Christians'. He is described as a painter and a pernicious and scandalous person of the parish of St Margaret's Westminster, and his motive is alleged to be 'debauching and corrupting as well the young persons as others of the lieges and subjects of the said Lord the King'.[20] Twelve years later *The Post Man, and the Historical Account* reported:

> *London*, October 13 [1696]. Yesterday about a Cart load of obscence [*sic*] Books and Cards, tending to promote Debauchery, were burnt near the Gatehouse at *Westminster*, by Mr. *Stephens* Messenger of the Press, in presence of a Justice of peace, and one Mr. Turner a Constable; they belong'd to one Bernardi an Italian.[21]

When Barnardi began trading is unknown, though a reference in Rochester's 'Signior Dildo' suggests that it may have been as early as 1673.[22]

Horner, in the first scene of *The Country Wife* (staged 1675), gives the impression that contraband of this kind was an expected part of any gallant's luggage after a trip to France. 'I have brought over not so much as a Bawdy Picture [or] new Postures,' he claims in his assumed guise of eunuch and mysogynist. He also infers that such imports were sought after by 'the quality', like Lady Fidget.[23]

On 9 March 1688 Henry Hills, Jr, Messenger of the Press, bought from 'a Widow near Mr. Hardins', i.e. Leicester Fields, 'A percell of Cutts' for which he had to pay 9s 6d. Since he was searching for obscene materials there can be little doubt that these were dirty pictures.[24] In Queen Anne's reign, three men were charged with publishing indecent pictures at the Guildhall Sessions; Matthew Heatley and Hans Mullins on 1 November 1707, and Peter Bouch on 20 November 1707. Mullins may have been a Dutchman or a German, as may Bouch.[25] Nicholls' print *The Compleat Auctioner* (c. 1700) clearly displays on his table of books a copy of *Aretine's Postures*. Though he is a disreputable looking individual and seems to trade in the Moorfields red-light district, this kind of sale seems rather too blatant. The first evidence I have come across of indubitably home-grown products,[26] occurs in depositions in the prosecution against *A Compleat Set of Charts of the Coasts of Merryland* in 1745.[27]

Despite the sparseness of information on the trade and its artefacts, there are numerous literary references to the use of erotic representations during the Restoration period. There are, for instance, frequent allusions in the bawdry and imported pornography to *Aretine's Postures*; in *Rare Verities*, readers interested in more details about copulation are referred to them as an authority.[28] The most interesting discussion of them, implying their availability in London, occurs in the dialogue in *The Whores Rhetorick* (1683) on page 171, which was an English interpolation into the Italian original of Pallavicino:

> *Mother Creswel. Aretin's* Figures have no place in my Rhetorick, and I hope will find no room in my Pupil's apartment. They are calculated for a hot Region a little on this side *Sodom*, and are not necessary to be seen in any Northern Clime.
> *Dorothea.* What do you mean by *Aretin's* Figures?
> *M.C.* Only, Child, Six and Thirty Geometrical Schemes which he drew for his own diversion.
> *Dor.* What have I to do with those hard names, are those tame things to be had here?
> *M.C.* Four and Twenty rough draughts may be had for money.
> *Dor.* Pray tell me of something I understand, and which is proper

> for this cooler Region. Though I have an itch to know what you mean by the Figures, for I am sure it is something else than what you have yet told me.
> *M.C. Aretin*, Daughter, among other things was a great Astronomer, and particularly had an exquisite knowledge in the nature of *Mars* and *Venus*, and in all the Seasons, and varieties of their conjunction.

Brothels particularly seem to have been customers for suggestive pictures. Some of these were paintings of the employees, suitably embellished and seductive no doubt, intended, like the advertisements outside strip joints, to encourage the hesitant customer. *The London Bawd* charges a new recruit to her harem £2 for the taking of her likeness. 'The ladies regent at the Bell and Falcon by Moorgate do meliorate their commodities by painting their pictures.'[29] One of the charges to the gull Francion in *The Wandring Whore* is 5s for 'Pictures as B.S. does'. Here it is also said of Mrs Creswell, 'You admit but very few but citizens and citizens' wives whose pictures you keep ready for your best customers to chuse from.'[30] Perhaps the famous portraits of Nell Gwyn by Verelst and Lely in her unlaced smock were greatly superior examples of the kind of pose adopted.[31]

Other brothel ornaments were calculated to arouse lust. Madame Decoy, Aretina's procuress in Shirley's *Lady of Pleasure* (1635) has in her house, 'artful chambers And pretty pictures to provoke the fancy'. Julietta, recently arrived from Venice, tells her colleagues of the illustrations common in brothels in Italy.

> In our private rooms we have a picture of the Italian padlock, Peter Aretines postures curiously painted, and several beautiful pictures stark-naked (not such Landskips as P—— in C—— at Priss Fotheringhams) one with a chamber-pot between her legs, one striving with might and main to enlarge the orifice of her *Mysterium Magnum*, that unfathomed bottom, one laughing at the large pretty cheeks and haunches she's got, and one pointing to another who has lost the hair off her Whib-bob and wears a huge black beard instead of a merkin.[32]

Mrs Wanton, too, in *The Yellow Book* (1656), has 'four or five naked pictures' in her establishment.[33] Madam Creswell, who with her sensitive bourgeois clientele had to take especial care not to offend their sensibilities, had, it will be remembered, a set of erotic drawings in her antechamber, which could quickly be reversed to show scenes fit for a cathedral.[34] The London Bawd describes taking a gentleman into a room with pictures 'representing all the Amours of Ovid's Heathen Gods and Ladies of Pleasure I kept in my house drawn in very amorous and inviting postures. One with her Golden Tresses dishevel'd upon her shoulders and her Breasts naked; another was drawn putting on her smock, a third tying her garters and a fourth in the arms of a Gallant.'[35]

Some imaginative writers attempted rather grander selections of visual aids. Thus, the author of *The Practical Part of Love* has a long description of the walled loggia of the library of the University of Love, which contains statues carved in various postures and a gallery of 'amorous and lascivious pictures as Venus and Mars lying naked together and caught in Vulcan's net' and others so lewd that '*scribere qua pudeat*'. Opposite, at a door always open, is a finely bound folio volume of *Aretine's Postures*, with chained *Emblemmata Amoris* and curious manuscripts with provocative frontispieces.[36] Aretino's description of the frescoes on the walls of the convent parlour is well known; one set appear to be copied from the original postures which had caused such a scandal in Rome. In the second dialogue of the first part Nanna describes how she was presented with what appeared from its cover to be a prayer-book, but when she opened it proved to be 'crammed with pictures of people amusing themselves in the modes and postures performed by the learned nuns . . . one woman was depicted shoving her precious parts through the bottom of a bottomless basket suspended on a pulley, and lowering them on to an enormous rod.'[37] The most extravagant scene-painting appears predictably in *Sodom*. The first scene is simply 'an Antichamber hung round with Aretines Postures'. The second scene in which the ladies first appear

> Changeth to a fair Portico Joyning to a pleasant Garden, adorn'd with many Statues of Naked Men and Women, in various Postures. In the middle of the Garden is a woman representing a Fountain, Standing upon her Head pissing bolt upright.

No more scene directions are given until the sixth and last:

> A Grove of Cyprus Trees, and other Cutts in shapes of Pricks. Severall Arbours, Figures and pleasant Ornaments in a Banqueting House I discover'd. Men Playing on Tabours, and Dulcimores with their Pricks, And Women with Jews Harps in their Cunts, A Youth Sitting under a Palm Tree in a Melancholly Manner Singing.[38]

Although occasionally pornographic or erotic illustrations were justified as instructions to youth, as with the neophyte Alexis in *Tullia and Octavia*—'I have only seen it in a Tableau where the History of Venus was depicted'[39]—they were more frequently thought of as incentives to the 'Obdurate lover' as Mrs Creswell called him.[40] Thus, according to Tullia, the Emperor Tiberius had a picture of Meleagre and Atalantis by Parhasius in his cabinet.[41] The most explicit description of this use is in *Tractatus Hermaphroditus* during the love-making of Barburosa and Margurita. The former, an hermaphrodite, is unable to achieve an erection after an hour of fore-play and so brings out 'a large book amply stor'd with obscene Portraitures wherein amorous combat was curiously describ'd in the utmost variety of Postures which ever were practic'd'.[42]

In the involved metaphor on women (here farms) *Erotopolis* (1684) discussed below, pictures of naked women are described as fantasy-objects for masturbation.

> Landskips of Betty-Land hang by bedsides, especially of those without farms. Some fall to till and manure the very Picture with that strength of imagination, that it is £100 to a penny they don't spoil it with their Instruments of Agriculture; others never so lazy or never so tyr'd before, upon sight of one of these Landskips shall revive again and go as fresh and lusty to their labour.[43]

Turning to what anachronistically may be called 'live shows', we encounter a wide range of productions. At its crudest the sort of performance that Priss Fotheringham put on at her 'Chuck Office' and conceivably the activities of 'Posture Moll' fall in the category of what used to known in the Far East during British Imperial days as 'special exhibishes'. It seems probable that some country dances also had strong sexual connotations. The old crone of Croydon described *Gillian's Dance* to Helena, Lucia's daughter, in *The Practical Part of Love*, as an extremely uninhibited affair. 'All obscenes that come not under the rigour of Law are exercised, as women riding bare-arsed on men's necks and Lip-frog with their Coats tuckt above the middle etc.'[44] Perhaps it was this kind of bucolic abandon that some Puritan critics had in mind when they inveighed against 'Mixt Dances'.

Rope-dancing enjoyed great vogue in the late 1650s and early 1660s. It appears to have consisted of men, like the famous Jacob Hall, who was briefly, on Charles II's ironic suggestion, Castlemaine's lover, and women pirouetting and pointing on ropes slung above their audience's heads. This gave the lewder males an unwonted opportunity to see normally hidden female flesh. This vision was so titillating that according to a punning song in *Choyce Drollery* (1656) it made the audience 'stand' in their excitement.[45] Given this warming up, it was logical for Bette of Wh—— and Bacon Lane to join the crowd at the spectacle 'to draw out a Duck or two' for custom.[46] Another Betty is recorded in a stanza of *Poeta de Tristibus* (1692) as dancing naked while a tumbler played. This talented Londoner also stood on her head and used the rod.[47] Apart from the rumoured antics of conventiclers, nude dancing was a speciality of some of the wilder rakes of the court circle. The ballum rankum, as this orgy was known, took place with whores as partners. The Ballers under Rochester's generalship held their balla ranka at Mrs Bennet's bawdy-house. Daredevil in Otway's *The Atheist* was a specialist.[48] If a lampoon of early 1681 is to be believed, which it probably is not, there were twenty-four French dancing-girls at Whitehall who performed naked before the King, a fringe benefit of the French alliance.[49] Nor is it known whether *Sodom* was performed at court, though it is extremely improbable that it was. However one tableau certainly ranks among the obscenest set of stage directions of the century.

> Six Naked Women, and Six Men appear and Dance. The Men doing Obeisance to the Womens Cunts, kissing and touching them often. The Women doing Ceremonyes to the Mens pricks, kissing them, Quidling and Dandling their Codds, and so fall to Fucking. After which the Women sigh, and the men look simple and sneak off.[50]

The regular appearance of women on the stage after the Restoration transformed the tone of the theatre, as has often been observed. The intention of this revolutionary development, according to the patents granted to Davenant and Killigrew in 1660, was that 'plays might be esteemed not only harmless delights but useful and instructive representations of human life'.[51] The theatre was a coterie affair, with a relatively inclusive and familiar audience, easily jaded, critical and appallingly behaved. They were, in Beljame's words, 'avid of enjoyment, eager to vary their pleasures and incapable of any sort of serious concentration.[52] Managements had therefore to use every conceivable device to catch and hold the attention of its rumbustious onlookers.[53] Actresses were a major weapon. Most of them could not act, having had no training or experience in the early years of the period, but they could at least display their pert charms. Their costumes exaggerated décolletage to the limit. Even more exciting was the strategem of putting them on in male dress. This probably began quite legitimately with the revival of old plays in which boy actors had been realistically scripted to 'masquerade' as boys. It was such a sensation, however, to see an actress in tights that very quickly plays were put on with all-women casts. Pepys was enchanted to see his first woman on the stage in man's clothes: 'The very best legs that ever I saw; and I was very well pleased with it.'[54] The actresses themselves thought of the stage as a route to prosperity and security, through catching the eye of a courtier in the audience. They therefore no doubt exploited the potentialities of 'sex stimulation' to the utmost, frequently with successful results. The fact that an all-woman cast performed Killigrew's extremely bawdy *Parson's Wedding* in October 1664 may have been a blow to the respectability of the fair sex, but it paid dividends in box-office takings and in the ambitions of the 'stars'.[55] Women on the Restoration stage turned the theatre at times into a kind of proto-strip show, and breached contemporary taboos just as thoroughly as the topless go-go dancers who now perform—with double irony—at the old Quaker 'Mount Sion', the Bull and Mouth in Bloomsbury. Lord Buckhurst fell for Nelly, according to a lampoon, after he had caught sight of her charms on stage through her drawers. He stole her from the actor Charles Hart with an allowance of £100 per year: a cheap price for the Earldom of Middlesex, for which he allegedly exchanged her with the king.[56]

A word about fashion, an everyday but highly significant form of sexual display. The *beau monde* and the *haute bourgeoisie* of the Restoration were well aware that clothes could be a great deal more provocative than nudity. Men as different as John Hall, the author of *The Wandring Whore*, Robert Burton, Montaigne and John Bunyan all agreed on this point.[57] The breasts were undoubtedly the female erogenous zones, in Laver's phrase, in our period, and for most of the century. John Ward explained décolletage with the directness of a rural bachelor: 'The breasts and paps of women are styled the teats of love; for which cause women, who studie temptation, doe so much discover them.'[58] Not quite the slant of another rural bachelor and 'poet laureate of the nipple', Robert Herrick, but true nonetheless. *The London Jilt* (1683) confirms the view of the vicar of Stratford-on-Avon with her account of her new corsetry and lacing after the still-born birth of her only 'mistake' had put her bosom 'in need of help'. She laced so tight, and uplifted so high, that she could 'rest her chin on 'em'. So far as we can tell from the few surviving prints of whores, who almost by definition exaggerate the display of the erogenous zones of the day, this was the common mode of ladies of pleasure. Confirmation comes too from the more respectable source of the author of the monitory verses 'Madam be cover'd' (1650). It is the showing forth of 'your naked twins' and their use as a metaphorical 'brothel badge' which offends him: 'These wanton signs direct men *gratis* The high way to your *numquam satis*.'[59] Yet the accomplished coquette realised that revealing too much defeated the object of the exercise.

> The Lilly-azure-vein'd, downe-naked brests
> Move me no more then dugs of other beasts.
> For what to every eye lyes ever bare
> Must needs be valu'd but as profer'd ware.[60]

Yet the hypnotic power of the clad female bosom is negatively demonstrated by a defensive strategy employed by a gentlewoman against an eager but unwelcome suitor, reported by Magdalena in the fifth part of *The Wandring Whore*. When he refused to take no for an answer, 'She uncover'd her breast naked, ranckled, rotten and corrupted, which he espying took leave of her, and never set eye on her after.'[61] The portraits of the schools of Lely and Kneller, and the cruder engravings and woodcuts which have survived, all suggest that ladies of the court and even members of the royal family all erred on the side of revelation rather than concealment. One of the many things that the Restoration restored was a view of the bust.[62]

Legs were deliciously taboo, making them all the more desirable. This was why their display in the controlled sexual environment of the theatre created such a sensation. As we have already noted, Gramont's *Memoirs* have several indications of the mesmeric power of the female leg if accidentally exposed. The most famous example was that of Arabella Churchill's being unseated while riding after coursing greyhounds. The Duke of York, whose taste for ugly mistresses was proverbial, had just begun his ostentatious ogling routine with the maid-of-honour.

> A fall at such speed must have been violent; and yet it proved entirely to her advantage, for, without being hurt, she gave the lie to all the unfavourable ideas that had been formed of her figure in

> judging from her face. The duke alighted to help her. She was so stunned that her thoughts were far from occupied with questions of decency; and those who first crowded around her found her in rather a negligent posture. They could hardly believe that limbs of such exquisite beauty could belong to a face like Miss Churchill's. After this accident, it was noticed that the duke's tenderness and affection increased for her every day; and towards the end of the winter it was clear that she had not been cruel to his passion or made him languish too long.[63]

There is little doubt that inhibitions against exposure were still very strong during the Restoration period. Nudity was very shocking. Rochester told Burnet that he and his fellow rakehells 'in their Frolicks . . . would have chosen sometimes to go naked if they had not feared the people'. When Buckhurst and Sedley did, they were arrested by the watch even though they were 'quality'. The penchant of this circle for displays of nudity—at Woodstock, for instance, as Rochester's guests, or at Ratisbon when Etherege was envoy there—was more probably aimed at shocking, as were occasional Quaker strippings, than at some vague gesture in favour of nature and the libertine philosophy.[64]

Whether the pornographic material that was available in Restoration London had any appreciable effect on sexual mores it is almost impossible to discover. Castlemaine was alleged to appeal to Charles II because 'she knew all the tricks of Aretino that are practiced to give pleasure'. Citizens' wives were in 1642 said, of courtiers and cavaliers, to 'dare meet the roughest gamester of them all in any *posture* whatsoever'.[65] Among the risqué leisure classes there may therefore have been some resultant experimentation. For the great mass of people, however, if the ballad and chapbook evidence is anything to go by, sex remained a relatively mundane and unvaried affair. Despite Aretino and his advertisers, the missionary posture ruled.

NOTES

1. P. 5. We have already mentioned Lowndes's suggestion that the translator was Richard Head.
2. Cecelia Tichi, 'Thespis and the Carnall Hipocrite', *Early American Literature*, IV (1969), 86–103; O. C. Watkins, *The Puritan Experience* (London, 1972), p. 6; Wright, *Middle-Class Culture* has many references to this distrust.

3. *Histriomastix* (1633), quoted in Lamont and Oldfield, eds., *Politics, Religion and Literature*, pp. 34–5.
4. Sig. A3^{v}.
5. Williams, *Journalism*, p. 120.
6. *An Antidote Against Lust* (1690), pp. 11, 38, 141.
7. *The Nature of Uncleanness Consider'd* (1708), pp. 64, 70.
8. *L'Academie des Dames* (1680), Dialogue VII, pp. 74, 86.
9. Foxon, pp. 19–25.
10. E. Goldsmid, ed., *A Pack of Cavalier Playing Cards* (Edinburgh, 1886) has some information in his introduction.
11. *Pinacotheca Maitlandiana* (1689), pp. 3–16.
12. London, 1693.
13. London, ?1697.
14. Bodleian, Douce Ballads, Vol. II, No 251.
15. Ibid., II, No 239.
16. Harvard Mss. Eng. 636 F*, f. 275; ballads were sometimes stuck up on alehouse walls or doors. 'Debauch' has been changed in a seventeenth-century hand to 'Daub'd', but 'Picture' has also been added in; the correct reading of the line is therefore hard to arrive at, though the general sense is not greatly altered. James is the surname of a miss.
17. Jeaffreson, *Middlesex Records*, Vol. III, pp. 275–6.
18. *London Bully*, p. 123.
19. P. 154.
20. Jeaffreson, *Middlesex Records*, Vol. III, p. 239.
21. Foxon, p. 11.
22. 'Signior Bernard has promised a journey to go And bring back his countryman Signior Dildo.' This identification seems far more plausible that Vieth's of a Spanish diplomat. *Rochester's Poems,* p. 57. If it is correct, the inference of the lines is that Barnardi made trips to Italy, perhaps to pick up fresh supplies and ideas. It is an intriguing possibility, that Barnardi, well-known at Whitehall, might have executed the 'severall lascivious pictures' at Rochester's lodge in Woodstock Forest. These were destroyed by his family after his death. Aubrey, cited in Pinto, *Enthusiast*, pp. 147–8.
23. This would support the suggestion in Chorier that France too had become something of a centre for this kind of visual pornography.
24. Foxon, p. 11.
25. Hayward Papers, Rochester Box II.
26. Apart from the amateur efforts at Oxford with a version of *Aretine's Postures*, Thompson, ed., Prideaux Letters, 30–1.
27. Summarised in Foxon, pp. 15–18. Figurines of couples copulating are mentioned in Simon Forman's Papers as being current in Shakespeare's London, but these were used for astrological or occult purposes. Rowse, *Forman*, p. 260.
28. P. 65; see also *Select City Quaeries*, I, p. 1; *The Ladies Champion*, p. 5; *Tullia and Octavia*, p. 94; *POSO*, p. 14; Robert Baron, *Apologie for Paris*, quoted in Carey, p. 214. This is a random selection from contrasting sources.
29. *Select City Quaeries*, III, xv.
30. Part I, pp. 10, 14; cf. Hayward, ed., *Brown, Amusements*, p. 444.
31. The former is reproduced in Latham and Matthews, eds., *Pepys' Diary*, Vol. VIII, opp. p. 334; an engraving by Valck of the latter is in the National Portrait Gallery, London, No 3811. Cf. *London Bawd*, p. 155, quoted below.

32. *The Wandring Whore*, Part II, p. 13.
33. Pp. 7–8.
34. *The Whores Rhetorick*, p. 172.
35. *London Bawd*, p. 155.
36. P. 38.
37. Rosenthal, ed., *Ragionamenti*, pp. 22–3, 52.
38. Dyce 43, ff. 134, 139, 159. The first line should probably read 'others Cutt', i.e. topiary work; 'I discover'd' in line 3 appears to be a mistranscription for 'are discover'd'.
39. Dialogue VII, p. 66. Robert Baron, who mentions *Aretin's Postures* in his *Apologie for Paris* (1649) was only eighteen when he wrote it. Carey, p. 214.
40. *The Whores Rhetorick*, p. 166.
41. *Tullia and Octavia*, Dialogue VII, p. 31.
42. P. 22.
43. P. 15.
44. P. 58.
45. Pp. 31–2.
46. *Strange and True Newes from Bartholomew Fair* (1661), p. 1. A male rope-dancer, leaping and vaulting on a tightrope twelve feet above the ground, appears in *London Jilt*, I, pp. 4–7.
47. P. 30.
48. 1684, pp. 3, 31.
49. Dyce 43, f. 558, 'At the Royal Coffee House'.
50. Dyce 43, f. 142.
51. Cited in Hunt, 'Restoration Acting', p. 179; my account closely follows Hunt's illuminating article.
52. *Men of Letters*, p. 38; cf. pp. 57–61.
53. The gallant in *The Character of a Town Gallant* uses the theatre to display his charms and pick up women. He sleeps during the play which he then damns.
54. *Diary*, 28 October 1661.
55. Beljame, *Men of Letters*, p. 32.
56. Dyce 43, f. 323. The validity of this libel is questioned in Sackville West, *Knole and the Sackvilles*, pp. 114–16.
57. Hill, *World Turned*, p. 314; *The Wandring Whore,* V, p. 8.
58. Diary, I, p. 103.
59. Quoted in Katanka, 'Women of the Underworld', p. 51' cf. *Englands Vanity*, published by Dunton in 1683 attacking naked shoulders, busts and *haute couture* in general, and *A Reprehension of Naked Breasts and Shoulders*, a translation by E. Cooke of Jacques Boileau, *De L'Abus des Nudités de Gorge* (Brussels, 1675), published in London in 1682.
60. *Spes interdictae discedite,* B.M. Add. Mss. 10309, cited in Carey, p. 381.
61. P. 8.
62. For woodcuts, see the title-page of *The Art of Courtship* reproduced in Thompson, ed., *Penny Merriments*, p. 108. This book of compliments shows two obvious court figures, and the woman's breasts are almost completely exposed; they are anatomically in the most extraordinary position.
63. P. 221; cf. p. 241 where Gramont eggs on Miss Stuart to ride at such high speed that the wind will raise her habit.
64. Pinto, *Sedley*, pp. 61–2; *Enthusiast*, pp. 166–7.
65. *St. Hillaries Tears*, p. 6.

11 Metaphorical

Because sex is, and was, a taboo topic, it has always invited the use of metaphor. Aretino's outburst on this topic is well-known, but bears repeating.

> Speak plainly, and say *cu, ca, po*, and *fo*; otherwise thou wilt be understood by nobody if it be not by the Sapienza Capranica, with thy rope in the ring, thy obélisk in the Coliseum, thy leek in the garden, thy key in the lock, thy pestle in the mortar, thy nightingale in the nest, thy dibble in the drill, thy syringe in the valve, thy stock in the scabbard, and the stake, crosier, parsnip, little monkey, the this, the that, the apples, the Missal leaves, the affair, the verbi gratia, the thing, the job, the story, the handle, the dart, the carrot, the root and the shit, mayst thou have it! . . . I shall not say in the snout, since thou wilt walk on the tips of thy shoes. Well, say yes for yes, and no for no, or else keep it to yourself.[1]

Despite this demand for calling a spade a spade, writers of bawdy and much pornography—though not of obscenity—remained remarkably coy, prefering innuendo and indirection. What is depressing about the home-grown variety, mainly bawdy, is the lamentable lack of inventiveness and originality they displayed. We have already quoted enough examples of this aspect of the metaphorical approach to 'unmentionables' to dwell any more on it.

This chapter deals briefly with a more extended use of metaphor, the type which artfully transmuted the male or female body, or more particularly their respective sex organs, into another recognisable field, and proceeded with more or less ingenuity to extract amusement from apparently respectable analogies.

This technique was by no means new with the Restoration. The classical elegists had used it, and there is a passage in Shakespeare's *Venus and Adonis* in which Venus compares her body to a deer park to her uninterested quarry.[2] Some of the drollery poems also explored these metaphorical possibilities in a crude way.[3] Yet, so far as I am aware, the first of several book-length metaphorical pieces was not produced until 1684. This was *Erotopolis: The Present State of Betty-Land*, published by Thomas Fox. It has been attributed to Charles Cotton, mainly on the grounds that part of the book is a burlesque of Virgil, but this evidence is rather slim. The title was amended in the Michaelmas *Term Catalogue* for 1684 to *The Kingdom of Love.*[4]

In one sense it is a parody of those books describing counties, regions or countries which were such a staple of seventeenth-century publishing, more recently used as a means of trying to stimulate emigration to British overseas plantations. *Erotopolis* is, however, primarily an ambitious bawdy joke. The name 'Betty' had strong sexual connotations in the seventeenth century, somewhat similar to our 'Fanny'. Whores and enthusiastic amateurs were frequently christened Betty in rogue literature, ballads and chapbooks.

This extended and elaborate pun follows the pattern of more conventional regional studies. We learn its geographical position, provinces, climate, soils, crops, flora and fauna, systems of tenure and husbandry, occupations and classes of inhabitants, common diseases, history and antiquities. Sometimes the strain of maintaining the allegory tells over its 174 pages, and the author strays into the easier paths of bawdry. Apart from the original idea, the general quality of the humour is pretty mundane. *Erotopolis* is basically hackwork.

Betty-Land, we learn, adjoins the Isle of Man, and its extent lies between sixteen and forty-five degrees. Its ruling planet is Venus, its tropic Capri*corn*— a pun on cornuting or cuckolding— and few of its inhabitants are born under the sign of Virgo. Its provinces include Bedford, Will-shire and the sparsely populated Guelder-land and its chief cities are Pego—slang for penis—and Lipstick. Temperatures vary. Sometimes it is bitterly cold, especially 'when the refreshing influences of wealth and youth decay' in the men, but sometimes it is so hot that if you touch the soil you will lose a member. The soil has magic qualities.

> If a man do but take a piece of it in his hand, 'twill cause (as it were) an immediate *Delirium* and make a man fall flat upon his face upon the ground, where if he have not a care he may chance to lose a limb, swallowed up in a whirlpit, not without the effusion of the choycest Part of his blood.[5]

Nonetheless, the soil is delightful to manure, and men take great pleasure in ploughing and sowing it, so much so that they will give

£1 or £1000 for a spot not 'so big as the palm of your hand' and tend it once or twice every night. Of the different kinds of soils, the light or dark brown seldom lie fallow, but short leases are recommended for the black 'lest your back pay for the tillage'; when barren 'the soyl cleaves and gapes moisture'. The main crop resembles mandrakes, and the commonest bird is the wagtail; the only fauna are horned beasts, except for the hare and coney, which 'are enough to stock the country as large as it is'. So far as fish are concerned there is 'infinite number of crabs and carps' in the one great river; anyway, the husbandmen 'are for flesh'. The main topographical feature is a great mountain which often swells for three-quarters of a year, portending a dear year ahead; when it starts swelling some male inhabitants are so terrified that they run away. The whole of Betty-Land offers 'a very fair prospect, the more delightfull the more naked it is'. Landholding is usually for life, though some hire private farms where neither spade nor dibble have entered before—virgin lands, as it were. The yeomen in Betty-Land are great spenders, and there is such a world of common there that 'husbandmen are not to be blamed for enclosures'. One of the greatest pests in this pleasant place are decoy ducks, especially alluring for Widgeon, Gulls and Dotterels. These creatures, though 'many times burnt in their own nests', spread their tails like so many peacocks, and are ruinous to husbandmen.

To this point[6] the author has maintained the analogy with brio and originality. Thereafter his inventiveness flags. The history of Betty-Land is mainly that of classical times. Gods like Jupiter and Hercules were industrious, even frenetic, ploughmen; Menander, Aristophanes, Anacreon, Plautus, Terence, Tibullus, Ovid, Martial and Petronius all wrote on tillage and husbandry of their times. The inhabitants then were generally very amorous and libidinous, and the spot belonging to Messalina was ploughed and harrowed twenty-five times in a day and a night. The husbandmen then were drained and exhausted with continual labour.

The nature of the allegory changes completely with the description of the inhabitants, which starts on page 59 and extends for most of the rest of the book. Instead of Betty-Land representing the female body, the shepherdesses of the country take over as the female of the species. This is far less original or clever, and the tone of the wit declines accordingly. The shepherdesses are industrious horn-makers, their art improved by such reading as romances and *The School of Venus*. They also make (man-catching) nets. The sirens, or whores, of the country are then described; they are most numerous and 'carry all before 'em'. The narrative at this stage collapses into a peep-show tour of the London stews in Lincoln's Inn, Lutiners Lane and Cole Yard, with the varied sights to be seen through crannies—the inevitable impotents, deflowerers, gulls and perverts. A swipe is taken at Catholics with the listing of Donnas Joan and Olympia as notable sirens, and a reference to the number of windfalls which the hurricane of confession has blown down. Fair Anglican play is observed with thrusts against Puritans, 'Sir Rogers or Hypocritical Devotists', the lecherous female members of Baxter's congregation and the minister who hands out wholesome piety to his flock, though his wife claims that he has the pox.

Towards the end there is a return to the original idea with a description of the sports and pastimes of Betty-Land, namely mounting and riding, running at the ring with the lance, card-games like 'In and In' and exhausting dancing sessions which are so lively that the shepherdesses 'can hardly go for the weight on their bellies'. The diseases are the giant-like Priapismus, the furor uterinus and the 'morbus, Neapolitan, Hispanic, Gallic, American, Mexican, Venereus, Lues Venerea, Gonorrhea simplex, Gonorrhea faetida, in English, the Pox'.

Like many bright ideas, *Erotopolis* goes on too long, way beyond the natural span of the joke. As a new departure, its interest is mainly for the future. The eighteenth century experimented with this type of metaphor in a briefer and more effective way. In 1732 appeared *The Natural History of the Arbor Vitae, or, The Tree of Life*, published in 'Dondon' for 'The Society of Gardeners', to which is appended *The Natural History of the Frutex Vulvaria* . . . By Philogynes Clitorides, published by W. James.[7] Thomas Stretzer's *A New Description of Merryland* was published in 1740 and reached a tenth edition by 1742 and his *Merryland Displayed* followed in 1741, and was reprinted in 1751. Curll, unspeakable but irrepressible, owned the copyright.[8] We have already encountered *A Compleat Set of Charts of the Coasts of Merryland wherein are exhibited all the Ports, Harbours, Creeks, Bays, Rocks, Settings, Bearings, Gulphs, Promontories, Limits, Boundaries &c.* (1745). No copy is known to survive, but the 1751 edition of *Merryland Displayed* describes the map of Merryland as being remarkably similar to the anatomical plates of M. Morriceau, the famous French man-midwife. The alleged author of the latter, Roger Pheuquwell, sums up the methods of the genre with the candour of the insider. 'There is not a baudy word in it; but . . . there not being a Page, scarce a Paragraph, without some smutty

Allusion, which it seems now-a-Days is not looked on as immodest.' Which doleful comment on the times aptly ends our analysis of works 'unfit for modest ears'.

In the preceding eleven chapters we have examined a welter of disreputable works published in England in the second half of the seventeenth century. It is clear that much of the bawdy was aimed at the lowest classes of the literate, as the obscene libels and lampoons appealed to the court circle. The style and allusions of the imported pornography suggest that a relatively high level of education and sensibility would be needed for understanding and appreciation. Some topics would be justified by their satirical content, though the sexual ridicule and abuse heaped on Puritanism, Catholicism, marriage or monarchy may well have masked deep-seated fears, guilts and doubts. As we run the gamut from simple-minded bawdy to sophisticated pornography, the purpose of sexuality changes dramatically, from quick, uncomplicated satisfaction of animal urges to the exploration of every kind of sensual pleasure. The focus alters too: from the sex-drives employed as narrative motivators for funny, cunning or lunatic responses, sexuality becomes an object of fascination in itself, a human activity to experiment with and examine microscopically. In the fantasy world of pornography, the obligations, the conventions, the prohibitions and the inhibitions of the real world could be evaded. The need for such cerebral escapism, however, argues both new sensual expectations which real life could not gratify, and a sense of guilt which could only seek their satisfaction in the private world of the book.

NOTES

1. Cited by Frantz, ' "Leud Priapians" ', 157.
2. Lines 229–40.
3. E.g. 'The Threading of the Needle', 'A Medly' in *Lusty Drollery*, pp. 126, 104.
4. It was reprinted in January 1741 in *The Potent Ally*; Foxon, p. 17.
5. Sperm was currently thought to be a distillation formed from the blood.
6. P. 34.
7. These have been groundlessly attributed to Thomas Stretzer. Atkins, *Sex in Literature*, pp. 218–19, sees a description of the phallus in *The Cabinet of Love* as the origin of these squibs, but Foxon's suggestion that they were skits on Philip Miller's *Catalogus Plantarum* (1730) carried more weight. They appear to have been reprinted in *The School of Venus* (not our book) in 1739, and again in 1741. Foxon, p. 17.
8. Foxon, p. 17.

Part III

Writers and Readers

12 Writers and Readers

Most of our authors preferred understandably to remain anonymous. The traceable minority fall into two groups: wealthy amateurs, like Rochester of Fane, or professionals dependent on the fragile crutches of patronage or publishers' whim. The painful fate of the protégés, has been described by Beljame;[1] Rochester aptly compared their lot to that of the whore: enjoyment and ejection. Publishers faced a competitive world, understocked with buyers, overstocked with producers; then as now, the author suffered. His copyright sold for derisory sums: a pound or two per ballad or chapbook, five for *Paradise Lost*.[2] Royalties averaged ten per cent, but impressions were small and prices minimal.[3] Some stationers waxed fat;[4] many writers, like Head, Brown, John Phillips, Dunton, Lee, Otway or Wycherley, died in poverty.

With so many authors unknown, generalisations are hazardous. Yet one similarity between many identified writers deserves mention: a surprising number came from Puritan or Calvinist 'low church' backgrounds. The pornographer, Thomas Nashe, was the son of an East Anglian Puritan preacher.[5] Marlowe's mother appears to have been a Precisian.[6] Rochester grew up under the zealous tutelage of his mother Anne St John and John Martin, master of Burford Grammar School.[7] Fane's mother was likewise a staunch Calvinist.[8] Three Rochester protégés, Oldham, Lee and Crowne, were the sons of dissenting ministers, the last schooled at Harvard under the unbending John Norton.[9] Christopher Fishbourne, who attempted obscene verse if not *Sodom*, came from a Cromwellian family, as did Wycherley.[10] Two nephews and pupils of Milton, John and Edward Phillips, joined the stable of the early smut-pedlar Brooke. Even Milton's associate, Andrew Marvell, son of the Puritan minister of Hull, could lapse into obscenity in his satires and write sexually suggestive lyrics.[11] Butler's alleged Puritan tutelage has never been verified,[12] but both Dunton[13] and Kirkman[14] came from Calvinistic backgrounds. Richard Head's ordained father was probably similarly inclined. Some, of course, had unimpeachable cavalier upbringings, like Sedley or Dorset. Nonetheless, the number and the often highly salacious nature of the writings of the Calvinist-raised group raises significant questions, to which we will return in the conclusion.

If the attribution of seventeenth-century erotica is a back-breaking and often unrewarded task, the tracing of readers is a labour of Hercules. Even nowadays, our knowledge of habitual pornophiles is based on such impressionistic hunches as 'if we lift the dirty old mackintosh, as likely as not, there's a pin-striped suit underneath'.[15]

The Stuart period had its 'dirty old mackintosh' myths about readers of disreputable literature. In popular legend, as reported by amoral eroticists and moral reformers, readership was ascribed to whores, young gallants, women of all ages and classes, nuns and Puritans.[16] Apart from doubts whether many whores could or would read anything, this strange assortment suggests a strong element of projection. Whores and gallants would be natural scapegoats for the respectable; insinuations about the fair sex or the pious feed a human need for ridicule and deflation.

Actual readers in a still predominantly devout society—we should not underplay the genuineness of repentance of a Rochester, a Sedley or a Buckingham—would likely be even more furtive than at present. Indeed secrecy itself could well have been titillating.[17] Pepys, for instance, left copies of neither *La Puttana Errante* nor *L'Escholle des Filles*; he kept his *Poems on Several Occasions* hidden in a locked scriptor drawer.[18] Contemporaries, like Rochester's family, or later generations, destroyed or suppressed compromising works and evidence.[19]

Proof of reading is often hard to demonstrate. Ownership does not prove readership—though with our subject it implies it—any more than non-ownership proves non-readership. Books could be borrowed, read in libraries or browsed through in booksellers. The mere mention of a title is insufficient testimony; if everyone who named *Aretine's Postures* had actually seen them, more than one set would surely have survived in contemporary catalogues.[20]

The two best types of evidence of readership occur in literary and private materials. Thus, for instance, Head's knowledge of *The Practical Part of Love* is obvious from his plagiarisms in *The Miss Display'd*. Rochester's apt allusions to the *Cena Trimalchionis* in 'Timon' argue his familiarity with the *Satyricon*.[21] A wide reading in classical pornography, della Casa's works on sodomy and Chorier's *Satyra Sotadica*, is the background to the Calvinist-educated Hadrian Beverland's *Peccatum Originale*.[66] Private papers as revealing as Pepys's Diary are of course rare. We can, however deduce from Ward's Diary that he had read the leading classical eroticists, *Hudibras* and Harvey's *Great* and *Little Venus Unmaskt*.[23] Robert Boyle admitted to youthful dalliance with erotic and bawdy verse, as did Milton.[24] Letters occasionally enlighten. One of Donne's reveals his familiarity with Aretino's *Ragionamenti*—which he shared with Jonson and Dryden—and also Sir Henry Wotton's desire to read it.[25] St Evremond's correspondence shows the delight of Waller and Buckingham in Petronius.[26] Appended notes by Thomas Style, the copyist, demonstrate his and Magalotti's interest in court obscenity.[27] A letter of Henry Savile's reveals Halifax as a customer for works 'forbid'.[28] We have already quoted Wesley's recollections of pornography circulating in London dissenting academies.[29]

Signatures in books witness at least ownership. Thus we know that Thomas Barlow, sometime Calvinist and later Bishop of Lincoln, had a copy of *La Puttana Errante* and Anthony a Wood one part of *The Wandring Whore* and Lord Burghley a *Ragionamenti*.[30] Wood's manuscript note 'I could never see any other parts but this' is as good a sign of keen interest in the contents as Henry Vaughan's handwritten index on the flyleaf of his copy of Sinibaldi's *Geneanthropeia*.[31] Bibliomaniacs, however, like Luttrell, owner of *The London Jilt*, Thomason, of many lewd ephemera of the period 1640 to 1660, or Francis Bernard, whose 13 000 books included numbers of pornographic works, may have been less concerned with contents.

Commonplace books and handwritten copies of disreputable material are all too often frustratingly anonymous, like the recorder of two versions of *Sodom* and an extract from *Satyra Sotadica* in a commonplace book now at Princeton. However, the handwriting of the Hamburg copy of *Sodom* appears to be that of Beverland,[32] and Puritan New Englander John Saffin's reading of *Poems on Several Occasions* is proved by extracts in his commonplace book.[33] Other surprising New England tastes have been uncovered from similar sources.[34] Scholars better versed in the literary and manuscript materials of Restoration England could no doubt expand this list of readers.

Unfortunately booksellers' records, giving buyers, do not survive. The Boulter and Chiswell invoices of consignments to Boston do not, in the cases of *Poems on Several Occasions*, *Venus in the Cloister*, *The London Jilt* and *Nugae Venales*, indicate orderers, though it is surprising to find the name of Mr (Cotton) Mather—later the leading minister of his generation—against the bawdy *Fifteen Real Comforts of Matrimony*.[35] The 1668 despatch of two copies of Ovid's *Art of Love*, the occasionally obscene *Merry Drollery* and collections of bawdy stories from London to the city of John Knox is unexpected.[36] Again, however, customers are not specified. Occasionally auction catalogues give buyers' names. In 1682 Dryden was the successful bidder for 'French novels, amours and galanterie', as well as Barrin's rendering of *Les Epítres et Toutes les Elegies Amoureuses d'Ovide*.[37] This route, however, has not led me to any pornophiles.

Two other sources remain: library and auction catalogues. The ten library catalogues tabulated (see Table 1) represent only a sample,[38] which a thorough search of Oxford and Cambridge college benefactions, wills, inventories and family papers would multiply. Two conclusions about the spread of holdings are immediately obvious. Firstly, classical and continental works preponderate, with Petronius as a clear favourite. The main English contribution to disreputable literature (*Nugae Venales* to *Fifteen Real Joys*) is completely unrepresented. The entries for court versifiers, anti-Catholic smears and quasi-medical works (inflated perhaps by the fact that Locke and Sloane were physicians) hardly redress the balance. Secondly, pornography and obscenity—especially contemporary works—are rare in comparison with bawdry. Indeed the least exceptionable works, amours and drolleries, are the best represented.

These conclusions must be qualified, however, by several special factors. Three of the catalogues—Gostling, Molyneux and Plume—are of benefactions; *Venus in the Cloister* or *Tullia and Octavia* are hardly suitable bequests for town or college libraries. One list, Etherege's, is almost certainly partial, with only thirteen English works in a total of eighty-eight. Gostling was only twenty-seven when he died in 1675, before the porn-peak of the 1680s. Coffin lived in remote Devonshire, reliant on his prudish London correspondent Lapthorne.[39] Harley was one of the great collectors of his generation, possibly more concerned with rarity and quality than with content.

If we examine the backgrounds of owners of pornography and obscenity in the list, the Puritan background is again evident. Pepys, Locke and Harley all came from devoutly Puritan families and were educated in that persuasion.[40] Sir Richard Ellys, of

TABLE 1. Library Catalogues

	Aristophanes	P Apuleius	Catullus, Tib, Prop.	O Martial	Ovid	P Petronius	Plautus	O Priapeia	P Aretino, Ragionamenti	Boccaccio	Gaya, Nuptials	Leti, Olympia	Leti, Putanismo	P Pallavicino	Poggio, Facetiae	P Puttana errante	Brantome	Cent Nouvelles	Putanisme d'Amsterdam	Rabelais
Blickling (Ellys)°						6			1	3			1	1		1	1			
Etherege			1							1										
Gostling†				1			1													
E. Harley°	8	7				8				5				2	1					
Locke°		1	1			4		1	2	1	1			1	1			1		2
Pepys°																		1		
Molyneux	1					3	1											1		1
Plume†		1	1	2		2	1					1			1					
Coffin	1	1	1	1			1								1					
Sloane°	1	1													1					
Total	11	11	4	4	0	23	4	1	3	10	1	1	1	4	5	1	1	3	0	3

	Amours, Galanterie	Celestina	Guzman Sp. Rogue	P School of Venus	P Chorier, Tullia and Octavia	Whores Rhetorick	Anti-Puritan	Drolleries, Jest-books	Nugae Venales	Crafty Whore	English Rogue	London Bawd	London Bully	London Jilt	Miss Display'd	Practical Part of Love	Wandring Whore	Fifteen Joys Rash	Fifteen Real Joys	Anti-matrimonial
Blickling (Ellys)°																				
Etherege	2																			
Gostling†	4							4												
E. Harley°																				2
Locke°	7							9												
Pepys°	4			1*				3												
Molyneux																				
Plume†	1							3												
Coffin	5		1				1	3												2
Sloane°					1*		1	3												
Total	28	0	1	1	1	0	2	25	0	0	0	0	0	0	0	0	0	0	0	4

	Oldham's Satires	O Rochester, P.O.S.O.	Adamite	Eng. Monastery Lisbon	Eve Reviv'd	Jesuits Morals	Nuns Complaint	Romes Rarities	P Venus in the Cloister	Aristotle M & P	Rare Verities	Venus Unmaskt & V.D.	Erotopolis
Blickling (Ellys)°													
Etherege													
Gostling†													
E. Harley°		3											
Locke°												9	
Pepys°		1					1	2					
Molyneux													
Plume†	1							1		1		1	
Coffin						1						1	
Sloane°											1	1	
Total	1	4	0	0	0	1	1	3	0	1	2	12	0

NOTES TO TABLES 1 and 2

1. Titles are arranged in the following order: Classical: Greek, then Latin; Continental: Italian, French and Spanish. Amours, Galanterie are sentimentally erotic romances of court or gallants' intrigues. English title order corresponds to chapter order. Drolleries, jest-books are bawdy anthologies in verse or prose; Anti-Puritan lumps together works like *Hudibras*, Royalist scandal-sheets or *The Rump*; Anti-Matrimonial complements *Fifteen Comforts* with similar bawdry.
2. Titles marked P or O are those defined as pornographic or obscene.
3. Starred listings are in the original rather than an English translation.
4. Owners who were clergymen are marked†, owners of pornographic or obscene books are marked°; booksellers' stock sales are marked*.
5. There is an under-recording of classical erotica as these were included some time after the start of listing.

Nocton, Lincolnshire, was a zealous convert from Arminianism in his thirties. His adviser was the Calvinist-raised emigré Michel Maittaire.[41] Hans Sloane was born in 1660, so, although his father was a Cromwellian official, his upbringing was unaffected by the Puritan dominance of education.

Even Gostling, Plume and Coffin owned books which strict Dissenters would have viewed with distinct distaste; amours, for instance, and bawdy drolleries, Latin and Italian eroticists. It comes therefore as some surprise to find Gostling the son of a Norwich Puritan family,[42] Plume presented to a benefice by Richard Cromwell[43] and a branch of the Coffin family leading colonists in Massachusetts.[44] Plume's and Coffin's theological holdings argue a continuing sympathy for Calvinism.[45]

In the 1670s the Dutch innovation of auctioning libraries of the recently deceased was imported into England, and rapidly gained popularity.[46] Catalogues, increasingly well-organised, were printed for these sales and London stationers like William Cooper, Edward Millington, Benjamin Walford and John Bullord became specialist auctioneers. Occasionally booksellers disposed of stock by this means, and provincial sales were held.[47] The catalogues vary greatly in length, but average about fifty pages.[58] The ninety-seven tabulated (see Table 2), from the unrivalled British Museum collection,[49] therefore contain nearly 250 000 titles. Those chosen represent all between 1676 and 1699 where ownership can safely be ascribed, as opposed to group or anonymous sales.

The catalogues do not, of course, indicate proof of readership, or even of purchase.[50] Under-recording may well have resulted from the removal of embarrassing titles by legatees, executors or auctioneers, or by their relegation to such categories as 'Fifty small unstitcht Books' or 'A Bundle of Pamphlets'. Occasional repeating titles may infer that other stock was smuggled into a catalogue. On two occasions books published after the bibliophile's death are listed.[51] On the other hand, fifteen sales occurred before the peak of 1683, and elderly men would anyway be less likely customers for smut. Forty-one, or nearly half, of the bibliophiles were clergymen. So, on balance, this group would probably record below average holdings of dirty books. An analysis of catalogues for 1700 to 1730 would almost certainly show a higher proportion of scandalous works listed.

TABLE 2. Sale Catalogues

Year	Catalogue	Aristophanes	P Apuleius	Catullus, Tib, Prop.	O Martial	Ovid	P Petronius	Plautus	O Priapeia	Total Classics	P Aretino, Ragionamenti	Boccaccio	Gaya, Nuptials	Leti, Olympia	Leti, Putanismo	P Pallavicino	Poggio, Facetiae	P Puttana Errante	Brantome	Cent Nouvelles	Putanisme d'Amsterdam	Rabelais	Amours, Galanterie	Celestina	Guzman Sp. Rogue	Total European – Amours	P School of Venus	P Chorier, Tullia and Octavia	Whores Rhetorick	Anti-Puritan	Drolleries, Jest-books	Nugae Venales	Crafty Whore	English Rogue	London Bawd	London Bully	London Jilt	Miss Display'd	Practical Part of Love	Wandring Whore	Fifteen Joys Rash	Fifteen Real Joys	Anti-matrimonial	Oldham's Satires	O Rochester, P.O.S.O.	Adamite	Eng. Monastery Lisbon	Eve Reviv'd	Jesuits Morals	Nuns Complaint	Romes Rarities	P Venus in the Cloister	Aristotle M & P	Rare Verities	Venus Unmaskt & V.D.	Erotopolis
1676	1. L. Seaman†	3	1		3	1		2		10																0																														
1677	2. H. Henchman†		1	3	1	1	1	1		8					1					1		1	6			3																							1		1					
	3. Cancelled																																																							
	4. Cancelled																																																							
	5. Cancelled																																																							
1680	6. S. Charnock†		1	1	1	1	1	1		6																0				2	1																									
	7. T. Watson†	2	1		2	1	1			7				1												1				1	1								1																	
	8. Visct. Downe°		2	1	1	1	1	1		7	1	1			1			1	1			1	2		1	7																														
1681	9. E. Palmer		2							2																																														
	10. N. Paget					1				1																																														
	11. S. Brook	2		2	2	1		1		10																				1																	1									
1682	12. R. Smith°	1	1			2	1			5	1						2						8			3					8	1		1																					1	
	13. W. Rea°					1				1					1			1		1			1	1		4					4			1																					1	
	14. J. Parsons									0					1								1			12					5			1							1												1		3	
	15. J. Humphry		1							1		2								1				1		4					5																									
1683	16. J. Arthur†					1				1		1											1	1	1	3				1	1																									
	17. S. Wilson									0													1			0				1	1																									
	18. W. Whateley†		1							1					1								7	1		2					5							1																	1	
	19. B. Walton†									0																0																	2													
	20. D. Rogers†									0		1											7			1					2			1										1					1	1					2	
	21. J. Collins									0																0																														
	22. C. Adams†									0																0					1																									
	23. J. Lloyd†°									0	1												5			1					1																			1						
1684	24. J. Gunter°									0													2			0	1*															1														
	25. R. Chace†									0						1										1																														
	26. M. Smallwood†					1				1															1	1					1																									
	27. J. Owen†									0																0																		1												
	28. F. Kendal*					2				2																0										1							1					2				1	1		1	
1685	29. J. Warner†°									0		1				1						1		1		4					1											1*														
	30. R. Lee†									0																0																														
	31. T. Parkhurst*									0					1								3			1											1	1								1				1						
	32. P. Hushar									0																0																														
	33. R. Davis*									0			1									1	3			2					1					1															1					
1686	34. E. of Anglesey°		1			3	1			5					1											1				4	6												1	1	1					1						
	35. R. Chiswell*									0		4														4					3					1	1					1	1			1		1								1

TABLE 2. *(continued)*

Year	Name	Aristophanes	P Apuleius	Catullus, Tib, Prop.	O Martial	Ovid	P Petronius	Plautus	O Priapeia	Total Classics	P Aretino, Ragionamenti	Boccaccio	Gaya, Nuptials	Leti, Olympia	Leti, Putanismo	P Pallavicino	Poggio, Facetiae	P Puttana Errante	Brantome	Cent Nouvelles	Putanisme d'Amsterdam	Rabelais	Amours, Galanterie	Celestina	Guzman Sp. Rogue	Total European – Amours	P School of Venus	P Chorier, Tullia and Octavia	Whores Rhetorick	Anti-Puritan	Drolleries, Jest-books	Nugae Venales	Crafty Whore	English Rogue	London Bawd	London Bully	London Jilt	Miss Display'd	Practical Part of Love	Wandring Whore	Fifteen Joys Rash	Fifteen Real Joys	Anti-matrimonial	Oldham's Satires	O Rochester, P.O.S.O.	Adamite	Eng. Monastery Lisbon	Eve Reviv'd	Jesuits Morals	Nuns Complaint	Romes Rarities	P Venus in the Cloister	Aristotle M & P	Rare Verities	Venus Unmaskt & V.D.	Erotopolis
	36. W. Whitwood	1			1	1				3							1									1					10							1																		
	37. E. Castell†									0		1					1						1	1	1	4																														
	38. J. Chamberlaine†	2	1		1	1	1	1		7				1												1					3																		1							
1687	39. T. Bowman*	4	1		6	7	5	8		31	1											1	10			2					8	2		1				1			1		7							1			1			
	40. C. Mearne*					1				1						1	1		1				7			3	1*	1*															4													
	41. W. Coventry°					1	1			2	2												5			2																														
	42. J. Maynard†°																									0								1								1	1								1	1	2			
	43. E. Wray	1				2	2			5		2			1								1			3															1		1	1												
	44. T. Jacomb†						1			1																0															1															
1688	45. Trade Sale*					1				1									1				5			1	1*				7																								1	
	46. W. Gulston†	1	2		2	2	1	2		10							1							1		2																														
	47. Ld. Maitland°						1			1		1										1	14		1	3	1*				4						1							1	1			1							2	
1689	48. Norwich Sale*									0		1													2	3					9										1		2	1												
1690	49. D. of Lauderdale°									0	1	1		1		1				2				1		7																								1						
1691	50. R. Cudworth†	1	1	1	1	2	1	3		10																0					1																									
	51. J. Lake†						1			1		1											1		1	2				2	2																									
	52. P. Mason							1		1		1			1										1	3					4												2	1												
	53. T. Bromley									0	1				1								3			2				2							1		1					1											1	
	54. D. Lapthorne		2	1	1	1	1	1		7		1			1											2					3												2												2	
1692	55. N. Rolls*									0											1					1								1			1						2		1			1		1						
	56. J. Barham°									0																0					6												2	1	1										1	
	57. J. Hoyle°			1	2	2		1		6	1				2						1	1	2		1	6	1*																						2	1		1				
1693	58. M. Blewitt†°	1		1	1	2		1		6	1	1					1					1	2			4						1																								
	59. R. Peade†			1	1					2				1												1																														
	60. Norwich Sale*									0													1		1	1					9			1																						
	61. S. Morgan									0													1			0								1															1							
	62. J. Cropper°	1				1	1	1		4		1								1			5			2					1						1								1										1	
	63. T. Sparkes†°		1							1																0				1												1		1	1								1		2	
	64. J. Dunstan									0																0					1			1																						
	65. J. Meggott†	1	1		1			1		4		1														1																														
	66. J. Reynolds†					2				2		1			1								5			2					5			1			1						1													
1694	67. T. Grey†		1				1			2		1														1					1										1					1		1								
	68. E. Ashmole									0		1			1											2											1					1	1													
	69. A. Palmer°				1	1	1			3																0					2			1																		1	1			
	70. T. Bennet†°									0		3											1		3	6			1																				2		1				1	
	71. M. Wright									0		1														1																														
	72. J. Starkey					2	1			3		1														1																														
	73. T. Britton									0													3			0					3		1	1			1	1	1				2					1								
	74. H. Wilkinson						3			3																0																														
	75. N. Coga†	1		1		1	1			4		1														1																														

1695	76. R. Belwood°		1		1	1	1			4													1			0					4													1	1		1			1						
	77. J. Tillotson†						1			1		2											1			2																														
	78. A. Littleton†				2	1				3		1														1					2	1																							1	
	79. J. Scott†									0													3			0																								1	1					
	80. J. Partridge									0		1											1			1						1		1			2						2					1	1				1			
	81. Ld. Stawel°		1							1		3				1	1		1				2		2	8					2												1						1						1	
1696	82. G. Ashwell†	1	2	1	2	1	1			8													2			0					6												1													
	83. Visct. Preston°	1				3	1	2		7		1				1						1	2			3					2																									
	84. - Norton†	1				1		1		3																0					1																									
1697	85. W. Bassett†			1				3		4																0					1												2	1												
	86. S. Annesley†				1					1																0																														
	87. A. Horneck†		1				1	1		3									1				2			1																														
	88. R. Grove†	1	2	3	1	1	2	1		11							2								1	3																									1					
	89. Ld. Brereton°		1					1		2	1						1						4			2					2																				1			1		
	90. A. Scattergood†	1	1	3	2	1	1	4		13		1											1			1																							1							
	91. M. Harding†°									0																0					2													1	1					1						
	92. - Rugeley		1				1	1		3										1						1					1																		1							
1698	93. N. Knatchbull°		1		2		1	1		5	1	2								1		1	12			5				5	8														1								1			
	94. W. Levinz†°									0	1					1		1	2				14	1		6															1					1									2	
	95. F. Bernard°	5	19	11	7	14	19	13		88	4	3				2	2	1		2	1	4	17	3	3	23	1		1		11	1		1			1						2	1	1	1			2	1	1		2			1
1699	96. J. Lloyd†	2	1			1	1*	1*		6													12			0				3	11			1									7		1				1				1		2	
	97. W. Anderton						1*			1																0																														
	98. - Du Prat	2	1	2	3	3	2	1		14		1					1		1				14	1		4					6												1			1*			2							
	99. J. Jones*				1	1	1	1		4													22		1	1				4				1				1											1				1			
	100. R. Hough°	1	3	2	3	2	3	2		16	1	1	2			1				1	1		23	1	1	8	1*	1*			11													1								1*			3	
	Grand Totals	39	57	36	53	77	66	59	0	387	16	47	3	4	15	9	14	4	8	11	4	14	247	14	22	185	7	4	2	27	198	7	1	17	0	3	11	6	3	0	7	6	48	15	11	6	2	8	18	12	8	5	13	1	29	1
	Less Booksellers	35	56	36	46	65	60	50	0	348	15	42	2	4	14	8	13	4	6	11	3	12	196	14	18	166	5	1	2	23	161	5	1	13	0	0	8	3	3	0	5	5	31	14	10	4	2	4	11	9	7	4	10	1	27	

The pattern of Table 2 shows marked similarities with Table 1. The classics again predominate, led by Ovid and Petronius; European editors and publishers, notably the Elzevir Press, prove the most popular, with the honorable exception of Farnaby's *Martial*. Boccaccio runs away with the prize in the continental section, with *The Spanish Rogue* a poor second. Aretino in Italian or Latin, but not English, is the favourite Pornographer. Neither *La Puttana Errante* nor Pallavicino found much favour in Italian or English. The number of amours is surprising for this type of readership. Representation of books in English is again relatively meagre. Only sixteen copies of pornography in this section were noted, ten in private hands, and most of these were untranslated. A mere ten *Poems on Several Occasions* are listed. *The English Rogue* and *The London Jilt* reach double figures among English bawdry, compared with seventy-four copies of anti-Catholic scandal, three times the total of anti-Puritan satire. Works on venereal diseases were comparatively popular, along with satires on marriage, but the average of two drolleries per owner is as unexpected as the taste for amours. Perhaps both categories represent youthful acquisitions; perhaps intellectuals' reading was more catholic than nowadays.

Several of these eighty-six book collectors achieved lasting fame; others were well known in their day as scholars, theologians and controversialists; the four bishops, Henchman, Walton, Warner and Lloyd; Seaman, Charnock, Smith, Whately, Rogers, Lee, Jacomb, Reynolds, Scattergood, Knatchbull and Annesley. Twenty-seven of them owned at least one pornographic or obscene book. I have traced the religious backgrounds of twenty-three. Of these, nine grew up in strongly Puritan families: Lloyd (23),[52] Anglesey (34),[53] Maynard (42),[54] Lauderdale (49),[55] Hoyle (57),[56] Palmer (69),[57] Belwood (76),[58] Knatchbull (93)[59] and Hough (100).[60] Levinz (94)[61] conformed during the Interregnum. Six more very probably came from Puritan backgrounds: Smith (12),[62] Maitland (47),[63] Blewit (58),[64] Sparkes (63)[65] and Bennet (70).[66] Five of the ten clerical owners were dons. All twenty-seven lived permanently or for significant periods within fifty miles of London, ten in the city. Eight were aristocrats or gentlemen, ten bourgeois and one came from yeoman stock.

Only fourteen privately-owned copies of pornographic or obscene books were in English. No doubt Latin, French or Italian helped to sanitise, along with the anti-Catholicism of many continental pornographers. The distancing age of classical or renaissance erotica might also help to rationalise ownership. However, four ugly ducklings, *The School of Venus*, *Tullia and Octavia*, *Venus in the Cloister* and *Poems on Several Occasions*, were modern publications to the Restoration. Ownership of any of these is reasonable grounds for suspecting prurient interests. Three of the five owners of *The School of Venus*, Hoyle, Hough and Maitland, came from Puritan families. Hoyle and Hough also owned *Venus in the Cloister*, along with Maynard and Palmer, likewise Dissenters. Hough also owned a *Tullia and Octavia*. Five of the six traceable owners of *Poems on Several Occasions*, Anglesey, Maitland, Sparkes, Belwood and Knatchbull, came from definite or probable Puritan backgrounds. The great majority of these assumed pornophiles, then, grew up in that persuasion traditionally the least tolerant of any kind of erotic writing.

This finding corroborates what we have already discovered from our analyses of the backgrounds of named writers, of literary and private sources and selected library holdings. It begins to appear that the sneer of Francis Kirkman, who both as bookseller and renegade Puritan had some reason to know, that for 'crop-ear'd fellows . . . fanaticks . . . stollen meat is sweetest' had more basis of truth in it than most of his utterances.[67]

NOTES

1. *Men of Letters*, pp. 88–135.
2. Ward, Diary, Vol. V, p. 1165; Richard Baxter, *Reliquiae Baxterianae* (London, 1703), p. 118; *D.N.B.*, s.n. Milton, Head.
3. Impressions averaged only about 1000 copies. McKenzie, 'Printers of the Mind', 14; F. Kirkman, *The Unlucky Citizen* (London, 1673), p. 177; K. I. D. Maslen, 'Edition Quantities for Robinson Crusoe', *The Library*, Fifth Series, XXIV (1969), 147–9.
4. Henry Brome, for instance, gave his daughter Allett a dowry of £3000 in 1683, Hotson, *Commonwealth and Restoration Stage*, p. 284.
5. Steane, ed., *Unfortunate Traveller*, p. 14.
6. *D.N.B.*
7. Pinto, *Enthusiast*, pp. 2–5.
8. She was John Rushworth's sister, *D.N.B.*
9. *D.N.B.*; S. E. Morison, *Harvard College in the Seventeenth Century* (Boston, 1936), p. 329.
10. Baine, 'Rochester or Fishbourne', 204; *D.N.B.*

11. Lord, ed., *P.O.A.S.*, I, pp. xliv–liii, 68, 102, 146, 164; 'To His Coy Mistress' and 'Young Love'.
12. Wilders, ed., *Hudibras*, pp. ix–xii.
13. Dr Stephen Parks kindly allowed me to read his draft biography of Dunton, since published; cf. P. M. Hill, *Two Augustan Booksellers* (Lawrence, 1958), pp. 3–20.
14. Gibson, ed., *Kirkman Bibliography*, pp. 51–2.
15. Mr. Geoffrey Robertson defending two gentlemen accused of selling pornographic literature, quoted in *The Guardian*, 19 Sept. 1975; cf. Reade, *Registrum*, p. x; *Report of the Commission on Obscenity and Pornography* (New York, 1970), pp. 25, 157. I am grateful to Maurice Yaffé and David Foxon and the librarian of the Tavistock Joint Library for help on the question of modern readers.
16. E.g. *London Jilt*, p. 108; *The English Rogue*, Part II, p. 342; Wycherley, *The Country Wife*, I, 1; *Onania* (London, 1730), p. 8; Congreve, *The Way of the World*, iv, 2; Foxon, p. 6; Wright, *Middle-Class Culture*, p. 113; A. Oldys, *The Fair Extravagant* (London, 1694), pp. 3–4; Hayward Papers, Rochester Box II; *Venus in the Cloister*, pp. 106, 125–7; J. Ostervald, *The Nature of Uncleanness Considered*, p. 122.
17. G. Gorer, Ch. III, C. H. Rolph, ed., *Does Pornography Matter?* (London, 1961).
18. A. Bryant, *Samuel Pepys: The Years of Peril* (London, 1935), p. 340.
19. D. Thomas, *A Long Time Burning*, p. 76. Cf. Foxon, pp. 11, 20.
20. That of Richard, Lord Maitland.
21. *P.O.S.O.*, p. 99.
22. E. J. Dingwall, *Very Peculiar People* (London, 1950), pp. 146–66; Beverland's uncle, the scholar Vossius, was also a collector of pornography. He read Ovid during divine service.
23. Diary, II, 520; III, 719; IV, 894A, 1019, 1030, 1283.
24. Thomas Birch, *Robert Boyle* (London, 1744), p. 31; Carey, 'Ovidian Elegy', p. 138; Clarke, *Classical Education*, p. 35.
25. J. Hayward, ed., *Complete Poetry and Selected Letters of John Donne* (London, 1949), p. 449.
26. Hayward, ed., *Letters of St-Evremond*, p. 184.
27. MS. Osborn, f.b. 66.
28. Cooper, ed., *Savile Correspondence*, p. 68.
29. Beecham, 'Wesley', 109.
30. First two are in the Bodleian; Foxon, Plate V.
31. E. Wolfe, 'Some Books of Early English Provenance in the Library Company of Philadelphia', *Studies in Bibliography*, IX (1960), 275–84.
32. Dingwall, p. 154; Ashbee, *Centuria*, p. 326.
33. N. Grabo, 'The Profligate and the Puritan', *Notes and Queries*, 207 (1962), 392–3.
34. S. E. Morison, *Harvard*, pp. 125–32.
35. Thompson, 'Puritans and Prurience', p. 46.
36. The invoices of Archibald Hislop are in the Register House, Edinburgh; I am grateful to Dr Stephen Parks for information on them.
37. T. A. Birrell, 'John Dryden's Purchases at Two Book Auctions 1680 and 1682', *English Studies*, XLII (1961), 193–217.
38. Sources: Blickling Hall Catalogue, courtesy of Mr Julian Gibbs; F. Bracher, *Letters of Sir George Etherege* (Berkeley, 1974) Appendix II; B. Dickins, 'Henry

Gostling's Library', Cambridge Bibliographical Society *Transactions,* III (1961), 216–24; B. M. Harleian MSS., 7661; J. Harrison and P. Laslett, eds., *The Library of John Locke* (Oxford, 1965); Pepys Library Catalogue, Magdalene College, Cambridge; L. A. Burgess, ed., *The Pitt Library* (Southampton, 1964); S. G. Deed, ed., *Catalogue of the Plume Library* (Malden, 1959); MS. 4, East Devon County Record Office, Exeter; B. M. Sloane MSS. 3972A.

39. R. J. Kerr and I. C. Duncan, eds., *Portledge Papers* (London, 1928).
40. Bryant, *Pepys: Man in the Making*, Ch. I; *D.N.B.*; A. McInnes, *Robert Harley, Puritan Politician* (London, 1970).
41. *D.N.B.*
42. P. Millican, *Freemen of Norwich 1548—1713* (Norwich, 1934) pp. 165, 225. I am grateful to Victor Morgan for assistance in establishing Gostling's Puritan origins.
43. Deed, p. v.
44. Kerr and Duncan, p. xii.
45. Plume owned numerous works by Baxter, Prynne, du Moulin and Owen; Coffin favoured Beza, Calvin, Dod, Preston, Sibbes, Owen, Shepard, Fox, Jewel, Ames and Baxter.
46. A Presbyterian minister, Dr Joseph Hill, is thought to have introduced the idea in 1673, after eleven years residence in the Netherlands.
47. These have been included in Table 2 to give an impression of booksellers' holdings.
48. Dr Francis Bernard's catalogue is the longest: 450 quarto pages.
49. *List of Catalogues of English Book Sales 1676–1900* (London, 1915). The late A. N. L. Munby kindly allowed me to use a xerox of his interleaved copy with his many additions and locations of other copies.
50. In many cases, older editions could have been inherited.
51. Bishop Lloyd (96) and Palmer (69).
52. Vicar of North Mimms, ejected in 1662. W. Urwick, *Nonconformity in Hertfordshire* (1884). My thanks to Mr Peter Walne, the county archivist.
53. 'A great Calvinist, the dissenting part receiving the far largest share of his favours' during the Restoration period. He took the covenant as a Presbyterian and was the son of a leading opponent of Stafford in Ireland. C. V. Wedgwood, *Thomas Wentworth . . . A Revaluation* (London, 1961) ch. VI; Pepys' *Diary*, November 1668.
54. Son of Rev. John Maynard of Mayfield, Sussex, leading dissenter of the county, ejected 1662. A. G. Matthews, *Calamy Revised* (Oxford, 1933).
55. 1616–82, leading Scottish Presbyterian.
56. *C*1642–*c*92, pensioner of Emmanuel College, Cambridge 1658, member of Gray's Inn, and from 1679 of the Inner Temple. Son of Thomas Hoyle, alderman, lord mayor and leading Puritan of York, and of an equally devout mother, R. A. Marchant, *The Puritans and the Church Courts in the diocese of York* (London, 1960) pp. 76–9, 81, 83, 86–7. My thanks to Dr. D. M. Smith, Director of the Borthwick Institute, and to Mr. W. W. S. Breem, librarian of the Inner Temple.
57. M. A. Balliol, 1641, independent minister Bourton-on-the-Water 1646–60, when ejected. Thereafter, minister of Baptist-Independent conventicle in London and Bristol; died 1678. R. Hayden, ed., 'Records of the Church of

Christ in Bristol,' *Bristol Record Society*, XXVII (1974). My thanks to Miss Mary E. Williams, Bristol City Archivist.

58. Admitted Middle Temple 1665, called 1670. Son of Josiah, vicar of Weston and headmaster Otley Grammar School, a leading Puritan preacher. F. Cobley and L. Padgett, *Chronicles of the Free Grammar School of Prince Henry at Otley* (Otley, 1923), p. 112. My thanks to Dr D. M. Smith, and Miss E. McNeill, Librarian, Middle Temple.
59. Sir Norton Knatchbull 1601–85, of Marsham Hatch, Kent, of moderate Puritan family, took convenant, served in Parliament and on county committees, subscribed to parliamentary cause, Calvinist theologian. Sir Hughe Knatchbull-Hugessen, *Kentish Family* (London, 1960), pp. 1–38. My thanks to Mr Felix Hull, Kent county archivist.
60. Barrister of Inner Temple, 1649–99/1700. Scion of leading Puritan family of London; his father and grandfather, merchants, both took covenant and supported parliamentary cause. Ms. Record Book of Parish Proceedings 1571—1677, St Margaret Lothbury, Guildhall Library, London; D. A. Kirby, 'Radicals of St. Stephen's, Coleman Street 1624–42', *Guildhall Miscellany*, III (1969–71), 105. My thanks to Mr W. H. G. Sadleir for research on my behalf.
61. 1625–99, Interregnum fellow and bursar of St John's College, Oxford, accepting *Directory of Public Worship*. President 1673–99. W. C. Costin, *The History of St. John's College Oxford 1598–1860* (Oxford, 1958).
62. 1590–1675. Cromwellian office-holder and obituarist; took strongly Puritan line in his controversy with Hammond over Christ's descent into hell in 1658–9.
63. 1653–95, later fourth Earl of Lauderdale; brought up by his uncle, the Presbyterian duke and married a Presbyterian Campbell. Later remained loyal to James II. My thanks to Dr Margaret Boddy for information on his later life.
64. 1653–93, son of Francis Blewit, brewer, of the Puritan parish of St James's, Clerkenwell, London. Attended Cromwell's old college, Sidney Sussex, Cambridge.
65. 1655–92, son of Rev. Archibald Sparkes, who conformed at Northrop, Flintshire, during the Interregnum, enjoyed certain augmentations and was consulted by the parliamentary triers. D. R. Thomas, *History of the Diocese of St. Asaph*; T. Richards, *Religious Developments in Wales 1654–1662*, pp. 30, 426. My thanks to A. G. Veysey, county archivist of Clwyd.
66. Son of John Bennet of Abington, Cambridgeshire, in the heartland of Puritanism. His brother was charged with refusing to supply horses to the parliamentary cause, but not convicted. His cousin Sir Levinus was a staunch Whig. *Victoria County History of Lancashire*, Vol IV (1971) p. 128; M. A. E. Green, ed., *Calendar of Committee for Advance of Money* (London, 1888) Vol. III. p. 1299; Green, ed., *Calendar of Committee for Compounding* (London, 1892) Vol. IV, p. 2688; G. W. Marshall, ed., 'Le Neve's Knights', *Harleian Society*, VIII (1873). My thanks to J. M. Farrar, county archivist of Cambridgeshire, Mrs D. M. Owen, archivist of the Diocese of Ely, J. K. Bishop, county archivist of Lancashire, and A. D. M. Cox, archivist of University College, Oxford.
67. Preface, *English Rogue*, Part II.

13 Conclusion

The fifty pieces we have analysed represent a back-handed compliment to Restoration publishers. By the 1680s they had become adept at the rapid translation and printing of European erotica. Before then they had obviously imported it in considerable quantities. The interest was commercial; they followed the recipe of Marsh and Kirkman and published for money. They made no libertarian claims. The nearest they ever came to a rationalisation was the time-worn hypocrisy that they were exposing evil to do good. Compared with the publishers of sedition, the Curtises, the Smiths and the Harrises, they ran only modest risks. True, during the Interregnum, Nathaniel Brooke was hauled before the Council for *Sportive Wit*; once he had informed, however, he seems to have escaped scot-free. Later, despite the watchful eye of L'Estrange, publishers could count on the leniency of grand juries in mild cases, and slight fines from magistrates if convicted. In 1688, for instance, Streater was fined £2 for printing, and Crayle £1 for selling *The School of Venus*; since this fetched from 2s 6d to 5s these token fines represented only a handful of copies lost. No doubt then as now conviction stimulated sales.

A few stationers made this kind of work their speciality: Streater and Crayle produced *Sodom* the next year; Marsh, Brook, Johnson, Kirkman and Rhodes were all precursors of Curll. Others had an isolated venture into the gutter—Wickens, Foxe, Cox, Cademan Briggs, Shell, Garfield and Jones—often soon after gaining freemanship. This was when they needed money-spinners to accumulate capital, or to build up their stock by exchanges. Kirkman described a regular and lucrative market for this off-colour merchandise:

> Sometimes I have gotten fourty or fifty shillings by being partners with one of the young booksellers in printing a pamphlet; and if it be an unlicensed thing, we sell them privately to customers in the shop; if a factious thing, we have our factious customers; if obscene and wanton, we are accordingly provided with those that buy them.[1]

The fact that a messenger of the press could pick up a dozen copies of obscene and pornographic books from ten different shops in three days in 1688 suggests that customers for the 'obscene and wanton' were not uncommon.[2]

In contrast with the publishers, the inventiveness of Restoration eroticists makes a pitiful spectacle. There was no original English pornography; it all had to be imported from France and Italy. Bawdy for middle- or low-brow consumption was likewise generally grindingly unoriginal; pervasive plagiarism, stock situations, stock characters, hoary puns and narrative diversions were the normal fare. Paradoxically Britain ruled the waves of obscenity with *Sodom*, Rochester's Poems and court satires. Her writers excelled at making sex shocking as they failed to make it either exciting or funny. They could disgust; they could not arouse or amuse. Their response to sexuality was smut, or burlesque, or rage, or outrage. They used it as a weapon; they smeared it, like excrement. The concurrent decline in erotic verse is surely no coincidence. For them women are mere sex objects, targets for ejaculation. But where are the machine-gun ejaculators? All too often they are jamming, or misfiring, or running out of ammunition or perversely hitting the wrong target. Impotence stalks the pages of Restoration erotica, leaving a debris of unsatisfied women.

Plainly many late seventeenth-century Englishmen shared an obsessive yet apprehensive view of sexuality. For all their libertine philosophising and summonses to merriment, they seem profoundly inhibited and uncomfortable about the subject. They cannot treat it in a matter-of-fact, balanced way; they cannot laugh about it without sniggering, or describe it straightforwardly, joyously, even innocently. Their reaction is disproportionate, discordant, distorted and disassociated. Pepys cannot appreciate the pleasure and the fun in *L'Escholle des Filles*; he is tantalised, drunkenly horrified; he ejaculates, he destroys. Shame is the spur.

This attitude seems to be new to the second half of the century. Of course, their predecessors could write and talk bawdy, could joke about Bacon's pederasty or Salisbury's alleged liaisons, lapse into unselfconscious vulgarity.[3] Yet, as we have suggested, tolerance for improprieties was generally low; the era had a well-built moral framework. About sexuality it had a sense of proportion; it was not obsessive. It did not dwell on perversions; it had no voyeuristic taste for experimentation; it was not concerned with impotence. There is a simplicity, almost an innocence, about this earlier generation's attitudes.

Many factors have been connected with this change of sensibilities and attitudes, several of which have already been mentioned. The world turned upside down in the 1640s and remained upside down for more than a decade. The Restoration constitution was a ramshackle affair; stable balance between liberty and authority, political consensus both remained elusive. Economically the country was going through its slow apprenticeship in commerce and imperialism. New-made wealth was spreading leisure down the social scale. Geographic and social mobility were perceptibly increasing. Traditional verities were being questioned by the adoption of Baconian experimentalism and a dawning sense that the environment was not inexorably uncontrollable. The rise of Arminianism reaffirmed a role for the individual will in seeking salvation. Community and cooperation were giving way to self-interest and possessive individualism. Human perceptions were changing as the educational revolution replaced a predominantly oral by a literate society. Human behaviour was being gradually changed by the conscious refinement of manners, the cult of self-control. The family was detaching itself from the community and the clan, turning in on its nuclear core. The ideal of marriage was rising to include mutual comfort and companionship between spouses. Within the household privacy was gaining recognition as an individual need.[4]

One effect of all this ferment was to transform people's conceptions of themselves, to elevate a sense of selfhood, to emphasise individualism. In the long run, the growth of this new kind of self-awareness, with its accompaniments of individual liberty and self-determination, is hailed as a great leap forward. Yet, at the time, the slow seethe of these forces of change could not but disturb and disorient those whom it was wrenching loose from conventional attitudes. Revolution, political uncertainty and constitutional stalemate fostered intolerance, paranoia and extremism. Commercialism undermined old values and relationships. Mobility produced rootlessness. Leisure might mean emptiness, boredom and uselessness. Scientific experiment and the written word sowed seeds of doubt. Self-control raised the threshold of shame and required the repression of the body. The nuclear family could become the neurotic, claustrophobic family, demanding new commitments from its members. Privacy could become introspective loneliness.

Puritanism was a leading yeast in this complex process. It was a counter-culture, which consciously or unconsciously encouraged many of the changes in Stuart society. Yet its perfectionism was God-centred. Its view of man's unredeemed nature was unflattering. From birth until God-given conversion humanity was depraved, a cess-pit of sin, selfishness and sensuality, the prey of devilish temptations, of carnal fantasies and wordly pleasures. The most that the saints could achieve of these unregenerates was to enforce outward decency and impress on them some inkling of their plight. Only God's grace could induce the miracle of spiritual rebirth. The stakes were the highest imaginable: eternal bliss or everlasting torment.

The commonest age for the onset of spiritual crisis about conversion was adolescence. Puritan youth was encouraged to search within, to rack its conscience, to discover its innate depravity and worthlessness. This painful introspection was a solitary exercise, often occurring when the wrestler was separated from his family by apprenticeship or residential education. It must regularly have coincided with the heightening of sexual drives and the conscious internalising of manners. This trauma of soul-searching and earnest, desperate hoping for God's miracle could induce insomnia nervous breakdowns, madness, even suicide.[5]

This assault-course in self-hate and craving for signs of God's love would plausibly affect the participant's attitudes towards sexuality. The convert's great love-affair must be with God. Earthly affections and desires must be kept firmly under control. Sexual pleasure and satisfaction could easily come to be identified with sin and shamefulness. Puritans incorporated highly erotic feelings into their spiritual meditations.[6] At the same time, they were peculiarly prone to describing sexuality in terms of uncleanness, filth and nastiness, and to using sexual terms in disapproving ways.[7] Sex thus intellectualised, displaced and dissociated may all too easily induce guilt and neuroses.

The generation after the death of Elizabeth and the breakdown of the Tudor constitution spread and fostered this bracing and inspiring alternative, especially among the literate classes in the south and east of England. It reached its apogee in the triumphs of the Civil War and the great experiment of the 1650s. If ultimately Puritanism failed to convert England to a Bible Commonwealth, it succeeded in imposing a new outward decency and exposing a generation of Englishmen to its system of values.

All of which brings us back to the paradoxical findings of our study: that a significant number of writers, readers and owners of disreputable works came from devoutly Puritan backgrounds, and that the only original English contribution to this growing genre lay in making sexuality outrageous, mechanical and disgusting.

The England of the Merry Monarch was a heyday for alcoholism, astrology, flogging, gambling, religious paranoia, persecution and ritualised violence. The times were out of joint; from the cracks and fissures emerged the vermin of pornography, obscenity and degraded bawdry.

NOTES

1. McKenzie, ed., *Stationers' Apprentices*; Kirkman, *English Rogue*, II, 213–14.
2. Foxon, Plate I.
3. Professor Lawrence Stone kindly loaned me Mr Julian Mitchell's working papers on early seventeenth-century court satire. James I once described Edward Coke as eating law, drinking law, pissing law and shitting law. The Diary of Rev. John Ward, typescript transcription by Sir D'Arcy Power at the Medical Society of London, Vol. III, pp. 831–2. Wayland Young has suggested that the taboo against four-letter words was weaker before the Civil War; *Eros Denied* (London, 1968), p. 32.
4. L. Stone, *Family Sex and Marriage in England 1500–1800* (London, 1977); N. Elias, *The Civilizing Process*, Vol. I (New York, 1978); P. Laslett, *Family Life and Illicit Love* (Cambridge, 1977); D. H. Flaherty, *Privacy in Colonial New England* (Charlottesville, 1972).
5. O. C. Watkins, *The Puritan Experience* (London, 1972); N. Pettit, *The Heart Prepared* (New Haven, 1966); D. B. Shea, *Spiritual Autobiography in Early America* (Princeton, 1968); W. F. Craven and W. B. Hayward, eds., *The Journal of Richard Norwood* (New York, 1945).
6. K. Keller, 'Rev. Mr. Edward Taylor's Bawdry', *New England Quarterly*, XLIV (1970), 382–406; N. S. Grabo, 'The Veiled Vision', S. Bercovich, ed., *The American Puritan Imagination* (Cambridge, 1974), pp. 19–33.
7. D. J. Hibler, 'Sexual Rhetoric in Seventeenth-Century American Literature', unpublished Ph.D. dissertation, Notre Dame University, 1970; Watkins, *Experience*, pp. 145–50.

Index